Praise for Lynn Charles and
Chef's Table

"Charles has done an awesome job with this delectable tale of two men with personalities that just don't quit. Your mouth will water waiting to see who will be the first to take a bite out of the ever-present temptation. Foodies and fans of m/m romance alike will savor every morsel of this story until the last chop drops on the butcher block."
—*Romantic Times Magazine*

"The novel's structure echoes a menu, from aperitif to digestif, and the food descriptions and antics of friends, family, and co-workers add spice beyond the central romance."
—*Publishers Weekly*

CHEF'S TABLE

CHEF'S

TABLE

LYNN CHARLES

interlude press

BOOK DESIGN by Lex Huffman
COVER DESIGN by Buckeyegrrl Designs
COVER AND INTERIOR ILLUSTRATIONS by Abby Hellstrom

To my husband: my first taste tester, my first reader, my first love.
Thank you for loving me most when I don't know what I'm doing.

Menu

I. Aperitif	1
II. Amuse-Bouche	6
III. Entrée	39
IV. Première Entremet	75
V. Plat Principal, Première Partie	88
VI. Plat Principal, Deuxième Partie	139
VII. Deuxième Entremet	176
VIII. Fromage	201
IX. Dessert	230
X. Digestif	258

▶•◀

"Food is everything we are. It's an extension of nationalist feeling, ethnic feeling, your personal history, your province, your region, your tribe, your grandma. It's inseparable from those from the get-go."

—Anthony Bourdain

↓

"If we could just have the kitchen and the bedroom, that would be all we need."

—Julia Child

I. Aperitif

*A light alcoholic beverage consumed before
the meal to stimulate the appetite.*

The night Executive Chef Evan Stanford sat in a nondescript Brooklyn diner listening to a story told by the most colorful man he knew was the night he realized how gray and colorless his own life had become.

"So, I'm out there dumping the trash—which pisses me off anyway because that's not my job anymore, you know?"

Evan used to enjoy the occasional staff outing after a long shift, the hierarchical brigade system of the kitchen breaking down into a simple social gathering with friends and co-workers. But the night his dishwasher Rosey started in on this stale tale, with his special brand of hubris and hyperbole fully intact, Evan found himself with little patience for it.

"It's your job if I *make* it your job, Ambrose."

Upon sight, Ambrose—Rosey—was an intimidating presence. He had the build of a former wrestler, because he was one; the leathered skin of a heavy smoker, because he was one; the hair of an aging rock star, because... well, the rock star thing never took off for him. Largely because in his younger days he had the tendency to steal guitars, not actually *play* them.

And, to further unbalance the universe, Rosey had the soft, caring eyes of a lifelong friend because, interestingly enough, he was one—even to someone so completely his polar opposite as Evan Stanford.

Rosey rolled his eyes, heaved a sigh in Evan's direction and stood to continue, his chrome-framed chair scratching against the old linoleum diner floor. "So, I heft up the bag of shit to toss it, you know?" He looked around begging for someone's eye contact, so Evan gave him some if for no other reason than to get to the end of the story. "And there's movement outta the corner of my eye."

Evan's towering and twig-thin maître d', Ross Wagner, lowered his menu, his deep bass voice rumbling with irritation. "It's New York City, Ass. Rats happen."

"Well, of course it was a rat. But, when I move into take a closer look, the thing I'm looking at is dead. Eyes all crusted over, mouth hanging open."

"Dead rats happen, too."

Evan peeked over the top of his menu at his sous chef, Robin Turner. "You can't tell me you haven't heard this bullshit before."

She blew a stray curl off her forehead and crossed her eyes to watch as it landed right back in the same place. "I can, and I am." Scratching at her head to rearrange her mop of tight, thick brown curls, she focused her attention on the storyteller once more. "And this better be good, Rosey, because I'm starving and dead rats are not my idea of a good appetizer."

"It'd be a better story if you'd all shut up and let me tell it." He waited until everyone but Evan was looking at him. "So, I squat down to get a better look, you know? I see the fucker move! And I get down there"—Rosey splayed his fingers in the air, his voice hushed—"and the son of a bitch moves again."

"You are so full of shit."

"Its legs flex; its body rises with breath. And I take a step back, not wanting it to spring up and bite me, right?"

"There but for the grace of God." Evan lowered his menu and leveled his gaze at his ever-so-colorful dishwasher. "Rosey, just sit down. We're trying to eat." He looked up apologetically at the arriving waitress, a beautiful Hispanic woman with long dark hair and a uniform one size too small. She seemed unimpressed not only with Rosey's story, but also with Evan's boredom.

"Last I checked, we're trying to *order*." Rosey sat down anyway and dropped his head back on the waitress's hip. "Meat-eaters' omelet. And sweetheart, I like my omelet firm—like your—"

"Finish that sentence and your omelet will be dripping down your head."

The waitress yanked the menu out of Rosey's hand and hit him upside the head with it. With a catlike grin, she crouched down next to Evan and poised her pen over her ticket pad. "What'll it be, Chef? I'm sure Boss will go off-menu for you."

Evan smiled back—equally catlike—and further perused his menu. "Seeing as I've never been here before," he let his eyes wander to her name tag, "let's stick to the menu this time, shall we, Mimi? I think I'll go with the turkey, tongue and Swiss. On grilled rye."

"Fries? Chips?"

"Are your potato pancakes shredded or mashed?"

"Please. Shredded. You think this is—"

"Hey, hey, hey now. Don't be mashin' mashed potatoes in pancakes. You're talking about my *home*."

Evan looked into the kitchen at the cook who was shaking a slotted spoon toward the waitress. His hair was thick, black and sweaty above a bright red terrycloth headband. His dark eyes shone and crow's feet properly crinkled, capped off with a happy, toothy smile. His accent was full-on Brooklyn, his shirt was also one size too small, and his sass and swagger finished the picture perfectly. For such a short-statured man, he was quite impressive. "So, where's home?" Evan asked.

"Me? I'm from Bay Ridge. I'm talkin' Oona's home. Ireland."

"Oona. So... boxty? Mashed *and* grated potato pancake, right?"

The cook's eyes widened and lit up even more. "You know boxty?"

"I'll know it intimately if you make me some."

"Absolutely, Chef. Make my grandmother proud."

"I look forward to it." Evan turned back to the table. His companions had all since ordered, and Mimi waited impatiently for his final decision. "I guess I am going off-menu after all."

The meal arrived and the conversation kicked back into gear, fourteen conversations rambling with only seven people talking. It was how they worked at the restaurant; it was how they socialized.

But as the meal wound down, Rosey remembered his abandoned story and charged it back up again.

"So I'm trying to decide, do I find something to poke at this thing and have it jump and attack my perfect face—"

"Oh God, you are shameless—" Robin chomped on her sandwich with disgust.

"Or do I run like a sissy boy? I mean, it's a dead, moving rat!"

"Could you, dear Ambrose," Evan paused long enough to dab away a drip of mayonnaise—house-made, he noted—from the corner of his mouth. "Maybe move this story to *after* we've all finished? Maybe even to the moment after I've left you people for the privacy of my own home?"

"Oh, don't be so fucking prim, Stanny—"

Evan shot him a fiery glare, eyebrow lifted, mouth firm and commanding.

Rosey was smart enough to flinch before he made it worse. "Oh come on. We're outta the kitchen, man. I used to de-pants you in gym class."

"We're not in gym class anymore, are we?"

"You still call me Rosey."

"Because that's what you *want* to be called."

Rosey sighed and looked around the table for some sympathy from his co-workers, receiving none. "Okay. Don't be so fucking prim, *Chef.* You're the sick bastard who gets off on the smell of blood dripping down a freshly butchered veal shank."

Evan smiled, but the venom never left his eyes. "That may be. I just have the decency not to discuss it while others are *dining.*"

"We're dining at a *diner.* There are no fancy—"

"A diner where the cook has obviously taken pains to use fresh ingredients and prepare them amazingly well. So you'll show him and your dining companions some respect."

"Yeah, *Ambrose.*" Mimi had sauntered back up to the table to refill water somewhere between *blood dripping* and *fresh ingredients,* and was beginning to take up the empty plates. "Or did I hear someone call you Rosey?"

"Yeah, baby. Ambrose Pemberton, III. But you can call me—"

"Shut it." Mimi continued bussing the table and with every bend she leaned over far enough to give Rosey—and everyone else—an eyeful of her ample cleavage. "We've got a *respectable* diner here."

The bell over the diner door rang, and a young couple disappeared into the dark night, leaving Evan and his staff the diner's lone customers. Evan shoved his last bite of boxty into his mouth and tossed a nod of gratitude to the cook.

Mimi dumped her armful of plates and silverware into a waiting bin and swung a spare chair around to straddle it and join their table.

"Okay, Rosey babe. Now that we're alone, out with it. The crusty rat. Dead or alive?"

II. Amuse-Bouche

*Light food served before the first course meant both to
prepare the guest for the meal and to offer a glimpse
into the chef's approach to the art of cuisine.*

Evan Stanford was a man who always knew where he was going.
And if on his journey the course changed, he swiftly adjusted to
the winds and continued on; maybe with a new goal in mind, but
always with a goal, always moving with a purpose.

He came to New York from his hometown of Quincy, Illinois right
out of high school. His goal then was to study theater and spend
his nights on the Broadway stage. He would pass off-Broadway,
touring companies, swing roles and waiting tables until his big
break came. Obviously. No one plans for those side trips.

What he really hadn't planned on was how expensive New York
City was. His parents had tried to warn him. They'd sent him off
with a nice nest egg and a great scholarship to NYU, but he soon
ran out of cash and found himself standing at a jobs board looking
for anything. Anything that would put a little more than ramen
in his mouth.

A new friend from his composition class sidled up to him and
told him about an opening where she worked. Robin was adorable,
hated writing essays as much as he did and seemed to roll on a
cloud of positive energy. So he followed her to the restaurant.

Fifteen years later, she was his sous chef and still one of his best
friends. And she still rolled on a cloud of positive energy.

In very short order, Evan's journey had switched directions. He
melded with restaurant life as if he were made for it. A few years
in, he landed a gig with an owner who saw potential in Evan and
had cash to spare. He sent Evan off to CIA—The Culinary Institute

of America—where he received a bachelor's degree in Culinary Arts Management.

His road was paved. His priority was set. He worked his way up through the ranks, skipping through a few short-lived relationships, mostly content with a single life. And now, at age thirty-three, he sat at the helm of a New York City restaurant, well-paid and respected by his peers and his staff. Goal achieved.

But a few mornings after his visit to that colorful Brooklyn diner, as he rolled over and smacked his alarm off, he had to wonder where all his excitement for it had gone.

It wasn't just that Evan felt listless and bored. He was unsettled. Untethered. And on some days downright moody, snapping at purveyors, being uncharacteristically rigid with the staff's schedule, going through the motions of running a kitchen with little interest or passion.

This wasn't how it used to be. He loved his sixty-hour work-weeks, the high-energy, on your feet, sweat-inducing *work*. He loved the constant creative energy, the ever-changing landscape of the business. Trends came in and out, and lesser chefs chased them like the wind while the old guard just kept doing what they did best. Only, they did it better and better, tweaking and twisting ingredients and ramping the flavors into new and exciting directions. He loved playing with food, creating new dishes, trying new takes on old favorites: *here taste this* and *what if we tried...*

Unlike many chefs who covered their bodies with tattoos, who tweaked on the newest drug on the street, who threw cash at new restaurant ventures as though they could print new money out of their convection ovens, Evan's focus for risk and creativity was always with the food. With flavor. With texture.

But, the sad truth was that, for reasons he could not conceive, the rhythm of the restaurant kitchen no longer felt like the beat of his heart. The cadence that had driven him for close to fifteen years was now out of sync, out of balance, making everything around him seem dull. Colorless. Disjointed. And on the worst days, downright grating.

He finally got out of bed, back cracking with each stretch, and took a look outside. Surely the weather was to blame for some of his malaise. A Midwestern boy, he always appreciated the four distinct seasons, and New York celebrated all four. Crisp, blustery winters warmed into vibrant, lively springs. Summer's heat wasn't a particular favorite, but it brought with it an abundance of fresh produce, markets full of color and life and potential creativity. And then of course, autumn in New York—well.

It couldn't be matched.

But this fifth season New York was experiencing, the time when spring just wouldn't arrive, when Mother Nature clung to the gray, dull, lifeless chill of winter, *this* he could do without.

As on strings of days before, it was an indescribably dreary morning, with a thick sort of rain teetering on the edge of snow and muting the view of the East River and the city from his bedroom window.

As he showered and got ready for the day, he recalled that diner a few nights before. He thought he'd been hiding his declining moods from his staff better, keeping a professional front on his less than professional attitude, but their thinly veiled invitation to go out and unwind after a particularly frustrating shift proved he'd been fooling only himself.

"Come on, Chef. Just a quick dinner. It's been too long since we've done that."

"I know this great diner down the street from your new place, Chef. Johnny's. Slick ya' up with some greasy food, you'll be good as new."

"Your routine is too tight, man. Loosen up. I'll even go to Greenmarket for you tomorrow."

While their intentions were good and true, he had been sure that a greasy meal at a greasy diner was not going to fix anything.

Except.

Except that ever since that night, he could not get that simple meal out of his head. It wasn't greasy. It wasn't cheap in quality or care. It wasn't even quick—the cook prepared most everything to order using fresh ingredients.

In a word, it was *spectacular*.

That potato crêpe—the cook's grandmother's boxty—was so light and delicate in seasoning and texture that it belied the weight of the main ingredient. The sandwich of tongue, turkey and Swiss that melted in his mouth—unusual in a city that seemed to relish its overcooked and under-seasoned tongue—was perfectly complemented by a house-made mayo and a freshly baked rye bread that was expertly toasted, with a crisp exterior yet soft and lush interior. It was a simple meal made in a simple kitchen by a proud, dedicated man.

It didn't hurt that that proud man was also easy on the eyes. So, with that memory and the hope of a breakfast of equal quality, he took the extra time before his shift and trudged down Flatbush Avenue to Johnny's.

"Ah, the chef has returned! What brings you back this morning?"

Evan turned toward the shout from the kitchen as the bell clanged against the door behind him. "Your boxty. I'm a sucker for a well-treated potato." He stripped his damp outer layers and sidled up the counter.

"Shoot. Here I was hoping it was my tongue." The cook winked and pushed his headband up with the back of his hand, moving his thick black hair higher. His face was dusted with a five o'clock shadow that had arrived about eight hours early, and his smile was bright enough to light up all five boroughs of the city and the darker corners of Evan's mood.

Evan caught a waitress's eye and nodded when she lifted a finger to tell him she would be right there. His attention was on the kitchen anyway. "Mmm... sorry to disappoint. A very close second, though."

"Excellent. So, what can I pleasure you with today?" The cook held Evan's gaze, quirked a sassy smile and went back to his griddle to plate a stack of pancakes. "Order up!"

Evan perused the breakfast menu, and as soon as he felt the cook's attention shifting to his neighbor, his own shifted back to work—checks and balances, lists upon lists, staff and product and efficiency. Within minutes his mind clouded with Il Boschetto's interests and he forgot his own appetite.

Occasionally, cutting through the drone of his mind, he heard the cook bantering with his neighbor—Walter, maybe?—and tried again to focus on the yellowed, well worn menu. It was breakfast, for God's sake. How hard could it be?

"You look like you need a spicy kick to your day."

I wonder if the cow's liver came in better today; it looked like shit yesterday. Cooked like shit yesterday, come to think of it. God, cinnamon waffles sound good. Too heavy now, not filling enough later.

"How about a spicy—"

Suppose I should just go with oatmeal. Probably bland and lumpy, though. I hope the fucking salamander got fixed. That's going to cost a small fortune.

"Hey, Blue Eyes. How about something a little spicy?"

Shit. It's Thursday, isn't it? I get to deal with Perci all day. I wonder if she has a drinking problem? Maybe I should just get some—

"Chef!"

Evan finally jolted out of his trance.

"Don't look at the menu. Look at me."

"What?" Evan looked into the kitchen. The cook stood there, arms up on the pass as if he were climbing into the dining room. His eyes were round and bright, but a hint of worry creased his brow. And he was staring straight at Evan. "I—I'm sorry. I thought you were…" Evan pointed helplessly to Walter and looked back at the cook, who was smiling now, shaking his head.

"I'm talking to *you*, Chef. Something spicy to start your morning?"

Now he couldn't seem to pull his gaze from the man, whose eyes held him there, reading him, his need for the day, like an open book—which Evan most certainly was not. And yet—

"Yeah. Um." Evan looked down at the menu again, searching for spicy, hot, Mexican, something to order because, yes. Spicy sounded perfect.

"Chef, come on now. Up here."

And Evan put the menu back, enjoying the man's thick accent and contagious confidence, both stronger today than he remembered from his first visit. "Spicy. Yes. That sounds good."

"Three-egg omelet. House-made chorizo. Sweet potato, scallions, cheese—I think I have some asadero if you want."

"You have house-made chorizo?"

"Just for staff. Keeps 'em happy, you know?"

It was *exactly* what he needed. "Well, they say the mark of a good chef is how well he cooks an egg."

"Hang on, now. I'm not a chef."

"Because you're one class short, Paddy!" The bottle-blonde waitress's accent was full Jersey Girl and the pop-snap-pop of her gum was reminiscent of a defective popcorn popper. She slid behind the counter, licked the tip of her pencil and tapped it impatiently on her ticket pad.

"Ignore her. Want some home fries with that?" The cook pulled two thick slices of bread from an egg custard and placed them on the flattop, quickly scraping down the left side to ready it for the next egg order.

"Yes. Please." He focused on the waitress who, while waiting on Evan to make up his mind, had blown a bubble half the size of her face. She sucked it back over her Botox-blown lips. "Is your fruit any good today?"

"It's not bad, Angel."

"I thought *you* were Angel," Evan said, pointing to her name tag.

"Aw, honey, we're all just righteous and holy around here, huh? What else? Coffee? Dish a fruit? Toast?"

Evan caught the cook's eye again and offered a smile—genuine, given his awful mood and the awful weather and the awful gum-popping so early in the morning. "Instead of those home fries, wanna whip me up a batch of boxty again?"

"Now see, you're asking me to go against tradition. At breakfast, boxty's leftovers."

"And I suppose you wouldn't have any of those."

"No, sir. Last batch I cooked was for you and if memory serves—you were a clean-plater."

Evan smiled and mimicked him. "Yeah. A clean plate-uh."

"You making fun of the way I talk?"

Evan offered his own wink and flipped his coffee cup over in hopes that the brew would match everything else good and right about this place.

Angel gave up trying to keep up with his order and shoved her ticket pad into her apron while she tended to a new customer. From the looks of his coat and hat, Mother Nature had decided on snow. The bitch.

"I tell you what, Chef. You let me know ahead of time what morning you might be back"—the cook slid a piping-hot bowl of oatmeal onto the pass-through and shook cinnamon on top of it—"and I'll bring all the ingredients to fix you a right Irish breakfast."

"You're doing an awful lot off-menu for me, now. This is only my second visit."

"Off-menu boxty's what brought you back."

Evan had a memory of a "right Irish breakfast," a full fry served from a tiny pub in Belfast. He had taken a whirlwind trip to Europe the summer after his graduation from CIA believing that even the best culinary institute in the country was incapable of honing the individual voice of a chef.

What he learned, more than anything, was that tradition and heritage were the root of it all. Skill could be taught. Voice was from the heart.

And this man's voice was loud and clear.

"Black pudding too?"

"I said a right Irish breakfast. White *and* black. Full fry. I'll pull out all the stops."

The cook continued to work, in constant motion as he juggled various egg dishes, a waffle iron, pancakes and French toast, sausages, bacon, ham. He looked about Evan's age, but it was clear he'd been cooking for years—he was efficient and quick, yet thoughtful about each specific order. Spinach in this omelet, fresh sliced banana for those pancakes, over easy, hard scramble, bacon extra crispy with the spinach omelet, chewy and fatty with the French toast.

"You want to come to the back, Chef? See how it's done with a two-man kitchen?"

Evan blushed at being discovered. "Another time. Show me what you can do with a couple eggs first." He wiggled his coffee cup, looking nonchalant but really mastering the art of passive-aggressive waitress baiting. "Did I hear correctly? The name's... Paddy?"

"Yes, sir. Patrick Sullivan. I'll get these right out to you, Chef."

"Evan. Stanford. Please call me Evan."

Patrick kept his eye on Evan, worrying his teeth over his bottom lip as he blindly reached up onto his shelf to grab two eggs. "As long as you're in your whites and I'm back here? You're Chef to me."

"That's entirely unnecess—"

"Miss Verito! Get back over here and get Chef something to drink, huh? This is why your tip jar is empty most of the time."

▶•◀

Evan went to the diner a few times after that to grab a quick break-fast or lunch before a shift—a calming start before diving into the fray of his own restaurant.

On a late-night visit after a long, soul-sucking shift, he heard Patrick calling Mimi from what sounded like a basement walk-in. "Camila, where the hell did Oscar put the brisket for tomorrow?"

"Hell if I know—I stay out of that arctic locker and you know it. Your chef is here." Mimi took Evan's upturned coffee cup and started to pour as he laid his coat and belongings across a neigh-boring stool.

"Wait. Better make that decaf."

"Oh, honey, look at you. No. You need a jolt." She poured the perfect roast into his cup and gave him a sympathetic smile. "Bad run tonight?"

"Hell. Pure hell."

Evan massaged his temples, his elbows resting on the laminate countertop, and focused on the pull of skin and muscle, the sounds of a diner winding down its daily run.

"Start with this. Black Forest."

Evan looked up and smiled sleepily back at Patrick's bright eyes shining at him. Within an instant, Evan almost forgot Perci, his incompetent line cook who just that night had actually overcooked an entire vat of cavatappi because, while sneaking out for her smoke break, she lost track of time trying to get her lighter to work. He almost forgot his immovable manager's backhanded compliment when rejecting two new, impeccable dishes for the spring menu: "We already have a perfect menu thanks to you! No changes necessary."

Evan almost forgot that, in less than twelve hours, he had to be back at it again.

He looked down at the plate Patrick shoved onto the counter between his elbows. Black Forest cheesecake. "Fresh cherries. Oh my God."

"Don't insult me. Of course they're fresh."

Without even glancing up at Patrick, he unfolded his utensil roll and tossed his napkin on the counter. Nor did he waste time placing his napkin on his lap. He looked at the dessert like a long-lost lover and stabbed the pointed tip of it, slowing when his fork hit the perfect resistance of firm, yet moist, cake. "Oh, God. Who supplies these for you?"

"Supplies? Sweetheart—we farm out nothing here. I made that late this morning."

"You made—" Evan lifted the fork and examined the decadent dessert before eating: a chocolate crust, at least a quarter-inch thick, made of biscuit cookies and butter, with the perfect crumble to nab remaining bits of filling with the last bites—to which he was already looking forward. The cheesecake was perfectly baked, dotted with plump, ripe cherries and swirled with a purple-red cherry reduction. "Rum?"

"Myers's."

"Shit." The slice was artistically topped with long, meticulously rendered chocolate curls. "Dark chocolate?"

"Of course."

"Fuck me." Without waiting another moment, Evan took the first bite and moaned as the cake melted into his mouth, the tart cherries dancing simultaneously with the sweet and sour of the cream cheese and the bittersweet chocolate. The rum hit last, and it was all Evan could do not to humiliate himself with his noises of pleasure.

"Well, that seems a little soon, don't you think?"

"Huh?" Evan looked up, dreamy and debauched. He couldn't remember anything he might have said in the last, oh, week or so, much less thirty seconds.

"You said—" Patrick blushed and patted Evan's left hand—the hand that had been flexing in pleasure as he enjoyed his first bite— before heading back into the kitchen. "I'm glad you're enjoying it, Chef. Can I get you something from the grill?"

Evan tried to compose himself, but the lure of the cake won and he forked another piece, closing his eyes to savor, to delight, to relish, remaining unconcerned with the flow of conversation. "N—no. Thank you. This is just what I needed. Again."

This was why Evan was a chef. Good food. Well made, with a respect for the ingredients and how they worked together, and how—if done right—food could not only satisfy someone's hunger, but soothe his soul as well. Patrick understood that.

He didn't just help Evan forget.

He helped him *remember.*

When Evan swallowed, he found Patrick staring at him from the kitchen.

"How come I never knew about your cheesecake?"

"'Cause you're always in such a fuckin' hurry."

"I'll make sure to change that. This is—" Evan lifted a chocolate curl from the top of the cake and ate, closing his eyes as the bitter-sweet chocolate melted in his mouth. "This is sublime."

Patrick beamed. He shook a basket of perfectly cooked fries, salted them heavily and dumped them on a plate. "On the house."

"No. You don't give things like this away."

"Not typically, no. But you're far from typ—" Patrick stopped himself and took a deep breath. "I mean it, Chef. On the house."

"Only if you stop calling me Chef." Evan pulled at the shoulder of his button-down shirt. "No whites. And you clearly are the superior cook at the moment."

"Shed the costume tonight, huh?" Patrick bent to inspect a sandwich on the grill and with a few swift moves had it up at the pass with the fries: a thick Texas toast grilled cheese with various cheeses oozing from its sides. "Order up!"

"If I could only shed the night." Evan took another bite, and Mimi locked the door, flipping the sign to *Closed*. "Oh! You're—I'm so sorry. I just assumed you were twenty-four hours."

"You're fine. Not for another twenty minutes. She just hates getting new tickets this late, and by this time of the day, I'm not in the mood to argue with her."

"You're sure? I should head home and—"

"I'm sure. I'm going to be here another hour anyway. Take your time."

And so Evan did, savoring each bite of the cheesecake. Mimi wiped down tables as he and the one remaining patron ate, but the scrape of chrome against linoleum did not even begin to intrude on his moment with the glorious dessert. In fact, it added a perfect soundtrack, one he'd come to love during his years in the industry: a restaurant shutting down at the end of the night, the smell of bleach vying for attention with the lingering smells of the food of the day. The echo of silverware hitting bins, hotel pans knocking into the sides of sinks, reach-in doors hissing open and sucking closed as everything is put in place for overnight storage.

These were the sounds and sights and smells that defined a good run, a hard-earned rest, happy customers and fulfilled cooks. He loved this. He loved this world. Somewhere in him, he still loved it.

He chucked a twenty-dollar bill on the counter and got Patrick's attention as he hiked on his overcoat. "Come visit my place soon. Let me cook for you."

"Aw now, Chef. I couldn't afford your restaurant if I worked double shifts for a month."

"It's not *that* expens—wait. You know my restaurant?"

"Il Boschetto on Forty-sixth. I, uh—I sorta looked you up."

Evan secured his hat on his head, the truth of Patrick's confession reaching down to his toes. "Chef's table. *Compliments* of the chef."

Patrick shook his head and wiped his pass clean with a smile. "Maybe one day, Chef. You have a better night now."

▶•◀

"Ordering one veal loin, two pasta taste, one chop on polenta!" Evan shoved the new ticket on the rail and checked a plate for accuracy. "That's one loin, two pasta, two chops, three osso, one liver and rib-eye mid-well, all day."

"Chop on polenta not scaffata, check?"

"Check. Where's my liver? This ticket should be right in front of me."

"One out on liver, Chef. Firing chops."

Evan had arrived at work that afternoon ready to roll, the taste of the Black Forest cheesecake days gone but its memory fueled a determination to set it all right again. He prepped with the staff, everyone falling into a rhythm of banter and storytelling that felt familial, easy. Prep bled into a comfortable family meal of quick food, last-minute tasks before opening and, of course, grandiose war stories of shifts past blown up so far from the truth, no one cared whether they were fiction or reality.

Then it was hard, fast work, noise and commotion and drive all in sync and reminding Evan of the good things about restaurant life.

The first push had just begun when Evan looked up from his expediting position. He surveyed his staff, quickly making sure everyone was on target, in line and ready to go before the kitchen kicked into balls-out organized chaos.

Rosey was already back in his cubby washing up from prep and family meal, singing along to the piped-in music. Poorly. With made-up lyrics. Evan could never figure out if Rosey didn't know the right lyrics or was just so much of an asshole, he made up new ones to entertain himself. When Evan heard, "Gonna have to face it, you're a dick with a glove," he voted for option two. Rosey was that much of an asshole.

On this particular evening, Robin ran grill, a second voice of Evan's barked orders, the perfect assistant director of his theater. She was tough. Fair. In love with the work, the atmosphere, the food. After all their years together, she was his cornerstone when things got crazy. And he was hers.

Evan loved to watch her husband Theo, Il Boschetto's roundsman. He was a physically diminutive man with an imposing intensity who got the job done efficiently, consistently and deliciously. Tonight he covered sauce, managing multiple burners as he choreographed every order, every dish, with not one movement wasted—poetry in motion.

And then there was Perci, a proverbial thorn in Evan's side and, in Evan's mind, the cause of his growing stress on the job. She was an older woman, pear-shaped, with horribly home-colored hair— he thought it was supposed to be auburn, but it always looked more like plum than anything. She had grown lazy and apathetic, a smoking powder keg threatening the pulse of his kitchen. She stationed side dishes with José Alvarez, her faithful assistant, and seemed to dance on *this* side of Evan's patience every few nights; she was like a slow-healing scab, almost unnoticeable one night, oozing and needing extra attention the next. At the moment, however, she seemed to be on task.

Overall it felt like a good start to a good night, eight cooks moving in tandem, talking to each other, the odd language of the kitchen their secret code.

"Selling liver, rib-eye. Jizz me, Theo."

"You wish, *golfillo*."

"Firing tables two and twelve!"

"To your left, to your left!"

Two more tickets clacked out on the printer, the rush charging forward with Evan's call.

"Ordering one breast, one roast fish, two pulled pork. Ordering one lamb chop, one pasta." Evan tugged two dishes off the pass, checked them, wiped down the sides and sent them off to waitstaff. "Table nine, please. Kitchen, that's breast, fish, pulled, lamb chop, loin, *three* pasta, chop on polenta, all day."

A pork chop landed, sizzling protein in a hot pan; Rosey dropped a hotel pan and swore, pans and utensils clicked and slammed against grill tops and flats, knives whacked steadily on wooden boards.

Rhythm, melody, harmony—it was the music of Evan's soul.

But then, as if a slow-motion accident were unfolding on a movie screen before him, the smooth start began to unravel.

As to be expected, it started with Perci. She burned a side of scallions and asparagus and set back the timing of that table's dishes just enough to put a kink in the chain.

If one table was off, so was the next. And the next.

It rattled her to the point where she forgot to taste and offered up salty, overcooked mush. Evan sent dishes back to be fixed, his impatience slowly ratcheting up with each plate—destroying any notion of a good shift and the hope that his foul mood could be cured by good cheesecake and a gorgeous smile.

Eventually, Perci's constant incompetence created a backlog on the line. Everyone had to push, push, harder, faster. Insults flew, runners dashed in and out with supplies to ease the burden and, more than anything, Evan's anger began to flare.

"Christ! Cook with some fucking *integrity*!"

"Behind, behind, behind, bitch. Step *aside!*"

Evan ramped up the intensity as he shouted orders, moving cooks, moving food, fixing, tasting, directing, getting the line back in order before the dining public became aware.

There were three goals when they were this far in the weeds: set up the tickets, knock them down and turn the damned tables.

"Hold table four, reorder on the two osso and lamb chop. That's *three* osso, one lamb chop, two veal loin, two liver, two rib-eye, mid, mid-well with shrooms, all day." Evan muttered under his breath as he pushed plates into a waitress's hand and experienced a glitch in his focus as he tried to reel it all in. "Table…" He scanned his tickets frantically. "Fuck, table—"

"Eight, Chef. I've got it."

While everyone else was on overdrive, pushing to keep things above water, nothing—not one thing—seemed to light a fire under Perci's ass.

"You need a pillow to rest your little weary head, Perci?" Even the runners carting nine pans refilled with *mise en place* and plates of compound butter were fed up.

As if on cue from the conductor, for her big, cymbal-crashing finale Perci flipped a pan too close to the flame, setting her zucchini and goldbar squash on fire. And then, in correction, she did it again with a second pan.

"Perci, get the fuck—" Evan took a breath, wondering if having her step away and take a breather would really help and deciding that if it wouldn't help her, it would at least help him. "Go take a smoke."

"I'm fine, I'm fine. I'll—I'm fine."

Evan shot a heated glare across the kitchen at the back of her head. "Turn around and convince me."

She turned and pushed her headwrap back further on her head, blowing air up onto her sweaty brow. "I've got it." She glanced at the grill and back to her burners, guessing at the readiness of the next plate. "Two out on the rib-eye mid-well, Chef."

Against his better judgment, feeling a little more at ease as things began to catch up and tickets slowed, he let it play out. He checked more plates, deaf to the sounds around him now, hearing only white noise and keeping a kind of tunnel vision on Perci. His heart sank as Robin tapped impatiently at her cutting board, the sliced rib-eye there waiting to be plated. "Perci, my rib-eye's dying—sides! Now!"

"I'm on it." The cook pulled a warm plate from the stack and expertly loaded a serving of garlic mashed potatoes on its center, trailing sautéed mixed vegetables around its edge. She slid the plate to Robin and looked up to her next ticket, adjusting her glasses on her nose and squinting to focus. It was a casual motion, showing no concern for the turmoil she had caused. "I can feel you scowling behind me, Chef. I said I've got it."

"I will *scowl* as long as I feel the need. Where's the pasta tasting for this ta—thank you."

A cook slid a tray of a trio of pasta dishes to the pass and Evan took it, grabbing blindly for the rib-eye that would surely be shoved into his open hand.

Only it wasn't there.

"My hand—my *hand*!" Evan snapped as he swiped down the pasta tray, waiting. "Right now!"

He looked up and found Robin waving the plate in front of Perci, sliced meat perched perfectly atop the mound of potatoes on its plate. "Mushroom, Perci. Dying meat here!"

And Perci, with all of her *I've got this* and *I'm on it*, was casually tossing a pan of caramelizing onions as if cooking dinner at home.

"What the fuck are you—shrooms, Perci!"

Perci snapped out of her haze, her eyes darting from the incomplete plate to Robin and to her burners that had no sautéed mushrooms on the heat. She spun around to Evan, eyes wide in panic as Theo shoved another table's order onto the pass. "I'm—I'm sorry. I didn't—"

"One osso, one chop, Chef."

"You didn't read your ticket. You didn't—" Evan quickly checked the new plates and slid them down to waitstaff for service, but when he looked back at Perci's station, expecting motion and hustle, she was still standing there, frozen to her spot.

And, just like the too-tight strings of an inexpertly tuned guitar, he snapped—one string after another uncoiling the last of his patience. As if tonight's errors alone weren't enough, months of lazy behavior, of avoidable mistakes, of the entire staff having to constantly crank it in tighter to save the rush from the weeds, all crashed in on him in that moment.

He bolted away from his station and yanked the plate out of Robin's hand, sautéed vegetables flying onto Perci's work table as he slammed it into the trash, plate and all. "Do you even *begin* to understand what we're doing here?"

"Yes, Chef. I'm—I'm sorry. I just—"

"You just *nothing.*" He grabbed two sauté pans from the overhead shelf and slammed them onto Perci's burners. "Robin, pull the rib-eye from the next order. You have more at the ready?"

"Yes, Chef." Robin squatted down to her lowboy, peeking up from the open door. "The incoming tickets?"

Turning around and snapping his fingers at a runner, he pointed to the printer. "Hand it over." With one hand on a sauté pan and the other grabbing the ticket, he read, "Two salmon, chicken breast, roast fish, osso."

He threw butter into one of the pans and quickly checked Perci's other working sides, shoving her aside, a useless rag doll in the way of service.

"That's how many osso all day, Chef?"

"I don't fucking know anymore. Can't you people figure it out?"

He ignored the new ticket that came through, tossing the one in his hand onto the pass while Robin called out the all-day orders. Throwing garlic into the hot pan, he looked around Perci's station for the mushrooms, cursing when he finally found them. "Your station is a fucking disaster."

"I am more than capable—"

"Are you? *Are you?* I have yet to see any sign of capable from you tonight." He got the mushrooms into the pan, stepping back as she grabbed at another pan of sautéed vegetables for the awaiting rib-eye plate.

He was in the way.

He seethed, tired of standing aside and watching it all fall to hell. He grabbed another sauté pan from the shelf and put it on the heat, not even sure what order it was for, crazily scanning the tickets on Perci's rail for a clue. "Fucking *shoemaker*. Constantly putting us in the weeds. Lazy. Incompetent—"

"Just fucking fire her. Jesus."

"Don't you have something else to do, Rosey? Get your ass out of here." Evan reached for a bottle of dry white and stopped dead when another hand landed on his, a gentle voice cutting through the fray to get his attention.

"Chef."

It was Robin, looking at him with angry, intense, pleading green eyes—the eyes of a friend and, at the moment, a very angry co-worker.

"Go back to your station, Evan. You're making it worse."

The commotion of the kitchen rattled around him, echoing in his ears: proteins sizzling, chatter between cooks spoken, not shouted as usual. His staff glanced up at him as if almost afraid. Uncomfortable. People he'd been working with for years, acting as if they were on their first day at a new gig with an unfamiliar, *untrusted* leader.

The music to his soul that had started his shift, was lost for the night.

Evan felt sick.

With a deep swallow he turned to Perci, who was oiling a heated pan, apparently humiliated enough to get down to business. "Are you back on track now?"

"Yes, Chef."

Robin turned back to her grill, swearing in at least three different languages as she mentally gathered the orders Evan had abandoned and surveyed the fires that were in mid-preparation. She ramped up her commands to get everyone back in step while Evan took his place at the window.

"Can we go again, Chef?" His head waitress, Natasha Kramar, stood expectantly, a line of waitstaff behind her, their white shirts skewed from activity and black aprons stuffed with order pads, pens. Their eyes—all of them—were huge, waiting for his lead. "We have a few more orders to put in, but thought we should wait until—"

"Yes. Thank you. Start them up again." Evan tugged on the knot of his headwrap and sighed, grabbing a clean ticket from the printer. "Did we comp that table some wine?"

"We did. The last few. Theo and I got the others served, but you're still—"

"Selling osso, chop, rib-eye!"

Evan grabbed and inspected the remade dishes. "We're behind. Yes. Table eleven, please." He adjusted his headwrap and read the first ticket, then the second, taking a deep breath and diving into the fray. "Picking up liver!"

"Selling liver!" Robin pulled the plate from Perci just as the last caramelized onion and bacon landed on the bed of crispy polenta and slid it to the pass. Evan drizzled the dish with olive oil and balsamic vinegar, grabbed the accompanying plates, checked the ticket and handed it off to the waitstaff.

Sweaty, exhausted, humiliated, Evan ran through the motions, breathing relief when incoming tickets fell behind the outgoing ones and the printer stopped spitting out orders. Tensions had eased, but not completely. No one would look him in the eye. Rosey continued to linger at the doorway to his cubby and stare, trying to get Evan's attention, but he couldn't spare it. Couldn't acknowledge.

He was the boss.

He'd acted like an ass.

However, there was one senior line cook who was far from innocent. And they probably had a good thirty-minute breather before the post-theater crowd came barreling down on them.

"Perci? In my office."

"Oh. Chef, I was hoping to take a smoke break."

"Your hopes are shattered." He dragged his wrap off of his head and shot her the one remaining glare he had left in him. "In my office. Now."

"How long will this be, Chef?"

Evan scrubbed at the dark brown mess of hair on his head, hours of sweat trapped in his wrap making him long for a hot shower and a soft pillow. Both were still hours away.

He offered Perci a bottle of water that she refused and opened his own. He took a seat behind his desk, fingering his hair back in place as much as possible. He was buying time before opening his mouth because, while he had planned to start with an apology, her lead-in made him second-guess.

But as he looked around his basement office, at the white cement walls covered with certificates, diplomas, awards and citations, at framed photographs and collages of years upon years in the industry from college gigs making barely minimum wage to his first "real" jobs, he had to third-guess and pay respect to those who had taught him well.

"I owe you an apology."

Perci blinked and sat up straighter, clearly surprised. "I—okay. I hadn't expected that."

"I was unprofessional. I was trained better than that. I was *raised* better than that. I take pride in being better than that. I am sorry."

"Thank you. You've been out of sorts lately and I—well, I never expected you to behave so childishly."

"Is this how you accept an apology from your boss? Typically? Because in light of your performance these last few months, the last person I need critiquing my behavior is you."

"No, it's—" She looked longingly at his small refrigerator. "No. Thank you for apologizing."

He narrowed his eyes at her and got up to get her a bottle of water, sitting on the front edge of his desk before handing it to her. "You do understand, however, that at most restaurants in the city, you'd be jobless now, right?"

She took it and pulled back a few swallows before answering. "I suppose so. But I have tenure here."

"Tenure? This isn't the teacher's lounge, Ms. Child." He sat behind his desk and leaned forward, his fingertips silently tapping together as he collected his thoughts. "Is there anything going on with you outside of the kitchen? Personal issues? Medical concerns? Family strife? I don't need details, but—"

"Nothing, Chef."

"Then explain to me why your head isn't in the game—and hasn't been for some time. You're costing me money. And the thing that just might affect your 'tenure' here—" Evan mimed the air quotes and promptly rolled his eyes at himself. "You're costing Mr. DiSante money."

"I don't—I really have no explanation. And I really, *really* need a cigarette or I'm not sure I'll be much better second round."

"So you're blaming your nicotine habit?"

"No. I'm not *blaming* anything." She squared her shoulders and raised her eyebrows, her voice rising with fake confidence. "You know, mistakes happen. You have to be more flexible and allow your staff to be human."

Evan sat back, almost choking on the two words he really wanted to say.

He was fair. He was tough as nails and he demanded excellence, but he was fair. And he had been beyond fair with this one, allowing her to stay in the kitchen much longer than he would have anyone else given the consistency of her errors. The edict he'd been given by DiSante upon being hired—that she remain on staff—was inexplicable.

"Flexible. See, if I *wasn't* flexible, if I was really running this kitchen the way I'd like to be running it, you'd have been gone by the last snowfall. So, I don't believe suggesting that I loosen up is going to benefit you here."

"If you think you're going to fire me—"

"Fortunately for you, I am unable to run this kitchen the way I'd like to, so we still need to work around management. But I guarantee you, from this moment on, things between you and me are going to be different. I will not have another night like I had tonight."

"No, because once DiSante hears about your behavior—"

Evan pulled Perci's employee folder out from under his laptop.

"I'm writing you up. You get two more—and that's me being flexible—and you're out. On the line. After shift. If I see you screw up at the market buying the wrong food for your cat—whenever it's necessary. The laziness, the incompetence, the lack of give-a-damn is over, do you understand me?"

"Yes, Chef."

"And just to give you a heads up? Speaking to me as if your—how many years of service?"

"Twenty, Chef."

"Twenty. Unreal." He picked up a pen and tapped it on his blotting pad. "Your twenty years don't mean shit to me if you don't produce, if you don't respect the line, if you don't respect the food. And you've proven to me that you *don't*."

He clicked the pen open and closed a few more times, weighing his behavior with hers. Regardless of his tirade earlier, he was still the boss. "In fact, from this point on, when I ask you a question on the line, there are three answers I want from you."

"Should I write them down?"

"You're not going to ruffle me any further tonight, so let it go, Perci." He stared her down a few moments more and started again, flaring three fingers of his left hand. "I only want to hear 'Yes, Chef.'" He put a finger down with each item on the list. "'Yes, Chef. And, yes, Chef.' Is that understood?"

Perci finally blinked. She attempted to replace the cap on her bottle of water, but her hands were visibly shaking and she was unable to steady them. She gave up and sighed. "Yes, Chef. I guess I owe you an apology as well."

"Accepted. But if you ever approach me again like your years of experience somehow make you superior to me in *my* kitchen? You will quickly earn another write-up."

She nodded and stood, smoothing her jacket and rolling her sleeves. "So, what happens if Mr. DiSante won't allow this?"

Evan shook his head. "I think you overestimate your importance here. You let me deal with Mr. DiSante. Your concern needs to be your station and the execution of *my* dishes."

"Yes, Chef. I'm—I'm sorry to have disappointed you."

Evan tossed the pen on his desk and waved toward the door. "Go smoke and get back on the line. We don't want two write-ups in one night."

Evan bolted out of Il Boschetto as soon as he could, taking the long ride on the Q to try to decompress and forget everything that had happened. He wanted to forget Perci's idiocy, forget the lost revenue that resulted from it, forget the anxiety and tension that crept into his bones the moment that first mistake was made.

But mostly, he wanted to forget his own actions. He had been so out of control. So unprofessional. So against everything he stood for as a leader in the kitchen—as a human being, bumbling through life like everyone else. It's why he offered Perci an out. Something personal affecting her work. Some burden she brought into the kitchen unawares.

But she never bit. She simply thought she was better, smarter, wiser. Untouchable.

Tenured.

He scoffed at the remembrance of that, earning him an odd stare from the apparently homeless woman three seats away from him on the mostly empty train. Perci's attitude and behavior, however irritating and condescending, were fixable. He hoped.

But his own behavior? He couldn't get a handle on it. Couldn't trace the steps back to how he got here, pushing cooks out of the way, taking over stations, flinging food and commands, impatience and ugliness, like some lame Gordon—he scoffed again, and the homeless woman moved further away from him.

He wasn't even a good Gordon Ramsay caricature.

So, instead of walking home from the DeKalb station, he stopped into Johnny's hoping Patrick was at the grill. The other cook, Oscar, was fine enough, but he needed a dose of Patrick. Of his food. Of his ability to *speak* through his food. His cheesecake, the special off-menu treats he'd whip up for Evan, all had a piece of Patrick in them. Evan didn't know his story, of course, but somehow he felt as if it were right there laid out in front of him, waiting for him to learn it.

Fate was on his side.

"Why don't you come on back, Chef? How long has it been since you've worked in a small kitchen, huh?"

And now he'd been caught staring.

Evan looked away, flushed and too tired to care. But when he looked back at Patrick, he was met with a friendly smile. "I should probably learn a more stealthy way to stare."

"Only if you want..." Patrick glanced up at a ticket on his rail. "Seriously, how long has it been?"

"Quite some time and—" Evan looked around. The diner was almost empty, winding down another day. "You still have some patrons. Thank you, though."

"Who cares? Besides, I figure you won't strain your neck that way."

But Evan wasn't longing for the days of a small space and a small staff, although upon reflection, it did seem like a simpler time.

For all of his psychobabble and emotional meanderings on the train, by the time Evan had arrived at Johnny's and sat down at a prime counter seat for the show in the kitchen, it had come down to this:

The view was *tremendous*.

Patrick's arms were strong and cut, lifting soup and stock pots as if they were wicker baskets. His skin rippled over flexing muscles that tested the strength of his shirt seams as they strained under the movement of his arms. The bastard even whistled along with the music as he worked—and it wasn't annoying.

Evan felt heat rise to his cheeks and ears, and Patrick simply smiled and waited, Evan assumed, for a reply or motion more responsive than a prepubescent mouth-hang.

"I'm only coming back if I can help."

"I'd be honored to have your help—if you don't mind working after your own shift. I've got morning prep to do."

"I don't mind at all." Monotonous prep work actually sounded relaxing.

Evan gathered his belongings and made sure no one was looking as he slipped behind the counter and into the kitchen.

"Is it okay if I use my own knives? I brought them home to sharpen and—"

Patrick sidled up to look around his shoulder. He was shorter than Evan realized but far from diminutive—broad-shouldered, solid and warm. Evan opened his bag on the work table, and Patrick's chest brushed up against his back as he pressed in for a better look. Evan gasped from the slight touch, the front- and back-of-house divide collapsing as they stood so close together.

Or maybe the room was warm. It was a kitchen, after all.

He should have thought this through more carefully.

Patrick ran a finger over the handles of the knives neatly stored in Evan's bag as if touching fine jewels, a treasure.

It was a treasure. The kit was worth thousands of dollars, containing all the portable tools necessary for his job, including a cleaver big enough to chop through a human femur like soft butter. The knives were weighted to Evan's individual preferences; each was an extension of his hands, and he protected them as though they were truly part of his body.

"I never had knives of my own, outside of what I use at home."

"Really? You deserve at least a good basic set. Every cook does."

"Maybe." Patrick pulled a chef's knife from his magnet on the wall and looked it over. "These get sent out for sharpening every six months or so—"

"Patrick." Evan took the knife from him before he could slice through the first onion in their pile. "That's a *home cook* schedule." He flicked his thumb across the blade and sighed. "Oh, honey..."

"You wanna talk to Johnny about it?"

"I take it that's the owner?"

"Yeah. Johnny Mangiano. Third generation owner. So tight he shits pencils."

Evan pulled another knife from the magnet and affected a strong Italian accent. "Johnny Mangiano, eh? Sounds like a mob boss."

"If I told you any more, I'd have to kill you." Patrick took the first knife from Evan, flicked the edge with his thumb and winced. "He's okay—most of the time. Just cuts corners now and then."

"Yeah, like with safety. These are a hazard."

"I know he needs to get on it. One of us is gonna get hurt. I hone them every day— multiple times—but—"

Evan lifted his eyebrows in judgment and Patrick sighed with a blush.

"I know. I've got a burner out on my six-eye, too. I adapt, but—" Patrick stroked his thick, dark eyebrows. "These are grooming masterpieces. I don't wanna lose one when it goes wild one day, you know?"

Evan laughed, imagining Patrick's eyebrows in flames while he chatted away mindlessly. "That would be a tragedy."

"It would."

"Here—use one of mine tonight." Evan handed Patrick a chef's knife, so perfectly cared for it looked brand new. "It's still sharp enough."

"I—I couldn't. It's too exquisite."

"You will. Or I won't stand here working next to you waiting for the bloodbath." He smacked the knife handle into Patrick's open palm, settling the matter.

"Rumor has it you enjoy—what was it? The scent?" Patrick weighed the balance of Evan's knife in his hand and folded his fingers around the handle, this thumb and forefinger properly gripping the heel of the blade. "Yes, it was the scent of freshly dripping blood, so—"

Evan quirked an eyebrow at him, pulling the other chef's knife from his bag and swiftly honing it. "Where did you hear—" And then he remembered. "Rosey. You overheard our conversation from that night?"

"Rosey's sort of hard to ignore. And you—"

"And me?"

"I'm afraid I was eavesdropping and staring. And burning your boxty."

"My boxty wasn't burnt."

"You ate the second batch."

"So you started at a diner, huh, Chef?"

"Well, it was a little boutique restaurant on East Twelfth. I was a busboy—a *lousy* busboy."

They were about halfway through preparing the following day's *mise en place,* filling nine pans with various aromatics, garnishes and fresh vegetables. "So, let me guess. You came to New York to be an actor."

"Of course." Evan worked on a box of onions, motioning to the unused root and tip ends. "Stock?"

"Yes. Use everything." Patrick slid his knife into the onion he was working on and moaned, "Effortless." It had become his mantra since they'd begun—every slice smooth and effortless. "And you found the theater of the kitchen was more enticing?"

"Well, not at first. I was—" Evan pushed onion skin into the trash and laughed at the memory of his first day on the job. "Have you ever seen a duck try to run?"

"I—" Patrick paused in his motions, his thick brow furrowed in concentration. "I can't say. If I have, I don't remember."

"Awkward. Like a penguin out of water, you know? Running alongside the pond, legs twirling, body wobbling. They look ridiculous." Evan mimicked with his hands and laughed again as he went back to work, expertly chopping his onion into a perfect medium-dice almost without looking. "I was a running duck. My first day I poured water on three separate customers in as many hours."

"I broke five plates in ten minutes—they didn't let me bus either."

"Exactly. Running ducks. Take ten steps to the back of the house and we're moving like the wind."

"Running Ducks. That'd be a great band name."

Evan snickered. "Kazoo band, maybe." He grabbed for another onion, making quick work of it with motions as natural as if he were—a duck in water. "If you make it singular, it'd be a great restaurant name."

"Ooh, yeah. The Running Duck." Patrick stepped into the walk-in dry storage and returned with a bin of garlic, dumping a few heads onto the table. "I've always wondered"—he grunted with exertion as he pressed the heel of his hand down on them one at a time, his weight breaking the heads into cloves—"why management always starts people out front. So few are equipped for it."

The snort Evan emitted was not only indelicate, it was downright derisive, and he hated the truth in it as soon as he heard it. "No one said restaurant management was smart."

Patrick whacked a few cloves of garlic and wiped his knife down, looking it over again. "If this is none of my business, just ignore me, but—is that what's going on with you? Management crap?"

"Nothing's going on with me." Evan's easy slicing motions slowed, and he chanced a glance up at Patrick, but quickly went back to it, focusing on the task at hand.

"You said you've lived here fifteen years? I see you for the first time a month ago, and now you're here a couple of times a week. And I'm not judging you or anything—or complaining—but you're eating a *damned* lot of cheesecake."

"Your cheesecake has some sort of addictive drug in it." Evan kept dicing, eyes on the curl of his fingers holding the onion.

Patrick laughed softly as he skinned the garlic cloves. "You don't have to talk about it if you don't want to, but it seems pretty clear something is going on. Just—the floor's yours if you need to talk. That's all I'm saying…"

"I've only been in Brooklyn a few months, and—" Evan stopped and dared to look up, finding Patrick's eyes on him, warm and gentle. Concerned. Understanding.

Oh, hell.

He chilled with fresh humiliation at his behavior earlier that night. A lazy, incompetent line cook was something he had dealt with more than once in his career. His overreaction was an embarrassment. But Patrick had become a safe place to land, even if only in easy banter, cheesecake and casual food. "She was already there when I was hired. I was told I could build the kitchen staff completely to my liking—hire and fire at will. Except for her."

Patrick began mincing again. "So, it's *indirectly* management."

"Yes. I feel like my hands are tied—"

"They're probably not as tied as you think they are."

Evan stopped and wiped his blade as Patrick stepped away to fetch bottles of water. "She stayed. Mr. DiSante actually believes—"

They knocked bottle mouths together before drinking, Evan wiping his mouth to hide his new interest in Patrick's Adam's apple, pronounced and inviting as it bobbed with each swallow. "Mr. DiSante actually believes that Perci is a descendant of Julia Child."

Patrick popped the bottle from his mouth with a hiss, eyes big and round in surprise. "What? Does Julia Child even *have* descendants?"

"No. Childless—ironically enough."

"So, because she's a *descendant*... "

"I had to keep her. The man's nuts and I've had it." Evan picked up his knife and split a peeled potato in half with a forceful *whomp*. "Before long, I'm afraid I'm going to shove her fat ass into the convection oven, turn it on and go on holiday."

Patrick blinked and scooped up his pile of minced garlic. "You're going all Sweeney Todd on me right now. And you have a very impressive sharp in your hand."

Evan nodded and continued to work the potato into a perfect quarter-inch dice.

"And you know how to use it."

Evan let a smile spread across his face and grabbed more potatoes from the bin. "Persephone Child," he sing-songed. "She's—I don't have issues with age, for the record—but she's in her late fifties and gives a bad name to every older line cook in the field."

"Experience has not been her friend?"

"No. It's made her lazy. And careless. And she has this overblown sense of entitlement just because she's been walking the planet longer than the rest of us."

Realizing he was standing there not doing anything, he got back to work. With every few words, Evan sliced a thick slab of potato in a long motion ending with a staccato as the knife hit the board.

"She has no urgency to her work"—*slice—thunk*—"and makes little mistakes that pile up." *Slice, slice, slice—thunk.* "No respect for the dishes, for how they work together"—*dice, dice, dice, dice*—"how each element depends on the others to complete a meal, a table."

As Evan talked, his motions sped, the perfect dice remaining perfect.

"You—you don't just cook food haphazardly. Timing is everything, from the moment a guest enters your restaurant until they walk out the door and open that table for another turn. She just doesn't give a—" He grabbed another peeled potato and started working on it, deliberate and focused. "You can't just stand on the line casually putting heat under food and assume the expeditor will tidy it all up for you."

He became almost manic in action as the words tumbled out of his mouth, taking out all the night's residual anger and frustration on a pile of potatoes and Patrick's listening ear.

And Patrick, having finished enough garlic to start the next day, began wiping down the bench and putting away the pans of *mise* while Evan carried on and finished the pile of potatoes, tunnel-visioned in his anger.

"She dances on my every nerve. I can feel my body tense when I know she's going to be on the line. She looks at me like I'm some sort of idiot and *she's* the one—" He scooped a pile of diced potatoes into a waiting water-filled pot, the *plop-plop-plop* echoing in the quiet kitchen. It stopped him short. He sounded bitter. Spiteful.

Awareness that he wasn't being entirely forthright about how poorly he had handled his own kitchen washed over him. Patrick's motions stopped as well and their eyes met from opposite corners of the small kitchen, as if Patrick somehow already knew the truth.

"I'm an asshole." Patrick raised an eyebrow in question and Evan explained. Or tried. "I'm standing here telling you about a woman you don't even know, painting her to be this evil incarnation of an obstinate teenager—and believe me, she's pretty awful—"

"You've put up with her for too long."

"That's just it. I have. But tonight—" Evan grabbed his water and took a deep slug. "I completely lost my shit. In front of her, in front of my entire staff. For all I know, the dining room heard me."

"Oh God..."

"I don't *do* that, Patrick. I mean, I know you don't know me and you have no reason to believe that I'm not just another pompous, pretentious chef, but—"

"Actually, I have every reason to believe you're not." Patrick grabbed a few of the last potatoes and tossed one to Evan, who caught it with a furrowed brow. "The first night I met you, you were with your staff—a group of people who all clearly respect each other very much. Who obviously love working together. That doesn't happen while working under a pompous pretentious asshole."

"She wasn't there." Evan did not look up, but continued to slice the potato into slabs.

"Why would she have been? She doesn't belong."

Evan looked up. "Maybe that's my fault too. I keep blaming her for my foul mood and she's sure as hell not helping, but—" He started slicing the slabs of potato into fat sticks.

"Can I ask you a question?"

"Yeah." He turned the sticks to dice and rolled his eyes at himself. "Hit me."

"Do you still remember that thing that made you decide that this"—Patrick motioned around his kitchen—"that this is it? Like, that moment the duck finally sinks onto the water? That you were where you belonged."

Evan made another cut and stared down at the pile of diced potato in front of him, the sheen of his knife glaring at him as it reflected the fluorescent lights overhead. He searched in the glare. In the potato. In the feel of the knife in his hand and the mat beneath his clog-shoed feet. In the sound of the knife hitting the board as he made one more cut to finish the job.

And he couldn't answer.

"I—I'm sorry. That was—I'm sorry." Patrick shook the pot of potatoes and looked inside to check their progress. Satisfied, he took the pile from Evan and dropped it into the pan, carrying the heavy pot to the range to sit until morning. "I hit a nerve."

Evan did not blink. Did not move. Did not stop staring at the board in front of him. "Right dead in the center of it."

"I'm so fucking sorry. I'm out of line." Patrick eased Evan's knife from his grip and rinsed off both of the chef's knives. He wiped them dry and laid them gently on Evan's knife bag. "If—if I haven't completely insulted you, go back to your story as I finish up." He shoved a stool under Evan's ass, patting his back when Evan mindlessly sat on it. "You need to talk and I need to shut the fuck up."

"No. You're right. I—I've been so stuck in the monotony of it all and—" Evan finally looked up into Patrick's eyes, relieved to find him waiting for him so expectantly. So patiently.

"I mean, it's obvious you love your work. I just wonder if maybe you need to remember why you fell in love with it in the first place."

Just like that first morning at the diner, with one simple thought Patrick stopped the world from spinning so Evan could start to see again.

Don't look at the menu. Look at me.

"I haven't even had my cheesecake tonight."

"It's okay. We sort of got sidetracked." Patrick wiped down the cutting boards and put them up on their shelf and with one final wipe of the table, went to the reach-in. "I have plain and chocolate mocha fresh from this morning. We have some individual servings in the walk-in—"

"Plain. No. Wait. Did you say chocolate mocha?"

Patrick smiled and pulled out the chocolate cheesecake.

Evan's mouth watered. "Oh, good. You have two pieces."

"You want them both?"

"No—no. Would you like to—" Evan stopped himself and met Patrick's gaze again. "We're almost done here?"

"Just have to start the dishwasher and lock up."

"Would you like to—can we take them up to my place? I'm just up the road and I have a fantastic dark Egyptian roast that would pair perfectly with the chocolate."

Patrick turned from the table and grabbed a carry-out box that he popped open and delicately loaded with the cheesecake. "I take it this means I didn't insult you."

"No. Not at all." Evan stood, put the knives into his bag and rolled it back up. "It's a nerve that needed to be hit."

Patrick's smile was soft—timid, almost. It had been so long since Evan felt as if he had a voice worth listening to—in the kitchen or outside of it. And standing here, with this man—this virtual stranger—he had a voice and an audience. An empathetic audience that didn't need him to be *Chef*.

Just Evan. The boy from Quincy, Illinois who was still trying to find his way.

III. Entrée

The start of the dinner, often lighter than the
main course: soup, soufflé or fish.

"Dini. From *amandine… reteta?*"

"Yes. It's an almond torte."

Patrick cocked his head like the critter staring at him from the floor, but in the opposite direction. Her light brown fur was offset by her black face and ears, and her eyes were big and round and appeared to be indelicately outlined with kohl. "Chef, I hate to break it to you, but that is not a torte. That?" He pointed at the dog. "Is actually a pug. In pink house slippers."

"They're socks, I'll have you know, and Dini doesn't like the hardwood on her paws—" Evan stopped hanging up Patrick's hat and coat in mid-motion; the expression on Patrick's face was equal parts hilarious, adorable and confused. "What?"

"Lady Amandine Reteta of Chelsea," Patrick began, voice affected, fake-British and quite haughty—for a Brooklynite. "Otherwise known as Dini, the pristine pug with pink house slippers, who belongs—importantly—to a Sweeney Todd-esque chef in the greatest city in the world, New York."

Patrick ended his pronouncement by squatting down by the dog and scratching under her chin. "This is a lot to wrap my head around." He smiled back up to Evan as the pug snorted off to her bed, clearly as impressed with her new visitor as he was with her. "That is a dog. Not a dessert."

Evan finally hung up Patrick's belongings, grabbed the cake box and turned to the kitchen. "I'm just going to take both of those pieces of cheesecake and eat them. Right in front of you."

Patrick laughed and stood, his knees popping noisily. "You can't hurt me by hoarding the cheesecake, you know. I have an in with the guy who makes them." With one more look at the dog before following Evan into his kitchen, he added, "She's sorta cute."

"Sorta? That's all you can muster?"

"For a pug."

The walk back to Evan's had been a chilly one, the damp April air holding on to every last gasp of winter. Evan pulled out a stool at his kitchen island for Patrick and began making panini. A warm sandwich sounded much more appealing than a cold cheesecake—at least momentarily.

"Just don't go to any trouble, Chef."

Evan turned from the refrigerator and shot a playful glare in Patrick's direction. "This is what I *do*."

"Sorry. I hate when people say that to me, too." Patrick settled on the barstool and tried again. "I'd love a sandwich, thank you."

"Besides, you've already cooked quite a few meals for me. It's the least I can do." Evan plopped a couple of different loaves of bread onto the island along with packages of cheeses and meats, lettuce and jars containing various homemade spreads and chutneys. "Anything you don't like?"

"Tripe."

Evan looked his items over dramatically. "Hmm, no worries there. And that means no haggis? How very un-Irish of you."

"No. Stop. Haggis is Scottish. We don't want that disgusting shit."

"My most humble apologies—I should probably know better. Tripe can be good if cooked right, though."

"Yeah, well, the one time I *did* eat it was in middle school. Which just so happened to fall on the same night I had the worst stomach flu of my life, courtesy of Patricia Horowitz."

Evan lifted a loaf of ciabatta. "Should I ask how Ms. Horowitz gave you the stomach flu?" He offered a whole wheat sourdough also, but Patrick flapped his hand in dismissal.

"I'm at your mercy. She, uh… tried to tongue-kiss me under the slide at the park."

Evan lifted an eyebrow and tossed the sourdough back in its drawer. "So did you swear off tongue-kissing after that, too?"

"No, just girls."

"Ah, smart man."

With a wink, Evan offered Patrick the heel of the bread and set about making their sandwiches. He sniffed the fig jam in pleasure before spreading the fresh slices of bread with it, topping them with prosciutto and shaved asiago cheese. "Red onion?"

Patrick nodded and looked down as Dini came into the kitchen to investigate the ruckus disturbing her beauty sleep. "So, Chef. Amandine Reteta. You have to have a million dishes just dancing around in your back pocket, but a Romanian chocolate sponge cake got the honors."

"It's an homage to my Aunt Millie."

"Mom's side or dad's?"

"Neither."

"Oh. *That* kind of aunt."

Evan laughed and laid the sandwiches down on the hot griddle, setting a heated cast-iron skillet on top of them. "No, not—" He tossed a small chunk of cheese down to the now-whining dog and sighed, looking up at Patrick again with a shy smile. "Thank you for coming over. I haven't allowed myself much time to socialize lately."

"That's a sign of a man who works too hard."

"And I moved out of the city to avoid doing just that—"

"So, here I am. Your Brooklyn diversion." Patrick's eyes were lively and flirtatious and Evan wondered how he had the energy after such long, exhausting days. "Tell me about Aunt Millie."

Evan shaved another few pieces of cheese and handed one to Patrick. "Aunt Millie lived across the street from us. She'd watch me after school, but even when I was older, I'd still go over there. Her house was magical. *She's* magical."

"And she baked?"

"She did everything. Sculpting and painting, cooking and gardening." Evan lifted the cast-iron skillet to check the sandwiches and put it back, unsatisfied. "She was a leftover hippie. All bohemian, with her bangles and flowing caftans. Incense burning—"

Patrick lifted his hand to his mouth and imitated taking a drag of a blunt. "Yeah?"

"Yeah. She smoked good shit, too." Evan smiled at the memory of his discovery of her love of good marijuana. The only thing that had kept him quiet about it was her promise of "a little taste" on his eighteenth birthday.

Evan checked the sandwiches again and smiled at the toasted bread, brown and crisp and perfect. "And Mom was grateful Millie could be there for me. She wasn't a typical mom—she worked weird hours and stuff—and I wasn't the typical son, so it worked."

He cut the sandwiches, plated them alongside a toss of spring lettuces and shook up a small Mason jar of vinaigrette. "Every time I went over there Millie had a new project for me. But mostly, we cooked." He turned to an iPod dock on his counter and flipped it on, closing his eyes and bopping his head in rhythm as the sounds of Cream wafted through the kitchen.

Without opening his eyes, lost in the memories of Millie's kitchen, of Millie's lessons, he said, "And this was playing. Every day. Every hour." He opened his eyes to see Patrick smiling at him—maybe even biting back a friendly laugh. "I still play this stuff in the kitchen at work. Just keeps us all moving, you know?"

"That's what we play too—something about it... "

"Yes. You can sing along or just let it time your work, twirl your favorite line cook into a spin during a lull—"

Before Evan even noticed him get up, Patrick took Evan by the hand and twirled him in to a dance with a warm smile and an even warmer hand pressed to his back.

"Prep in rhythm with The Stones... "

Evan laughed and moved them to the refrigerator, spinning and moving to the music as he gathered bottles of beer, watching Patrick's ass as he swayed his way back to his stool. "She always said three things: *Be true to yourself; moisturize nightly and taste everything.*" He popped the caps off of the bottles and slid

Patrick's beer and plate over to him. "She taught me everything I love."

When Patrick pulled the beer from his lips with a pop, Evan had the decency to blush at Patrick's amused smile and lifted eyebrow.

"Well, not *everything*."

"Like tongue-kisses under the slide?"

"She definitely didn't teach me about those."

Patrick finally bit into the sandwich. As he chewed, he twisted and turned the edges around, looking for a drip of jam squirting out of an edge to lick at. "You have to give me your jam recipe."

"I'll do you one better." Evan took a bite of his food and went to his pantry. He dug into the back corner of the top shelf and pulled down a jar of the preserves. "Take some home. Can't give you a recipe. I sort of wing it as I go."

"So, is this culinary school or Millie?"

"Millie. We'd preserve all sorts of things. Tomatoes, stone fruits and berries. She'd make jams and jellies, pickles and chutneys, different varieties of pesto and spreads."

"And *amandine reteta*."

"Well, that one was special." Evan joined Patrick at the island, and they ate as they talked, forgetting all about cheesecake and that it was already two a.m. "I was in fourth grade, I think. And I'd tried out for Linus in *You're a Good Man, Charlie Brown*. I knew the lines, I knew the songs. I was a shoo-in." Patrick tensed, as if anticipating the outcome, and Evan nodded in affirmation. "I ended up on set design. They said I'd be great at that. And I was, but the day I found out—"

"Who wants to be consoled with that bullshit?"

"So, after school, I went to Millie's like usual, and it must have been written all over my face. She let me wallow—just that day. I said I wanted chocolate cake. I kept waiting for the lecture about having cake for dinner, but it never came."

"So you made *amandine*."

"I'd never had a homemade cake before—Mom always did stuff from the box, you know?" Evan took a pull of his beer and pulled up a stool next to Patrick, relaxing for the first time that day. "I miss those simple pleasures sometimes—forget to allow myself."

"Maybe that's why you keep coming back to my restaurant."

"I come back to your restaurant because it's *good*, not simple."

"So you say."

"And besides, the cook's kinda cute."

"Sorta like a pug."

Evan laughed, pulled a slice of prosciutto from his sandwich and fed it to Dini, who was walking around in circles trying to decide between begging and napping. "Anyway, like everything else with Millie, I not only got a chocolate cake, but I learned techniques. I almost freaked out when she held the bowl of whipped egg whites upside down over my head."

"I bet they didn't budge."

"Not an inch. Perfection. I learned how to temper eggs with the almond cream and temper chocolate with the ganache. And then—and *then*—when we pushed the ganache over the edge of the filled cake and it fell down the sides and seeped into the seams"—Evan was lost in his memories, almost acting out the motions—"catching it on my finger—oh God. It was better than any stupid part in a stupid old play."

"Food heals."

"It does. It did that day." Evan licked a drip of jam from his fingers and nodded, the memories warm in his mind, sure he could smell the cake baking in the oven.

"She sounds like an amazing woman."

►•◄

"Polenta."

"Pardon?" Patrick tugged on Dini's leash as she made way to sniff into someone's garbage.

Evan had popped into the diner the day after yet another stressful and mind-numbing shift and sampled a new cheesecake masterpiece—lemon with a delicate hazelnut crust. Before he could think twice about it, he invited Patrick to join him for Dini's walk the following day, a task he happily took from her professional walker on his days off.

And to his great pleasure, Patrick didn't even hesitate before accepting.

"The other night, you got me thinking. About Millie."

Patrick tightened his grip on Dini's leash and hooked his other arm through Evan's. "So, naturally—polenta."

Evan smiled and pulled his arm closer, Patrick readily following. "Do—do you want me to take the leash?"

"No. Then I'd have to let go of you too."

Evan ignored the fact that they only had to change sides and they could still hang on. He simply hummed, enjoying the pull of Patrick's arm in his and the way the sun's last rays peeked over the roofs of the quiet neighborhood, giving Patrick's face a golden glow. "She'd make it maybe once a week. She always timed it to be done just as I got home from school. We'd pour it out on the counter to cool, and—"

"Did she slice it into portions with twine?"

"Oh, twine with wooden spoons on each end for weight, and then she'd grill it or pan-fry it. I always had to poke at the mound, watch it jiggle like Jello. She'd smack my hand away, but I always got the dirty pot anyway."

"Okay, you've lost me. Cleaning is never the best part."

"Ah, but see, here's the thing. If you let that thin layer dry over the heat? You can peel it off; it tastes like Fritos. I don't know how many times I burned my fingers on it, because once it's cool, it's sort of gross, but—"

"Okay, clearly my childhood was deprived. Oona would never have let me pick at a dirty pot."

"Well, no one says you're too old to start now."

"Health department might take issue."

"Pft. You could walk into our kitchen any given night after service and find me and Rosey battling it out for the last hotel pan waiting to be washed."

"Now that I'd like to see."

"It usually involves a lot of Spanish cursing and elbows. Total class. All the way."

▶•◀

"This is a day for coddle." Patrick lifted his camera to his eye and focused, the leather case still attached and bobbing gently in the breeze.

They had finally exchanged phone numbers, and Evan was pleasantly surprised at the call that came through on his next day off.

"So, I'm out here at Pier Six. I have a beautiful spring day, this skyline and my Yashika. The only thing missing is you."

After an explanation that Patrick's "Yashika" was a vintage film camera, Evan packed an impromptu picnic and was there before he could talk himself out of it. It seemed like a date. He missed dating. He cherished this budding friendship. Dates could completely screw that all up.

He'd tossed in a good bottle of Beaujolais anyway.

Evan looked out at where Patrick was focusing and waited for the snap of the shutter to ask, "Coddle. That's a stew, right?"

"Yeah. Better reheated than the first time around. Makes the gravy thicker."

"So, one of Oona's specialties?"

"Yes. And her mother's, and *her* mother's. Peasant food. Potatoes, sausage, rashers, onion, stock and thyme. That's it." Patrick continued to frame shots of Manhattan's skyline from their spot in the park as he talked, snapping pictures, advancing the film and readjusting the tripod. "Oona would have it on the stove at least once a week from October through April. Daideo—that's Gramps—he wouldn't eat it unless it was reheated. She'd get so angry with him." He stopped long enough to imitate his grandmother, complete with hand gestures and furrowed brow. "*I worked on this all day, Raymond.*"

Evan laughed at the affectation, imagining a round, fiery woman, apron stained with that day's meals and years' worth of grease spots. "Tough old broad, I take it?"

"The toughest—and the most tender. He'd just roll his eyes at her, knowing better. You dump the ingredients in, let it sit for an hour and it's done."

"So, what'd you do? Fridge it up and pull it out later in the evening?"

"Yep. We'd go out and work in the garage or ride bikes, play stoop ball. Anything to kill time and then get it out, heat it back up and—" He kissed his fingers put his hand over his heart. "Heaven in a bowl."

Patrick went back to his camera. After the next shot wouldn't take, he rewound the film, put it into its canister and pocketed it before loading another roll.

Evan sighed as it plopped into place. Patrick side-eyed him, snapped the back of the case closed and advanced the film to the first frame. "I'm taking your picture today. You're not getting out of this."

"Who said I was trying?"

"You've been dodging the lens like a broken eggshell floating in the white." Patrick started disassembling his tripod with the ease of a professional.

"That's because broken shell clings to broken shell. C'mere." Evan pulled his phone out of his back pocket and opened an arm for Patrick to snuggle into. "Is this backdrop good, Mr. Photographer?"

"It's the city—of course it's good."

Evan lifted his phone and their faces appeared on the screen, making them both smile. "Say Taleggio."

Patrick laughed and Evan snapped the picture. It was a little blurry with a lot of smile.

It was perfect.

"Send it to me." When Patrick's phone buzzed, he smiled again looking at the shot. "So, you saying we're broken?"

"No." Evan took Patrick's hand and walked. He wanted to find the perfect spot by the river for their picnic. "We just have similar stories. Our history. Our passion—which I'm afraid I'm losing and it scares the hell out of me—"

"I seem to remember an evening not too long ago when you violently—pardon me—*passionately*—prepped *mise* in my kitchen. I don't think you've lost your passion."

"Maybe I've just misplaced it." Satisfied with the hill and the view, Evan shrugged his bag off his shoulders and began to unpack.

"Do you think it's just the mess with Perci?"

"She's clouding my view of things, but—I've dealt with stupid line cooks before." Evan plopped the final piece onto their blanket and sighed. "You heard Rosey's rat story, right?"

"Yeah. That was one *vile* story."

"I feel like that rat. Like something's eating me from the inside out, making me do things I don't want to do. This churning, bubbling cauldron of—" He peeled open a package of soppressata, grumbling for the right word. "Of something."

"Well, I think you've got one up on that rat."

"I'm not dead?"

"You are not dead. Or maggot-filled, for that matter."

"No. No, I'm not. I actually feel pretty good… today." Evan settled his gaze on Patrick's eyes.

"I do too." Patrick winked, shifting off of his shins and onto his ass. "So, what can I do to help?" He snooped into the packages of meats and cheeses Evan had pulled out of his satchel, laughing when Evan smacked his hand away from the box of cookies he'd stowed.

"Dessert, young man. After the meal." Evan handed Patrick the bottle of wine to uncork. "And just keep doing exactly what you've been doing."

"Easy enough, Chef."

Once everything was in place, Evan lifted his glass to Patrick's. "*Cin cin.*"

"*Sláinte.*"

They ate in relative silence, people-watching, laughing at silly dog antics and the Many Walks of Children, giving them ridiculous names.

There was the *I've Had to Pee for an Hour* dance, and of course, *I Told You I Was Going to Have a Meltdown Today* stomp, and Evan's personal favorite, the *Where's My Fucking Tiara?* march.

It was easy. And warm. And whether Evan was right or not about this being a date, he no longer cared.

They packed up, and as Patrick handed the folded blanket back to Evan, he clung to it for an extra second, getting Evan's full attention. "Thank you, Chef. This has been a welcome break."

"I'm glad we both had the time off." Evan hiked his bag up on his shoulder and they started their walk back, buttoning their jackets as a breeze blew in from the river. "Can I ask you a favor, though?"

"Sure. Anything."

"Will you please call me Evan—not Chef?"

Patrick sucked in a breath in surprise and stopped, stepping in front of Evan and resting his hand on Evan's arm, eyes big and round and full of apology. "You've asked me before—I am so sorry."

"No. It's not a huge thing. I just—" Evan nodded to keep walking, hooking his arm in Patrick's. "You're becoming a friend and—"

"It puts a distance between us?"

"Yes. And it's good on the line, but you're not—" Evan sighed and snuggled in tighter as a breeze blew in from the water. "It's nice having a friend away from work. You get it without the 'boss' factor mucking it up." He hoped his next thought wasn't true. "Of course, there's the risk that I'm coming off like a complete nut job... "

"You are hardly a nut job—sometimes a good ship hits rough seas."

"I hope that's all this is."

They walked a little farther, in no hurry to put an end to the day, Patrick stopping to open his camera for another shot. "And I'll stop calling you Chef if you promise me one thing."

"What's that?"

"That we keep this up. Socializing."

"Is that what this is?"

Patrick smiled, blushed even, and Evan thought he might melt on the spot—he was feeling very adolescent and silly. "Yes, Patrick. I'd like to keep this up. Very much."

"Good." Patrick unhooked Evan's bag from his shoulder, taking the burden for himself. "So, I've been thinking. What can one expect from the chef's table at Il Boschetto?"

Evan's mouth and eyes popped open and a smile took over his face. "You'll come!?"

"I'd be honored to. Now that I'm your official confidant and all." They began walking arm in arm again, the setting sun coloring the sky with brilliant shades of pink and purple. "But I have one condition."

"You sure have a lot of conditions today."

"This is a good one, though—Perci doesn't touch my meal."

Evan laughed. "No worries. It's *chef's* table. I do it all."

"Then bring me your best."

"Nothing less."

"Oh, and one more?"

"You're pushing it, buster."

"Do not *ever* bring that rat up again."

►•◄

On another shared day off—something that was becoming a regular occurrence—they sat at a small round table by the window in a coffee shop they'd visited together once before, quietly sugaring, stirring and taste-testing their coffee. Patrick popped the cellophane wrapper of his biscotti and blushed at the look Evan gave him.

"Don't judge me. I love biscotti." Evan's eyebrow remained cocked as he sipped his coffee while Patrick removed the lid from his cup and dipped the sweet bread. "You're judging me."

"I'm not judging you." He was judging him. Biscotti. Prepackaged. He was judging him *hard*.

"You are and—" Patrick took a bite and closed one eye, chewing slowly. "Dear God, please judge me."

"We should have just gone to the diner."

"No. I needed a break. We just need a better coffee shop."

"Because they're so hard to find in this city." Evan smiled around the lip of his cup, his eyes dancing as he offered a napkin for Patrick to dump the biscotti into.

Then he risked taking his own bite. And made a face so strained, it stretched muscles he'd forgotten he had.

"Okay, now I'm judging *you* because you knew that'd be bad."

"We need a better coffee shop."

Patrick took one last regretful look at the tasteless biscotti and sipped his coffee, less content than he had been when they sat down. "So, I have a confession."

"You really like cardboard-flavored biscotti?"

"No. I do not—although I'm considering swiping that back and sucking it up anyway because—"

"You will do no such thing in my presence."

They shared a smile and Patrick looked down, spinning his cup on the table. "I've been stalking you."

"Pardon?"

Patrick blushed and rolled his eyes. "Well, not really *stalking*." Evan crossed his arms in mock indignation and Patrick hurried to continue. "I mean, I looked you up after that first night. Because—" He sipped his coffee and sighed. "Because I wanted to be able to spout off that the chef from whatever restaurant you were from liked my boxty."

"And who would you spout this off to?"

"Probably just my mother. No one else would give a damn."

"I'm hardly a big deal."

"Mmm. I don't know about that." When their eyes met, Patrick licked his lips and rushed ahead. "Anyway, I hadn't read your biography then. I figured I'd never see you again—chefs don't tend to frequent the place—" He fidgeted with the lid of his cup, popping it off and on—and on and on when it wouldn't settle back into place.

It was the first time Evan had seen Patrick's bluster falter. It was sort of cute.

"That's because too many chefs are pretentious blowhards."

"You most definitely are not that."

"Oh, I have my moments, as we've clearly seen."

Patrick quickly looked up and, catching Evan's eye, darted his gaze back to the table. He tried his lid one more time, finally achieving success. But he still fidgeted.

Evan put his hand on Patrick's. "What did you find that's made you so nervous?"

"I'm not nervous—"

"You're nervous *and* a horrible liar." And then it hit him and he sat back with a groan. "It's the Beard Award, isn't it?"

"Yes." Patrick picked up the empty sugar packets from the table and started stuffing the ripped tops into their respective pouches. "I have a fucking James Beard winner in my kitchen, flicking at my dull knives, prepping *mise* like a rock star while I use his thousand dollar chef's knife to hack away at vegetables like a preschooler with Play-Doh."

"Okay, wait. Did I make you feel that way? That night?"

"Well. No. No, you've never—"

"Then I'm not sure I understand." Evan pointed at Patrick's fidgety hands.

Patrick sighed and finally met Evan's eye, the tension in his shoulders easing as a shy smile curled his lips. "It *intimidates* me. Why didn't you tell me?"

"Because—" Evan opened his palm for the sugar packets that Patrick had nervously folded into miniscule rectangles. "Give me those. You're making *me* nervous." He put them in the napkin with the biscotti. "And I didn't tell you because it's not important. There was no intentional omission—"

"Oh! No! I didn't think you were purposely... no. It's just—if I had such an honor, especially the Rising Star Award? Chef—" He shook his head and started over. "*Evan*, those are the Oscars for you guys."

"They are." Evan bit his lip. He hated this. It threw their balance off-kilter, and being with Patrick was a balance he was beginning to depend on, a place to reset from the unrest of his job.

"How old were you?"

"Twenty-eight. I'd just started at Il Boschetto."

Patrick nodded and sipped his coffee.

And Evan waited for more questions. None came.

"See, this is why I don't say anything. If it was up to me, it wouldn't even be on the website. It makes things… weird."

"I don't mean to make things weird. I keep telling myself that I should be honored you keep coming back for my food and—"

"And you should be. You should also be honored that that guy… Walter? The one who wears that fur-lined atrocity of a coat and smells like Stouffer's lasagna and piss? You should be honored he shows up every day, too."

"Walter has the hots for Angel."

Evan ignored him. "Because there are a million choices in this city—all within walking distance of wherever he lives—and he chooses your place. Your food. I've heard him ask if you're the one cooking, so don't give me any of this Angel bullshit."

"Well, if he's asking for me, that's ridiculous. Oscar does a fine job."

"*Fine* is stretching it. But *you* make the food sing, and that's my point."

Evan let the silence linger for a few more moments, but when Patrick's attention drifted to the world outside the window, he pushed for one more point.

"All I'm saying is, don't sell yourself short, especially in comparison to me."

Patrick kept his gaze on the street, but a devilish grin spread across his face in spite of his clear effort to stop it. He finally turned to Evan with one more sad attempt at looking upset. "But I am short—in comparison to you."

Evan rolled his eyes and laughed, sitting back with relief. "Okay, smart-ass. Let's level the playing field a little. You haven't been totally forthcoming either."

Patrick frowned in question and then—"Ah, here it comes."

"One class short of your degree, *Paddy*. What happened?"

"You won't accept that it's just one of those things, will you?"

"No."

Patrick sat back too, crossing his arms and legs instead of talking.

"Hey. If this isn't something you want to talk about—"

"No, no. It's only fair." He picked up the sugar packets again, unfolding one and refolding it before looking back up at Evan.

"I'm not keeping score," Evan said.

"I know." Patrick smiled shyly and flicked the paper back to the trash pile with the biscotti. "Johnny's was hurting when he hired me. They were putting out stale doughnuts and blueberry muffins, using industrial-sized cans of veggies—you know the routine."

"Packaged biscotti... "

"He wouldn't know a biscotti if it bit him in the ass, but yeah. Third-rate shit wasn't cutting it, especially with the way the food scene was growing."

"Competition only makes us better."

"Right. Johnny needed to compete and he didn't know how. And, I'd been baking with Oona since I was a kid. Was doing quite a bit at the café in Williamsburg. So, I asked him if I could make some fresh treats for breakfast—desserts, too. He gave me three weeks to make it worth his while."

Evan nodded, knowing how it went. "I bet it only took ten days."

"Word travels. It took off like wildfire. So I started making the cheesecakes, coming up with new flavors, making pies, cakes, pastries—the whole menu expanded. He's raking in the cash, even Zagat writes us up real nice. So, he sends me off to FCI."

Evan blinked, sure his mouth was hanging open. "You went to the French Culinary Institute."

"Well, it's no CIA, but yeah."

"Stop it."

Patrick smiled. "I had to back off on my hours at the diner, but Johnny paid for my whole ride. Said I reminded him of himself, which," Patrick sat himself forward, his elbows on the table, and whispered, "was a little frightening. Lovely man. Not someone I want to emulate."

"Why do I get the feeling he's short, balding and smells like medicine?"

"Because—" Patrick barked a laugh and chugged his coffee. "Because he is. *Such* a stereotype, but you know—thank God for him."

"Yes. So, you're a pastry chef?"

"No. He had a heart attack. I never finished."

Evan waved his hand in dismissal. "Semantics. How many years ago was this?"

"About the same time you got your Beard, sounds like."

"So did he just pull the money, and you couldn't go back?"

"No. Money's not—" Patrick stopped himself and tipped his cup all the way back for the final dregs of coffee. "Money has nothing to do with it." He took a breath as if to continue that thought, but stopped again, rolling his eyes as the espresso machine whirred and interrupted their conversation. "I just figured we'd settled, me and Johnny. He helped me get my feet planted and I helped save his business."

"So, if you've settled, why are you still paying him back?"

Patrick's eyes narrowed and he spun his empty cup on the table, holding Evan's gaze firmly. "Where are you going with this?"

"Well, I mean, you don't have to be stuck there—if you've settled your debt to him. He got you through school; you got his business back on the map. Maybe it's time to move up."

Patrick sat back as if he'd been waiting for this to come between them. "You saying I'm not good enough? Because I don't have some piece of paper and I work at a diner?" His accent thickened and his posture pushed beyond proud into arrogant, legs spread, fingers tapping angry rhythms on his coffee cup.

And Evan was completely blindsided by it. "No. I'm not even implying that. I'm saying—" Patrick scoffed, but Evan pushed on. "I'm saying you're *more* than that place."

"Maybe I like it there, huh? Maybe I like making simple food. Maybe I like that feeling of making people happy with the stuff that reminds them of home. I'm not ashamed of the work I do there."

"Nor should you be. I don't understand why you're getting so defensive." There was a flash of regret in Patrick's eyes, so Evan tried again. "Don't you want to work someplace where you have functional equipment? Where the clientele appreciates the work you put into your food? The skill behind those desserts?"

Patrick rolled his eyes like a bored teenager listening to his father's lecture. "And they don't now?"

"They know they *like* it. Hell, I thought you farmed out your desserts, they were so fucking good."

"See there." Patrick sat up and took a swig from his cup, crunching it up angrily when he found it empty. "Right there. You assumed I farmed it out because a short order cook couldn't possibly—"

"No! Do not—no." Evan took a breath and sat back, weighing his words, growling at the espresso machine that whirred into action again and wondered why they'd not heard it at all before now, when it fed the crumbling of their conversation. "It's the *place*, not the cook. You are amazing. I haven't been saying that because I have nothing better to say to you."

"You lost me."

At least he was listening. "Okay, you don't expect Mozart to be busking down at the Dekalb Q, or... or...Van Gogh to waltz into your house ready to paint your bathroom Seaturf Blue."

"What if that's how they *want* to make their living, huh? Does that make them less talented? I mean, just imagine how amazing your wait for the train would be—or how stunning that bathroom would look if Van Gogh did the paint job."

Evan sighed, tapped out. "It doesn't make them less talented. It just makes them..." He was out of argument.

"Makes them what—*Chef*?"

Evan was ready to fire back, hurt that the title he'd worked so hard to earn was suddenly a weapon to cut him down, to level a playing field he didn't even want to play on. And this from Patrick, of all people.

He revved up a shitty retort, and a flock of loud teenagers came barreling through the door, giggling and pushing and flirting and pimpling so disruptively that he had to stop. And reconsider. And stare at this man who was so angry with him, for reasons he didn't understand.

So instead he lifted a finger and shot Patrick a glare. "We're not done." He got up and snuck in front of the chaotic horde and bought two bottles of water. Reset the conversation, maybe. Give them both something new to fidget with on the table. Anything.

When he came back, he purposely nudged Patrick's feet with his own, making him look up. Evan caught a glimpse of apology in his eyes—but only a glimpse. "This is what I want you to hear. Do I have you?"

"You have me." Patrick tipped the mouth of his bottle to Evan's before he drank.

"You grabbed my attention that first night I was there with my staff. You're quite a force to be reckoned with, you know?"

Evan smiled then, blushing at the fact that his first, first, *first* impression was that the dude with the headband was gorgeous. "But then, I tasted your food and I *heard* you. You put yourself in everything you make; from the fifteenth plate of eggs over easy each morning to your newest cheesecake creation, you're there. Every time that damned bell rings behind me as I walk in, I know I can shed my own shit, focus on you and your food and remember why I love this insane life."

"Evan..."

"And Patrick, that's why I continue to come back. I can't speak for anyone else, but if you can serve people an escape from their day-to-day lives just by cooking your food, you're doing right. So, if you want to stay and cook your food and serve up your spirit until the day you can't stand anymore, and you want to do it at Johnny's, then by all means, you do that and you do it proudly."

Patrick looked down and back up at the teenagers, quiet now and gathering chairs around tables. He sighed and shook his head, finally looking Evan in the eyes. He seemed shy and unsure, so different from the cocky little bastard who had sat there moments before.

"All I'm saying is… pushing past the diner would be doing a *better* thing. For you. Because you're capable. Because you deserve a better situation than the one you're in. And you have the ability to do it."

Patrick nodded and took a swig of water, pulling up closer to the table as if in apology for being so far removed. "Thank you. I'm sorry. I'm—can I?" He cleared his throat, suddenly bashful. "Can I ask one more—I don't want to ramp this up again."

"Ask me."

"You pushed. You drove. You went for it. And you are—while I enjoy being in your company so fucking much, when it comes to your work, you are still clearly unhappy."

"Yes. I am."

"And why is that?"

"I still haven't figured that out."

"I'm happy there. Mostly. I mean, it does get mundane, and now that I've played with some good knives, I've been bugging Johnny to just buy us new ones." He took a swallow of water. "And now that you mention it, Walter really does smell like piss."

"Poor guy."

"But I guess I just wonder… when is it good enough? When do you know it's time to stop pushing?"

"I—I don't know. I guess it's different for everybody. And if you've found your 'good enough' at the diner, then—"

Patrick looked up and smiled crookedly and shyly, his voice so soft and friendly. "Maybe you should be intimidated by me instead. Maybe I've got it all figured out."

Evan's sigh of relief was big and loud and tinged with laughter. "Maybe that's another reason I keep coming back." He took a drink and caught Patrick's gaze as it fell to his throat when he swallowed. "Look, I'm—I'm sorry if I insulted you. It was the exact opposite of what I was going for."

"I know." Patrick took another pull of his water and turned his attention outside. The streets were getting busier as the day wound down. "I'm sorry I twisted it."

Evan reached his hand across the table and closed his eyes in gratitude when Patrick took it in his own, warm and calloused from years of stirring and slicing, lifting and butchering. A career mapped by the topography of his hands. "Are—are we okay?"

Patrick kept his attention outside, his voice quiet but sincere. "We're okay." He bit at his bottom lip, a little too pensive for Evan's comfort.

"Are you okay?"

"We're okay."

"Patrick."

Patrick took a quick breath and pulled his attention from the increasingly busy street back into the coffee shop. To their table. To Evan. A softness in Patrick's eyes mirrored his gentle grip on Evan's hand. "Say that again."

Evan didn't understand.

"My name. Say it again."

Evan's skin warmed from the inside out. This was unexpected after their argument. He uttered the name with all the affection he felt for this stubborn, proud man. "Patrick."

Patrick breathed in the sound like air, a smile settling on his face, a peace amidst the clamor of the shop and the rubble of their bitten words. "Yes. I'm—I'm okay."

"Good. If you want to talk about this again, it's on you. I won't bring it up, okay?"

Patrick waved him off. "No, you're fine." He took another breath and smiled devilishly. "I'm good. Besides, the way I see it? If I do stay where I am, I don't have to listen to some pompous, over-educated *chef de cuisine* tell me my meringue peaks aren't stiff enough."

Evan laughed, relief washing over him as he laced his fingers through Patrick's, their eyes locking with their fingers. "Stiff is, um... stiff is good."

Patrick chuckled deeply, softly, looking down at their hands and back up. He brushed his thumb over Evan's skin. "Stiff is very good."

▶•◀

"Where are the fucking condoms?"

Evan groaned and made to move, but just couldn't bring himself to do so. "Look up. Blue box—they changed the color."

"Convenient when speed is a priority. Christ."

"You okay?" Evan finally roused himself from his paperwork, his back stiff from being bent over the desk all afternoon. He peeked outside of his office to see if Theo had been able to find the box of latex finger cots he was frantically searching for.

"It's Perci." Theo plucked the box from the first aid cabinet and dug out a wrapped condom. It looked exactly as the name indicated, only smaller to go over a finger, keeping the blood from a wound in and the dirt from the world out. "Idiot was dripping blood into the fucking polenta."

"The polenta? Fifteen minutes before service!?" Evan was out of the office in a flash, following Theo through the hallway and up the stairs, his footsteps loud and heavy, his heart and mind racing to come up with an alternative.

"Yeah, we got another pot on, but—"

Evan took a calming breath before he got to the kitchen. He did not want to repeat his humiliating outburst of weeks past. There was already enough natural intensity driving pre-service activity. "Fuck. Eighty-six it for the first hour. Double up the mash. How are we on gnocchi?"

"Ahead of the game." Theo caught Perci's eye and showed her the finger cot in his hand, putting the box where it belonged in the kitchen. "Sanitize first."

She rolled her eyes, sucking the side of her bleeding finger into her mouth. "I know what to do."

"You've proven otherwise." Theo growled and adjusted his striped headwrap, his dark eyes firing anger. He was never one to settle for less than perfection.

Evan took one more deep breath. "Start with the gnocchi and the mash as a sub. Let Natasha and Ross know for front-of-house." He looked over Theo's shoulder. "And Perci?"

"Yes, Chef?"

"As soon as you're clean, I want you in my office."

"Yes, Chef."

"Excellent answers."

Theo looked over his *mise* and turned to Evan. It was almost time for service, when Theo would mentally disappear into line mode, creating sauces in his head before they were ordered. "I'm sorry I missed it, Chef."

"She knows protocol." Evan stepped into the kitchen to begin his nightly walk-through, making sure things were to his satisfaction, tasting as he went. "It's not your responsibility to think for the woman."

"No, but—"

Evan stopped at the saucier's station, grabbing a tasting spoon to dip into a bubbling pan of sauce. "Carlos, check your seasoning on the puttanesca. Hitting a bit acidic to me."

"Yes, Chef."

Theo began to apologize again, but Evan lifted a finger to stop him. "My kitchen—my responsibility." When Theo backed down, he continued, "Is every station covered tonight so I can finish downstairs?"

"We're good, Chef."

"Good. We don't want to have to resort to putting Rosey on the line."

"Oh God, no."

"HEY!"

▶•◄

"Chef! What'll it be tonight?"

Evan smiled up at Mimi, amused as always by the warmth in her smile and the bite of her tongue. If she weren't already, one day she'd be someone's Millie. Someone's Oona. He was sure of it. "Reuben. Potato pancakes. Iced tea."

"You want our menu pancakes or Patrick's off-menu crap?"

"Have you *had* his boxty?"

"No, I have not."

"Well, you try that first, *then* call it crap." He peeked around her to look into the kitchen, but couldn't catch a glimpse of the real reason he was here—a post-shift wind-down by the name of one Patrick Sullivan. "Menu variety this time, please."

"He's here, *cariño*. Just had to run downstairs for tomorrow's chicken."

"You have a coop down there?"

Evan ducked and laughed when Mimi swatted at him with her ticket pad. "Smart-ass. Walk-in freezer. I'm surprised he hasn't taken you down there."

"I've seen plenty of walk-ins in my day."

"Ah, but it holds such fond memories for him. He hasn't told you?"

"No... ?"

She stuck his ticket on the order holder and rested back against the counter. "He was hot shit up in Williamsburg, so he's still thinking he's a big shot down here—all full of his ridiculous Brooklyn swagger."

"He does have a nice swagger."

Mimi's eyes lit up. "I *knew* it. You're not just coming back here for the food, are you?"

"I do come back for the food." Evan blushed and picked at the scrappy menu in front of him. "But if it's taken you this long to figure it out, I'm sort of disappointed in you."

She lowered her gaze, her hand firmly attached to her hip. "I'm disappointed it's taken you this long to make a move."

He'd given up denying it—the growing affection between them washed slowly and steadily through his veins and had only ignited further after their tiff in the coffee shop. It felt amazing.

They had begun sharing quick texts during free moments in shifts:

Patrick: So the cops were just here.
Evan: What? Are you okay?
Patrick: Mimi slugged a guy. Tried to put her tip in her cleavage.
Evan: Isn't that where she always keeps them?
Patrick: You're missing the point.

They had also begun having late night phone conversations as they settled into their respective beds, moaning and groaning from the day's aches and pains, physical and otherwise. Just the other night, Evan had mused,

"I spent my shift wondering what kinds of seasonings one should put in a meat pie."

Patrick was quiet for a moment while Evan giggled, waiting for him to realize what he was talking about. And then—

"Are you talking Mrs. Lovett's meat pies?"

"Of course. But then I look at how wide Perci's old saggy ass is, and I'm thinking that while fat equals flavor—"

"Evan!"

So now, Evan didn't lie to Mimi. But he didn't respond either. He simply winked and rested his chin in his hand, waiting for more of her story. "Walk-in. Sexy swagger."

Mimi shook her head and started wiping down the already clean counter. "Right. Paddy comes in all high and mighty and Johnny sends him down to fetch some patties for burgers. Except, I'm down there taking my break. With my girl, you know?"

She stopped her work and winked at him, and Evan raised an eyebrow.

"Oh, don't act so shocked. You know what goes down back of the house."

"Yes, I've seen my fair share over the years."

"And never participated, huh?" She tossed the rag into a bus bin and poured him a glass of ice water.

"I don't think I ever said that. But I believe you were the one caught with your skirt up around your waist."

"Yes, yes I was. Poor Paddy—all that bluster went gusting right out of him. I could have sworn he peed himself."

"What's this *poor Paddy* crap I hear when I'm not around?" Patrick kicked the steel basement door closed and dumped the frozen birds onto his work table, the sound echoing through the window like bowling pins falling on a lucky strike. He peeked into the dining room and lit up with a smile, wiping his hands down the length of his apron. "Hi."

Mimi cackled at him, and the charm of Patrick's blush creeping up his neck and cheeks broke when his middle finger flailed in the air in her direction.

"You have an order ticket—*tu novio* is hungry."

Evan wiggled his fingers in a wave, desperately trying to stifle his laugh. He was still imagining Patrick stumbling in on Mimi and her lover, unable to tear his eyes away, equally horrified and turned on. He'd encountered a similar scene himself at his first restaurant, the chef and his saucier going at it over the pot basin, checks around their ankles, white jackets still almost perfectly in place.

Patrick went to his station, glancing between his waitress and Evan, finally shaking his head as he grabbed the ticket from the rail. "I don't think I like the idea of you two conversing when I'm not around."

"Oh, don't get your boxers in a bunch, Boss. We weren't conversing. We were—"

"Commiserating. Sharing war stories."

"Mmm, I bet. You like your Reuben stacked?"

"I like it however you make it."

"Stacked it is. Like my waitresses." Patrick flagged Mimi down and pointed across the diner. "Ms. Romero, the gentleman at table six has been tapping at his menu since I went downstairs. Get on it."

When Evan was finished with his meal, Mimi brought him a slice of red velvet cake—unordered, but upon sight suddenly necessary. "You need a break from all that cheesecake, Chef. I cut ya' an extra big slice."

Evan caught Patrick's eye and dug in. "Is there an end to the variety here?"

"Nope. Infinite. I'm actually an alien." Patrick washed his hands and took off his apron and headband, ruffling his hair as it escaped its trap in the sweaty terrycloth, and joined Evan in the dining room.

He was a bit of an adorable mess.

"You off for the night?"

"No. We're slow and there's this really cute guy in my dining room." He pointed to the end of the counter. "Come down here, huh? A little more private."

Evan moved down with him and offered a bite of cake. "Where's the cute guy? Maybe I should check him out?"

Patrick took the offered bite and his lips curled around the fork, not taking his eyes off of Evan. "Damn, that's good." He swiped his finger into the piped icing at the base of the cake and looked at it piled there, and then up into Evan's eyes, before popping it into his own mouth. "How was your shift?"

"No cute guy?" Evan wagged his eyebrows and took a bite of the cake. It was perfectly light and fluffy—just as expected.

"Oh, very cute. I just want to look at him, not talk about him." Patrick watched Evan sneak his tongue out of his mouth to swipe at a stray crumb. "So, your shift? You seem a little more… buoyant tonight."

"Well, besides the delicious dinner and dessert"—Evan licked his lips again just to see if Patrick followed. He did. "After a debacle tonight, Perci has only one more strike."

"You look entirely too pleased about that."

Evan focused on the cake again, taking a break from Patrick's intense gaze. "The dumb-ass contaminated an entire vat of polenta—which is the bad news." He stabbed a piece of the cake and poked the full fork into the air as he spoke. "And I was getting a really good rage going, but then it hit me. One more strike. God only knows what it'll be, but it'll be her last."

Evan indelicately shoved the bite of cake into his mouth and Patrick laughed and handed Evan a napkin. "What's ridiculous is that you've had to put up with her for so long."

"I finally spoke to DiSante's heart—his wallet." Evan wiped his mouth with a blush. "Finds out she's losing him money and he's suddenly all about getting her out of there." He sighed, swirling his fork into the cream cheese frosting. "I'm aiming at a good mood; I don't want to talk about Perci."

"So, let's not talk about Perci." Patrick pulled up a stool and thanked Mimi for the coffee she brought them, also unordered but suddenly necessary.

"Yes, let's talk about Millie instead. She's been on my mind a lot thanks to you, and I think I need to find time to go see her."

"How long has it been?"

"I talked to her over the holidays, but haven't seen her in... God, it's been... three or four years. You know how hard it is to get home—"

Patrick laughed. "I grab a cab."

"Oh. Right. Smart-ass. Well, for those of us who have to fly, it's a hassle. I mean, when's the last time you took off even two days in a row?"

"Um."

"Right. So, it's been years. Now she's in assisted living, and... I shouldn't wait any longer than I have. It's going to be weird to see her anywhere but at her own house."

"I can imagine. That was like a second home for you, wasn't it?"

"It really was." For a moment, Evan disappeared into memories of Millie's home, the sights, sounds and smells of so many days of his childhood and teen years, and later a required stop every time he did fly home from New York. "She had the best kitchen—knocked out a half bath for her pantry. A cook's dream."

Evan sipped his coffee and gathered his memories, trying to focus on his story and not Patrick's eyes, which were dark and engaged and occasionally slipped down to watch his mouth.

"Every summer she'd go to the shore for a month or so. On the few days leading up to it, she'd plant me in front of this massive closet of food to help her clean it out. 'Four things tonight, Evy.

No peeking in containers and first touch gets the pick. We'll make a masterpiece.'"

Patrick forked the last piece of cake, almost forgotten between them, and lifted it to Evan's mouth, watching him intently. Then he pressed up the crumbs and laughed when Evan nabbed the fork and ate them himself. "You are passionate about your crumbs."

"Nothing this good should ever go to waste." Evan sighed and took a sip of his coffee. "I'm sorry I'm rambling on. I just don't think I've taken the time to realize how much I miss her."

"Maybe you've let yourself get so busy so you won't miss her so much."

Evan settled his mug into the saucer slowly, its rattle mirroring the rattle that went through him at those words. "You know, I don't think I like how you get right to the heart of me so easily."

Patrick smiled, his eyes soft and warm. "I'm sorry, do you want me to stop?"

"I don't think you are sorry." Evan smiled back. "And, no."

Patrick poked at one more cake crumb and popped it into his mouth with a wicked grin. "So did you and Millie make any masterpieces?"

Evan cocked his head side to side, considering. "Rarely. Sometimes. By the time we played, the pantry was almost empty. Normally it was *loaded*. Vinegars and oils, dried fruits and nuts, flours, chocolates, pastas." He sighed, envisioning the organized chaos of it. "She *always* had the best truffle oil."

"Mmm, truffle oil. Kryptonite."

"Of the gods."

Patrick took Evan's plate and dumped it into a bus bin. "So, what happened when you pulled a crappy mix?"

"One of the first times, I got oyster sauce, flaxseed and Nutella. I dove in blind, thinking it was peanut butter—make some kind of peanut sauce, you know? That night we did take-out."

"Wise choice." Patrick drained his coffee and tossed the mug into the bin. He hopped off his stool and settled his elbows on the counter across from Evan, so close that Evan had to refocus just to see the whole of his face.

And when he did, he couldn't hide the sharp intake of air, the warmth rushing through him, the desire to reach out and scratch at the scruff on Patrick's jaw. "Hi."

Patrick smiled and ran his fingers through his sweaty hair.

And then he winked.

And Evan blushed, missing the first bit of what Patrick was saying.

" ... Just stand next to Oona in the kitchen. The chatter about nothing. Lessons that have less to do with deglazing a pan and more about using a little heat and acid to scrape up the crap from your life."

"How long has she been gone?"

"She passed just after I came back to help Johnny. Sometimes, I just miss the food. Cooking it. Eating it—"

Evan lifted his elbows to the counter too, his hands folded in front of him, chin resting on his thumbs. "You know, if you want to cook it... it wasn't that long ago that you promised me a full fry."

Patrick's eyes trailed up to Evan's and down to his mouth again, pupils dilating as Evan brushed his lips up over the knuckles of his thumbs, tasting his own skin with his tongue.

Evan was speechless, breathless, caught in Patrick's intense gaze. They lingered there, their eyes unwavering, soft shy smiles curling at their lips.

Patrick bit at his bottom lip before speaking. "Am, um—am I reading things right here?"

Evan blinked, trying to hide his bubbling joy behind his folded hands. "I'm not sure. What are you reading?"

Patrick smiled as if in on the secret. Which of course he was— that was the whole point. "Well. I'm reading... that if I do what I've wanted to do since that first night you showed up here—"

"Since the first night?"

"The first night."

"Hmmm... go on."

Patrick blinked and licked his lips as if to fully prepare his statement. "Since that first night, I've wanted to lean across this counter and kiss you."

Evan lowered his hands to the counter, just avoiding brushing his fingers along the dark hair on Patrick's arms. "Interesting. And what happens after the kiss?"

"Well, if I'm reading right," Patrick paused and reached to trace Evan's jaw, but changed course and ran his fingers down the curve of his shoulder. "If I do that, not only will you be okay with it, but maybe, in time—" He stopped his motion and looked back in Evan's eyes, smiling when they locked, all shyness and insecurity driven away. "In a *short* time, if I'm an advanced enough reader—it might lead to me having an opportunity to fix you that full fry."

"Hunh." Evan felt the blood rush up his cheeks to the tips of his ears. And maybe lower as well. "So. Maybe in a little more private setting than say—the middle of a diner in downtown Brooklyn?"

"A little."

Evan leaned closer; their breath almost mingled as they spoke. "You know what I think?"

"What do you think?"

"I think you're a very good reader."

"Yeah?"

"Yeah." Neither of them budged, and Evan's heart raced. The conversation between them continued with their eyes, which dragged up and down each other's faces from eyes to lips to necks and back. They blindly reached for each other's hands, their fingers twisting and twining together, want and lust calculating how to best make this happen—yesterday.

"Sadly, you'd better move on that first idea, because my phone alarm is about to bring reality crashing in on our moment."

"Oh?"

"I need to sleep—Greenmarket at seven tomorrow."

"Seven a.m.?" Patrick kissed Evan's knuckles and Evan had to close his eyes as Patrick's lips dragged across his skin. "That's harsh."

"That's life." Evan opened his eyes and let them linger on Patrick's mouth as his own imagination fired and snapped. How soft and sweet, powerful and tender those lips would feel against his. He dared drag his eyes up to Patrick's and found them crinkled in an amused smile. "Stop flirting and kiss me."

Patrick groaned as he closed the small distance between them, fulfilling Evan's imagined fantasy perfectly. The kiss was soft and sweet, with just enough power to make his toes curl. And when he pressed in again, leading with the tenderest brush of his tongue, Evan ignored the fact that they were in public and made a noise that would embarrass the sassiest of streetwalkers.

They pulled back with a loud smack, flushing at their display, Patrick's voice raspy and deep. "Come back in the kitchen."

"I can't stay."

"I know. I just want to send you off properly."

Evan didn't miss Mimi's cackle as he stood and gathered his coat, slipped behind the counter and disappeared into the kitchen, the swing door flapping loudly behind him. And when Patrick pressed him up against the reach-in, hands cupping at his neck and jaw, thigh slipping between Evan's, he didn't rightly *care* that she knew. Hell, the few patrons still enjoying their meals at this hour probably knew.

They kissed and tasted, cream cheese frosting-flavored and coffee-accented kisses, Evan's fingers sinking into Patrick's hair with matched groans at its silky softness and the scratch and soothe of Evan's fingers on Patrick's scalp. After a few more moments, desire building a slow burn between them, Evan's phone buzzed in his pocket. Its low hum broke them apart, breathless, forehead to forehead, their bodies still moving together in a slow roll.

"I've got to... *oh God...* I have to go. I'm sorry."

"I understand."

"I know. Thank you."

"Besides, I'm not looking for fast food here."

"No?"

Patrick shook his head, his eyes dark with want, and scratched his fingers at the nape of Evan's neck.

With one more lingering kiss, Evan slid his hands down Patrick's arms, sighed and stepped back. "I understand."

"I know. Thank you."

Evan smiled and grabbed for his coat that he'd haphazardly tossed onto Patrick's work table. "I'll call you after shift tomorrow." Patrick pulled Evan in for one final kiss, stealing just one more taste. "That is some damned good frosting."

Evan dipped his pinky into the reduction and tasted. Still dissatisfied with its consistency, he lowered the heat a step and pulled a stem of thyme from the pan.

Ross came in from the dining room, a stack of menus under his arm. "You have a visitor, Chef."

"Mmm-kay. Taste this—summer menu, hopefully. Drizzled over veal chop, grilled corn, fresh figs—some olive oil at the end?"

Ross swiped a finger across the spoon, tasting and smacking his lips in consideration. "With those sides? Maybe a bit sweet?"

"Okay, that's what I was getting too. Thanks." Evan went back to his creation, opening another bottle of balsamic vinegar into yet another saucepan and dropping in a bay leaf. As he walked away from the burner to get more thyme, Ross cleared his throat.

"Chef. Your guest. Where shall I—"

"Oh! Yes. Can we offer them a caprese while they wait? Some wine? I want to finish this before I—" Evan shoved a finger into his mouth, dripping with honey he'd swiped from the wooden dipper.

"Special delivery, Chef."

Evan snapped out of his creative haze and looked up, a bright smile curling around his finger. "Patrick!" He looked him up and down. "Where in the hell have *you* been today?"

"Got an unexpected day off. Johnny came barreling in with some of the old cooks and took over. I, uh—" He looked down at himself and shrugged at his mud-caked jeans and boat shoes. "Oscar and I spent the day outside. Which"—he stepped into the kitchen and kissed Evan's cheek—"is why I'm here with a delivery. Where should I put them?"

"*Them?*"

Patrick turned back to the hall and thanked Ross for letting him inside before the doors opened for dinner service. Then he disappeared for a moment and returned with two boxes and a proud smile.

Evan turned off the burner under his reduction and peered into the boxes. "Morels? You went morel hunting?" He picked up a few of the spongy mushrooms as if they were jewels. "These are huge—gorgeous! Where did you find them?"

"About an hour out of the city. There's this old apple orchard we found a few years ago. Seems to have been forgotten. They thrive there."

"Do you do this every year?"

"We try. It's been so damned rainy this spring that they were everywhere. We ended up with a ton."

"You're giving us, what?" Evan lifted up a couple mushrooms and breathed them in, their earthy, woodsy smell, pure and fresh, his brain already clicking on how to use them in the next few nights' prix fixe menu. "Five pounds?"

"Yeah, we split the rest. I'll dry 'em and we can use them for a quite some time. You can have more if you want."

"No, no. These are—*God*. They're still warm from the sun." He picked through a few more and looked up at Patrick, still in awe. "Thank you."

Robin wandered over and gasped. "Holy shit, those are beautiful!"

"I know." Evan introduced Robin to Patrick, flipping through the mushrooms as they shook hands, beaming like a schoolboy who had just discovered the perfect mud puddle. "And now he's our best friend."

"Forgive my grimy appearance in your kitchen."

"You keep bringing treats like this, you can come in covered in dog shit, for all I care."

Patrick scrunched his nose, stepping closer to Evan to take hold of his hand and whisper in his ear. "So, this visit isn't completely altruistic."

Robin took her leave, and Evan tugged Patrick down the stairs and into his office. "Come into my lair."

"Oooh, how excit—"

Evan cut him off with a hard, desperate kiss, pulling back breathy, needy. "Do you know how early seven a.m. is when you haven't been able to sleep at all beforehand?"

"Did I keep you awake?" Patrick fluttered his eyelashes innocently, and Evan considered kneeing him.

"Yes, you bastard."

"I'm sorry."

"Mmmm… I'm really, *really* sorry I had to take off last night."

"That's okay." Patrick cupped Evan's jaw in his hand and kissed him again, softly and tenderly, dragging his bottom lip across Evan's mouth. "We'll have plenty more opportunities, I'm sure." He stepped back and took a moment to look around the small office, at the evidence of a very successful career. "Which is one of my less altruistic reasons for coming. Is there room at the chef's table tomorrow evening?"

"There's always room for you."

"No, I mean—I want you to myself. Just you, your station, your food." He stopped his wall-gazing and took hold of Evan's hand again. "Your attention."

Evan raised his eyebrows. "Well then." His eyes darkened. "I do believe that can be arranged. Tuesdays are our slowest nights, so—"

"Excellent. What does one wear to the chef's table at Il Boschetto?"

Evan stepped back to inspect—to consider. "Hmmm… how about whatever Oona would have had you wear."

With another quick kiss, Evan slipped his work apron up over his head and tossed it into a bin in the corner. He grabbed a jacket from a row of hooks on the wall and shrugged it on, lifting his chin when Patrick stepped in to snap him up.

"And, uh—to make up for having to leave last night?" Once snapped, Evan wrapped his arms around Patrick's waist and pulled him close. "I have Wednesday off." At Patrick's gentle press of a kiss to his neck, he sucked in a breath and dared to pull back from his lips. "You?"

Patrick didn't even try to hide the groan and the grin that squinted his eyes and puffed his cheeks. "How 'bout that? So do I."

IV. Première Entremet
A small vegetable or side dish served between
courses to cleanse the palate.

Evan's advice to wear whatever Oona would have had him wear should have been helpful. Instead, it only made Patrick stand at his closet longer.

Oona, in all of her simple, beautiful, homespun glory, would have been in a complete dither about what to wear to such a "fancy" place as Il Boschetto. And Evan had been right; it wasn't *that* expensive or high-end, but it most definitely would have been off the scale of attainability to Oona's sensibilities. Besides, she would have had to put on *lipstick*. Completely beyond attainable.

And so it was with his family. Humble. Unpretentious. You do what you need to do to get through. The best legacy was that of responsibility, knowing you contributed to the little corner of your world. Be polite, be thoughtful and work hard. And there is certainly never a need to impress anyone.

"Just be grateful you have a roof over your head."

"No sense getting worked up; nothing's going to change."

"Stop drawing attention to yourself, Patrick."

So, he tended not to. Tended to gravitate to other people who blended in. Attractive enough, successful enough, cute enough. His relationships mirrored that. Nice enough. Comfortable, fun, satisfying.

But also forgettable. Short-lived. A blip in the span of his life.

In a word: unimpressive.

So when one Chef Evan Stanford came blowing through his door, lording over his own kitchen staff with a commanding yet loving gaze, every lecture about blending in, about keeping the status quo and about being satisfied with what you have went out the window.

Evan Stanford *impressed*.

He impressed in his whites, tall, broad-shouldered and slender-waisted, crisp—pristine, even, especially before a shift. He impressed in the way he carried himself, in the way he owned who he was, even the broken and unhappy and conflicted parts.

He impressed in his kiss—which really didn't surprise Patrick all that much. Confidence is sexy. And Evan was sexy. Full lips, deep blue eyes that veered into almost navy when he was turned on—a fact Patrick was happy to know, even if only in the brief moments they'd stolen since the evening he took the plunge and made his move.

While Patrick hadn't had a chance to eat much of Evan's cooking yet, he knew it to be impressive. You don't get a James Beard Award by blending in, by swimming in the murky waters of those around you.

And so Patrick anticipated an impressive meal. A sexy, beautiful meal. A meal that was more than he could ever supply in return. And he tried, as he picked the right, then the wrong tie—*yes, no, yes; too casual without; it's just dinner inside a fucking kitchen, for God's sake, yes; Oona would tell you to wear the tie*—he tried not to let that fact get to him. He wanted to enjoy the gift Evan was offering, just as Evan had so graciously accepted, and then come to favor, the food he'd been making him these few short months.

He eventually settled on a burgundy and gray get-up—not too formal, not too casual—and he wore a tie. Oona would have told him to. And she would have tied it better than he had.

He spent most of his train ride fidgeting with the tie and wiping his sweaty palms on his pants legs. And laughing at himself for being so worked up.

Once he got to Il Boschetto he was given the red carpet treatment, which only served to ramp up his jitters. Ross greeted him by name and took his sweater and newsboy cap in exchange for a glass of

Prosecco. A kind waitress led him to his seat at a table for two partitioned off from the rest of the dining room and close to the noisy kitchen. He could occasionally hear Evan's voice breaking through the commotion, in charge, in control. Patrick stared at the swing door, aching to watch him in action.

"Chef Stanford will be taking care of you this evening." Natasha, Evan's head waitress, was a beautiful woman with long, lush black hair—thick-figured, as Oona would have described her. Her smile was warm and genuine as she pulled out his chair. "But if you need anything while he's preparing your courses, I will be here to attend you."

"Thank you." He sipped his wine and wiped his hands on his pants, wishing his ridiculous nerves would wipe away as well. "Does he know I'm here?"

"He will in a minute. Would you like to speak to him before we begin?"

"Whatever is customary is fine."

She shifted the votive candle on the table a hairsbreadth. "He's nervous too. Don't tell him I told you, but he overcooked the pork chops for family meal tonight. They're razzing him up a storm in there."

Patrick laughed, a little relieved. "Well, hopefully he got that out of his system then."

She squeezed his shoulder as she stood, a laugh hiding in her voice. "I'll go tell him you're here. Your antipasti should be right out."

He took a sip of his wine, hoping the wait wouldn't be long. He felt awkward and on display, even though he was visibly cordoned off from the other patrons and—*oh.*

"Natasha said you might want to see me before we begin?"

He had seen Evan in his whites numerous times already—often stained and work-worn after a full shift—but tonight—oh, *tonight* Evan was dressed in full formal whites with executive black pants. His jacket was perfectly bleached, pressed and fitted, as though he'd just taken it out of the tailor's bag. It was lined with a burgundy piping down the placket that matched the Il Boschetto insignia, and ironically enough after all of his fretting over what to wear, Patrick himself.

Topping off Evan's ensemble was a toque, tall and straight-sided with multiple pleats around its circumference, the number of which, Patrick had heard, mythically referred to the number of ways the chef knew how to prepare eggs.

Normally Patrick found a toque pretentious and absurd, but as Evan stood in front of him, clearly unnerved by Patrick's staring, he was beautiful. Regal. "I, um—I said you could if you wanted. Or if it was customary. Or—" He swallowed thickly and rubbed his hands on his pants again. "Or something." When he stood, he knocked his thigh soundly against the corner of the table. "You look amazing."

Evan grimaced and took Patrick's hand, squeezing his fingers. "So do you. I love your shirt—" Evan reached up to smooth Patrick's tie and stopped himself, clearly flustered. Patrick got it—he felt like a middle-schooler going to his first dance, wilting grocery store flowers his only offering. "And—and you shaved."

Patrick blushed and brought Evan's fingers up for a gentle kiss, smiling at the scent of garlic on his skin. "Thank you. Oona always liked me clean-shaven and in a tie."

"She was a classy broad too, wasn't she?"

"No." Patrick ached with the desire to kiss Evan—kiss him as soundly as his thigh had connected with the corner of the table. "She was a simple woman. Plain. And a man with facial hair was never *simple*. It was lazy."

Evan stepped in closer, but just as Patrick closed his eyes for the incoming kiss, Robin popped her head in from the kitchen, stopping her announcement almost before she started it. "Chef, your clams—oh. Oh, I'm so sorry. Your um... your clams are on the heat."

Evan snickered but didn't move, still inches from Patrick's lips. "Thank you, Robin." The door flapped as she backed away and Evan closed the space between them with a soft but brief kiss, brushing the smooth skin at Patrick's jaw with the backs of his fingers. "Time for work."

"Don't forget to enjoy it."

"For your second course, I've made you *raviolacci*—a mushroom ravioli served in a truffle butter sauce." Evan stepped aside as Natasha poured a new glass of wine. "And my sommelier has selected a Gaja Barbaresco to accompany."

The antipasti—littleneck clams with white wine, garlic and scallion, delicately topped with a light *pangrattato*—had been divine. Upon his first bite, Patrick understood why Evan was a James Beard winner. His food was prepared with exquisite simplicity, masterful technique, artistic plating and a clear knowledge of his ingredients and how to make them harmonize as though they were created to be together. Patrick knew that this was going to rank as one of the best meals of his life.

And to his own surprise, his nerves faded away.

So it was with great anticipation that Patrick looked down at the small ravioli, licking his lips and cutting one open before Evan could escape to his kitchen. "Mushroom ravioli. Are these—"

"Your morels. Yes. I think we have enough for a full service tonight on our pasta menu, so—"

"You used my morels."

"Well, they were so beautiful and flavorful and—"

"And truffle butter sauce."

"You said you liked truffle oil."

"I do." Patrick looked up at Evan and smiled graciously, oddly moved that this meal had been prepared specifically for him. "Thank you."

"*Buon appetito*." With a nod and a smile, Evan turned to head back into the kitchen, slipping out of his professional role briefly enough to toss a wink over his shoulder.

As expected, the ravioli was magnificent, with a perfectly smooth texture. And just as it should have been, it was cooked and treated as a vehicle for the mushrooms and truffle oil, the real stars of the dish.

Every dish was simple yet exquisite, elegantly plated and thoughtfully constructed. Even the light toss of arugula with lemon and olive oil, served to cleanse his palate between courses, was carefully prepared and presented.

When Evan brought his main course—a lamb shank osso bucco, slow braised with risotto Milanese—Patrick reached for Evan's hand before he could disappear again. "Can you sit with me? Or are you still busy?"

"I'm—" Evan looked back toward the kitchen and then at Patrick, sighing with a smile. He sat down, removed his toque and unbuttoned the top of his jacket.

A small tuft of hair stood on end on the side of his head and Patrick wished to press it down, just for the excuse to touch him. "There you are." At Evan's questioning glance, he reached across the table to fix Evan's hair.

"Thank you." Evan patted at the spot and smiled. "Where have I been?"

"Working." Evan took a breath to explain, Patrick assumed, but he didn't need an explanation. He had everything he needed right in front of him. "But you're here now."

"I am. Our pastry chef took care of your dessert, so—"

Patrick shoved the plate to the center of the table and offered his fork. "Please?"

"I've had my taste."

Patrick started to argue, but Natasha appeared again with another plate of ravioli. "Do not yell at me, Chef. Robin insisted. And Rosey. And Carlos. And that new cook whose name I can't remember. And—well, I didn't disagree with them, although Theo thinks we all need to mind our own business." She smiled and set the plate in front of Evan, pouring them both fresh glasses of wine. "You didn't eat at family meal."

"Tell everyone thank you." He turned back to the kitchen and his amused smile quickly switched to a warning glare. "And tell Rosey that he needs to be working, not snooping."

"Yes, Chef. Mr. Sullivan, is there anything else I can get you?"

Patrick laughed as Rosey slipped back behind the swinging door. "No, I'm good. Thank you."

Natasha disappeared, her scolding "Get your stupid ass back to that sink, Ambrose Pemberton," ringing through the galley as she chased him down. Evan stabbed at his food and shook his head. "When the cat's away…"

"They love you. Rosey's been peeking through that door the entire time I've been here. Robin too."

"I'm very lucky. And picky about who I hire."

"And Perci?"

"Fuck Perci."

Patrick laughed and forked a bite of his meal. "So, how's she doing in there?"

"I gave her the night off—you asked for my attention tonight."

"That's a good—" Patrick looked up from his plate into Evan's eyes and realized he was no longer talking about kitchen dynamics. He rested there, his food cooling on his fork until Evan nodded at it.

"Eat—it's better warm."

"Oh. Yes. I'm—yes." Patrick dipped his fork in for a few more grains of risotto and ate, instantly forgetting about kitchen dynamics and Perci, and even momentarily forgetting about Evan's eyes, because this food—this *food*. The lamb practically melted in his mouth, succulent and rich, the marrow buttery sweet. It had a purity, a simplicity, and yet everything was remarkably complex and layered in intense flavors that showed the care with which Evan worked—as though it wasn't work at all.

Food was his canvas. His playground.

And when Patrick did take a breath and look up at Evan, casually eating the meal his kitchen had insisted he have, he realized that that was exactly how he saw Evan as well. There was a kind of simplicity about Evan, a boy from Illinois who had made a successful life out of the opportunities handed to him. But underneath was this burning, churning, layered complexity—art and passion, talent and finesse. No wonder his food was so delicious.

It was an extension of himself.

"For dessert we have a *torte di zabaglione e cioccolato*—" Natasha stopped and smiled when Patrick feigned a snooty posture at the name. "Okay, fine—" With her hand on her hip and a glint in her eyes, she finished her presentation a little more naturally. "It's a chocolate mousse cake with Amarena cherries and chocolate sauce. And two forks."

When Evan lifted a finger to say something, she lifted her own to scold. "Chef, the kitchen is *fine*."

She smiled back at Patrick and continued, placing two new wine glasses on the table and pouring. "For the final selection from our sommelier, we have a lovely Bracchetto d'Acqui."

"Thank you, Ms. Kramar. Tell them I'll be in there shortly."

"I will tell them no such thing, Chef. Take your time. Mr. Sullivan, it's been a pleasure meeting you."

"Patrick, please. And the pleasure's all mine."

Patrick watched her disappear into the kitchen while Evan scraped at the top of the cake with his fork, visibly entertained by his own thoughts.

"She's a character."

"You're a character," Evan replied.

Patrick snickered and watched as Evan continued to draw shapes into the top of the cake with that infernal smirk on his face.

"What?"

Evan blushed and finally tasted the scrapings from his fork, catching Patrick's eye. "Nothing." The soft laughter that bubbled under his words told a different story.

"You seem amused by something. I mean, it is chocolate mousse, so *I'm* quite amused, but—"

"No. It's—it's nothing. I might offend and I have no intention—"

"Okay, now you definitely have my attention." But then Patrick took his first bite of the mousse cake and lost himself in the light, creamy chocolate dream melting in his mouth. "Oh my *gawd*."

Patrick opened his eyes from this bliss and there sat Evan, biting back a hearty laugh and shaking his head, his eyes alight with his secret joy. He popped his finger into his mouth to suck off the sauce he'd been dragging it through and wiggled his eyebrows, his finger still firmly planted in his mouth.

Patrick dropped his fork—the man was simply exasperating, sitting there all smug and sexy and sucking at his fingers.

"You going to share your secret with the class or are you just gonna keep driving me crazy playing with your food?"

Evan finally forked a piece of the cake and looked up at Patrick once more before eating, moaning theatrically around the velvety mousse. "God, that's good—although I'm sure you could do better."

"Do not get sidetracked by the chocolate." Patrick smiled as he stabbed for another bite. "Or one of your lectures." The blush that slid up Evan's neck and cheeks seemed to rush through him instead. "Now, tell me what you're laughing at?"

"It's just that—" Evan grabbed another forkful of cake and looked beyond Patrick as if the proper answer might be hiding behind the partition.

"Evan... "

Evan ate and sighed around the melting chocolate. "I've just really enjoyed watching you tonight. All prim and proper and mannerly."

"I thought I was here to watch you."

"And you have been."

"So, does my ability to do prim and proper surprise you or something?"

Evan smiled and took a sip of wine—stalling, Patrick was sure of it. "No." He reached his hand across the table and rested his fingers on Patrick's wrist. "Yes. A little. It's just that—" Evan looked up at him, slow and a little tentative. "I never thought I'd fall for a Brooklyn boy."

Patrick chuckled softly and squeezed Evan's fingers in his. "You were afraid that would offend me?"

"Well, it does come with some judgment on my part and—"

"Never mind that." Patrick rested on his elbows and Evan mimicked him, the dessert now sitting ignored between them. Patrick cupped Evan's hands in his, his eyes never leaving the pool of Evan's deep blue gaze. "Say that last part again."

"The judgment, or… "

"That you never thought you'd fall—"

Evan bowed his head and blushed, red tingeing his ears when he looked up again. "I said I never thought I'd fall for a Brooklyn boy."

Patrick wanted to jump out of his skin. He knew. Of course he knew. He felt it in the smile that spread across Evan's face whenever they saw each other. In his special, personalized care with this meal. In the sigh he'd emit at the end of a long day and a short phone call before bed. In his insistence on Patrick knowing that he was excellent at his craft and was appreciated.

Patrick felt it in these moments. He knew.

But he was a Brooklyn boy after all. So he opted to play it cool, tilting his head just a little, hoping to shoot for a little cocky. "Yeah? You falling for me?"

Evan laughed heartily and relaxed as he pulled Patrick's hand to him, tenderly kissing the skin. "I'm fawlin' fuh you. Hawd."

Patrick's heart danced at Evan's Brooklyn mimicry and he felt himself getting lost in the lips pressing his fingers again and again. "We really need to work on the accent." Patrick looked down at his dessert, a little longingly, he feared. Evan pulled away, inviting him to eat. So he did. "It's funny you say that, actually."

"Oh?"

"I was talking to Oscar the other night, and I said the same thing."

"You falling for a Brooklyn boy too? Do I get to meet him?"

"Don't be cute."

"I can't help it."

"You're especially cute with that toque on."

"Stop. It's ridiculous." He picked up the toque and offered it across the table. "You'd look good in it."

"No. That's not my place."

"Oh, come on." Evan held it closer. Patrick pulled away. "No. Thank you."

Evan pulled back, looking a little hurt and a lot embarrassed. "Sorry."

"No, it's—" Patrick speared a piece of cake, dragged it through the chocolate sauce and waited for Evan to look him in the eye again; he needed to start again. When their eyes met, Patrick offered the bite, mindlessly opening his mouth when Evan did and feeling heat pool low in his belly as Evan closed his eyes to fully enjoy the decadence of the dessert.

"What I said to Oscar was... I never thought I'd fall for a chef."

A peaceful joy spread across Evan's face and Patrick could do nothing but reflect it. He felt it spread throughout his entire body. "You fawlin' fuh me too, huh?" Evan teased.

"Like a rock."

Evan finished the last of his wine and set the plate aside to scoop Patrick's hands up in his and studied his face as if seeing him anew and brushed the back of his finger over Patrick's jaw with a contented sigh. "So, after dinner drink? We have an amazing Amaro—"

"No, thank you."

"No?" A buzz came from under the table and Evan shifted, ignoring it.

Patrick smiled, pleased at his immaculate timing and his patient tutelage of Oscar in sending out timed text messages. "No. I had something else in mind. Answer your phone."

"No. I'm with you right now."

"Answer. Your phone."

Evan studied him, but Patrick remained firm, glancing down to where Evan's phone sat in his pants pocket.

"Kiss me first." Evan's voice was low, raspy, and Patrick would have been a fool to resist such a simple request even though he knew a coy little power play when he saw one.

He leaned in and gave him a loose-lipped, chocolate-y, amaretto-laced kiss.

Evan pulled back just a hair, his breath ghosting over Patrick's lips. "What, um. What else did you have in mind?"

With another brief kiss, Patrick sat back and placed his napkin atop the cake plate, hoping to appear casual when in reality he wanted to take this man by the jacket collar, right here, right now, and have his way with him. "Answer your phone."

Evan sighed and reached into his pocket to read the text. "What's this?"

"Just to clarify, you are off tomorrow?"

"I am. You?"

"I am." Their eyebrows twitched—together—as if in a mirror. "When are you done tonight?"

"Been here all day; shooting for ten o'clock."

"And you take the Q?"

"Or a cab... depending."

"Take a cab; it's quicker." Evan put his phone away, picking at the cake under Patrick's napkin and licking the mousse off of his fork as Patrick talked. "Pack an overnight bag with some extra house slippers for Dini. And do whatever you need to do to make her mobile."

"Sedation, typically."

"Seriously?"

"No."

Patrick sighed at Evan's impishness and grasped at his wrist, stopping him from popping a cherry into his mouth. He brought it to his own, sucking a little longer than necessary on Evan's fingers. "Bring the damned dog."

"You know, you could have finished a drink by now."

Patrick ignored him. "Hail another cab."

"This is getting expensive."

"And you're being difficult." And Patrick loved it. "Take the damned Q down to Prospect Park, if you think Dini can handle the train. Just end up at that address." Patrick pointed to Evan's pants pocket. "Number Four E."

"Are you leading me to the location of my murder?"

"You're the Sweeney Todd in this relationship, remember?"

"I remembuh."

Patrick wanted to reach over and kiss him again—kiss the smartassed look right off his face. And then he remembered that, even with the surrounding noise and the nosey Rosey, they were alone. So he did just that.

Evan licked his lips as if to chase the taste of the cake. "But I still don't see why you're refusing an after-dinner drink."

"There are drinks there. Served by a very efficient bartender."

"But this meeting is hours away."

"He wants to be sure he's not intoxicated and ready for your arrival."

Evan's eyes darkened and he shifted in his seat with a soft moan. "Is, uh—is the bartender cute?"

"Sorta like a pug." Patrick took Evan's hand in his again, kissing each fingertip, his eyes resting firmly on Evan's as he watched the movement of Patrick's lips on his skin. "Is that an okay plan?"

"More than okay."

Heat sparked between them, between their eyes, between their tangled fingers, and swirled around their feet. Patrick breathed softly, both exasperated and entranced. "Thank you for the spectacular meal."

"You're welcome. It's the first meal I've enjoyed preparing in a long damned time."

"Then I'm even more honored. You can always tell when a chef loves what he's doing."

Evan leaned across the table and kissed Patrick again, brushing his nose against his cleanly shaven cheek. "I loved cooking for you."

"Mmm... excellent. I'll see you in a few hours."

V. Plat Principal, Première Partie
The main course.

Evan had always had a strange relationship with sex.

Oh, he'd come to love it like any other healthy thirty-something man does—come to crave it, as a matter of fact—but his relationship with it had a wobbly start.

Realizing that he thought about boys differently than the boys he thought about thought about *him* was crippling enough.

But when he discovered how he was expected to *show* that attraction, all his systems fired simultaneously. Fear, anxiety, arousal, lust, disgust, curiosity and revulsion all came crashing down around him and he shut down, occupying his time and thoughts with very nonsexual things. Like spending time with Millie. Or studying super hard for that algebra test. Or coming up with new ways to prepare chicken, because his mother's chicken breasts were overdone and over... everything. He was *over* his mother's chicken breasts before he was twelve years old.

Much to his dismayed young heart, desire still prevailed; so he focused on the act of kissing, on soft lips and scorching eyes, wet, brushing tongues, whispered secrets and soft suckles on the tender skin of a masculine jaw. He was good at it. He knew so. He was told so.

He kissed the cute exchange student from Guatemala on the opening night of *Little Shop of Horrors*—he was Seymour to the other boy's Audrey II—only one velvet curtain and two feet away from not only the director of the show, but also from his best friend—who, of course, got all the juicy details that night after the show.

He kissed the boy he met on the plane when he moved to New

York. "We'll discover the city together," the boy had said. Only he'd given Evan a fake phone number and was lost forever in the sea of eight million people. The sneaky and stealthy kissing while the flight attendants worked the aisles? That had stayed with him for months.

Once settled in the city, he kissed a neighbor at his first apartment, and then a fellow theater major in college, and then of course the darling barista at the coffee shop on Twenty-first and Tenth who always drew hearts around his name on his cup and was the first to get a little more of him than his lips.

And then he found himself in the restaurant world. Sex was everywhere. The story of Patrick's first day at Johnny's was not unusual. That world was filled with all sorts of people for whom decorum was rarely a priority after a string of sweaty twelve-hour, high-intensity shifts. He witnessed heterosexual sex, lesbian sex, even a ménage à trois; but when he stumbled in on Hector and Ramiro, the resident sous chef and *garde manger*, deep in the throes of the blow job of Hector's life, their steely-hard, reddened dicks out and proud, Ramiro slurping and sucking with an intensity that took Evan's breath away even upon memory, he decided that kissing and humping pelvises would no longer cut it.

And he was liberated.

His first forays were bumpy and clumsy, occasionally slutty, and against everything his kindhearted and well-intentioned parents ever taught him about self-respect, but good God *damn*. Orgasms— giving them, watching them, receiving them, even cleaning up after them—were so much more amazing when shared with someone else.

He slept around; he dated a little. He fell in love once and then a second time, with the last man to break his heart. And the sex was good, exciting. Thrilling, even. He was good at it. Men wanted him more and more once they had him.

And yet.

And *yet*.

He always knew, even in the throes of the most mind-blowing

orgasms in the arms of the most amazing bodies, the most sexually charged partners, that something was still off. Missing.

So, as he stood just inside Patrick's kitchen, Dini scurrying around to find a familiar scent so she'd feel safe, he felt a little anxious too.

There was no pretense as to why he was here. Oh sure, he'd taken the time to appreciate Patrick's gorgeous photography, which decorated the long entry hallway into his apartment. He was sincerely interested in the taking, developing and framing of the beautiful pieces of art. He was.

But dog-ear-scratching and décor-commenting and small-talk-deflecting couldn't push away the real reason he was here. It wasn't just for sex, although clearly that was on the agenda.

He felt a connection to Patrick that he'd never felt before. He knew he struggled with being emotionally available to men. In fact, his ex had spat the words "emotionally frigid" at him as he walked out Evan's door for the last time close to two years before.

But with Patrick he'd found an instant ease. An instant peace, calm and connection. And it wasn't just that he was a fellow cook and understood the restaurant world. It wasn't just that damned boxty either, although any idiot would be remiss in not coming back for more of it.

It was the way Patrick saw him—got to the heart of him, as he'd pointed out earlier that evening. He helped Evan see himself more clearly. The world around him. His circumstances and his options related to them.

He wanted to be the same for Patrick. He wanted that in a way he'd never wanted it before.

He wanted emotional intimacy. A nest of warmth in which to land as they fell deeper and deeper with each smile, each brushed touch, each flirtatious kiss. So he was anxious in his hope. In his desire.

The slam of a cabinet door stopped Evan from staring at a photo of a row of brownstones decked out in their spring finest, window boxes filled with colorful flowers and greenery.

"What's your pleasure?" Patrick held up a bottle of brandy and a bottle of amaretto, his smile bright, his dark, cocoa brown eyes inviting Evan to come closer.

You.

"Surprise me."

Patrick mixed drinks and answered Evan's questions about the history of the building he lived in and about his photography hobby and why he insisted on using film instead of going digital. They watched Dini chase her tail while Evan desperately tried to explain that *stupid* in canines was completely adorable—"I mean, look at her, Patrick"—while Patrick remained mostly unconvinced.

"But she's not even nipping for her tail, Ev. She's just… spinning on her ass."

But when they began chatting about the goddamned weather—which had paid them back for the horrible transition into spring with a string of beautiful days, flowering trees and comfortable temperatures—Evan had had enough conversation.

He sipped at his perfectly made Italian Sunset, the gradient of yellow to orange to red slowly merging as he tipped the glass to his mouth. "So few bartenders make this right." He paused to watch Patrick drink his own concoction—unsure what it was beyond brandy and ice—and followed the bob of his Adam's apple along the length of this throat. "You always seem to know what I want."

Patrick stepped into his space, taking the drink from his hand and tasting it for himself. "Rumor has it I'm a good reader." Evan was seated on the stool before he even knew there was one behind him, eye-to-eye with Patrick now, spreading his legs to let him step even closer. "And I'm really tired of small talk."

Patrick's lips landed on Evan's perfectly, firm and confident, his hands hot and needy on Evan's arms, sliding up to cup Evan's face, where he pressed his thumbs onto his cheeks and gently guided his head right where he wanted it. Evan melted into it, wrapping his ankles behind Patrick's calves to pull him in even closer.

They stayed there kissing, gasping, grasping at each other's clothes, their mouths running up and down jawlines, their breath warm and damp over skin and flushed cheeks. Patrick tried to straddle Evan's lap on the stool, but finally gave up when he almost toppled them over for the fourth time. They laughed and kissed and pawed their way through the apartment, shirts and shoes flung various places, until they were in Patrick's bedroom, breathless, panting, pausing for a moment and looking into each other's eyes.

With a gentle nudge, Evan pushed Patrick onto his back on the bed and crawled on after him as Patrick worked his way up to the headboard, heat and lust and carnal hunger radiating between them.

God, he had missed this.

He pulled on the drawstring of Patrick's sweats, his eyes scanning the length of Patrick's body as it reclined underneath him: beautiful, sculpted, dark hair dusting across his chest and leading a trail down into his pants.

He was perfect—masculine and fit, hard muscle and soft skin, the bulge of his erection inviting under the soft fabric of his sweats. Patrick's tongue wet his bottom lip and all Evan could do was fall onto him and capture his mouth, sweet with alcohol. He worked his way down Patrick's body, licking and sucking each nipple as Patrick gasped beneath him, his fingers sinking into Evan's hair. With each rise of breath, Evan pressed kisses down Patrick's abdomen, stopping when his lips reached the waistband of Patrick's pants.

He looked up at Patrick and smiled, drawing his tongue away from the waistband and back up the line of hair to his navel, his breath of a laugh warming the wet skin.

"You are a tease," Patrick said.

"You are delicious." With a leer, Evan hooked his fingers into the waistband and wiggled off Patrick's sweats, greeting each inch of uncovered skin with soft kisses. When Patrick's dick sprang free, smacking lightly against his stomach, Evan moaned in delight.

Yes, he'd missed this very much.

Evan worked his way down, lavishing kisses on Patrick's hips and the line of muscle leading between his legs, groaning when Patrick opened his legs wider for him, "Yeah... let me get at you."

And then the purpled flesh on Patrick's thigh caught his eye and he remembered when Patrick cracked his leg on the table earlier that night.

"Oh honey." He kissed at the large, fresh bruise on Patrick's leg, tentatively touching it, feeling the heat pooled there. "You really—"

"Yeah, it hurt like a bitch." Patrick lifted his head to look and flopped back into the pillows as Evan continued to kiss on and around the discolored skin.

"Am I hurting you?" Evan looked up and smiled at the sight of Patrick's head tossed back, fingers clutching the sheets, answering his question without a word. "My hero. You didn't even flinch." Patrick only spread his legs wider, rolling his hips to meet Evan's lips as he continued kissing and working around the bruise up the length of Patrick's thigh and back, as if *not* touching his lips to Patrick's skin was inconceivable.

Because it was.

"I was—*fuck*—trying to be suave."

Evan giggled against his skin. "Well"—he planted one more kiss and looked up through his eyelashes—"we can just say *I* gave it to you."

Patrick groaned. "Play your cards right and it won't be a lie."

Evan blinked and lifted back up over Patrick's body, dipping down to gently tug on a pebbled nipple. "Don't move." He stood and made quick work of his own pants, pausing when he caught Patrick's dark and needy gaze. He licked his lips and lowered his pants in one swift motion, Patrick's dark, rich baritone moan going straight to his dick.

He crawled back onto the bed and between Patrick's legs, running his hands up Patrick's spread thighs. "You like that?" He licked and suckled gently at his hip. "To be marked?"

Patrick hissed and tossed his head back into the pillows, lifting his hips to meet Evan's mouth, a writhing, begging mess. "God, yes."

"Damn." He kissed down and around again, striping the tendon along Patrick's stretched inner thigh with his tongue, looking up for one more word of approval. "So. Matching set?"

"Fuck."

"Eloquent."

Patrick tugged on Evan's hair and propped himself up on his elbows, their eyes landing on each other's, dark and hungry. "I thought we were done with conversation."

"Mmmm... yes." Evan slowly licked his hand, his eyes never leaving Patrick's, and wrapped his fingers around the shaft of Patrick's cock where it jutted from his body, absolutely stunning in its insistence on getting some attention. "I have more important things to do with my mouth anyway." As he slid his fist up and down the thick shaft of Patrick's cock, he lowered his mouth to Patrick's thigh where he nipped and sucked, drawing the flesh into his mouth only to soothe it with his tongue again and again, coloring Patrick's skin with red and purple marks.

With one more look to appraise his work, Evan focused on the weight of Patrick's cock in his hand: heavy and solid, achingly hard. He tuned into the noises Patrick made, watching his hips work and twist—*stop watching, just take me*. Teasing with a gentle kiss on the tip of Patrick's cock, he giggled low in his chest when Patrick hissed and bucked. Slowly, methodically, he drew his tongue up the underside vein and worked his mouth down and over him, holding for a moment and then sucking back up to lick around the swollen head.

It was one of his favorite things to do with a man. The thick, solid shaft covered by smooth skin, weighing on his tongue; the run of veins moving beneath his lips; the curve of the crown and the slit, delicious and hot, dripping for him in approval. It always made him feel powerful. Sensual. Carnal.

Evan pulled off wetly, sloppily, feeling Patrick's cock throb in his hand as his grip tightened, twisting and sliding over him. "Mmm... so good." Patrick grunted a string of curse words so colorful, Evan wasn't convinced they were all in English.

Evan took him in again, and set up a rhythm, slow, torturous, Patrick's cock throbbing in his mouth and in his hand as he gripped at the base, moans of pleasure and desire echoing between them. Patrick's hands splayed and sunk into Evan's hair and his hips pumped in rhythm until he gave up, lost in the pleasure Evan was bringing him.

God *damn*, Evan had missed this.

Patrick's moans turned to desperate gasping and finally, after a choked-off attempt at Evan's name, he patted Evan on the shoulder and tugged on his hair. "Babe. Ev—I'm gonna... God, you're amazing—let's not—"

Evan popped off, smiling and still stroking, his spit slicking the hot skin beneath his fingers. "No?"

"Let's not finish before we get started, huh?"

Evan kissed at Patrick's hip again, breathing him in: sweat and man. "Sorry."

"Never apologize." Patrick covered Evan's hand over his cock and stroked with him, a seductive heat in his eyes. "I just want—"

Evan pulled himself over Patrick and settled between his legs, their cocks instantly aligning as if drawn together. "Fuck—"

"Yes. I want *all* of you."

Evan groaned and let Patrick pull him in for a kiss, his tongue sweeping into Evan's mouth as they rutted together, legs clamoring for purchase to push harder. Patrick's hands were hot on his back, down over his ass, tugging him in, slipping a finger into his crack and up again as they moaned, chasing the sensation with each roll of their hips. He kissed and nipped at Evan's jaw, his breath hot on his neck and when Evan pulled back—when he could bring himself to—Patrick's eyes were bright, his mouth parted and lips puffy.

It *had* been too long since Evan had felt this, felt strong thighs bracketing his own. Since he had felt a man hard and solid and ready beneath him, wanting him, needing him. Since he had tasted and smelled the essence of a man, felt muscles flexing and moving under his touch where soft and hard blurred into one sensuous notion of pleasure.

It was all a heady combination and Evan couldn't quite get enough of it.

He finally slowed their motions to rest for a moment in the overflowing warmth of *him*, of Patrick, of his deep brown eyes, wide and round, blinking slowly as his eyes focused.

Evan ran a hand up Patrick's arm to trace the frame of his face and rolled his hips once more. He dipped for a kiss and pulled back with a gentle tug at Patrick's bottom lip.

"Evan..." Patrick was almost pleading. He reached between them to grasp at their cocks as Evan began his rhythm again, pushing and chasing, licking at the salty, rough curve of Patrick's neck. His pre-dinner shave had grown out enough that it was beginning to scratch at Evan's tongue. *"Please. I need you."* Patrick planted his feet on the mattress and pushed gently at Evan's shoulders to lift him.

Evan sat back on his haunches, stroking himself a few times and running his hands up and down Patrick's thighs, both enamored of Patrick and empowered by his desire. Patrick was simply gorgeous—gasping, closing his eyes and swallowing as he tried to gain control, still softly stroking himself.

"Please."

"God, yes." Evan looked at the bedside table, where he assumed he'd find supplies—and maybe some footing—and tried to think and to process while Patrick lay there, a delicious combination of soft heat and rugged sexiness. His brain was short-circuiting. "In here, yeah?"

Patrick nodded and pointed to the drawer. Evan dipped down for another kiss, another taste, his body landing on top of Patrick's again as they pushed and ground together, chasing relief, still avoiding the end.

"Shit. Sorry. You're just—" Evan lifted again and smiled down, catching his breath as Patrick ran his knuckles along Evan's jawline. "Fucking stunning."

He fumbled in the drawer and stopped once more for another kiss. Then he knelt between Patrick's legs as lube dripped from his fingers. "Fucking. *Stunning.*"

Patrick smiled up at him seductively, peeking up through his lashes like a coy minx. He took hold of his own cock and slowly dragged his hand up and down his length as his soft moans swirled around them, encouraging Evan to "Hurry, please, and just start with two—I already—"

"Jesus." Evan kissed the tip of Patrick's cock where it peeked out of his curled fingers, smiling up at him as he slipped his hand between Patrick's legs to press and massage the soft skin of his perineum. "While I worked tonight?"

"Yes." He hissed and spread his legs further, impatient, needy, *gorgeous.*

"So eager. Look at you."

Evan ran two fingers around the puckered rim, kissing the groan from Patrick's mouth as he slipped in one fingertip, then two, waiting, sensing Patrick's body relax around him. With a slow, gentle push he was in, finding an easy, steady rhythm. He went deeper and deeper, gently curling his fingers with each drag.

"Oh fuck." Patrick let go of his cock and rode Evan's fingers, slowly, desperately. Every few strokes brushed over his prostate—barely—there one second and gone the next. Patrick was lost in the teasing pleasure of it.

Evan worked his mouth up Patrick's abdomen, licking around each nipple and over each shoulder, placing a tender kiss on his temple. As if the breath on his skin woke him from a dream, Patrick opened his eyes again, dark and shining in the dimly lit room. "More." He pulled him down for a kiss, sucking his tongue into his mouth. "You. I want *you.*"

Evan groaned and sunk his fingers in one more time, kissing and licking back down Patrick's body, giving a quick swirl of his tongue around the head of Patrick's cock: dripping, purple, hard. With one final curl of his fingers, he dragged them out, Patrick's back arching with the motion.

"Evan. Let me, let me..." Patrick scrabbled for the condom and unwrapped it, quickly sheathing Evan with an exquisite grip and stroke that Evan would get lost in if it weren't for the pleading lure in Patrick's eyes—*now, please now.*

"Give me a pillow, sweetheart." Evan took the offered pillow and propped it under Patrick's hips, stopping again to look at this beautiful man. This man who had already stolen his heart, who was beginning to pull him out of his day to day doldrums simply by offering himself freely and without expectation.

With one more whimper from Patrick, Evan shook out of his reverie and lined himself up, focusing on the man beneath him: his sounds, his movements, his eyes and mouth all saying *yes* and *please* and *more just like that.* Then he sank into him, offering himself in return.

Freely and without expectation.

It was slow. Heated. Intense. Every time Evan pulled back, he felt Patrick tighten around him, his body not just taking him in, but also moving with him, tuned in and synchronized. Every push in brought him deeper, closer, and felt more intimate than the last.

And Patrick *cared* for Evan in a way he was unfamiliar with. He brushed mussed hair from Evan's brow, placing tender kisses onto his skin whenever he could reach, whenever he was close enough to Patrick's mouth. His touch was firm, yet tender, and his eyes— oh, his *eyes*—always sought to be on Evan's; affectionate, hungry, stealing a bit of his soul with every thrust, with every kiss.

Evan couldn't look away. Couldn't get enough of the tight heat surrounding his cock or the warm, genuine yearning to be closer, to feel more deeply, to hold more tightly.

The pillow was tossed, replaced by Evan's thighs and then nothing as he bent over Patrick's body to scoop him up into his arms, folding his thighs back, sinking into him again and again, so tight, hot, slick, the slow rhythmic smack of their skin echoing with their groans of pleasure.

Evan kissed his way from the crook of Patrick's neck up his jaw, landing on his mouth as though he'd never kissed him before, exploring and searching, his teeth dragging across Patrick's bottom lip and pulling a whimper from him.

They were tiring, yet energized, as if this would be the only time, the only chance, the first and last.

Patrick yanked the pillow from behind his head and tossed it over the side of the bed, his head flopping back and rolling to the side as he grabbed for Evan's thighs, pulling him closer and closer still—

"Evan. Your dog—"

Evan didn't even look, knowing full well she'd been in the room with them the entire time. Instead he focused on the man, the sounds, the moment. "She's taking notes."

Patrick looked back at Evan and laughed, each chortle making his ass clench tighter around Evan's cock. "Healthy social life?"

Evan pushed in hard and deep, spreading Patrick's thighs and hiking him up closer, resting Patrick's legs on his shoulders with a snicker. "I named her after a *tart* for a reason." He whipped his head to fling an errant lock of hair from his brow and began pumping more shallowly, more slowly. "Do I need to stop and kick her out?" Then he pulled out and snapped his hips in hard just to make his point.

Patrick grabbed at Evan's thighs and dug his nails in, his gaze intense, desperate. "Don't you dare stop."

Evan smiled down at Patrick, the breath knocked out of him by the simple light in Patrick's eyes, dark yet shining in the dimly lit room. "Do I have you back now?"

"I never left." Patrick slipped his legs off of Evan's shoulders and reached up to pull Evan down for a blistering kiss, one hand sinking into Evan's sweaty hair while the other slipped between them to wrap around his own cock. "Don't want to be anywhere else."

Evan kissed the tip of Patrick's nose and propped himself up on his elbows, fingering through Patrick's hair with an awkward hand. "Me either."

And then Evan righted himself and ran his hands up and down the length of Patrick's legs, finally curling his arms around his thighs and holding him close as he pumped into him. Patrick's hand flew over his own cock while the squelch of their bodies moving and smacking together, the rhythmic grunts of exertion and pleasure, echoed in the room.

They moved hard and fast, chasing the coil of pleasure that tightened and tightened between them, inside of them, around them, until finally Evan looked down at Patrick, close, so close, and watched the head of his cock push through his fist. "Patrick. Yes. Come on—that's it." He stuttered and squeezed at Patrick's thighs, fingernails digging into his flesh as he twisted inside and finally, *finally*, pulse after pulse, crying out as his body spiraled in hot, blurred pleasure.

Patrick's hand on his own cock was hard and firm and flying, and, with one final buck, he tossed his head back as strings and drops of pearly white painted his stomach and chest.

Evan pushed in one final time with a grunt, holding there until Patrick settled and peeled his eyes open to rest on Evan's. They were sated, blissed, and Patrick smiled the sweetest, most lovesick gaze Evan had ever seen. And he knew he was mirroring it.

He pulled out and disposed of the condom, curling around Patrick with a kiss and a satisfied moan. "Sorry about Dini. I'll kick her out next time." He sighed as his body molded perfectly around Patrick's sweat-slick and pliant one.

"Well, we don't want to send her out into the world unprepared."

"I *am* her world."

Patrick turned in Evan's arms to face him, cupping his face in his hand as he kissed him softly and tenderly, brushing their noses together. "I guess she's not so stupid after all."

Evan woke to a wet tongue on his palm and jerked away in panic; for that first moment, he forgot where he was. And then his eyes focused on the soft earth tones of Patrick's room and the abstract black and white photographs on the walls. Dini snorted, and he shifted his naked body in the sheets, sighing and scrunching deeper into the mattress in almost childlike contentment.

The pillow next to him was empty, missing the man who had

been snoring softly next to him all night. The man who had made him smile more, come more, gasp and groan and *breathe* more than he had in an age.

But the smells coming from outside the room were reassuring and alluring enough for the moment. Evan stretched, sat up and popped his back, scratching Dini's ears as she licked his ankles where they dangled over the side of the bed. After rummaging around in his bag for some flannel pants, he stumbled into them and followed his nose to the kitchen.

Patrick stood at the stove, disheveled in a torn T-shirt and low-slung sweats, whistling away as he managed a frying pan that popped and crackled with frying sausage and rashers. A tea kettle sat to boil, and other ingredients were spread over the counter space, waiting to go into the pan.

The muscles of his back rippled and flexed as he worked, and his ass jiggled as he lifted the pan to poke at the sausage with a trained finger, inspecting its level of doneness.

Evan slipped behind him and wrapped his arms around Patrick's tiny waist, pressing a soft kiss to the curve of his neck. "Smells amazing."

"Did I wake you?"

"No, Dini's tongue did. I was hoping for yours, but..."

"Ah, well. I figured that could wait until you were more awake to enjoy it." Patrick lowered the heat on the pan and turned in Evan's arms, kissing him fully. "Good morning."

"Good morning." After a peck on the tip of Patrick's nose, Evan stepped back and looked down at the dog. She had shimmied her way between them and was panting as though she'd just run a mile. "I should take her out."

"Already did. Go back to bed."

The man had taken his dog out. And was fixing the largest breakfast he had ever seen. He'd been awake not more than five minutes, and it was already the best day ever. "Can I help?"

"No, I want to give you breakfast in bed." Patrick turned back to the stove and shook the pan, sliding the meat onto a plate and into a warm oven. He gave Evan a pointed look. "Go on. You're messing with my plan."

Evan gave the spread one more glance before considering going back to the warmth of Patrick's bed. "This isn't recommended by the Heart Association, is it?"

"Hardly. But it's good before a real active day."

"I don't think I'll be able to get out of bed after all of this."

Patrick dropped a knob of yellow, creamy Irish butter into the hot skillet. "*Now* you understand my plan."

Evan went back to bed.

And shortly thereafter, once Evan was properly settled in with Dini tucked at his side—panting anxiously as though the food had been specially prepared for her—Patrick arrived with a loaded tray, complete with a small vase of brightly colored tulips.

The meal was magnificent: sausage, rashers and black and white pudding. A perfectly fried egg, delicately framed by a brown, crisp cuff, the yolk creamy orange and topped with only the thinnest of skins, molten and runny, waiting to be popped and drip over all the grilled tomatoes and sautéed mushrooms.

Evan devoured everything, chasing it with homemade brown bread, Irish butter and perfectly brewed tea.

After eating, feeding each other and slipping pieces of sausage and pudding to Dini, they shoved the trays onto Patrick's dresser so they could promptly disrobe, make out like horny teenagers and take a well-deserved nap.

They awoke peculiarly tangled together and greeted each other with lazy kisses and soft, meaningless whispers, only to doze off again mid-sentence. And later again, not missing a beat, Evan tasted Patrick and knew he'd never encountered a delicacy so succulent and divine. He found Patrick hard and pulsing, dripping and hot in his mouth, down his throat. Afterward, he stretched his body back up to Patrick's mouth, sloppy and sleepy, debauched.

Content.

They napped again only for Evan to be awoken by Patrick's hand wrapped around him, tugging and stroking, pulling the pleasure from him like fine taffy. His orgasm spilled onto Patrick's fist, his own thighs and belly, and Patrick licked him clean. They curled together again, both spent and invigorated, ready for a shower. Or maybe another nap.

Evan was pretty convinced they'd never leave the bed. He wasn't even a little disappointed at the thought, because the evening, the middle of the night and the morning had all been sheer and utter bliss.

He woke first and caught himself staring like a creep, watching Patrick sleep. He tried not to laugh at himself, but he wasn't sure what any other man in his situation would do. Patrick not only cared for all of Evan—even the ugly sides—but also made him feel comfortable enough to expose all of himself. Even the ugly sides.

His ex wasn't wrong; he had always been emotionally frigid with men. And then Patrick, with his exuberant friendliness, his tender compassion, his unabashed joy, split open that tightly wound box inside Evan, leaving his emotions gaping and raw. He felt an intimacy with Patrick that he hadn't allowed himself to feel with another man.

Evan bent down to place a kiss on Patrick's slightly parted lips as the softest snore rumbled in his chest and he stirred to life, stretching and groaning and pulling Evan into him when his eyes opened just enough to see him.

They finally welcomed the world into their bed, reading the news together on Patrick's phone, commiserating over an article about aging chefs and how soon their bodies give out with the physical toll such a life brings. Like most articles about chefs, it ended with the question so many cooks discuss late at night in dark, seedy bars when they are sweaty and sore and spent from a run of interminably long shifts.

The question was about the food that hit you at your core; the final taste you wanted on your lips before you left this life, the one you wanted to carry with you into the next.

The last meal of your life—what would it be?

"So, how about you?" Patrick turned off his phone and tossed it on the bedside table, pulling Evan into his arms as they snuggled into the sheets yet again. "You ate my last meal this morning."

"Last meal? Today? Are you going to be cliché and die in the throes of an amazing orgasm?"

"Mmmm. That sounds like a magnificent plan."

Evan draped a leg over Patrick's and kissed his chest, the coarse hair tickling his lips. "So for your last meal, you want to protein up with a full-fry... "

"Yes. After a start with oysters and Guinness. Because if we're shoving food in our maw for the final time—"

"Oh God, oysters. Excellent choice. Where are these oysters coming from?"

"Well, ideally they'd be eaten standing in the marsh from where they'd been pulled in Galway Bay. Barring that... I'd get them from The Lobster Place at Chelsea Market. Oona always just used whatever she found at the grocery and it was good enough."

"But for your last meal..."

"Right. The best. With the bread we had this morning, slathered in butter."

Evan moaned at the thought and figured, since he'd already had the full fry... "Can we do that? I can pick some up oysters and we can—"

"It's even better after a night of drinking."

"Oh God, yes." Evan lit up and licked his lips just imagining it. The initial hit of salty seawater. And then, after that first chew—the one some fear and skip over because of the slime factor—the sweetness taking over. And then. And *then* the finish, different for every different type of oyster, and for every different location they are harvested from: fruity or nutty, buttery or mineral.

Oysters were one of those delicacies you could never fully appreciate until you'd enjoyed the absolute best.

And Patrick appreciated them in a way that made Evan feel as if he'd never had them before. "So, oysters and Guinness, a full fry, and for dessert?"

"Gelato from that place in Park Slope."

"Flavor?"

"Yes."

"Today?"

"Shower and we'll go?"

Patrick fussed with the water temperature while Evan waxed poetic about his last meal and tenderly kissed along Patrick's shoulders as they flexed and rippled in motion. Evan's last meal was simple, really. He would start with a charcuterie plate with the finest meats and cheeses and maybe even a fabulous pork and brandy terrine—if it was done right.

For his main course, however, he wanted a dish Millie had made when he was a boy—a perpetually changing cassoulet/*ribollita* hybrid with beans, vegetables and cheap cuts of meat that sat all day in herbs and stock. Her best versions made their own gravy, which she served with her buttery whipped garlic and rosemary mashed potatoes.

"Oh, and the gravy would just ooze into the potatoes, making this—this *slop* of meaty, hearty…" Evan's voice faded into the memory and he barely even noticed Patrick's lips trailing along his clavicle.

"Lumps or no?" Patrick pulled Evan under the spray of water in the shower and tilted his head back so he could run his fingers through Evan's hair, lathering it with shampoo as he massaged his scalp.

"Definitely lumps. Lumps made it Millie's. And you know—*ah, God*—you get that creamy, buttery whip and then, *ooh!*" Patrick used his thumbs to massage right behind Evan's ears and down his neck. "God, that's good. A lump—a nice little surprise bite."

Patrick gave him a surprise bite, nibbling gently on his ear, before carefully rinsing his hair of the suds. Evan groaned and stuttered out more details about what he had affectionately named "Millie's Mess" as a boy.

"All rinsed," Patrick said.

Evan lifted his head and turned to him, kissing him softly. "The French have nothing on Millie." Evan wiped away the water dripping from his brow and found Patrick's pupils were blown wide with lust. "And you stopped listening anyway, didn't you?"

Patrick blinked as if coming out of a trance and soaped up the bath sponge. He turned Evan to face the wall. "I'm listening. And getting hungry. What about dessert?"

"You're going to think I'm a kiss-ass."

Patrick grazed his lips across Evan's back as the water cascaded down it and suds slid down Evan's crack, over the curve of his cheeks and onto his thighs. Patrick followed the flow of the water with his hands, pushing the last remnants of the lather onto the shower floor, kissing Evan's ass and pressing his lips to his wet, soapy back all the way up to his neck. "I used my own damned food as a favorite. Go."

Even in the hot shower, Patrick's breath in Evan's ear made him shiver. He grabbed Patrick's arm and wrapped it around his chest, arching his ass and hissing when he felt Patrick hard and ready. With one shift, Patrick's cock was between his cheeks, his slow, undulating motion letting the soap and water work with them, slick and steady.

All conversation was forgotten. Evan reached back to find Patrick's mouth, the water running down his neck and chest, his cock quickly hardening as Patrick rutted between his ass cheeks, insistent, grunting *sexy* and *gorgeous, can you come for me again* and *fucking beautiful* between kisses full of tongue and the grazing of teeth. Then Patrick took hold of him firmly and worked him fast, back and up in rhythm with their bodies, the water drowning out their moans and cries as they came, first Patrick, then Evan. The evidence washed down the drain and they turned to kiss the breath back into each other before stumbling out of the shower to dry off and laugh at how absolutely ridiculous they were.

It wasn't until they were knocking spoons into the same scoop of tiramisu gelato that Evan finished his answer.

"Your white chocolate raspberry cheesecake."

"What?" Patrick looked up and Evan sneaked another spoonful, forgoing his pistachio in favor of the chocolate, espresso and mascarpone mixture in Patrick's dish.

"My last dessert."

Patrick stopped mid-spoon and looked up at Evan, his face almost comical in its incredulity. "Of *all* the desserts you've had— you've *made*."

"It's the best cheesecake I've ever had. Anywhere."

Patrick looked down and took a spoonful of Evan's pistachio. "You know, you're already getting me naked. You don't have to butter me up."

When Evan grabbed Patrick's wrist and turned his spoon into his own mouth, Patrick laughed and took Evan's bowl to the counter.

"Hello? My gelato." But Evan sat back with a smile, his heart filled again with the warmth he'd felt that morning. *Yes, this is so right*. It was invigorating. It was electrifying.

Patrick returned with a bigger dish, clearly amused with his decision. "Okay, let's do this right." He handed the bowl over. "Your pistachio, my tiramisu and some toasted coconut with chocolate shavings, because what were we thinking that we didn't get those to begin with?"

"Toasted coconut?" Evan scraped cream from each of the three scoops and closed his eyes as the cold, sweet gelato melted in his mouth. "You are..." He swallowed and opened his eyes, his breath hitching when he was met with the simple, happy smile of this beautiful man. "Where have you been all my life?"

Patrick's eyes softened and he offered a small bite of the coconut to Evan. His expression went right into Evan's soul. "I've been right here. Waiting for you."

►•◄

Evan was used to distractions in the kitchen. His job was buoyed by auditory distractions: printers clicking a constant tick-tick-tick of new orders; cooks chattering about the food, their horrible mothers-in-law and how drunk they'd gotten the night before; expeditors shouting orders and the general clang-sizzle-hiss of food prep all served not only as a droned soundtrack, but also a constant distraction. You learned to work with it, if not for it.

But this distraction—Patrick's lips moving up the curve of his neck, hot breath tickling his ear right before the damp warmth of his tongue traced the shell of it; Patrick's arm wrapped firmly around his waist, hand dipping knuckle deep into the waistband of his lounge pants, the other covering his own hand on the sauté pan handle, "helping" him flip the asparagus over the heat—was a distraction he could not get used to.

Not that he wanted to. Not at all.

It was delicious. Patrick was delicious. And delightful. And decidedly perfect in his bed, out of his bed, in his arms, *on* his arm. In the weeks following that first night, they had captured every moment they could together—at the diner, at their new favorite coffee shop, stealing away for a quick walk between shifts and relishing the rare occasion of a full night and morning to delight in each other.

On this particular morning after, Evan was trying to determine if the asparagus was done and ready for the lemon vinaigrette. And Patrick was there, all over him, humming and rubbing and kissing and distracting.

"You know, I think I've found one negative of this little arrangement."

"What's that?" Patrick bit down on Evan's earlobe just right, making Evan almost lose his grip on the sauté pan. Patrick giggled and drew his teeth across the tender skin. "Careful, love."

"Neither of us will let the other serve breakfast in bed." Evan turned from the stove and put his hands on Patrick's shoulders, pushing him gently away. "Now shoo. I'm going to burn your asparagus."

"Is that a euphemism?"

"Patrick Sullivan. Take your soft lips and your wandering hands back to bed where they belong."

Patrick stepped back with a snort and grunted as he bent down to pick up Dini, knowing full well she was to be included in this breakfast-in-bed moment. "Come on, puppy. *You'll* let me smooch you."

Dini snorted, whined and wiggled her way out of Patrick's arms, landing on the floor with a thud.

"She knows I don't like to share. Now get. I've already riced my eggs and they're going to dry out."

Patrick tossed his hands up in the air and feigned a southern belle's distress as he turned and walked toward Evan's bedroom. "Oh my *stars*, we don't want dried out eggs mimosa! The *travesty* of it all!"

Evan beaned him in the back of the head with a discarded asparagus stalk.

Evan's body ached. Deliciously.

Sometimes the stolen moments they'd find in the schedule were simply indulgent, when they were completely absorbed in each other, in laughter or in quiet, in fucking hard and fast or in spreading each other out, slow and languorous, in whispered words of affection and amazement. In shouts of pleasure and rapture.

But God, did his body ache.

So this time, Patrick held Evan propped on his lap, his strong arms wrapped around Evan's body helping him lift, meeting him with a roll of his own hips, pressed together with shallow thrusts and hot, breathy kisses. It still got them there, Evan first, with a hand around his own cock giving just that extra push to the end while Patrick watched, encouraging him, going over the edge right after Evan as he so often did.

Look at you, just look at you.

They stayed there, Patrick's spent cock slipping out, hands in each other's hair as they kissed and came down and the room settled back into place, the bed beneath them a nest of warmth and security.

With one more lazy kiss, Evan groaned and lifted himself off of Patrick's lap, curling right back around his side as Patrick tended to a quick cleanup. Within minutes, Evan was pressing his lips to Patrick's chest, to his smooth, warm skin, and Patrick was shifting to accommodate Evan's weight, to hitch and arch yet again as Evan's tongue swirled around the perimeter of a nipple.

"Some day, Mr. Sullivan, I'm going to tongue-kiss you under the slide. Show Ms. Horowitz how it's done."

Patrick looked down at him, eyes heavy-lidded, smile lazy from orgasm. "Come up here, Beautiful." Evan hiked up and Patrick kissed him once, tenderly, chastely, his eyes focusing as he drew his fingers around the frame of Evan's face. "Let's go."

"What? Right now?" He snuggled back into the crook of Patrick's arm, drawing imaginary designs on his chest. "I'm comfortable."

Patrick wiggled them both up to sit. "Yes. Now. It's a gorgeous day. The pier's what? A twenty-minute walk from here?"

Patrick hopped out of bed and Evan fell back into the free space, pulling the covers up and laughing at the look it got him.

"Oh, come on! You can't just suggest something so perfectly spontaneous and then not follow through!"

"I can." Truth was, he was enjoying the view while Patrick bent to retrieve his clothes and disappeared into his permanently oil-stained, flour-covered work pants, marked with hours of hard work and good food.

And then his own clothes landed on his face.

Evan laughed and pulled them under the sheets, snuggling in deeper. "You know, I could just tongue-kiss you here. In bed. Where we don't have to stop at kissing." He inched himself closer to the edge of the bed, where Patrick was digging in Evan's drawer for a clean T-shirt. "And then we can scrounge for food. And tongue-kiss some more. For days. Until our bosses call, wondering if we've run away to the circus."

"Yeah, but under the *slide*. It's like kismet."

Evan sighed. "Dini *could* use another walk."

Fully clothed, Patrick yanked back the sheets and straddled Evan's still-naked body, bouncing like a child on Christmas morning. "And see? It'll be even more awesome because we'll have a bag of dog shit dangling between us."

"You really know how to seduce."

But when Patrick bent down and captured Evan's lips in his own, the warm brush of his tongue and the soft rock of his hips setting every last nerve on edge, Evan couldn't help but follow the man's every whim. "Did you even bother put on underwear?"

"Follow me to the slide and find out."

They took a long route to the pier, meandering through streets in Brooklyn Heights, and had to cart Dini in their arms most of the way. Stamina was not a pugly sort of quality. Or a ladylike one either, to hear her tell it.

And she told it, by plopping down on her backside and refusing to budge, her round face and chin lifted in defiance, her pink rhinestone-studded collar gleaming in the sun.

Evan tugged on her leash. Dini sat.

"We've walked her this far before—what's the deal?"

"It's getting warmer. She overheats."

Patrick bent over to pick her up, giving Evan a look that felt a lot like judgment. Fond judgment, but judgment nonetheless.

"I didn't know pugs were so lazy."

"Mmmm…"

She squirmed and Patrick put her down. She walked happily, noisily for another block and then—*PLOP*, right back on her behind.

Evan gave in to her need for a rest and leaned against a wrought-iron fence, tugging Patrick by his shirt to come close. "We need a warm-up before we get to the slide anyway."

"You afraid you're going to forget how to French kiss?"

Before Evan could respond, Patrick's lips were on his, demanding, stealing his breath, his sense and his witty retort as though none of those things ever belonged to him to begin with. Evan pulled his head back with a smack, keeping their bodies pressed close. He was in no hurry to get to the pier or to tug Dini along for the ride. "You'll keep reminding me if I do? Forget?"

"Without fail."

They finally journeyed on, speaking to the older gentleman they'd caught staring at them from across the street as they kissed.

"Gentlemen... "

"Good afternoon."

"Headed to the pier?"

"Pretty day for it."

His voice was rough and graveled, as though it had been skimmed over a cheese grater. But his eyes were crystal blue and shone in the sun, teasing, yet dipping away shyly as he went back to watering the flower boxes perched on the windows of the corner property where he stood.

"He does know those plants are dead, right?"

Patrick knocked against Evan's shoulder as they walked away, giggling at the man and taking Evan's hand in his. "If it makes him happy..."

The park wasn't particularly crowded, but they meandered anyway, waiting for the right amount of solitude. Or for Dini to finally collapse in a heap—Evan wasn't sure which was going to come first.

Finally, Evan couldn't take the wait anymore. "We're not teenagers sneaking out of the house, for God's sake. Just come here."

He grabbed Patrick's hand, yanked him toward the slide and tied Dini's leash to the ladder. When he reached for Patrick again, he was halfway up the ladder, crooking a finger in invitation. "Come on."

"Oh hell, no. I am not getting my ass stuck on the way down."

"Your pert little ass isn't this wide. Get up here." Evan looked up at him, the blue sky and the sun haloing his hair, his eyes gleaming through the shadow he threw, and couldn't even consider resisting.

He hit the second-to-last stair and pushed Patrick down the slide with a squeal, giggling and following closely behind, landing with a jump and almost toppling them both over. Walking, wobbling, tangling, they righted themselves under the slope of metal where the sun's heat had yet to hit. The ground was soft under their feet and Patrick looked as Evan imagined he had as a teenager: dreamy and wide-eyed, hair perfectly mussed, T-shirt askew from goofing off. God, he could *devour* him.

Without wasting another moment, he cupped Patrick's jaw in his hand and kissed him. The kiss was soft and tentative, as if it really were their first and they were confused and scared and oh so eager teenagers. And while it wasn't a first kiss, Evan's heart fluttered in just the same way. He tasted Patrick's lip with the slightest brush of his tongue, stepping closer when Patrick parted his lips.

Patrick was warm, and vibrating with the sweetest moan, innocent and indecent all at once. But mostly indecent. Evan pulled him closer by his ass and when they pressed together Evan gasped, their lips still brushing as he spoke. "You *didn't* bother putting on underwear."

"I did not."

"Tsk. Think of the *children*." Evan swooped in for another kiss, open-mouthed and desperate, and sucked at Patrick's bottom lip as they parted again.

"I have more pants-less activities in mind for later today." *Kiss, nibble, kiss.* "I don't particularly *care* about the children."

When they heard the stomping of little feet on the ladder overhead, they reluctantly stopped, sharing one more soft kiss before parting and untying Dini.

"So. Better than Patricia Horowitz?"

"Much better. I wore underwear for hers."

Patrick: I'd given up, you know.

Evan smiled at the text, remembering their last moments together that day, only hours before.

They'd said their goodbyes reluctantly, ridiculously. Patrick kissed him and walked to the door, coming back again pretending he had another question. He kissed Evan again and then he was off, only to rap on the door saying he'd forgotten to kiss Dini. Which was the most ridiculous thing of all, because as hard as Dini tried to kiss him back, Patrick was never particularly fond.

Nights apart after such glorious days, days of kisses under slides and lazy lovemaking and weird old men watering dead flowers, Evan's bed felt huge and empty without Patrick at his side, heating his cold feet with his furnace-hot legs or taking the piss out of him about his luxurious taste in ice cream.

"What's wrong with a simple chocolate? Can't she... what's her name?"

"Jeni. It's a midwestern thing."

"Can't Jeni Whatsername just call it chocolate? No, it has to be Askinosie Dark Chocolate. Ndali Estate Vanilla Bean."

It never sounded quite as frou-frou in Patrick's accent. Which only made Evan love it more.

"It's fair trade Ugandan vanilla *from Ndali*. A guy named Askinosie provides the cocoa and chocolate. There are reasons for the—"

"It's so she can charge ten dollars a pint, is all I'm saying."

Evan was hoping his dish of Brambleberry Crisp would somehow calm his adolescent pinings and give him the peace to sleep. Alone. With a snoring dog. Who, if he played it right, just might warm his feet.

Cold-thumbed and a little lonely, Evan scooped entirely too large a spoonful into his mouth and replied to the text.

Evan: Given up on?
Patrick: This. Falling.

Evan stared at his phone for a few moments, sucking the latent cream from his spoon. God damn the man, he needed to go to sleep, not write love notes via text.

Evan: Yeah. So had I.

And then—

Evan: It can be complicated.

Patrick: I don't want it to be complicated.
Evan: It doesn't feel complicated. It feels—really good.
Patrick: I want to see you. Tonight.
Evan: Patrick... we both have to be in before the sun rises.

Patrick didn't answer. Evan stared at the unblinking screen.

God *damn* the man. He shouldn't invite him back to his apartment, either.

Evan: Come on over. I was just going to read.

He shoved another spoonful of ice cream into his mouth and before he could even settle back onto his propped pillow to begin his twenty-minute wait, his security speaker buzzed.

Evan laughed and hopped out of bed, his bare, cold feet loudly smacking the wood floors as he rushed to the door to buzz Patrick in. Shoveling more ice cream into his mouth, he wondered if the elevator ride up to his twenty-ninth floor apartment got longer at night, because it was taking—

"You're ridiculous."

"I can't stay. I shouldn't stay." Patrick looked into the bowl. "Bleesberry from Lilongwe?"

"Brambleberry—no. Asshole." Evan yanked the bowl away. "You can't have any."

"What's a brambleberry?"

"It's not real, Patrick. It's blackberries, black raspberries and currants, and why am I telling you this?" He shoved a spoonful into Patrick's mouth.

"Shit, that's good. Streusel? Oat streusel?"

"Yes."

"She still makes up names to charge more. *Brambleberry*, for God's sake." Patrick was still standing at the entrance; Evan's feet were still freezing and they were arguing about ice cream.

"Did you come up here to annoy me?" Evan was smiling anyway. Because this man had upended everything he believed. About ice cream. About his heart. About kisses in the park and Brooklyn boys. Probably, if given the chance, he would upend any notion Evan might have about a life lived without him in it.

"Not initially, but this is sort of fun."

Evan looked into his bowl. "One more scoop. Want?"

"No. Want you."

Evan tossed the bowl into the sink. Dini stirred and instantly settled again as their muffled moans and stumbles carried them into Evan's bedroom.

It was fast and desperate, hard and passionate, pants at the ankles and thighs, shirts pushed up and out of the way, just *on your knees* and *where's the lube?* and *come on, come ON* and *need you,* the headboard banging loudly along with pleas cried out to an unknown god. And it was over all too soon. They fell onto the bed in a heap, spent and sweaty and so unbelievably happy, breath settling into a more peaceful rhythm as Evan lazily drew his fingers through Patrick's hair.

"Thank you for not giving up."

"Thank you for giving me a reason not to." Before he fell asleep in Evan's arms, Patrick was up and standing in front of the mirror, coaxing his hair back into place with his fingers, spending more time flirting with Evan's reflection than was probably wise if he aimed to leave. And when Evan got up to wrap his arms around Patrick's waist, needing to be near him again already, now, always, Patrick closed his eyes and rested his head back on his shoulder.

"Tomorrow?"

"Tomorrow."

►•◄

Evan looked around at the mess in his kitchen, at the mess of Patrick, apron dotted and speckled with fruity sugar syrup and smeared with berry juice and God knew what else, and laughed because the mess was so monstrous that taking it seriously would be somewhat depressing.

It had started innocently enough.

On an innocuous day off from work, Evan *accidentally* tasted a succulent, juicy, ripe strawberry at the market... when he was hungry. And then he ate another. And then conversed with the farmer. An hour later, he was at home with a peck-sized basket of the fool things, not to mention blackberries, raspberries and some mango for shipped-in variety.

And thus started the First Annual Evan-and-Patrick-Cook-Themselves-Sick Escapades of Summer.

Patrick taught Evan the fine art of making Irish breads—brown soda, white soda, brown bread and what became Evan's favorite, barmbrack.

"It's typically a fall bread, but it's always delicious," Patrick had told him as he drained the raisins and dried fruit peel from their whiskey-and-tea soak, the early summer sun shining into his kitchen window.

And Evan showed Patrick some of Millie's favorite preserve techniques. They made chutneys, jams and spreads, all the things they couldn't do in their restaurants, and indulged in the pleasures that had brought them into the kitchen as boys.

But in addition to a monstrous mess, even with preserving, they ended up with more food than they could handle.

"What are we going to do with all of this shit?" Patrick cut off a heel of brown bread and slathered it with a schmear of strawberry jam still lingering in its pot.

"They *are* preserves… "

"Yeah, but the bread." He shoved the treat into his mouth and moaned. "Oh God… and we're not giving any of it away. You don't mind if I get fat, do you?"

Evan served himself up some of the same and gave Patrick a sticky, sweet kiss. "More cushion for the pushin,' babe."

"Hey, how about that guy we see on the way to the pier? He looks as if he could use a little pick-me-up."

"The one who waters dead plants in his window boxes?"

"I'm thinking that's the first sign he could use a pick-me-up."

They cleaned, and whined about it—"Don't we have porters for this shit?"—and prepared a box of bread and jam for the peculiar man they often saw on Middagh Street.

"What if he's not there?"

"We'll feed it all to Dini. She's less concerned about her figure—being that she's shaped like a potato."

"*You're* cleaning up after her."

"She's your dog."

"It's your bad idea."

But the man was there, sitting on his stoop and gnawing on a toothpick as he cleaned his fingernails with the blade of a pocket-knife. "Gentlemen… "

Within moments, they learned that his name was Roger and he was fifty-eight years old. And, while scratching under Dini's chin and giggling as her hind leg tamped at the ground in utter delight, he admitted to once having a teacup Yorkie, which seemed completely preposterous given his gruff, rough-edged demeanor.

"So whose flowers are these, Roger?" Evan dared to pick through one of the boxes, trying to figure out what had been there. "Flowers" was about as far as he got; the plants had clearly lost their battle for life before winter ever hit.

"Ehh, the owners of the place. They asked me to keep 'em nice 'til they got back."

"Any, uh…" *Maybe marigolds? Millie hates marigolds.* "Any possibility of getting some new ones in there? Seems a waste of water to keep tending to these."

"They'll be back soon. I probably, ehh… shouldn't mess with them."

Evan shot Patrick a look of concern and eyed the box tucked under his arm. "Oh! Yes! We, uh… we had the day off today, and since it was raining we got to baking and sort of overdid things." Patrick shoved the box at Roger, who looked at it as if it might contain a bomb. "We've enjoyed seeing you on our walks and thought maybe you might enjoy? There's Irish soda bread and a couple different jams… "

When Roger didn't take the box, Patrick opened it to show him. "The brown bread is still a little warm."

At that, he looked up at Evan as if asking permission, and then at the box. "I'm a felon."

"You're a—" Evan cocked his head in confusion and shared a glance with Patrick, who looked no less confused or more concerned than Evan was. "Okay. Felons can't enjoy bread and jam?" Evan pushed the box forward again, pleading with his eyes.

"Well, yes. But. No one just *does* things like this for me." He finally peeked into the box. "Oh. My. Those look—" He took the box and breathed in, his sinuses rattling like maracas.

"Well, we did. We are." Evan peeked into the box as well. "I think we gave you strawberry preserves and a mango-raspberry jam."

Roger dipped his hand in the box and tore off a chunk of bread. They all juggled everything around, finally getting a jar open so Roger could dip the bread right into the jam. He looked it over before finally popping it into his mouth. "So you're not afraid of me?"

"Should we be?"

Roger sized them up while shoveling bread into his mouth as though it was his first meal in days, licking his fingers as he talked around it. "No. I—I robbed a bank. It's just that most people—"

"Roger, I *hire* felons and addicts and immigrants in my kitchen. Unless you're planning on robbing us—"

"Oh! Oh no, reformed. It was, ehh—it was for a girl."

Patrick laughed and offered him a handkerchief. "Did she appreciate it?"

"Visited me once in prison and I never saw her again."

"See, this is why I swore off women."

"You swore off women because the first one you kissed gave you the stomach flu."

Now Roger was laughing and tried to hand the handkerchief back to Patrick. "No—you can keep it."

He shoved it into a back pocket already stuffed with a gray, holey cloth. "So, are you guys... I mean, I've *seen* you, so. Are you boyfriends?"

Evan smiled and crouched down to Dini, who was splayed out on the cement sidewalk and waffling between a good panting fit and a good nap. "Yes. Dini's our den mother—makes sure we behave."

"I, ehh, I never knew anybody like that before."

"You probably have; you just didn't know it." When Roger didn't respond, Evan took another look at the window boxes. "Let me get you something for these. They'd be so pretty—"

"Thank you, but ehh, the owners said they'd be back. They'll be back. Pretty again in no time."

"Okay."

"Honestly. No worries. And, ehh... thank you for the bread. You made my day."

▶•◀

"Lobster tail!"

"Pft. *Amore mio...* " Patrick pouted and Evan frowned. They stood at the Court Pastry Shop counter, drooling over the piles upon piles of sweets stacked up on trays in the glass display case. Cookies and pastries, cakes and pies, and behind the very patient clerk, a freezer case full of Italian ices.

After finding great chemistry together not only in the bedroom, but also in the kitchen, this was the last place they should be. But now they were here, they surely weren't going to walk away empty-handed.

Even if Evan didn't remember the proper name for the cone-shaped delicacy he was staring at. "Not lobster tail? Shit. Wait. It's a—wait. I know this—"

"You are an executive chef at a respected *Italian* restaurant in New York City and you don't—"

"Oh, shut up and order one. I cannot be expected to know everything."

"*Sfogliatelle*, my sweet. Speak to this masterpiece with respect." Patrick nodded to the clerk and she pointed to the largest one in the case. "Yes. Perfect."

Once outside, Patrick pulled the pastry out of the bag and sniffed deeply, desperately trying not to choke when powdered sugar fluttered up his nose.

"Smooth."

Patrick broke the pastry in half. Evan gasped as it crackled perfectly in Patrick's hands. "Can you make these?"

"Sure can. Pâtisserie II Practicum. Passed with flying colors, I'll have you know."

They ate the delicate pastry with its orange-ricotta filling and moaned, licking fingers and sneaking sugar-clouded kisses. "Teach me."

"They take forever."

Evan considered, a coy smile spreading across his face. "Lots of downtime in the midst of it?"

"Well, I mean, the dough takes an entire day."

"Right, laminated dough?"

"Yes, butter, dough, turns, cooling, rolling all day. But even after I make the dough, there's resting and cooling and baking—"

Evan playfully ran his fingers up and down Patrick's thigh. "We could find other things to do."

Ridiculous as it seemed when they cooked all day every day, after that first afternoon together in the kitchen when they made enough bread to feed an entire neighborhood, they couldn't get enough of it. Learning something new, something intricate and demanding fed them both. Evan's insistence on getting things just right matched the precision necessary for baking, while Patrick's desire to learn to trust his palate was tested when they played with new flavors and ratios in tried and true recipes.

Patrick scooped one more schmear of ricotta filling with his finger and offered it to Evan. "I'm sure we could." Patrick swallowed thickly as Evan's eyes fluttered closed, his lips curling around and sucking at his finger. "Mmmm... let's make time."

And so a few nights later, after closing, after midnight, after everyone had gone home, they stood in Evan's restaurant kitchen ready to take on the task of making the multilayered, decadent pastry called *sfogliatelle*.

"I feel like I'm on some weird covert mission."

Evan took the bag of goods from Patrick with a swift kiss and unloaded containers of ricotta, an orange and a few vanilla beans. The sound of the items hitting the stainless steel table echoed through the empty space—noises you would barely hear in the din of a rush. "Honey, we're a restaurant. We have all of this."

"I know, but you inventory and this is for us, so—" Patrick washed his hands and pulled a package of chilled dough from a cold pack.

After suiting up with aprons and headwraps, they were ready to work.

"Okay, we can either use a pasta machine or we can hand-roll this thing."

"Hand-roll. What do you take me for?"

"An Italian chef who didn't know *sfogliatelle*."

"Well, no but… " Evan glared playfully at Patrick and tossed a healthy fistful of flour onto the work table. "I'm not a pastry chef." He stepped back as Patrick smacked the dough onto the table and floured up a rolling pin. "What's *paysanne*?"

Patrick looked up at Evan and rolled his eyes, putting a pan of butter and shortening onto low heat. "Okay, smarty-pants. How do I know you're not just making up words now?"

"Would I do that?"

"You would."

"But I'm not." He peeked into the reach-in and grabbed a carrot, picking up a chef's knife on his way back to the work station. "These are what we call clues, Master Baker."

"You callin' me a masturbator?"

"I hope so." Evan cut the carrot into large chunks and looked up as Patrick gave up on his dough to watch. He leveled a chunk of the carrot to get a firm cutting surface and sliced a few slabs about as thin as elongated Scrabble tiles. "Any guesses?"

"Well, logic tells me it's some sort of fancy knife skill."

"Yes." He cut the corner off of one slab, turned it diagonally and cut oblique diamond-shapes. Making quick work of a few more slabs while Patrick watched, he scooped them up and sprinkled the cut carrots into Patrick's hands. "*Paysanne.*"

"Show-off. What would you use that for, anyway?"

"Garnish, if you're a pretentious bastard." Evan cleaned up his trash and handed Patrick his floured rolling pin again. "My point is—"

"That I could watch you do that all day, but my dough is getting warm." Patrick popped a piece of carrot into his mouth and began rolling out the dough, turning it a quarter turn every few passes to get it as even as possible—first making an oval, and then, with a few practiced maneuvers, a rectangle of sorts.

And Evan stared and blatantly objectified Patrick's arms and shoulders and back as art in motion.

Patrick stood upright and spun the dough on the floured surface.

"Okay, now I need your help." He pointed to the other side of the table. "You go over there, I'll stay here and we're going to stretch this thing out."

"Like pizza dough?"

"Only much, much thinner. I want to see the table through it." Patrick demonstrated the technique, using his knuckles to pull the dough toward him while Evan hung on to the opposite side. "If we pull together—"

"How big?"

"Width of the table by about four feet should be good. Getting it thin enough is more important."

They worked and pulled, spun and stretched. Occasionally Evan caused a slight tear on his edge and grimaced and Patrick soothed, "It's okay. We'll lose the edges anyway. Gentle, gentle."

Finally, the dough was almost chiffon-thin, the edges draping off the lip of the table, large puffs of air trapped underneath it that Patrick smoothed carefully with his hand. His touch was tender and caring, just as Evan knew it to be late at night and early in the morning when he was naked and flushed, watching his motion on Evan's skin and checking the response beneath his fingers, caressing him as if he were a treasure.

"Okay, you have the fat?"

Evan started from his daydreaming and pulled the pan of melted butter and shortening from the back burner. He met Patrick on his side of the table for a slow, desirous kiss. "You love this."

Patrick pressed in for one more kiss and took the pan. "Yes. Not for every day, but now and then, yes, I like *creating* something this involved."

Evan looked down at the gigantic sheet of pastry and the pan of melted fat. "We need brushes."

"Brushes? Pft." Patrick took the pan and dipped his fingers into the hot, buttery oil. "God's tools. Much more efficient." He puddled the oil onto the pastry in patches, smoothing it out as he went with a delicate touch: a casual covering here, there, up on the corner, over on the side. He offered the pan to Evan to cover his side of the pastry, and their fingers brushed, slick with oil. They paused now and then to stroke each other's hands, hungry, wanting looks darting between them.

Patrick wiped his hands on his apron with a smile. "Now we roll." He wiped down Evan's knife and reached across the table. He eyed the proper width and gently dragged the knife down the length of the pastry, making an almost perfectly straight cut. "Okay, now you hold onto your side and I'm going to tug as I roll."

"This thin and it's not going to rip?"

"Not if I made the dough right."

Evan gently took hold of the strip of dough and Patrick deftly worked his edge of it into a skinny snake shape, rolling and pulling the dough thinner and thinner, tugging as he went. His motions quickened as it rolled into a fat cigar shape, skinny and uneven on either end. Patrick sliced off the ends and the edge Evan had been hanging onto, setting it onto the larger sheet and slicing down its width to start another strip.

They set to rolling again, one roll going onto the next strip and the next, making it fatter and fatter with each pass. They shared few words—"A little tighter, babe," and "How long does this rest?" And before he even realized it, they had worked their way across the sheet of dough and there was only one final strip to roll.

Evan was enthralled.

It wasn't as if he hadn't watched artisans work before. He had a staff of them. His own pastry chef was renowned in the city, coveted even. He'd spent many a break, many a pause in the day watching the man create and paint, sculpt and design beautiful, decadent sweets for his patrons.

But watching Patrick through the lens of the intimacy they now shared, he saw not only a craftsman manipulating a slab of flour and fat into this delicate, gossamer sheet, but also the man who, only a week ago, had held the weight of him in his arms, pushing him up against the shower wall, slippery, desperate and so fucking strong and masculine. He heard not only the clipped way he spoke to his staff when the diner was busy, calling out orders, quickly correcting Oscar or his assistant, harping at his waitresses to hustle it, to quit flirting, to get their heads in the game, but also the way he took the time to come out of the kitchen and patiently listen to Walter tell his one interesting story, how he almost saved a man from falling from the train platform at the Thirty-fourth Street station—thirty-five years ago. Patrick listened as if he'd never heard the story before.

Every time.

Evan saw the man who served unordered slices of cheesecake and pie to his elderly regulars, waving off their offers of payment and then slipping the stubbornly left cash into his waitresses' tip jars.

And the man who sat on a stoop with a felon, trying to one-up him on Brooklyn lore and finally conceding victory to Roger, who had a couple decades on him and a slightly dirtier past from which to spin his tales.

He saw an artisan. A gentleman. A Brooklyn boy. And so, *so* much more.

Brow furrowed in concentration, Patrick dipped his fingers into the oil one final time and created a glued edge. His forearms flexed ever so slightly as he tugged against the edge Evan held. He rolled and rolled until he reached the end and Evan let go as Patrick swiped the uneven sheet with the sharp blade of the knife.

"I love you."

Evan gasped at his own words, out before he could stop himself, he was so overwhelmed and dazed and *taken* with this man.

Patrick looked up and set the thick roll aside to rest, a smile spreading across his face as he walked around to Evan's side of the table.

He made to cup Evan's face in his hands and stopped himself, wiggling his greasy, floury fingers in explanation. When all Evan could offer in return was a crooked smile, Patrick finally gave up and wiped his hands on his T-shirt.

But Evan didn't care, and he wanted, he *needed* Patrick to know that. He needed him to know that the mess, the skill, the *passion* of the work bled into every facet of who Patrick was. Of the man he had fallen in love with.

And when Patrick did cup his face in hands still slick with buttery oil and dusted with flour, covering Evan's cheeks with a splotched white mess, Evan fell even deeper under Patrick's spell.

"You beautiful"—*kiss*—"beautiful man"—*kiss*—"I love you too."

"Yeah?"

"Yeah." Another smile, another kiss, and then, "Don't act so surprised."

"Not surprised." Evan took hold of Patrick's wrists and kissed, with tender warmth, every spot of discolored skin there; scars from years in the kitchen, stripes from hot pans, spots from splattered oil and grease, the war wounds that all professional cooks endured and that told their stories. "Relieved."

"So, you did doubt."

"No." Evan stopped, looked up into Patrick's eyes and had to confess with a blush. "Yes. Maybe a little."

"Evan... "

Evan continued to make love to Patrick's wrists and hands until Patrick stopped him, brushing at Evan's cheek with his thumb. "Look at me."

He looked into Patrick's eyes—how could he not? Evan loved him, this beautiful, amazing man, and he loved Evan back.

"I've loved you since you stood in my kitchen and imagined a stack of potatoes to be Perci's head."

At that, Evan laughed and pulled Patrick in for a hug, his own greasy, flour-covered hands sinking into Patrick's hair. "I'm still surprised you put up with me that night."

"Are you kidding me?" Evan pulled back. The sincerity in Patrick's eyes, the intensity of his gaze, made Evan quiet, no matter how many arguments to the contrary he could conjure. "Evan, you laid your heart out all over my *mise*—like an offering. I'd have been a fool not to take it."

It was cheesy and ridiculous and heartfelt, and Patrick's eyes were shining, huge orbs of cocoa and laughter, and he had a smudge of flour on his cheek, and all Evan could do was swallow him up in a kiss so deep, so intense that after only moments they had to pull back just to catch their breath.

Patrick continued to cover his face with tender kisses, the dusting of flour scratching their skin and catching on Patrick's stubble. "So… " Evan laughed and put his hand on Patrick's chest to keep just a little distance. "Patrick." It was creeping into middle-of-the-night territory, for heaven's sake. He looked down at the wrecked work table and the thick roll of dough and sighed. "So what now?"

"We kiss." Patrick stepped in and kissed him again and again, laughing into Evan's mouth when he caved and let him. They pressed their bodies together, wrapped up in canvas aprons and exhaustion and flour. So fucking much flour.

Evan relished the warm twist in his gut that came just from being held like this. It was amazing just to feel cherished. Just to have someone who was a companion, a friend and now a lover who fit into his life as though he was made for it. As though *they* were made for it. For each other.

He gave in to it all, to Patrick's kisses and his touch, easing back now as they whispered more, almost gratuitous *I love yous* into his kitchen, his second home, his throne room. He stopped and swallowed thickly, pressing one more tender kiss to the fullness of Patrick's lips, never wanting to stop, yet wanting to finish this project so they could fall into a bed together and show the depth of the confession they'd just professed. "Your pastry. What's next?"

Patrick pouted.

For the love...

"Fine." Patrick stepped back and sighed. He picked up the thick roll of dough and set it atop a swath of cling wrap, covered it and placed it in the reach-in. "We freeze it and make a filling."

"And that downtime you promised me?"

Patrick closed the door and pulled Evan to him by his apron string and then his ass, fingers cupping under its curve with a gentle squeeze. "After that, plenty of time."

"How long?"

"As long as I fucking want." Patrick pulled at the knot on Evan's apron again, this time loosening the string with almost a magician's sleight-of-hand and letting it drop to the floor at their feet.

They'd made and cooled the base of the filling, taking another make-out break only to have to stop, frustrated and turned on, wondering why they'd chosen a night when they actually had *time* to explore and soak in each other to make stupid pastry. But, true to their perfectionism, they finished the filling, sliced the dough into rounds and pressed the rounds into shell shapes. Now, after multiple taste tests, they had finally filled each shell with the sweet cheese mixture, cleaned up all that flour and put the shells in the oven to bake.

"They'll burn."

Patrick unbuttoned Evan's jacket and kissed his neck as he exposed more skin, growling at the T-shirt underneath. "Don't care." He pushed the jacket off of Evan's shoulders and yanked at the drawstring to Evan's pants.

Evan sucked in a gasp of air and breathed out his name like a sin.

"That's ah, um..." Patrick yanked Evan's pants down, underwear and all, his stripes puddled around his ankles, ass and legs bare to the heat of the kitchen. "*Fuck.* An awful lot of work to just—"

Patrick kissed his way down Evan's abdomen and, kneeling on the floor, took Evan's semi-hard cock in his mouth, walking his lips down its length until he swallowed around the head. With a drawn-out, exquisite suck he pulled back up, sculpting Evan's body with the heat of his mouth. He traced his hands up the muscles of Evan's thighs and hips, sliding under his shirt to ghost over the skin of his stomach, his sides and back down to his ass, pulling him closer and closer. Evan was fully hard and gasping, reaching back to grab onto the stainless work counter for balance.

Just as in his work in the kitchen, Patrick was skilled, efficient, guiding Evan to the edge quickly and expertly dangling him there, pulling back to kiss up and down his length, cupping his balls in his hands and then tenderly sucking them into his mouth, morsels to be savored. He guided Evan's legs further apart with a firm hand, drawing fingers at the crease of his thighs while tasting the slit of his cock, dripping and darkened, before taking him into his mouth again.

Evan could only hang on, eyes closed to the realities of where they were, the cliché of back-of-the-house sex—not a new experience by far, but one that still threatened to make him laugh at its audacity, its disrespectfulness and the utter sensuality of being so overtly raunchy and *dirty* where health inspectors scrutinized every corner, every nook, every cranny. The silence of the room, typically a place of constant motion, incessant noise and myriad scents and sights, all clamoring for attention, magnified their solitude. Their gall.

And this exact spot was even more ludicrous; Evan's bare ass was perched—of all places—on Perci's work station, while his pants pooled around his ankles and his cock slid in and out of his boyfriend's hot, wet mouth.

"Patrick! Pat—shit!"

"That's it. Come on, babe... " And Patrick's mouth was around him again, the warm, wet heat dragging up and down the length of him, fingers digging into the flesh of his ass until Evan let go of the counter to grasp at Patrick's flour-covered hair, holding him still as his orgasm washed over him, through him, Patrick swallowing around him, taking it all.

He pulled off with a gasping pop as he licked Evan clean, slowly and tenderly, moving his mouth to Evan's hips and thighs when he was too sensitive for more.

With a pop of his knees and ankles, Patrick stood, pressing kisses up Evan's abdomen, lifting Evan's shirt up and over his head and using it to wipe flour from his cheeks. "You're a bit of a mess."

Evan swallowed and smiled, lazy and sex-weary, eyes droopy. He pulled Patrick in for a kiss, groaning anew at the taste of himself on Patrick's tongue. "And whose fault is that?"

Patrick giggled and looked around. The work stations were immaculate, inspection-ready, while they stood disheveled, flour-caked and *done*. "Better a messy cook than a messy kitchen."

►•◄

In the midst of all the happiness and love and sex and brown-eyed man of wonder in his life, Evan still had to deal with a job that droned on in the background of his now very preoccupied mind. Repeatedly, the drone would crank up to an irritation, and then the irritation would crash into a full reminder of the lack of balance that had brought him to Johnny's Diner in the first place.

He'd named the imbalance "Perci," even though on most nights she seemed to have found her rhythm again. Still, every hour he had to spend in the kitchen with her had him on edge.

So today, with a string of long shifts ahead of him, he popped into the diner for a quick bite, a sneak-Patrick-attack and, as always, communion with the collection of personalities that frequented the place.

Evan waved at Angel as the bell on the door clanged behind him, surprised to see Rosey sitting alone in a window-side booth. "Well, they'll let anyone dine here, won't they?"

"No accounting for taste—I just sat down." Rosey patted the table across from him and Evan joined him. "Just headed in?"

"Yeah. How was opening?" Evan unbuttoned the top of his chef's coat and grabbed a menu.

"Smooth. Fine. Double order of zucchini came, though. No garlic."

"Christ. Not like it's not the same fucking order practically every day. Robin on it?"

"Always." Rosey looked over the menu and back at Evan. "So, the rumors true?" He pointed to the kitchen. "You shtuppin' the cook?"

"Why, you want some pointers?"

"No. Thank you. I like a little vagina with my dick, if you don't mind."

The ever-familiar pop of chewing gum announced Angel's presence. "Why is it, Rosey, that every time I come near your table, you're talkin' about sex?" She pulled the pencil from behind her ear and wiggled her hips to the faint piped-in music.

"That's because sex is all he ever talks about." Evan winced when Rosey kicked him under the table and then promptly ignored him. "What's hot on the menu today?"

"Paddy. Every day." She winked and Evan rolled his eyes.

"I'll just take the special. Whatever it is."

"What if it's like..." She chewed her gum noisily and bopped the eraser of the pencil on her cheek. "Oh! Like baboon balls or... or... flamingo toes?"

"Then double it. Those are my favorites." Evan put the menu back, wondering why he ever bothered to look at it, and smiled back up at Angel. "I'll trust whatever he makes."

"I just want a burger, man. Medium rare. No onion. Unless you don't mind onion breath, sweetheart." Rosey leered and Evan rolled his eyes again.

All he wanted was quick lunch and a piece of that new southern peach-pecan cheesecake Patrick had been going on about, and maybe a sneaky kiss in the dry storage before his shift started.

"Your onion breath is none of my concern, *Ambrose*." She ripped the ticket off the pad and swatted him on the head. "I'll bring ya' both some water."

Once she walked away, Evan settled back into the corner of the booth, cracking his back with a moan. "So, you've become a regular here now? How come I never see you?"

"I come for breakfast mostly. I suppose you get yours in bed nowadays."

"I do. So does he, if you must know."

They shared a look of understanding—that Evan would only speak so much of his personal life, and Rosey would understand the unspoken. Because somehow, he always had. "You do seem happy, Chef."

"I am. And, as reluctant as I am to admit it, we have you to thank. It was your idea to come here that last group outing."

"Remember me at the wedding."

"Who's getting married?" Patrick plopped down next to Evan and rubbed Evan's calves propped up on the bench. His hair was matted in a sweaty ring around his head, his biceps pushed his shirt's limits of seam strength and his five o'clock shadow was, as usual, early to the party.

He was downright edible.

"With any luck, this guy right here." Rosey pointed his thumb to Evan only to be met with a glare and a sour "Rosey!"

"WHAT?"

"Well, hell. I hope I'm invited." Patrick sat up and passed the glasses of water Angel slid onto the table. "Hey, I know! I can provide the food!"

"I'm sure my future husband will be thrilled."

"Husband? Oh no, fella. I don't do any of those *homo* weddings, now. That's just against nature."

"You didn't think it was against nature last night."

Rosey howled. And Evan and Patrick shared a look that could be interpreted in no other way than *let's go do it again. Now.*

Rosey cracked his hand on the table, jolting them out of their shared daydream. "So wait. If you're out here, who's cooking our lunch?"

"Oscar. I'm on break. And—since I have you both here, I can finally hear the story about how you went from pantsing Evan in Quincy to washing dishes in his restaurant in New York City. Evan will only describe it as a long story that only you should tell."

It was Rosey's story to tell. Few people really knew it and discretion was part of the deal between them.

Evan sat up, unbuttoned his chef's jacket entirely and stripped it off, removing the employer and employee division—they were just old friends sharing stories. "I always told you you'd work for me one day, didn't I?"

"You did. Almost every time." Rosey chugged back his water and settled deeper into the booth. "There he'd be in the middle of the gymnasium—or better yet, the freshman hall—pants at his ankles, some designer boxers shining in the fluorescent light. He'd mouth off with some pronouncement of glory. 'Thank God I wore the Calvin Kleins,' or 'You're lucky my dad never taught me how to throw a punch.'"

"I was intimidating."

"You were. He'd bend over to pull 'em up and someone always got a good whack at his ass first."

"Memory serves, it was usually *your* hand on my ass." Evan smiled around his glass of water. "I think you have a latent longing for boys."

"I have no such thing."

Patrick laughed. "So, did you ever do a full Monty?"

"Once. I got good at grabbing my waistband in time." Evan and Rosey shared a look. "It was better than being slammed into the lockers and being called a faggot every day."

"I never called you a faggot."

"I know. Probably why I brought your sorry ass back here."

Angel arrived with the food and they stopped chattering to get everything situated. Rosey downright pouted when Angel refused to join them.

"She's working, Rosey." Patrick swiped a forkful of Evan's cole-slaw and grimaced. "I told him to go easy on the mayo, dammit." He took a swig of water and pushed Evan's plate away, as if that would make the slaw fix itself. "So, what turned it all around?"

"*Godspell.*"

"Jesus saves." Patrick crossed himself.

Evan snorted and then corrected Rosey's answer. "Actually, *Godspell* didn't turn it around. Rosey's school prank gone wrong turned it around. *Godspell* followed."

"It was a dare. And I was an asshole."

"You *are* an asshole." Evan took a bite of his sandwich and smiled. "Continue."

"I was just supposed to go into the storage of Mr. Periman's room and spray paint a couple of set pieces, you know?"

"What were you going to gain?"

"Melissa Bainbridge's panties. And hopefully a way into the ones she was wearing," Rosey explained. "So, I went in one night and fucked 'em up, you know?"

"Except he's not only an asshole, he's an idiot. He got caught—forgot the night custodians."

"Turned around on my final spray. Swiped a big-ass stripe of red right across his fuckin' face."

"Red was not his color."

Patrick patted his scruffy cheeks. "You've gotta have the right complexion for red."

"Right. And pizza-faced alcoholic does not blend with red." Rosey motioned to Evan that he had a drip of something on the corner of his mouth and groaned when he tilted over to Patrick for a swift kiss clean-up. "Jesus, guys. Anyway, to pay my debt to society, they stick me on the set design crew for *Godspell.*"

"Oh, I bet Mr. Periman was thrilled."

"Fuck Mr. Periman. I never got Melissa's panties."

"Rumor has it she never wore any, so his whole effort was probably for nothing."

Patrick pinched the bridge of his nose and laughed. "How was my high school experience in Brooklyn less exciting than this?"

"Not everyone has the privilege of growing up with Ambrose Pemberton."

"'The Third,' Chef. Don't forget 'The Third.'"

"Yes, I'm sure the first and second Ambroses are quite proud of you."

"Oh, there isn't a first or second. Mom doesn't even know who Dad is—she just stuck it on there for decoration."

Evan had heard all this before, so watching Patrick was entertainment all on its own; his eyebrows danced all over his forehead as he tried to make sense of it.

"So, Rosey gets on set and, as expected, is obnoxious. They make him paint the brick façade for the opening number. Brick by brick. Shading, hue, grout lines."

"Periman was a pervert. He just wanted to see my ass bent over all damned day."

"Yes, I'm sure his wife and children would agree with you. I come in one afternoon to practice with the accompanist and he's there all sprawled out, covered in orange and brown paint making a royal mess of things."

"Do you *know* how many fucking bricks I had to paint?"

"Hundreds, Rosey. Hundreds, I'm sure." Patrick reached across the table and stole one of Rosey's fries.

"You know, you make this shit—there's probably plenty in the kitchen, you don't have steal from your own customers."

"It tastes better off someone else's plate."

Patrick ate and Evan rolled his eyes, continuing Rosey's story. "And I took pity on his sexy ass and helped him for a bit, showing him a few things I'd learned from that damned Charlie Brown show."

"And then I got good at it. I was laying brick like a madman. Then I had to put that contraption of a cross together and Evan helped me figure it out and before long—"

"Before long, it was show time. And other than pushing set pieces around, Rosey's punishment was over."

"And I was pissed."

"Why?"

"The jackass ended up loving it."

"Because of you. Before then, no one had ever taken the time to show me nothing. It was always, 'Just shut up and do it, Rosey.' 'Figure it out yourself.' 'Why can't you do anything right?' And Chef here just dropped to the ground, got his fancy pants ruined and taught me how to do it right."

"And I had to promise I wouldn't tell anyone that he loved it, so Periman wouldn't ask him to do it again."

At Patrick's questioning eyebrow, Rosey offered, "Cool factor, dude. If the guys found out I was into that sort of shit?"

"Of course. So, you had his secret."

"I had his secret. And I kept my pants on for the rest of school. And no one shoved me into the lockers anymore."

"We graduated and I went to Omaha. Failed everything."

"I never did figure out what you were trying to accomplish out there."

"Surviving. Came home and did community college—thought I'd try some sort of art major, you know? Failed at that too."

Evan offered the last bite of his sandwich to Patrick. "He's still an amazing painter."

"Yeah, I dabble. And I tried finding work. I have something for a few months at a time, but I could never keep a damned job."

"That's because you were trying to find happiness at the bottom of a bottle." Evan and Rosey shared a look again—concern, memory, disappointment, friendship. "I came home one Christmas and a mutual friend told me he'd been sleeping at the county shelter."

"He cleaned me up. Bought me some clothes and dragged my sorry ass onto a plane with him." Rosey shoved his last few French fries in his mouth and looked out the window.

Evan could feel the heat of Patrick's stare on his skin, but he didn't acknowledge it; he was lost in his own memories of how scared he was for Rosey. How important it felt to help him. The argument he'd had with his dad when he decided to bring Rosey to New York.

"So, I gotta ask, Chef. Why'd you do that for me? I was a mess."

Evan tossed his napkin onto his plate and sat back, resting his hand on Patrick's thigh. "I knew the restaurant life was exactly what you needed. It's made from derelicts turned right. 'Here's what you do; this is what will happen if you don't do it.' Knowing that was available to you, I couldn't just leave you there."

"You gave me what? Two months to get my shit together?"

"Yes. There was no way in hell we were living together any longer than that."

"Oh God, now *that* I'd have liked to have seen."

"No. You wouldn't have. But, I got him in as our *garçon de cuisine*." Evan reached across the table and patted Rosey's hand, patronizing and loving all at once. "Our little kitchen boy."

"Fuck off."

"I will not. Thanks to me, you have a nice life." He grabbed his water, but stopped before drinking. "Whoever your dad is—he'd be proud of you, you know."

"Fuck my dad."

Evan chortled, knowing Rosey was at his limit for sentimentality. Proving him right, Rosey let out a belch and tossed a twenty-dollar bill on the table. "Yeah. I gotta go. Since Angel won't let me take her out, I gotta find me some entertainment for my night off."

The silence hung heavy after Rosey blustered out, but Patrick took Evan's hand between the plates on the table and rubbed Evan's knuckles with his thumbs.

"You *saved* him."

Evan offered a slight smile, knowing it to be true but never having admitted it fully. "Maybe so. It was exhausting. He still is exhausting."

"You're one helluva man, Evan Stanford."

Evan blushed and shook his head. "Can I just say I'm really grateful I didn't have to save you from anything?"

"Mmm…" Patrick lifted Evan's hand to his lips and kissed his knuckles. "Don't be so sure about that."

VI. Plat Principal, Deuxième Partie
The main course.

"Two out on osso. Perci, still waiting on that *farro*."

Evan watched from his expediting station as Perci took the plate he had sent back and put on another spoonful of undercooked grain. As the next cook grabbed for the plate to finish it, Evan held up a hand to stop her and slipped a spoon into the edge of Perci's plate, tasting the *farro* and shaking his head. "Are you fixing the error or just continuing to serve me the same unacceptable shit?"

"I added an extra minute, Chef. I prefer my *farro* to have a crunch."

"*You* prefer?"

"Oooohhhhh. Look out."

As if directed to do so, the kitchen full of cooks shouted in unison, "Shut it, Rosey!"

Rosey lifted his hands and disappeared into his cubby with a stack of hotel pans to wash, singing along to "Rock the Casbah" with his own special flair. "Drop the pasta, drop the pasta."

Not only was this was the third plate of undercooked *farro* Evan had sent back to her, but twenty minutes into the rush, Perci had inexplicably swiped minced shallot from Theo's *mise*—an act that, had Evan witnessed it rather than hearing the fallout after the fact, would have resulted in her being sent home on the spot.

You do not swipe someone else's *mise*.

So, Evan was on edge again, a condition he honestly hadn't found himself in since—well, since The Night of the Bloody Polenta Debacle. Because since that night, his focus had been on Patrick. On his heart and his soul and how amazing it felt to draw focus off of himself and onto someone else. How fulfilling it was to play and create in the kitchen with another cook. How intensely he could feel the words "I love you," and know them to be true.

He hadn't been looking for a relationship; he honestly hadn't even wanted one. But the past few weeks proved that sometimes *not* having a goal allowed you to run into some pretty amazing things.

Unfortunately, focusing on Patrick and his lips and his ass and his hands and tongue and laugh and heart and—focusing on *Patrick* was not going to get this run back on track. And it most assuredly was not going to get Perci to suddenly hone in, pay attention and give a good goddamn.

He blindly grabbed orders as they came ticking in, moved plates as they hit the pass, talked to his kitchen and waitstaff in tandem and waited for Perci to finally acknowledge him after challenging his palate.

You not only do not swipe someone else's *mise*, you also do not challenge the chef's palate.

"Natasha! Table fifteen! Carlos, we have stuffed pepper, *galletto*, salmon. That's pepper, chicken, *two* salmon, two rib-eye mid-rare, one medium rib-eye, one osso, all day. Where's the sauce for my swordfish?"

Theo slid his plate to the pass, properly plated and sauced. "Selling sword."

Evan stuck a thermometer into the fish, read it, pulled it out and called out again. "Come on, breast for this table, let's move." And as the plated chicken slid down the pass, Perci finally met his gaze, as if waiting for his disapproval of the sautéed greens accompanying the plate in his hand.

He piled the greens more neatly, wiped the edge and put both plates under a warmer to await the osso.

"My osso is dying, Perci. Did you put heat under the pan this time?"

"It's not ready; I thought you wanted it mushy."

Tension throbbed at his brow as he waited for the proper answer. It never came.

"Did you come looking for a fight today?"

A line cook's bellow broke through. "Selling three pulled pork!"

Evan grabbed the plates and wiped the edges, handing them to a waiter. "Table six is coming; this is for…" He checked his tickets again. "For table nine. Thank you."

And then he was back to Perci, a new ticket in hand. "Because, sweetheart, this is my kitchen. And in my kitchen, we cook the food to my order. Kitchen, two veal chop. Order up another osso because Perci has sufficiently killed this one. That's one osso, two veal chop, one pepper, one chicken, two rib-eye mid-rare, one rib-eye medium." He leveled his fiery glare in Perci's direction, but her back was turned as she tended to sides other than *farro*. "All day."

She turned, delicately placing sautéed green beans on a roasted half-chicken, and pushed the plate toward Evan. "Need I remind you, Chef—I've been cooking and eating *farro* longer than you've been alive?"

Another ticket clacked in on the printer. The front-of-house did not seem to know, care about or consider what might be going on in the back. Evan steeled himself and checked to see what had been put on to fire before reading. "We have the rib-eye and salmon on fire, yes?"

"Yes, Chef."

"Ordering roast fish, liver, veal chop, osso. That's roast fish, one liver, three veal chop, two osso, pepper, chicken, all day."

José, Perci's assistant, was swamped and unable to pick up her slack as he so often did. And Perci refused to move another serving of *farro* from the vat of cooked grain to a pan to toss with butter and mascarpone, instead tossing shallots into a hot pan with oil while the dishes for the entire table slowly died under the warmer.

Evan shot a look at Robin and she slipped into the expeditor's role, allowing Evan to walk away to the back entrance, where staff stored their belongings. He peeked into Rosey's cubby, pointing where he was headed. "Which one's hers?"

"That obnoxious paisley thing. Middle shelf."

"Of course it is." Evan retrieved Perci's knife roll and returned to a kitchen so busy it really couldn't pay attention to the impending drama.

"I'll kindly ask that you put my knives down, Chef."

He smiled—pleased and smug—and set her knife bag down on her workspace, landing it squarely on the pile of zucchini she had been slicing. "You're done. Get out of my kitchen."

She blinked, as if she truly didn't believe him, and continued to toss a pan of caramelizing onions.

"Perci. Get out." He pointed with his eyes to a chef's knife resting on her cutting board. "Is that one yours as well?"

"Yes, Chef."

"That's the answer I've been looking for." Evan could see her hands shaking as she let go of the pan to wipe down the knife. Years ago he might have felt bad about the timing, the public humiliation, but not anymore. "Too little too late, I'm afraid."

"You—you really don't know who you're fooling with, Chef."

"As soon as you walk out, I won't be fooling with anyone." He turned to go back to his station, pulling a tasting spoon out of its container to test the vat of *farro* that had, by pure chance, been sitting on the heat just long enough.

He nudged José's elbow. "Heat that with some butter and mascarpone; should be able to save this table."

"Yes, Chef."

Perci made her exit, the steel door slamming behind her. Everyone breathed a quick sigh of relief, but that was all they were allowed. Another ticket clicked in from the printer, setting everyone back into gear.

Evan shot a look back up at José. "You ready to impress me?"

"Yes, Chef. For—for good?"

Evan smiled, remembering being that anxious to impress. That ready to show someone who could move him forward. "For tonight. One step at a time, kid."

"Yes. Yes, Chef!"

"Okay, back to work. Show's over." Evan grabbed the swordfish and chicken from the warmer, smiling as creamy, perfectly cooked *farro* landed on a plate for his osso bucco. "Table six, please. Kitchen, we have two rib-eye, medium, mid-rare. One seaboat, one salmon. That's medium, mid-rare, seaboat, salmon, two chop, all day. Can we all say thank you to Robin for saving the day?"

"Thank you to Robin for saving the day."

"Assholes."

►•◄

Tony DiSante, owner and manager of Il Boschetto, was not a particularly memorable sort of man. He was in his late fifties and of average height. He always wore a baby blue dress shirt with a navy blue tie and navy blue slacks. He wore his graying hair in a greasy, comb-over and he walked with an odd, hobbling gait. His handwriting was atrocious, his ability to micromanage far outweighed his ability to *actually* manage and yet he had somehow kept Il Boschetto on the New York City theatergoing and tourist map for decades.

Evan figured upon hire that he had done it by using the reputation for great crowds to lure up-and-coming chefs, get them to redesign a great menu, and then ride on that train for as long as the chef, or the eating public, would allow.

That was Evan's experience thus far at Il Boschetto. He'd had a few restaurants bidding for his leadership and had chosen Il Boschetto based on location, salary, cuisine and yes, DiSante's reputation. He redesigned the menu, kept many traditions in place, upgraded the quality of ingredients, tweaked the flavors and created a few new dishes. His nomination for the Beard had already been determined before his hire, and after the menu came out, he found himself with the coveted medal perched on his home office shelf.

And then it all seemed to... stagnate.

The funny thing about stagnation, Evan was learning, is that you don't realize it's happening until you're stuck in cement drying solid around your feet.

Persephone Child had been gone for two weeks. Evan decided to let the dust settle from that upheaval before going to DiSante with a short summer menu that he would have preferred to get moving before Perci left. Robin and Theo helped him prepare a tasting menu for Mr. DiSante with some of the new flavors he had been developing. "For a new prix fixe, if nothing else, sir."

DiSante ate that night, snooped around the kitchen and left.

Two days later, he called Evan into his own office. DiSante's was too much of a paperwork-mountain nightmare to ever have someone else in there.

"Evan, you're doing great work for me. You've built a great team. The tables are full every night."

"Thank you, sir."

"And I truly enjoyed the meal you prepared for me. That grilled corn and fig side with the, um... what was the... drizzle? Sauce?"

"Balsamic reduction."

"Yes. That." He kissed his fingers with a loud smack and Evan wanted to roll his eyes. How could a restaurant manager not even know what a balsamic reduction was?

"Thank you." Evan waited for Mr. DiSante to continue but it was as if he'd forgotten it was his turn to speak. "Sir? With all due—I mean. I have to get upstairs and prep. Can you—"

"Oh. Yes. I'm sorry. It was lovely." DiSante got up from his chair and went to the door. His hand was on the knob before he spoke again. "But the answer is no. Budget is set, crowds are assured. No new prix fixe. But thank you so much for the delicious meal."

"Is this something we can work out—"

The click of the door cut Evan off, leaving him alone in his office. He sat in the silence, formulating new *discussion points*—never arguments—to approach another time. Cost-cutting measures, numbers from other restaurants' account books when their menus changed more frequently, anything. Anything monetary, since that seemed to be the only language the man spoke.

His phone buzzed in his pocket; it was Robin. "Yeah?"

"Oh. You answered. Yeah, Carlos called in. We're short. Can you get away from him?"

"He's gone. I'm on my way up."

"You okay?"

"Nope."

"Fuck."

"Yep."

►•◄

Evan: *I'm seeing some 51–60 here at Agata.*
Patrick: *Oooh, you thinking shrimp risotto?*
Evan: *Yeah. Need anything else? Lemon? Stock? Wine? You good?*
Patrick: *I'm good.*
Evan: *Okay, paying and then I'll hit the Q and be home.*
Patrick: *Love you.*

As if to amplify the news from DiSante and a heavy shift with a short staff, the trains smelled like wet dog. New York smelled like wet dog. If Evan was brutally honest with himself, *he* probably smelled like wet dog. The heat of the summer had fully descended and it seemed to have been raining for three days straight, making everything steamy and dank. It all perfectly mirrored his mood, intensifying the unpleasantness of both.

"You look like a drowned rat."

"I feel like that'd be an upgrade."

Patrick kissed him anyway and took his knife bag, groceries and drippy jacket. "Go shower. I'll put the stock on low heat."

"You have a Sauvignon?"

"Pinot."

Evan curled his lips in distaste. "That'll do, I suppose." He kicked off his clogs and headed into the bathroom, checking his phone and angrily thumbing out a text, mumbling about the dog walker. "Put Dini's socks back on her... ruin my floors. Again."

Evan stood under the shower head and sighed, willing the water to wash everything away. Was it true that the only place he would feel satisfaction was in Patrick's arms?

It wasn't that he was begrudging either of them that satisfaction, or being ungrateful, but finding joy only in someone else seemed— unhealthy. Unlike him. He was an independent man, for God's sake.

It was work. Of course it was. It was DiSante; it was breaking in a new guy, even though he welcomed the chance to teach again. The flow of their crew was back on the mend and yet—

And yet, every day he felt like a dead man walking, trudging to his last meal; only in Evan's personal hell, he had to make the meal and never got to eat it, never knew the comfort and warmth of dishes as perfect and fulfilling as Millie's Mess.

Evan rushed through the rest of his shower, figuring he might as well enjoy the part of life he enjoyed, the time he had with Patrick. He joined him in the kitchen, and instead of feeling relief in his presence was instantly set on edge.

"You said you had stock." With his head tilted and face scrunched, Evan bypassed another kiss and headed right to the stove to peek into the simmering pot.

"That... *is* stock?"

"It's shrimp risotto—this is chicken stock."

"I was out of fish. It'll do." Patrick peeked into the pot and shrugged and Evan groused, helping himself to Patrick's pantry to gather shallots, rice and—

"No *vialone*?"

"Arborio."

Evan grumbled again and thunked the box onto the counter. "It breaks down too fast."

"Are we cooking for an audience or just our dinner?" Evan ignored him and opened the shrimp, picking through it to make sure it had been properly de-shelled. "What's going on tonight? You've never been this particu—"

"It's fine. Just—" Setting the shrimp aside, he grabbed a shallot and a knife from Patrick's knife drawer. After the first cut, having to use the strength of his arm, not the sharpness of the knife, he growled and searched for a honing blade. "Honestly, you're going to cut off a finger with these things."

Patrick shook his head and put a pot on, melting butter and finished the shallot, scraping it into the pan. They worked quietly, Patrick bumping their hips together, trying to nuzzle into Evan's neck, dragging his hand across Evan's back whenever he passed him.

Evan knew what he was trying to do and he wanted to respond. He wanted to play. To flirt. To turn the heat off the food and make out. But instead of helping, Patrick's attentions were only poking at the stink of Evan's day.

The rice heated and toasted, and after a sour-faced sniff of the Pinot, Evan glugged in a cup of it, stepping back for Patrick to stir it to a boil.

He busied himself chopping some parsley and prepping a quick green salad while Patrick stirred the simmering rice, the aroma of the wine wafting over them and dissipating as it evaporated into the rice. And just as Evan was going to comment on how good it smelled, how it was soothing the prickly edges of his shitty day, Patrick picked up the pot of stock and poured the whole of it into the simmering rice.

"Patrick!! Oh my—" he dropped his knife onto the board and looked into the pot, Frodo watching his precious ring sink into the fiery pit of Mount Doom. "What the hell? You don't put all of—"

"What? It's just a shortcut." Patrick stirred and turned the heat up a little.

"There are no *shortcuts* for risotto. It's to be added *gradually* so the starches—" Evan turned from the stove and grabbed another shallot, slicing off the tip, peeling and angrily mincing, his knife a blur whacking rhythmically on the wooden cutting board. "I just figured you would know how to—I mean, I know you don't have it at—"

"No. Of course not. Risotto's too complicated a dish for a pedestrian diner."

"Oh for God's—don't start that shit now."

"No. I get it. I hear exactly what you're saying."

"No, you don't. That is not what I meant." It wasn't. But instead of feeling sensitive to it, to the fact that Patrick took it that way, Evan's mood cranked even tighter as he gathered the minced shallot on the board.

"I do know the traditional way to do this. I just thought we were going for a quick dinner." Patrick stopped stirring and smacked the spoon onto the stove. "What are you even *doing*?"

"Starting over. You've ruined it."

"I've ruined—" Patrick looked at his perfectly cooking rice and the new pile of shallot while Evan bent into a cabinet looking for another pot. "You know what? Do it your way." He turned off the heat under his pot of rice, snagged a quart container of stock from his refrigerator and slammed it onto the counter. "I'll just sit this one out since I'm clearly uneducated in the proper technique for preparing Your Highness his dinner."

"What? Your High—no. I'm just—" Evan grabbed the stock and poured it into the pot on the back burner and set it to simmer, wondering how to finish that sentence. He was just what? "I'm just tired. It was a horrible day and I'm—"

"You're not the only one who worked all day."

"I'm aware. I just—"

"No, I get it, *Chef*. I'll make sure to study up on proper culinary techniques before I come to work. In my own kitchen."

Evan dropped the knife onto the cutting board and finally looked up, finding fire in Patrick's eyes, his jaw clenched and shoulders tense. His heart flipped in his chest, panic and confusion and embarrassment coursing through his veins.

"Goddammit, Patrick." He shucked the knife into the sink before turning the heat off of his stock. He wiped his hands on a towel, trying to gather what little sense of decency he had left. "I didn't mean to—" He'd done it. He danced on the one raw nerve he knew Patrick carried around with him. He was typically so carefree and easygoing, it was easy to forget that he was as vulnerable as anyone else. "I'm sorry. I'm not fit for company. Maybe—should I just leave?"

Patrick ran a hand through his hair, gesturing to the half-started food, and then, as if he remembered everything all over again, he stiffened and walked to door and placed his hand on the knob, ready to open it. "Maybe it would be best. I don't appreciate being treated this way in my own home."

Evan's heart sank. This was the one place, the one person, the one *thing* in his life that felt right. And with one stupid meal, he'd kicked at their cocoon of comfort, scattering it all over Patrick's kitchen. "I—I'm sorry I ruined—I'm sorry."

▶•◀

Unsurprisingly, Evan's mood didn't improve. He snapped at clerks, wincing as soon as he heard the horrible tone and words coming out of his mouth. He grumbled and growled when anyone sat within three feet of him in an empty subway car. Even Dini avoided him outside of mealtimes, and his staff was keeping their distance as well.

Two days after he walked out of Patrick's apartment, Evan ended a particularly slow shift in his office, stripping off his whites and checks and sighing in relief as his bare legs hit the air conditioning. He couldn't wait to get home and into the shower.

"Chef, we need to—oh. Shit. Sorry. I'll come back."

"Robin," Evan laughed, and hiked up his shorts. "Get in here. This isn't new scenery."

She peeked back in with a reluctant smile and motioned to the chair across from his desk. "I suppose it's not—do you have a few minutes before you leave?"

"Yeah." He offered her a bottle of water and threw on a T-shirt before joining her at the desk and opening his own bottle. "What's up?"

"Well, that's pretty much what I wanted to ask you. You've been—"

"An obnoxious bastard."

"Yes. I thought after you got rid of Perci, things would be better."

"So did I."

She cracked her water open and took a drink. They stared at each other for a few long moments until Robin finally tried again. "What was your deal with her, anyway?"

"You don't think I should have fired her?"

"That's not even close to what I said, and you know it." She took off her jacket and tossed it on Evan's mini refrigerator, looking at him again. "She probably should have been gone before you were hired. But we've dealt with idiots like her our entire careers. There's one in every kitchen—at least for a week—but she got to you like no one else."

"Her attitude was just... it was offensive. She didn't start out that way. She just sort of slipped into it like a mudslide. One day it's a solid surface and life comes and rains on it and before you know it, it's just—"

"You know, your flair for the melodramatic always was fucking entertaining."

"What? You wanted to know what my problem with her was. I'm trying to tell you." He unscrewed his bottle top and flung the cap toward his trash can, missing horribly. "Do you still love it, Robin?"

"Tonight? No. I hated every minute of it, thank you."

"You're welcome. I mean the job. The work. The insanity. Does it still ignite every nerve in your body?"

"Usually. Yes. And you're part of the reason why... or you used to be."

"I wonder if she ever had that. I mean, she worked line for twenty years. You'd think passion had to drive her at some point."

Robin sat back and crossed her legs, taking a long pull of water. "Wait, is that it? You're afraid she's a view into your future?"

"What if she is?"

"Oh for the love of *God*, Evan. You have passion. You have a voice. You have everything all of us dream about. She never did." Robin capped her water and tapped the bottle on her knee, squinting and running what Evan knew to be a million thoughts in her head before she chose the one she'd share. "You're afraid you're drying up already."

"How do you keep it alive? You're stuck cooking the same food all the time too. How do you—when do you *create*?"

"When I go home. For my kids. I invite my parents over a lot, Theo's folks. I have parties—I invite you, but you never come anymore."

Evan mentally traveled back to the kitchen with Patrick. To the breads and the preserves. To the *sfogliatelle* and the dinners that didn't end up with apologies and wasted rice. He created with Patrick. He created *for* Patrick—the meal he had served him at the chef's table was undoubtedly one of his best in years. It was still in him.

Somewhere.

"I don't want to dry up."

"He rejected that menu, didn't he?"

With practiced ease, he patted at his hair as DiSante tended to do with what little he had and mimicked the man's nasal, Italian-tinged accent. "You made a great menu when you came, son. Keep making that food. People know what to expect."

"You know that's not going to change."

"So what am I supposed to do?"

"You know I love you, right?"

"Yes?"

She scooted up to the edge of the chair and bounced her water bottle on the edge of his desk to make her point, her eyes fiery, curls bouncing everywhere. "You either have to change your situation or your attitude. You're starting every shift impatient and ending them downright rude and I know chefs are known for being massive cunts, but you've never been that."

"And I am now."

"No. Stop with the melodrama. You're not—" She sighed and sat back again. "You're not. You needed to fire her and you did. Now you've got to stop treating the rest of us like she was our fault."

"Or like DiSante is your fault."

"Or that. Look, I'm worried about you. You are the best chef any of us have worked for. And I can't keep going home snapping at my kids and pretending their perfect faces are your evil scowl."

"Patrick and I haven't talked in two days."

"Evan... "

They sat and stared at each other again, sizing each other up. Evan was wrapped up in his own head so tightly he wasn't sure he could untangle a clear thought if he had to.

"Who's that woman you always talked about from home? When's the last time you even *went* home?"

"Millie. Too long. You know what it's like getting away from here for more than a day at a time."

"Go home, Evan."

"I keep talking about going to see her."

"Go home. She's who turned you on to food. Go home. Find yourself again. And then get your ass back here and shout about *that*. We'll figure out how to make DiSante listen."

"And if we don't?"

"Go *home*, Evan. Do that first."

"And you'll make sure the kitchen's covered?"

She glared at him and he finally nodded. "I hear you. Right. Go home." He tossed his empty bottle into the trash, making it this time. "Thank you for talking to me. I—I miss talking like this. I miss you."

"I miss you too, you asshole."

▶•◀

During his post-dinner lull the next night he received a text, the first word from Patrick since their ridiculous argument.

Patrick: This is stupid.

Relief washed over Evan so profoundly, he laughed. When he heard himself, he realized that he hadn't really laughed in days.

Evan: You're stupid.

Patrick: Your dog is stupid.

Through his own fog, he had the clarity to know he loved this man. Desperately, imperfectly, completely. The few days without texts like these, without late night phone calls that ended with "I love you," without a quick walk to air out the day, were a ridiculous exercise in stubbornness.

Evan: She misses you.

Patrick: And her owner?

Evan slipped down to his office and dialed Patrick's number, his heart flipping in his chest when he answered in a quiet, deep, soothing voice. "I have *vialone*. And a decent Sauvignon. And fish stock."

"Her owner is an idiot." And then, "You bought—after how horrible I was?"

"I can't believe I let you walk out the door for risotto."

"You let me walk out the door for being a dick."

"Over risotto." Patrick sighed into the phone and Evan imagined him running his hand through his hair. Even over the phone, he ached to straighten out the mess he'd made. "You stepped on a nerve."

"I know. And I can't promise I won't do it again."

"I can't promise I'll handle it any better, either."

"I want to do better for you."

"Me too."

A silence lingered between them. A good silence. One in which, were they together, a smile would be shared and, Evan imagined, Patrick would reach out for just a few fingers of Evan's hand to silently say, *We're okay—just tread lightly.*

"Bring the stuff to the restaurant? Or not, I have all of that here. Just—come? And... and I'll explain everything."

"I'll see you around 11:30."

"Patrick?"

"I love you, too."

▶•◀

"Hey babe! You were right!" It was a few days later, and Patrick had spent much of his day off walking and taking pictures. "Roger planted the impatiens you left him. They really perked up the place."

Evan had spent his day off doing other things. He only grunted at Patrick's perky entrance.

"I grabbed a pic on my phone to send you, but you know cell reception on the train—*oh, babe.*"

Patrick stopped in his tracks with an intake of air so loud it normally would have pulled Evan's attention from the mess in front of him. "Evan?"

Evan knew the kitchen was nothing short of a complete disaster—he'd made it that way, after all. Dirty sheet pans stuck out of the sink waiting to be washed. Measuring cups and mixing bowls and various utensils littered the perimeter of the sink, coated with a variety of powders and glazes. The kitchen table was covered with crumbs, a metal straight edge, and cooling trays of at least two hundred one-inch squares of cake. On the stove were no less than three pans, one with a candy thermometer resting on its rim. Drips of a clear white substance smattered almost every flat surface.

He stared down at his project—his failed project. His stupid idiotic idea of a project to bring Millie to him, because taking time off to go home, even with Robin's offer of help, seemed like an insurmountable task. He even tried calling the center where Millie lived, but she was in the activities room or, Evan suspected, off flirting with the man in 12B whom she had mentioned over Christmas.

"His eyes are bluer than yours, Evy. I didn't think that was possible."

On his one day off, when his only project should have been sleeping and lounging and possibly fucking the oblivious ball of energy of a man standing in front of him, he had decided on this.

Evan could feel his hair flipping and flopping all over the place. He noticed his apron was askew, as if he'd been through a physical battle. And there was a battle raging inside him, while on the outside he was visibly calm. He lifted a spoon from a glass measuring cup and a gloppy, gummy ooze plopped back down into the cup. "Remind me what I do for a living."

He dipped the spoon into the cup and lifted again, not looking up.

"You—you're a chef. What are you—" Patrick approached the island and dipped his finger into a bowl of buttercream. "What spurred—petit fours? God, that's good."

Evan pointed to the table of cakes as his answer. "The cake is good, too."

Patrick helped himself to a cube and brought one over to Evan, feeding it to him. "The cake is perfect. *Génoise*?"

Evan nodded and lifted the spoon again, as if another attempt would somehow smooth out the mixture. "I can't—" He sighed and dropped the spoon, the clanking against the bowl screaming his frustration. "It's not—Millie used to do this in her sleep and I thought I'd remember, but—"

"Okay. It's just a little... "

"Gloppy. And when it's not, it's seizing up." He motioned to a pile of grocery bags on his back counter and took another ragged breath. "I bought those stupid melting wafers as a last resort, but dammit, I want to do it like she did and I can't seem to—" Evan finally looked up, his eyes red and damp.

He felt ridiculous and stupid and embarrassed and really, really just wanted to be alone, but the thought of Patrick walking out right now terrified him.

Terrified him to the point where his heart rate increased, his breathing caught in his chest and tears stung his eyes, which was the stupidest thing—getting teary about poured fondant—and maybe Patrick *should* leave, because he felt an urgent pressing at the seams of his sanity and he did not, under any circumstances, want Patrick to be a witness to it.

Leave me alone.

Don't go. Everything I feared is happening.

I can't find myself.

"Okay, first. Wafers don't have to be your last resort." Patrick stepped into the kitchen, planting a soft kiss on Evan's neck. He found the melting wafers and spoke, his words measured and cautious. "Although, never use Wilton. These are—honey, they're made of Satan's ear wax."

He knew Patrick was trying to soothe him with humor, but his churning anxiety broke through to the surface anyway, spiked and biting and unreasonable. "Well, I'm terribly sorry." He grabbed the dish of failed fondant and slammed it into the sink. "That's all I could find at the grocery."

"Evan, I was just—"

"I *said* I don't want to use them anyway. Millie never did, and I just don't understand why this simple task—"

"Petit fours are far from simple—especially in this humidity. And poured fondant can be a moody bitch—"

"Don't *even* suggest that it's like its maker—" Evan continued to slam dishes into the sink, whacking the faucet on and ruining any chance of saving the icing with a rush of water.

"I had no inten—Evan! What are you—" Patrick grabbed at the wooden spoon in Evan's hand, but Evan held fast. "Is this about Millie or is this about me?"

"I don't even know any more." Evan loosened his grip, but kept possession of the spoon. "It's not about you."

"Then why am I the target again?"

"Because you're in the way."

Patrick stepped aside and lifted his hands in submission. "Do you want some space? Time?"

"Yes."

Patrick swore under his breath and headed to the door.

"No! Please. Dammit. Stay."

Patrick heaved a breath and turned back to him. "Evan, I have to be honest with you, my patience with these outbursts of yours is about shot."

"You're not the only one." Evan took a deep breath and dared to look at Patrick, hating the anger he saw in his eyes. "I'm sorry."

Evan flipped on the disposal and whined pitifully as the thick, failed mess slid into it, the whir of the engine spinning it away for good. "I need to get out of here. Walk. Something. I feel like I'm going to jump out of my skin." He wiped his hands on the towel looped through his apron belt and took another deep, ragged breath, so grateful Patrick was still standing there.

"And I can't keep biting at you, but that's all I seem to be *capable* of doing and I can't stop and if I don't stop you're going to walk out that door and I'll have ruined the one good thing in my life, all over a stupid idea that probably has some sort of perfectly acceptable recipe in a box in a musty attic in Quincy."

Evan angrily wiped a tear from his cheek and looked at the man standing across his disaster of an island, afraid to see anger there but finding eyes full of warmth, shoulders strong and waiting to support him, and what he deserved the least—loving patience.

He felt ridiculous. And stupid. And childish. And so completely out of control of just about everything in his life—which he knew was ridiculous as well—and he really, really needed Patrick to hold him, but he'd given every indication that touching him would be a nuclear mistake. He was frozen in his spot, his legs almost cramping with a need to get out. To run down the twenty-nine flights of stairs into the busy streets, catch a subway or a cab and go, go, go, go, go. The fight was over—he needed the flight. And, as so many times before, Patrick read him like the open book he was not and made the first move. With a few steps Patrick was there, softly kissing his lips and pulling him into his arms.

Evan breathed him in, let the strength in Patrick hold him up and quiet his racing, churning heart. And not for one minute in the many they stood there did Patrick ask. Or judge. Or push.

They ended up on Evan's couch and Dini's persistent licking at his bare ankles pulled Evan out of his bubble of self-loathing and self-pity. He hiked her up against their intertwined bodies and she curled in, snorting and sighing with no more in judgment in her love for Evan than Patrick had.

"Thank you for not leaving."

"Leaving doesn't work for us." He kissed his temple. "I love you."

"I've been broken since the day you met me."

"If we waited until everyone was *un*broken, we'd never connect with anyone."

"I'm *difficult*."

Patrick snickered at that—his own personal pouty Meg Ryan—and kissed the tip of Evan's reddened nose. "Yes. And you're hurting and I want to help you, even if all that means is to sit here and not know why."

They sat in silence—almost silence, given Dini's perpetual noise-making—peace slowly taking the place of anxiety and sense taking the place of crazy.

"What's a good brand of melting wafer?"

"Merckens."

"You know where to get some?"

"I do."

Evan considered for a moment, scratching Dini's ears, his feet rubbing up and down Patrick's calves. "Can we go now?"

"Yep."

He kissed Patrick swiftly, kicked himself free of the dog, the tangled man and the humiliation, then took off his apron. "We'll talk on the way."

They didn't talk on the way.

Evan mulled quietly and Patrick stayed close. They picked out good melting wafers and Patrick insisted on getting Evan a new candy thermometer. And Evan insisted they were going to try it Millie's way one more time.

"I don't like taking shortcuts when there is a perfectly proven method already in place."

"I've noticed that about you."

"Shut up."

They didn't talk on the way home because the train was particularly busy and they spent twenty of the twenty-five minutes pressed up against other people, glancing desperately at each other and trying not to laugh at the man sandwiched between them as he bopped along—quite animatedly—to the reggae tunes ringing in his earbuds.

It wasn't until they'd made both a traditional poured fondant and a version using the new melting wafers, until they'd covered every square of layered *génoise* and decorated them with buttercream ribbons and rosebuds, until they'd taste-tested and decided that both versions were equal to Millie's petit fours that starred in Evan's every tea party as a boy, and until they'd settled onto Evan's couch with large glasses of iced tea that Evan tried to venture into the conversation.

While they sat, Dini took to chasing something unseen, dashing from room to room, sliding gracelessly on her bright purple socks into whatever furniture might catch her and getting up and at it again, running, panting, running, crashing, shaking and running in and out of rooms. She only stopped long enough to look at Evan and Patrick as if they were completely *daft* for sitting there when, obviously, an important chase was on.

"I think your dog has a mental health issue."

Evan laughed and clicked his tongue to have Dini join them on the couch, but she had better things to do. She cocked her head in question and took off, skittering around the corner into the hallway again and thumping into a door. Or maybe a wall.

"This is why her nose is flat."

"Her nose is perfect." Another bump echoed down the hall. "Did you have a dog as a kid?"

"No. Mom was allergic. Personally, I think she didn't want to be bothered."

"We didn't either. Mom always wanted one and Dad would not budge." Evan set his tea on the coffee table and snuggled into the crook of Patrick's arm, a mooring for his rocky emotions. "The neighbors had one, though. This long-haired mutt—had some kind of herding dog in him. And he'd chase squirrels like it was his job."

"It *was* his job—he was herding them."

"Right. Except squirrels are smart. Run up the tree; no more dog. So, he'd just stand at the base of it and bark his fool head off."

"Did he ever catch one?"

"No. Which was the joke. He wouldn't know what the hell to do with it if he had."

"Probably not."

They sat quietly for a few moments and Dini skidded into the end table one more time before curling up on her blanket, panting and happy. "I'm afraid I caught the squirrel and now I don't know what the hell to do with it. So I'm just running around barking at absolutely nothing."

"So," Patrick teased, lingering on the word, "you're more like Dini, then."

"Yes. God, I'm a prissy, snorty pug. No wonder I'm moody."

Patrick laughed brightly and sat up. "C'mere." They turned and sat cross-legged, their knees bumping, a blush creeping up Evan's face until Patrick cupped his cheeks in his hands and brushed his calloused thumbs under his Evan's eyes, wordlessly asking for eye contact. "You most certainly are not a prissy, snorty, wrinkly pug." He kissed Evan's blushing cheek. "But you have seemed a little... misguided lately."

"How diplomatic of you." Evan took Patrick's hands into his lap and drew indiscriminate swirls on them as he gathered his thoughts. "I even used to enjoy the pursuit, you know? Getting where I was headed was just as much fun as being there."

"Wait, this is you having fun?"

Evan rolled his eyes at himself. "Well, once upon a time."

"So, what changed?"

"I was ready for the insane schedule—thrived on it. It ramped up after the Beard with special events and master classes, but that went its natural course and petered out."

"I would love a master class with you."

"After today? You're a glutton for punishment."

"Maybe. I bet you'd be an excellent teacher, though."

"Yeah, I'm pretty good at it," Evan confessed. "Anyway, DiSante started taking advantage. Every little crisis was a new phone call. A quick trip in on a day off became a full shift." Evan sighed and grabbed for his tea. "I had to fight for time off. I got home less and less frequently. I knew I was losing a grip on things, so I thought putting a little geographic space would send a message."

Patrick brushed back a lock of Evan's hair that had decided to rebel sometime during the buttercream rose decorations.

Evan closed his eyes at the touch. "Come to find out"—Evan opened his eyes and put his tea back without drinking—"I moved here to meet you."

"And I'd been waiting."

Evan moved in for a kiss, soft and wet, a whispered "I love you," and "I'm so sorry," ghosting between them. But when they pulled back, Patrick wouldn't look at him.

"And in light of your lingering unhappiness... "

"Patrick... " Evan scratched gently at Patrick's jaw and he looked up, worrying at his bottom lip. "No, wait. Don't do that." Evan wiped the worried furrow from Patrick's brow with his thumb.

Patrick lowered his head and chuffed, a faint smile shining through again. "Don't do what?"

"Worry. About us." Evan grabbed Patrick's tea and shoved it into his hand. "See, I haven't told you the best part about that dog."

"No?"

"After he was out there barking awhile, you'd hear his master calling into the yard. And with one more yelp up the tree, Rigby would run—faster than he ever ran after that squirrel—into the house where he was warm and happy and fed and loved." Evan stopped and rested his eyes on Patrick's for a moment, affirming what he was about to say. "I heard our neighbor tell Dad once that Rigby had a bad habit of chewing up socks and used sanitary napkins, but it didn't matter. They *loved* him."

Patrick's intense gaze dissolved into a wicked smile. "So, I'm your master?"

Evan's head dropped and he snorted louder than Dini. "Is that something we need to discuss?"

"Mmmm... I might be open to the idea."

"You do like the mark of ownership, don't you?"

"Well..." Patrick's eyes flashed dark. He was obviously torn between continuing the deep conversation and letting it slide into innuendo and maybe nakedness. "I... I do, but if I were the master, it'd be *your* creamy complexion that would be blemished, wouldn't it?"

Evan whimpered and rubbed his foot right along the crease of Patrick's thigh. "You're kind of an asshole. I was trying to go all rom-com on you and you've taken us to Grindr territory."

"My most humble apologies." Patrick smiled at him, and crawled up Evan's body to kiss the tip of his nose before settling down on his chest. He sighed when Evan wrapped a leg around his calf. "You were saying... They loved Rigby."

"You love me, even in the middle of my mess. You're *home*, Patrick."

"I love being that for you."

"Maybe once I get my shit together I can be the same for you."

"You already are."

Evan took another deep breath to finish, not really believing him—not really sure how it could be so—and not really having the energy to argue the matter. "Anyway, after I moved I spent a damned lot of time blaming Perci for everything."

"You weren't totally off-base. She represented your biggest fear."

Evan sighed. "She still does." He glanced up to the kitchen, now spotless, but only hours before... "In case you couldn't tell."

"Evan, that woman never had a voice to lose. She never had anything to say, anything to offer. Not professionally, anyway." He kissed Evan softly. "You need to let that go. Figure out what to do with the fucking squirrel."

Evan nodded, his fingers tangling in Patrick's hair. He rested his head back against a throw pillow, feeling as if the weight of it all might win. "Maybe my squirrel got bored with my indecision and split."

They rested silently for a few moments, and then Patrick asked,

"Did you ever feel like you were barking up a tree when you were with Millie?"

"No. She was home—my second home. Where I could just be my best self." Evan giggled imagining Millie's reaction to his afternoon's disaster. "Even if my chocolate seized."

"Then I think Robin's right. You talked about going to see her a few months ago."

Evan smiled at the ceiling. "I did, but *someone* distracted me."

With an air of mock innocence, Patrick got up to take their watered-down tea glasses to the kitchen, laughing as Evan grabbed for him in the empty air. "I feel like you're accusing *me* of doing such a thing."

"I am, sir."

Patrick stopped halfway across the living room. "Ooh, sir. I do like that! I'm thinking this master thing—"

"Stop." Evan laughed and got up to join him. "I want you to come with me."

"What? No. I think you need to do this alone. This is your chase."

When Patrick started back to the kitchen, Evan rushed ahead of him and stepped in front of the refrigerator before Patrick could grab at the handle. "I don't *want* to do this alone. You've helped me get this far. You've opened me up and"—Evan kissed him—"you've loved me when I've been ugly, and I really, really need her to meet you."

"What if she doesn't like me?"

"That's why you don't want to come?"

"It's not that I don't *want* to—" Patrick worried his bottom lip again and Evan smiled.

"Let's ship one of your cheesecakes ahead. Just in case."

▶•◀

They were drunk.

Getting coordinating time off to go to Illinois was a feat of epic proportions, so they went out to celebrate their great outsmarting of the managers.

They celebrated *hard*.

"You're perfect, you know." Evan poked at Patrick's shoulder, pushing off the edge of the fountain that he'd been drunkenly walking like a balance beam to prove his sobriety.

Which wasn't proven at all.

"I am *not* perfect. Remember? I think Bond films are this country's greatest contribution to the cinematic arts."

"That questionable lack of taste aside—"

"And I take lazy shortcuts in my day-to-day cooking and baking."

"Okay, now you might be making a point." Evan took Patrick's hand, stepped a quick cha-cha and spun Patrick under his arm. "Bringing up *my* recent horrible behavior with you to prove how imperfect *you* are is just bad fucking form."

"There. I told you. I hang onto things to bolster my own arguments. See? Not—" With a not-so-gentle tug from Evan, they finally poured themselves into two metal chairs, grateful for the small table between them to lean on. "Not perfect."

"Okay Mr. Not Perfect, prove it." Evan poked sloppily at Patrick's shoulder. "Guilty pleasure meal. The one you'd never tell your favorite FCI instructor about. The one they'd use against you to strip your degree."

"I don't *have* my degree."

"Because you are a dumb-ass."

"Yes. Therefore. Not perfect. Also, you said you wouldn't bring that up again."

"I'm drunk. And I was only—"

Patrick kissed Evan's—well, Evan thought he might have been going for his lips, but he ended up landing on a weird spot on his shoulder. "Forgiven." He also didn't answer the original question because, Evan figured, he'd already forgotten it. "Is that kiosk open? I think I'm thirsty."

"I think you're sexy. I am particularly fond of your lips."

"You are particlu—particular-ly," Patrick smiled triumphantly when he completed the word, "fond of my lips all over you. Your fondness for my sexy has nothing to do with me."

"It has everything to do with you because—"

"Papaya King."

"What?"

"Guilty pleasure. Although, I do not believe in guilty pleasures. If it brings me pleasure, why should I feel guilt?"

"Because you chose Papaya King over Gray's Papaya. That, my sexy not-quite-a-pastry-chef man, might be grounds for a divorce."

"When did we get married?"

"You wanna get married?"

Patrick blinked and then looked over Evan's shoulder and started to giggle. Like a five-year-old boy who had just caught his grandmother in her underwear.

"What?"

"Turn around. Watch."

Evan turned and looked in the direction Patrick was pointing. A tiny man—who, based on his attire, worked for the company running the nearby kiosk—was beginning to shut down the park for the night—as shut down as a Manhattan park could be, in any case.

He tidied the tables and chairs and picked up scraps of trash. But what was so entertaining was when he closed the umbrellas that blossomed out of every few groupings of chairs.

Each time, the man walked up to an umbrella, stepped close to the pole and unwound the cord pulled taut to hold the fabric open. THWUMP, the canvas flopped over his head, swallowing him like a deflated mushroom cap.

After tying the cord, he crawled out from under the material and went on to the next one, completely unaware of the silly scene he was painting with each oversized umbrella.

"Wonder what we do from day to day that looks equally ridiculous to someone on the outside."

"Massaging our meat."

Evan squinted at Patrick, who was still enraptured by the tiny man and his disappearing head and shoulders. "I'm going to go get us some water while you think about what you just said."

Evan got up, kissed Patrick quickly, but lingered at his lips to scold. "Papaya King. You disappoint me."

"You smell like framboise."

"That's because I just drank three too many French martinis. You're a horrible influence on me."

Patrick bit playfully at Evan's bottom lip. Evan was off and back again in a flash. Before he even sat down, Patrick asked, "Don't you just rub it down first? Run your hands over the smoothness of the flesh, feel the weight of it under your fingers?"

"Are you talking about your Master Baker skills again? Because I'm pretty sure I know how to—" Evan opened Patrick's bottle for him, pushing it under his chin before sitting down with a heavy plop. "Drink. You're creeping me out."

"Massaging your meat."

Evan lifted his eyebrows and took a huge pull of his water.

"Before you butcher it, don't you just—" Patrick motioned with his hands, smoothing around and down the round of an imaginary pork shoulder on the table in front of him.

Evan's smile curled around the lip of his water bottle. "Yeah, I guess that would look weird to an outsider."

"Like massaging your lover before—"

"Stabbing him with a butcher knife."

"Right on, Sweeney." Patrick tossed back three or four swallows of water. "I'm drunk."

Evan looked back around for their little man and pouted when he didn't see him any longer. "Sell me a Papaya King dog."

"King Combo. One onion, one kraut, curly fries with cheese—"

"Cheese sauce? The shitty kind?"

"The shittiest. And a mango." Patrick took a pull from his water and capped it back up. "Or a papaya. Probably mango. The skin snaps when you bite into the dog and the kraut is perfect and juicy and the bun gets soggy and oh God, it's—"

"Just like Gray's. Why do people argue over this? It's the same damned thing."

"You're just not particular enough about your wieners."

Evan licked his lips, an evil glint shining in his eyes.

Patrick adjusted in his seat.

"I prefer to call them meat in tube form. And I like *your* wiener."

Patrick burped. "So, what's your order, Bourdain?"

"Not much different. Two kraut, mustard, papaya."

"Is that your guilty pleasure?"

"No, your wiener is."

"You turn into a horny nine-year-old when you're drunk. It's a little gross."

Evan ignored him. "I could devour an entire box of Kraft Macaroni & Cheese. Or…" A smile spread across his face at the memory. "Yes, this is better. Chef Boyardee SpaghettiOs. With meatballs, otherwise you're just wasting my time."

"Oh God, I haven't had those since—since *high school*."

"There was a little market around the corner from my first apartment and I'd get a load of those single serving tubs every time I got sick—which was often, that first year or two. Mr. Moriarti got so used to seeing me. 'What is it this time, Evan? Sniffles? Flu? Broken heart?' They were perfect when splorting a can of soup into a pan was too much effort."

Evan sat back and remembered one spell in particular when he had emptied Mr. Moriarti's shelves. His roommate had to keep running out for him while he curled up on his bed after another three-night stand came to a screeching halt and his heart was left flopping around on the floor of their studio like the dead fish it really was.

The warmth of Patrick's hand on his arm and the resonance of his baritone shook him out of the recollection. "We're drunk. We're cooks. Metropolitan on Bedford is open. Let's go make this shit."

"Dogs and SpaghettiOs?"

"And boxed mac and cheese, because why the fuck not?"

Why the fuck not indeed. They planned their meal on the train ride into Brooklyn and raided the shelves as the booze in their system began to fade.

"Why do you have three heads of cabbage?"

"Kraut. I thought you were the chef."

"Patrick, kraut takes three *weeks* from scratch. I want to still be drunk when I eat this shit."

"Right. I knew that." Patrick started to put the cabbage back and stopped himself. "That would be something I still use from a can at Johnny's. Kraut. Love me anyway." He grabbed a jar of prepared kraut and a box of red wine instead.

"*Boxed* wine? Really?"

"SpaghettiOs, Evan. Really. Did you get buns?"

Somehow they not only got everything they needed, picked up Dini and got it all prepared without injury, but they also set up a picnic on Patrick's living room floor to devour it all.

"If anyone in my kitchen finds out about this, so help me God, Patrick."

"I already texted a pic to Rosey."

Evan blanched and bit into what he feared was probably his third dog, unashamedly talking with his mouth full. "You did not."

"I did not."

"SpaghettiOs don't taste as good when you're not sick or broken-hearted."

Patrick reached over and scooped some from Evan's plate onto his own. "I could break up with you." He stabbed three meatballs and sucked them into his mouth. "And then we could have make-up sex afterwards."

"You know"—Evan finished his wine and fingered up the final slop of kraut from his flimsy paper plate—"when I was first starting out, killing someone else's food on the line, this is what I wanted to cook."

"Pretend pasta and minced meat tubes?"

"That's it. I'm breaking up with *you*."

Patrick stuck out his tongue.

"Drunk food. The stuff you eat when you're just fucking hungry. Only good, you know? Quality. People would come in and think, *I just want some pot roast,* and I'd give them the best pot roast they'd ever had. Better than their grandma's. And it wouldn't matter if they dripped gravy onto their necktie because it was after hours anyway. Besides, their weird Aunt Myrtle gave it to them and they only wore it out of guilt."

"That's a pretty elaborate fantasy to not follow through on." At Evan's judgmental gaze, Patrick belched and took a different route. "Why didn't you do it?"

"Squirrel." He plucked a meatball from Patrick's plate. "Why didn't you finish your degree?"

Patrick swallowed the last of his wine and smiled. "Wrong master?"

Evan moved their plates up to the coffee table, caught Patrick's lips in a kiss and rested back against the couch. "Thank you for this. For allowing me to just let off some steam. I've been awful."

"Figured we'd better get it out of our systems now. Something tells me Millie won't abide a foul mood."

"She'll tell me to get over myself. 'Go make something, Evy. You're driving me nuts.'"

"God, I can't wait to meet her."

▶•◀

It was in the silencing of it that he finally heard it.

The tea kettle whistling.

He knew Patrick had come—was relieved, even—but he didn't move to greet him. He didn't move when he heard him talking to Dini, her hind leg tamping on the hard wood floor as he probably scratched under her chin where she liked it. He didn't move when he heard Patrick swear, his footing faltering as he walked down the hall toward the bedroom where Evan was sitting.

"Evan? What is going on—you left the tea kettle on and your laundry is in the middle of the—" Patrick stopped suddenly and groaned. "Oh, Dini... been waiting too long to go out?"

Oh yeah.

He had been laying out clothes for the trip and decided to make some tea when the dryer buzzed and Dini started pacing. Then his phone rang.

And now Patrick stood in the doorway to Evan's room, looking at him, worry and confusion written over every inch of his body. Evan wondered how long he'd actually been sitting there.

"Evan?" Patrick pointed helplessly back into the hall. "Dini must have needed to go out—" He stepped into the room and Evan wanted to run to him, but he couldn't seem to move from his spot on the bed, where he was surrounded by a week's worth of clothes for their trip.

Patrick looked down at Evan's lap and peeled the phone from his hand. He had to give it a tug to free it from his clinging fingers. "Who called?"

Evan finally looked up as Patrick sat down, landing on his linen walking shorts. "Mom." He would normally be irritated that he'd have to iron the shorts again; except the plane trip would ensure that anyway, and suddenly he remembered that maybe they wouldn't be taking a plane trip anymore.

"Millie's dead."

Patrick gasped. His hand went to Evan's arm, where its warmth instantly began to melt the ice Evan had felt in his veins since his mother's call. "When?"

"This morning. Middle of the night? They—they found her this morning at... at the center. Still in bed. Never made it in for breakfast."

"In her sleep."

Evan nodded. "What she always wanted. Just... not there." Patrick's fingers were tangled in Evan's; he couldn't be sure when that had happened. "You said Dini needed to go out?"

"Well, not anymore." Evan finally started to get up, but Patrick gently squeezed his hands. "I got it already."

"I'm sorry. You shouldn't have to clean up after my dog."

It wasn't like he could get up to function anyway. His mind was a whirlwind of questions that would never have answers.

Did Millie hurt? Had she given the staff signs that she was unwell? Or did she, in typical Millie fashion, leave them laughing the night before, completely unaware of her ultimate plan?

Did she think of him? Did she remember that Evan loved her? Understand that Evan owed his *life* to her?

Had he ever really told her that?

"I waited too long."

"Evan, no. Don't do that. She knew you have a life here. She knew."

"I don't know what to do. I think I'm supposed to cry or something." He looked at Patrick, hoping he'd have an answer, but all he had was love. It was written all over him, in his touch, in his eyes, in the faint, patient smile on his lips. "What did you do when Oona died?"

"I laughed."

"Patrick... "

"She had this old cardigan. Her aunt had made it for her or something? She wore it September through May. Cooked in it. Went to the market in it. Church. That thing was *gawd* awful. Pilled and stretched out, buttons hanging by the threaded shanks she kept reattaching, I don't even remember what color it was supposed to be. It was just—gray. Colorless."

"Bet it smelled awesome."

"It smelled like food." Patrick stopped for a moment as if to sniff at his memory. "Mostly garlic, come to think of it. We'd tease her about it, which is probably why she always wore it. 'I will die in this sweater. You will bury me in this sweater.'"

"She did not... "

"I got the call. Ran to the house, up the stairs, everyone's gathered around the bed and as soon as my eyes landed on her, all I could do was bust out laughing."

"Was your dad mad?"

"No—once I started, everyone else did too." Patrick's eyes reddened at the memory but his smile still shone through. "They were just waiting for someone to break."

Evan smiled then too, imagining the scene, the release from the expected, the feeling of breaking free from the ice of grief. "Did you bury her in it?"

"Of course we did. Hell, the only thing scarier than a pissed-off Oona was the idea that she'd come back and haunt us."

Evan laughed, full and deep, and felt a huge chip of ice break free in himself. He swallowed Patrick up in his arms and breathed him in as he settled, a single tear slipping down his cheek. "I wanted you to meet her."

Patrick pulled back, kissing Evan softly. "I know."

"I was going to tell her I was coming, even picked the phone up last—" Evan hiccupped and covered his mouth with his hands, his eyes quickly filling with tears. "I picked up the phone last night to tell her—"

Patrick pulled him back into his arms and rocked Evan gently as his breath stuttered with silent tears. "That would have been a nice surprise."

"I wanted her to know I'd found you."

"Maybe your mom told her and that's why she knew it was okay to go. You've got a new home."

"I do." Evan pulled back with a beleaguered sigh and eyed the mess on his bed and all over his room. "Now what are we supposed to do? We have a flight to Illinois in"—he looked at the clock on his bedside table and sighed—"twelve hours."

"Your neighbor's taking Dini, right?"

"Yeah, before we leave."

"So, let's go anyway. We're off work, we have a hotel for a few nights—"

"A Hampton in Quincy, Patrick. This will not be luxurious."

"You might still find what you're looking for."

"A hug from my mom wouldn't be so bad either."

►•◄

"How were you still single when I met you?"

Every moment from Evan's apartment to the airplane had been a test of his patience, fortitude and equanimity—qualities Evan never had in abundance, if at all.

Nothing went right.

Patrick forgot his phone, jacking up the cost of the cab as he ran back up to Evan's apartment to retrieve it.

It took three tries to get to the proper terminal thanks to a clueless cab driver—or maybe one who was passive-aggressively bitching about Patrick's delay—and an indifferent airline employee. And it just so happened that the clueless cab driver was right, a fact which Evan continued adamantly to deny on the shuttle back to the original terminal.

And then there was the debacle at the ticketing counter where, for the longest four minutes of Evan Stanford's life, he was told that, not only was there no seat for him, but the next available nonstop flight to the tiny airport in Quincy wasn't until Thursday.

It was Sunday.

And then—

"Oh. I'm terribly sorry, Mr. Stanford. Yes. Here you are." A faint smile, waived baggage fees for both departing and returning flights and a bump up to first class, they were finally headed to the gate— where Patrick set off alarms like Fort Knox.

With a meat thermometer.

Once that was settled, they sprinted down the terminal to the gate as they heard their names being called, the gate attendant giving them a proper scolding: "We were just about to close the door to the airplane, *gentlemen*."

But what took Evan's breath away, what had kept him mostly speechless throughout the entire ordeal, was the way Patrick had handled every single hurdle. Before Patrick went upstairs to retrieve his phone, he tossed extra cash on the front seat of the cab. And when he came back, he engaged the irritated driver in such an interesting conversation about what "homeland" and "dreams" meant that Evan wondered if that was how they ended up at the wrong terminal.

The entire time Evan stood at the ticket counter, spelling and respelling his name, handing the clerk credit card after credit card, explaining over and over again how, when, where and most importantly *why* he had made the arrangements, Patrick's hand was on his back, a warm constant, a silent support, a reminder that this woman was not the source of his anxiety and that somehow, some way, he was going to get home to—

Well, he still wasn't sure what this trip was going to be about, but Patrick was here, warm and constant, to be with him for whatever awaited.

And when the alarms screeched throughout the security checkpoint, Evan was convinced that it was only Patrick's charm that kept him from having to do a squat-and-cough strip search. It could have been Evan's own heart-piercing glare, but based on all evidence up to this point, it was Patrick. His smile. His humor. His easy nature and ability to simply roll with it all.

So, once they had settled into their first class seats, their carry-on bags had been properly stowed and their fingers were properly intertwined on the oversized armrest between them, Evan asked his question. "How were you still single when I met you?"

Patrick looked at him as though the answer was as simple as, *The sky is blue, Evan. Can't you see?* "I told you already."

"Remind me."

Patrick turned in his seat and captured Evan's hand in both of his, his eyes shining with raw emotion. "I was waiting for *you*."

Evan rolled his eyes at Patrick's ridiculous answer and sat back in his seat, his head nestling perfectly into the contoured headrest. "So you were waiting for someone difficult?"

"I prefer to call it *challenging*."

"What if I become impossible?" Evan side-eyed Patrick, pleased that he was playing along. He'd been plenty "impossible" already.

"I'll see it as provocative."

Evan quite liked that word. He quite liked Patrick. And he liked that Patrick quite liked *him*, even when he was less than provocative. "Hrm. Or maybe... intriguing?"

"Can I get you gentlemen a drink before takeoff?" Evan opened his eyes to look at the flight attendant, not intending to order, but when Patrick's Brooklyn-laced baritone oozed sexiness at a simple drink order, "Whiskey sour," he decided to join in.

"Manhattan, thank you." Evan watched her step back to the seats behind them and when he settled back in, Patrick reached over the armrest and brushed Evan's cheek with his lips, his breath warm on Evan's skin when he spoke. "More like... alluring."

Evan hummed in consideration, the tension from the past few hours slipping away like a thief in the night without his take. "Enticing?"

"Arousing."

Evan turned to Patrick, his eyes now alight with love and joy and a happiness that propelled him above the swirling cacophony of the day and the reason for this trip.

He traced the line of Patrick's jaw, the stubble scratching his fingertip, and breathed him in, whispering one more word.

"In*tox*icating."

The flight attendant interrupted their intimacy with a quiet apology and tentatively set their drinks down between them. Patrick smiled and thanked her.

"To Millie," he said, raising his glass.

Tears prickled at Evan's eyes, but a smile prevailed as he lifted his glass to Patrick's. "And Oona. That they might live forever."

VII. Deuxième Entremet

*A sweet dish served between courses to
cleanse the palate, usually a sorbet.*

It wasn't that Evan Stanford was difficult—well, mostly it wasn't
that.

It was that he was *passionate*.

And sometimes, Patrick knew, passions overwhelm. They
could take the reins from reason and courtesy, from patience and
empathy. And when they did, passions could become a negative
force: fiery. Impulsive. Illogical. Unprocessed.

From Patrick's perspective as a man whose passions ran deep,
like a well-hewn valley steadily formed and carved by the flow of
wind and water, those occasionally out-of-control passions were
what put the color in people. The spark. The light that could guide
them out of the easy dreariness that life can become and into the
vibrancy of a life well lived.

And Evan brought color into Patrick's life. He came into his
darkroom, smacked on a contrast filter and blew the very satisfactory image he was about to process into a vivid masterpiece,
balanced with shadows and highlights and a full spectrum of color
and hue. It had happened the first time Patrick saw him, and every
time after it only intensified.

And that was just it. Patrick's life was fine before Evan showed
up in his diner. Satisfactory. Contented. But now he could see, he
could feel, he could taste this life of passion. And though it was
occasionally messy, he was addicted.

This great passion even manifested itself in the mundane. And
maybe those were the loveliest bits of all—the little sparkles of
color on the edges of the day to day.

Take Dini, for example. Evan didn't simply have a *dog*—or, as any reasonable chef rarely home would, a cat—he had a *brachycephalic* dog named after a stuffy Romanian dessert. A brachycephalic dog who wore a new pair of socks every day (Patrick still called them slippers because Evan's impatient sigh was always worth it) and a "diamond"-encrusted pink collar and walked the streets of downtown Brooklyn with her scented poop bags fashionably attached to her leash in a pink camouflage poop bag-holder.

"Brachyceph—what?"

Evan had sighed and explained as though Patrick should be as familiar with the term as he was with blancmange and *gliadin*.

"Ah. So, a face that looks like she ran into a patio door five hundred times."

"You could sleep on the couch tonight, if you prefer."

He didn't prefer. He never preferred. Because sleeping with Evan, whether they were actually sleeping or reading or eating breakfast, or fucking or making love—or better yet, both—or simply staring at vapid reality shows on television while curled up together as though it were the last day on earth, was a gift he would never trade. Especially not for a snide remark about that damned dog.

Evan's gift to him was color. Intrigue. Arousal. Intoxication.

Passion.

He was so far gone for this man, so enraptured by him that he often wondered how he had succeeded in living as full a life as he had without him.

The clarity came as soon as they arrived at the Stanford home in Quincy. Patrick saw Evan's passion anew in the tenderness he showed his mother, Joanna. She had tried to look as though she hadn't been impatiently awaiting their arrival, but her cover was gloriously blown when her feet seemed to lift from the ground the moment Evan stepped inside the screen door.

He understood—he thought Evan hung the moon and stars as well.

And then there was the passionate intimacy between Evan and his father, evident in every exchange. Their welcome hug was full-bodied and firm, with Evan's face tucked into the bend of Martin Stanford's chubby neck, and they were silent but for deep inhalations of breathing each other in and sighs of absence and familiarity.

They communicated without words, but with glances and touches, eyebrow lifts and nods filling in for phrases and questions.

Isn't he amazing, Dad?

He makes you happy?

The happiest.

Then he's amazing.

Patrick felt analyzed in that moment, but completely appreciated—and, if he were totally honest with himself, a little jealous. His family loved, but not like this. Curt nods, faint smiles of approval, brows furrowed in disapproval and lectures about not rocking the boat permeated his familial memories.

It made for a monochromatic life.

And yet this family, in its Midwestern, suburban normalcy, welcomed him instantly, tucking him into its heart as though he'd been there all along.

By the end of their first day there, and without anyone knowing quite how it happened, it was decided the Stanford home would be the gathering place for those who wanted to remember Millie. She had no surviving family to speak of, but for someone like Mildred Bishop—a woman whom the entire neighborhood loved and ultimately cared for—a gathering must take place.

So after a few haphazard *what ifs* and *maybe we coulds*, punctuated by grunts from Marty, Joanna and Evan began the task of planning the event while Patrick sat by and waited for his orders, falling deeper and deeper into the lure of this man and the things that made him tick.

"I can get a honey-baked and do a pan or two of funeral potatoes and maybe that green bean casserole everyone loves. I have those petit fours you sent us—"

Patrick bit back a laugh as Evan visibly struggled with the pedestrian—or, as he affectionately called it, "Walmart"—menu his mother was concocting. Her blue eyes danced with how excited she was to be helping her son. Evan's eyes matched hers, but pled for her to understand before he actually spoke his mind and hurt her feelings.

"Ooh, and what about those pig and chicken sandwiches everyone loves?"

"Pig and chicken sandwiches?" Patrick's mouth watered at the idea—maybe some kind of barbecue mix, slow roasted, perfectly seasoned. And with the combination of his and Evan's creativity, the sauce would be—

Evan answered almost apologetically, indicating the layering of the sandwiches with the motion of his hands. "Bread—white only, preferably Wonder Bread—ham salad, bread, egg salad, bread." His smile was pinched, almost as if he were in pain. "Finger sandwich size, frilled cocktail toothpick in the middle."

"Oh. I see." Patrick willed a polite expression, but saw Evan turn away to hide his own laughter and knew he'd failed.

"Can I—" Evan gently pulled the pen from Joanna's hand to get her attention, and Patrick snickered at the similarity between Evan and his mother. They not only looked alike, they *were* alike. When they were involved in something they had tunnel vision and were blind to all else.

She looked up at Evan and pressed in to his touch on her back. "You want to do this?"

"If you don't mind?"

"I'm just trying to give you a break from the kitchen, sweetheart."

"I know and I do appreciate that, but this is what Millie and I did. It's what I do. I—I need to do this. If that's okay."

Evan and Patrick headed out to the grocery, where Evan composed a menu as he lingered in the aisles, making mental checklists of what Joanna would already have and what he'd only find in New York, adjusting for poor-quality produce and less than stellar butchering.

"A funeral is not the place for foodies, Evan."

"Pig and chicken sandwiches. Honestly."

"Yeah, sorry, but that just—" Patrick had been shivering off and on since he'd heard of the atrocities.

"And Millie hated them. I don't know what she's thinking." Evan plucked up what had to be his tenth or twelfth or twentieth tomato and sighed. "And why can't I find a decent tomato? It's late July, for fuck's sake."

"Surely there's a farmer's market somewhere."

They cooked and they prepped and they shared stories. It was exhausting and invigorating. As the people began to gather, tasting the food they had prepared, stopping conversation to take second bites and savor, Evan melted into the fabric of the community he grew up in as if he'd never left. And Patrick soaked it in: more contrast, color and light for his soul.

Evan jotted down makeshift recipes for those who asked and sent the Misters Madison, the first gay men he'd ever met in Quincy, home with a small box of petit fours after promising his mom he would ship her replacements from New York.

He kept up with the ribbing of other neighborhood men, giving as hard as he got.

He cooed and sighed over pictures of grandbabies and Mrs. Hamilton's twelfth cat.

Evan shone. His laugh was crisp and bright. His stories of life in New York were hand-picked for each audience: a tale of a bad night in the kitchen, complete with colorful language and hyperbolic humor, for the Misters Madison; and a story about Dini, a trash bag and a hot summer day for Mrs. Collins, the elderly neighbor he thought had passed about three years before.

"Stop laughing. I think I sent her daughter a sympathy card."

He prepped. He cooked. He delegated and praised. He served, he waited, he sunk his gloved hands into steaming hot water to wash dishes, and he never missed a beat in conversation. He was glorious. In his element. Bright, happy, at ease—everything Patrick believed him to be.

It was clear that in the daily grind, in the push, every day of his life, to be the best, serve the masses James Beard-winner quality food, order up, fire it now, hustle hustle hustle—Evan had lost his voice. Forgotten it. Or at least, forgotten what it sounded like.

But being here, cooking the foods that Millie taught him and adding his own special flair, it all slipped back into place, the squirrel-chasing dog coming home again.

As the last guests departed, and Marty walked the lingerers to their cars so "the kitchen staff" could clean up, Patrick remembered something Oona had told him not long before her death. He was on a path to a culinary career and she had fretted about him. She was worried that training and bosses and "the job of it all" would take his heart.

"We all cook from a history, Paddy. With a story. The trick is getting someone who doesn't share your history to feel and understand and taste it."

She always reminded him that whatever he cooked, whomever he cooked for, it should always be based on who he was. And while preparing Johnny's food at the diner occasionally made that task difficult, he tried every day to do it—in his desserts, in his special touches with the ordinary dishes and in his knack for knowing the little extra something special diners needed to get their day back on track.

And here, now, Patrick felt Evan's history. He understood it. He tasted it. If Evan could redirect his passions back to his history—

Well, he would be unstoppable.

▶•◀

"So, this is Millie's house."

Patrick stepped inside the ranch home and smiled. It was everything he had imagined and just as Evan had described it: eclectically decorated, with treasures and tchotchkes sprinkled over every flat surface. Plants nestled in corners, near windows and hanging from macramé holsters. Behind the couch was an easel, holding a brightly colored abstract painting.

"Did she paint that?"

"Yes. In fact... " Evan squeezed into the corner behind the couch and pulled a few smaller canvases from the floor. "I did this one." He looked at it one more time with a snicker before handing it off to Patrick. "I was having an angry day."

The painting was dark and stormy, with blues, purples and grays smeared across the canvas quite artistically, and a bent, barren tree giving the nondescript figure of a boy inadequate shelter. "How old were you?"

"Judging by the moodiness? Probably fifteen. Sixteen."

"It's still beautiful."

"Mmm. I still can't believe she paid someone to come clean this place and never put it on the market. It's just been sitting here for nine months." Evan swiped a finger across the end table and wiped dust onto his pants. "And obviously they didn't clean often enough."

Patrick quietly followed Evan as he continued his tour through the hallway with the bath and an art room filled with pieces of pottery, a pottery wheel and a table littered with fabric and ribbons, paper and stamps, clay tools and a huge jar of assorted brushes. He quickly pointed out Millie's room and a guest room where he had stayed a few times when his parents needed a kid-free weekend.

He saved the kitchen for last, smiling sadly as they entered and taking a deep breath as if hoping to smell something warm and inviting coming from the stove.

"White sage and cedar—her favorite incense."

Patrick didn't smell it, but this wasn't his experience to have. "Is this the infamous pantry?" He opened a double door and smiled. It was still well-stocked.

"God. It's organized exactly the same as it always was."

"If it ain't broke... "

Evan nosed around for a moment, touching bags of pasta and rice, snooping through the oils and vinegars, opening a few cans of candied fruits and nuts. He picked out a dried apricot and popped it in his mouth and offered one to Patrick. "Still fresh–ish."

"You should make something."

"What? No, it seems—" He pulled a box of granola from the top shelf and popped its top to dump some into Patrick's hand. "Intrusive?"

"Yet we're scrounging anyway."

"We are." He pinched a bit of granola from Patrick's hand and ate. "This is stale. Nothing would be fresh enough to cook with anyway."

"Not for your restaurant, but—" Patrick shoved the rest of the granola into his mouth. "But for the reconnection. You're a chef now—this game will be a breeze."

"But I know this pantry—it's sort of cheating."

Patrick saw a kitchen towel draped over the oven handle and got an idea. "Okay, so let's complicate it a little." He grabbed the towel and, before Evan could argue, tied it around Evan's eyes, kissing the nape of his neck under the knot for good measure. "Okay, pick three."

"*Patrick...*"

"Go on. We can run to the store for the fresh ingredients." He pushed Evan closer to the closet with a gentle nudge. Evan lifted his hands blindly, tenderly feeling around the shelves for ingredients.

With a crinkle, his hands landed on a bag of pasta and he grabbed it, moving to his left where the bottles of oils and vinegars were stored.

"Even blindfolded, you're cheating."

"Too late now. You can't change the rules." Evan grabbed a bottle and handed it over. "Besides, this could be *anything.*"

"Yeah, pasta and an oil or vinegar—real complex."

Evan tugged Patrick in for a kiss, totally missing and landing somewhere in the eyelid-bridge-of-nose-forehead area. "You're always shorter than I think."

"Every day. I don't grow overnight like a Chia Pet."

"No. Just your beard. Point me the right way again, smart-ass."

"Just for that, I should rig the pantry."

Evan lifted the towel from one eye and shot Patrick a playful glare. "Millie would never move shit."

"Oh, I bet if you were blindfolded she would have." Patrick ducked Evan's swatting hands and laughed, pushing him the right way into the pantry. "Okay, one more ingredient, babe. I'm getting hungry."

"If the rule wasn't that I had to eat it too, I'd purposely find something disgusting."

"Like?"

He pawed at the shelf with the nuts and dried fruit, chocolates and a box that he lifted and touched. "Food coloring?"

"I'm not telling you."

"I think I could make anything work at this point, but not that." He tossed the box back on the shelf and lifted a canister, taking a deep breath when he popped off its lid.

"Oh wait now, no, no, no. You can't sniff test it!" Patrick yanked the can out of Evan's hands and glowered as Evan laughed and feigned innocence. "Even if this is the best ingredient in there, you cannot have it." He looked down into it. Candied... he took a taste. Watermelon. He wouldn't have wanted it anyway, the brat. "No more sniffing, mister."

"Fine. I'll take this, then." He handed another canister over and removed the blindfold, planting a kiss on the right spot this time. "Oh, and I would have picked Fruit Loops. But they're on the top shelf and nothing up there is ever worth the effort."

"Yeah, okay pasta and Fruit Loops would have been—well, you could have ground them for rainbow bread crumbs."

"Oh God."

Patrick lifted the lid of the canister and groaned. "Almonds. Almonds, red wine vinegar and pasta. Little..." He read the package, squinting as he stumbled over the pronunciation. "Minchi—minchi-uh—*minchiareddhi*. What the hell is that?"

Evan grabbed at the bag and cackled. "She does not have—" He looked at them more closely and laughed again. "Oh my God, she always was a saucy old broad. Look." He opened the package and pulled out a few pieces of pasta. "Little penises."

"Little—what?" Patrick took a couple in his hand and laughed at the rolled, thin dried noodles. "Long, skinny, uncut penises. Oh my God."

"Might have to thin the sauce I have in mind for them—but yes. This will be great. We have to invite Mom and Dad. And do *not* tell them about the pasta." Evan fell silent for a minute and smiled, his eyes reddening with threatening tears. "God, I loved this woman. I think I learned more about being a gay man from her than from actually being one."

Patrick held up a noodle and nudged Evan with his elbow. "Please don't tell me she told you how to eat di—"

"Patrick Sullivan, I will put Fruit Loops in your penis noodles."

"Actually, I think the noodles would go in the—" He showed him with his circled finger and thumb. Just in case.

"Stop."

"Wanna take a walk? It's cooled down a bit out there." Patrick dropped the rugs he'd taken to the back porch to shake out onto the kitchen floor. Hopefully this would be the last of Evan's spot cleaning rampage through Millie's home.

He wasn't sure what purpose it served, except to keep Evan's grief—and maybe a little guilt—in check. But he was going to keep helping until Evan could find it in himself to walk out and lock the door behind them.

"Dad, why don't you come with us?" Evan patted his dad's rounded belly and draped the dishtowel over the remaining pots drying from their pantry-inspired dinner—penis pasta with roasted tomato almond pesto. And roasted chicken breast because Marty wanted protein.

With a grunt, Marty agreed to go, mumbling something about exercise, egg white omelets and kale chips.

Patrick really liked Marty. He grumbled like his own father, but he loved... well, he loved like Evan did. Easily. Beautifully. But not flawlessly.

They took a quick route around the block, Evan and Marty pointing out homes of interest and the corner where Evan had skidded out on his bike, earning him a trip to the emergency room and a bright purple cast on his arm.

"It was, of course, a weekend Joanna had to travel for work. Do you know how hard it is to hyperventilate *and* keep it from a sobbing six-year-old boy calling for his mother?"

"You did fine, Dad."

Marty carried on, gossiping about Mr. and Mrs. McCafferty's very public meltdown and divorce and putting Evan and Patrick both in stitches.

"She was always such a mean old hag."

"Well, she had to live with him for thirty years. I'd be a mean old hag too."

As they neared the Stanford home, everyone still enjoying the stories and the memories that Patrick imagined as vividly as if they'd happened to him, he found his voice. "Evan, you act like you're not, but you really are a people lover, aren't you?"

"I most certainly am not."

"Like hell you're not."

Patrick did a quick double take as he heard Marty's voice echo his own.

"Good God, I can hardly deal with one of you—" Evan rolled his eyes and let go of Patrick's hand, charging ahead of them while Patrick and Marty stood there and laughed at him.

"See? Look how happy you are right now." Patrick jogged ahead, grabbed Evan's hand back and laughed at the impatient eye roll it earned him. "You *love* people."

"I do not love people, especially you two right now." But he was smiling; underneath that obnoxious fake glare, he was smiling. "You're both creeping me out."

"You love your neighbor. Vicki? Dini is, as we speak, probably luxuriating at her apartment—without socks on—"

"How *dare* you suggest such a thing!"

"It's *July*."

"Wood floors."

Patrick and Marty rolled their eyes, simultaneously muttering about the spoiled dog and her spoiled owner until Patrick pointed out, "Which Vicki does not have." At Evan's incredulous look, he continued. "I was there, remember? My point—you wouldn't let just anyone take care of that damned dog."

"That's because I love that damned dog more than I love most people."

Patrick tried to scold with his eyes and Marty was being no help, chortling and shaking his head.

"Okay, fine. I love Vicki. Because she loves my dog."

"You love Rosey."

Marty laughed and Evan snorted. "Okay, *now* you have officially lost your—"

"You saved him. And you kept him when he figured out how to save himself." Evan opened his mouth to make a retort but stopped, looked at his dad and nodded, so Patrick kept going. "You love Robin and Theo and Carlos and Natasha and Ross, and I even saw it that first night, your little haughty attitude crumbling all over my diner once the stories started flying—"

"I am not haughty."

"Your dog wears slippers."

Evan looked absolutely betrayed by his father. If you can smile through betrayal. "They. Are. Socks."

"You're missing the point, babe."

Evan grunted. "They're *mine*. Of course I love them. Well, except for the FNG. I'm not so sure about him."

"FNGs need time—"

"'FNG?' Is this some new Internet thing? Because I finally figured out that when your mother texts 'SMH' she means 'shaking my head' and not 'suck my hair,' which never made any sense, especially since hair is not something I have in abundance—"

"Dad, stop. Oh my God, you still type with your index fingers too, don't you?"

"My thumbs don't work right or something."

"'Fucking New Guy,' to answer your question, Marty." Patrick had to talk or he would have to laugh at these two completely adorable, lovable pains in the ass standing in the middle of London Drive.

"Fucking new—what? You don't even call the new guys by name? Evan, that seems—"

"Rude. Except that everyone ends up with a nickname at some point. We're still weighing the value of 'Kinks' once FNG wears itself out."

"Kinks?"

"Rosey caught him and one of our new servers—" Evan stopped himself, a blush creeping up his face, and Patrick laughed, not even knowing the end of the story.

"This is the best trip ever."

"It just weeds them out, Dad." Evan looked back and forth between Patrick and Marty. "What are we even talking about? Wasn't I being judged or something?"

"You. Loving people. And I think that—stop rolling your eyes at me. Do I need to give you more examples?"

"No, just better ones because you're pointing out *my* people. I love you too, but that doesn't count in whatever it is you're trying to tell me."

"I don't count?"

"Ohhh-kay, that's my cue. I'm out. I'm confused and I'm tired and Mom said she wanted me to water the garden. You guys going to stop by before you head back tomorrow?"

"Breakfast?"

Marty thanked them again for dinner and turned back to his house, mumbling, "Fucking new guy" over and over as if he were weighing whether or not he should use it at work. Patrick decided he'd mention it at breakfast the next day as a decent option, because nothing will balance the scales with a cocky new guy better than killing his name and calling him "FNG."

"Rosey caught FNG doing what?"

"Getting pegged out back by that new server—the blonde?"

"Who brings a strap-on to work?"

"Apparently Blondie does."

Evan took Patrick's hand and they started another loop around the neighborhood. Patrick could feel Evan side-eyeing him. Thing was, he was still stuck on the audacity it would take to cart sex toys to work... and then use them there.

"Keep talking, because you're about to buzz out of your skin envisioning that one."

"Right. Okay, Roger," Patrick teased.

"Roger? I don't even *know* Roger. He's crusty and mumbly and he needs to blow his goddamned nose and—do we even know if he's homeless or just fond of that corner stoop?"

"Stoop or no, he reminds you of your father—"

"Oh gross, he does not—"

Evan stopped walking and stared at Patrick, who could only smile because he knew that look. The look that said *Shit, you're right, and now I'm going to have to admit it.*

He loved that look.

They started walking again. "Fine. Minus the sinus issues."

Patrick scoffed. "You have a pug and you whine about sinus issues."

"And the potential homelessness. And the mumble—Dad's starting to mumble under his breath a lot, isn't he?"

"He does do that a lot," Patrick agreed. "But you even mentioned the resemblance after we first met him. His plaid shirts with the mother-of-pearl snaps, and his pocket protectors, and that he always has a story. All that bread and jam... you bought him flowers, Evan."

"He was watering dead ones!"

"How many petit fours did he get?"

"My freezer isn't big enough—"

"How often do you get off at the wrong train stop to take him extra food from work?"

"Okay, fine. I love Roger." Evan waved his fingers in the air and mockingly drew out the "O" in "love." "What is your point? This stupid town makes people's brains fuzzy."

Patrick shook his head and pulled Evan's hand up for a kiss on the knuckles. "No. In fact, I found some clarity here. About you. Maybe even about myself."

Evan hummed and twined his fingers more tightly in Patrick's, tugging him around the corner to a new street. "I *have* been quoted as saying that you're a good reader."

"I like reading you. And I've loved watching you, this trip— seeing you come alive with these people you've known all your life."

"I'm afraid I'm totally missing your point again."

"Okay, let's take it back to New York. How often do you come out of your kitchen?"

"When my shift is over."

"You're being obtuse on purpose now, aren't you?"

"Maybe a little."

Patrick loved this man so much he would close up everything in New York and live in a godforsaken town like Quincy just to be with him. "How often do you come out and talk to the people you're cooking for?"

"Never, anymore. I did when I started—but I have control issues and—"

"You do?"

"Are you making a point or making fun of me?"

"The other night at your parents', you created that menu for those specific people. And? You loved doing it."

"But I know these people. It wasn't hard to take Mom's ideas and just deconstruct them into something less... "

"Cream-of-crap soup-based?"

"Yes," Evan said. "I don't see how—"

"I wouldn't have made that specific food. You knew what they'd want. What they'd expect. And then you gave them better."

"A lot of it was Millie's stuff, and... I am a chef. Food is sort of my *thing*." They walked a few more steps and then Evan stopped, panic flashing over his face. "You're not suggesting that I move back here, are you, because—"

"No, Babe." Patrick sighed with a smile and tried again. "I'm not saying you should be cooking for *these* people, but you need to tap into them. Into where you came from."

"Into Millie."

"Yes. She taught you how to do the food. And your parents taught you how to do the love. If you combine those things, they'll be creating James Beard Awards just to honor you."

"Stop."

"No." But Patrick let it rest between them as they walked. To him it was clear. Like a mother sauce needed the right ingredients, the right heat, there needed to be a perfect blend of Evan's passion and his people, his food and his love for it all. When one element was missing or out of sync, the sauce would break.

And something was sorely missing.

"Okay, say you're onto something," Evan said. "Because if I really think about it... "

"You felt it too, didn't you? Like a running duck finally slipping into the water."

"I did. That burning in my chest. That drive to just—to get it right. I saw their faces in my mind when I cooked and then when they ate and appreciated it, didn't just devour it before their eight o'clock curtain."

Patrick beamed and Evan rolled his eyes.

"Okay, Answer Man, how in the hell am I supposed to fix it, though? I'm sort of in a static situation."

"Can you get out of the kitchen? Talk to the tourists about what show they're going to see. Find out who your regulars are—why the guy who always sits at table seven on Thursday nights orders the rib-eye cremated."

"Because he has no taste—who kills a piece of meat like that?"

"That guy does," Patrick said. "Because that's how Ma used to cook steaks the one time a year they could afford them when he was growing up."

"Listen to you. You're the one who loves people."

"What's Mrs. Hamilton's eighth cat's name?"

"Fiona."

Patrick hummed, quite pleased with himself.

"Shut up. I could be making that up."

"But you're not."

"I'm not." Evan stopped and looked at Patrick, who was feeling a little cocky; he couldn't quite help it. "Add that I'm not cooking my own food anymore… "

"Well, it's yours, but—"

"Right. I created it, got the Beard, and he won't budge outside of a few seasonal sides and the rare chef's table."

"It's like the menu won, not you."

"Yes!" They got back to Millie's and Evan settled back against their rental car, taking Patrick's hands loosely in his own. "I need to create new food."

"You're too good not to."

"I have a mortgage now."

"And a reputation that could get you hired anywhere."

"You know anyone who needs an executive?"

Patrick didn't have an answer to that. He wasn't even sure the answers he was able to offer were good and right, but he did know that Evan's talents were being wasted cooking the same food day in and day out, even if they were his own recipes.

And it was this man's talents—his passion, his desire to do more, to be more, to grow more—that challenged Patrick's own concept of "good enough."

When is it good enough? How do you know?

After watching Evan fight and fuss and fume over these answers for himself, Patrick was beginning to see that maybe you never did know. That maybe you just kept pushing and striving for as long as you possibly could. That "good enough" was not the goal; the journey was.

He opened the door for Evan and offered as encouraging a smile as he could muster. He could see the wheels of Evan's mind turning as they buckled themselves into the car.

"Am I at least making any sense?" Patrick asked.

"You are. I'm not sure what to do about it, but maybe coming out of the kitchen now and then is a start. I'm not you, though. I can't be Mr. Personality."

"I'm not suggesting you be me. I'm just saying that if you know who you're cooking for, you might be less likely to lose track of why you're cooking at all."

"Right." Evan turned the key in the ignition and put the car in reverse, laughing when he forgot to hit the brakes before doing so and a quick roll-jerk-stop interrupted his thoughts. "I wonder if DiSante will even notice that I'm leaving the kitchen."

"What that old buzzard doesn't know won't hurt him."

Even during the memorial gathering, their stay in Illinois, had been dominated by a hush that seemed to blanket them, cushioning their steps. It was so different from their pace in New York that it took Patrick a few days to get used to it.

As they drove back to the hotel that evening, Evan was quiet; but he seemed to have a new energy buzzing just beneath the surface. His left leg bounced at every traffic light as if willing it to change now, now, now. He casually held Patrick's hand, draped over the middle console, but constantly stroked and squeezed it, rearranging the positions of their fingers, his arm.

Patrick wanted to speak but felt that the charged silence was something he shouldn't break, as if Evan's thoughts were taking the place of speech, filling the space between them with what was needed for the short journey across town.

They parked and got to the elevator without any conversation, Evan leading as they walked, kissing the top of Patrick's head as he pulled him close for the ride up to their floor. He led the way to their room, and as soon as the door clicked closed behind him, the quiet energy shifted.

He pressed Patrick to the hotel door, clasping their hands over Patrick's head and taking him in a fiery kiss. His eyes sparked with need and intent and he whispered Patrick's name like a prayer, slotting his thigh between Patrick's legs and almost lifted him as he crowded in closer. His lips trailed the lines of Patrick's jaw and the curve of his neck, where he paused long enough to lave and then suckle while his hips rolled and pressed, his cock hard against Patrick's hip.

And all Patrick could do was ride it out. He was pliable in Evan's hands, letting him speak his heart in action. He'd kiss and nip anywhere he could, but this was Evan's show and Patrick was happy to just go with it.

Evan let go of his hands to lift one of Patrick's legs around himself and grind again, their dicks, thick and demanding, almost aligning through the fabric of their pants. Patrick wanted to get at Evan, to feel the heat of him in his hands, but Evan grabbed Patrick's other thigh and held him up against the door with the force of his upward thrusts, hard and desperate, until it just wasn't enough. Patrick could only give in, his head against the steel door, his body a willing slave to Evan, whose breath was hot on his face, whose fingers dug into his thighs, whose voice when he finally spoke was wrecked and raspy and rattled deep in his chest.

"Hold onto me."

It was the easiest thing he'd ever had to do, holding onto Evan. He tightened his legs around Evan's waist, kissing him sloppily, wetly, as they stumbled to the bed, graceless and not caring.

Shoes tumbled to the floor and Patrick clamored to have Evan's lips back on his, to have his clothes off now, please now, to have Evan all over him, through him, around him. His hands were everywhere, picking at hems and buckles, and he laughed when, after all the fumbling, the damned clothes were still there, just skewed, giving peeks at and hints of the flesh he so desperately wanted under his fingers.

"*Fuck.*" It was just a roll of Evan's hips, but it hit just right; the friction on his cock sent jolts through his body and he could do no more than laugh and flop back helplessly as Evan took over, ripping his own shirt over his head and hiking Patrick's up so he could cover his abdomen with his mouth, with kisses and licks and suckles of flesh until Patrick wiggled out of his shirt.

The fabric hit the floor and Patrick took hold of Evan's face, stilling him for a moment, searching his face. His eyes were dark and desperate, his lips parted and red-wet.

So hot. So crazed. So completely *his*.

"What is it?"

"You. I love you. I want you. I—" Evan rolled his hips down again and they both groaned, lost in the pleasure of it, the hard, hard heat. "God, you just—"

He never finished. Patrick pulled him down for another heated kiss and wrapped his legs around Evan's hips as they moved together, letting the friction of the clothes between them add to the pleasure, to the anticipation. To the need.

Patrick tried to find purchase, to grab whatever it was Evan was chasing, to tune in, to focus. "Babe, shhh." He pulled Evan's face from the curve of his neck but their bodies never let up, grinding and lifting in heated friction like teenagers in the backseat of a car. "Come on… " Patrick scanned Evan's face and felt his breath, hot and heavy over his skin, his eyes, even hotter. "It's been a lot this week. Let me take care of you."

"You *always* take care of me."

He did. He was made for it, he was sure. "I love you," he said, as though that explained all.

"You love me." Evan smiled and dove back into the warmth of Patrick's neck, inching down to his clavicle, running his tongue along the valley of bone there. "You *love* me."

"I love you."

Evan continued his journey down Patrick's abdomen, speaking between kisses and suckles, presses of his hands over Patrick's skin, brushes of his thumbs over his nipples, watching his own motions as if discovering Patrick's body for the first time. "You *know* me."

Patrick arched into his touch, seeking the full weight of him again, relishing the steady rhythm of Evan's words, fingers and mouth, the hardness of his cock running along the line of his own again and again.

"I *love* you." He did. So deeply, so completely, as he'd never loved before. He wanted to do everything to make this man happy. And he fed off his passions like a babe at the breast. Nourished. Nurtured. Energized to do anything Evan desired.

Evan pulled up again, smiling down at him with a love in his eyes so deep Patrick had to blink it away—it was almost too intimate, even though it was all for him.

Dipping down for another swift kiss, Evan softly commanded, "Look at me," and unbuckled Patrick's pants as he pushed his hips into nothing with each button's release, their rhythm already so integrated he couldn't stop. "You *get* me." He kissed Patrick again as if lost in his own amazement, and curled his fingers into the waistband of Patrick's pants and underwear, tugging them down, catching the tip of Patrick's cock in his mouth as it sprung free.

"Evan... *fuck*."

Then it was scrambling and swishes of fabric and sheets, broken moments to grab for lube and a condom, *roll over, baby* and *yes, please*, Evan's hands warm and commanding on Patrick's back, his cock, slick with lube, rutting along the cleft of Patrick's ass and catching on his sensitive hole; and then, with slowed, deliberate motions, he entered him until Patrick was full, full of the passion that clung to Evan's body, to his skin, his hair, that still carried the scent of Millie's white sage and cedar incense, lovingly reignited after their pantry dinner.

Buried inside, Evan curled around Patrick, pressing kisses to his neck and shoulders, breath hot on his skin until Patrick couldn't take it and turned, kissing him crookedly, messily as Evan stilled his hips to a slow grind, in and in and in, closer, closer, closer still, making one body from two.

"Evan... "

"I love you." And he finally pulled out, his nails dragging down Patrick's side, gripping his hips, controlling their motion, push and drag, *I love you, I love you, so much, I love you,* and when Patrick lifted his head and saw their reflection in the mirror, Evan was staring between them, watching his cock retreat and then slowly disappear into the deep heat of Patrick, running his fingers down between them as if in awe.

Evan looked up and met Patrick's gaze in the glass, stopping as a slow smile spread across his face. "Hi, Beautiful."

Patrick chuckled deep in his chest and clenched around Evan, pressing back and getting lost again as Evan squeezed the fullness of his ass and pulled him closer in a slow drag until Patrick whimpered at the pleasure rolling through his body.

He wanted more, reached back to pull Evan's thighs in tighter, wanted Evan's lips all over him, the weight of his body, the whole of his cock plunging into him over and over, and Evan complied, harder and faster, bending to kiss the back of Patrick's neck and coming up again to find that sweetest of spots that made Patrick call out and dig his fingers into the pillows, pull them to himself so he could rest, surrender, let Evan give and give and take and take and all the while Patrick was filled with the love, the intensity, the *passion* of Evan.

Of them.

Patrick knew the moment Evan was about to come; he read him, knew him, his body and the sounds he made, the way his breath hitched, the pitch of his rising moans, his nails digging into Patrick's ass as, with one final groan, he cried out. Patrick worked his hips slowly, easing Evan through, meeting him in a crooked kiss as Evan collapsed over him and wrapped his arms around his waist until he caught his breath.

"Mmm, don't move. Don't... " Evan pulled out slowly and slipped his fingers down Patrick's crack and into his hole, kissing his shoulder blades, hooking his fingers slightly forward, a question in his moans. *Is that it? There? I love you.* His tongue laved around Patrick's hole and he cried out, too much, not enough.

Patrick arched and bent to direct him and then Evan landed with perfect, rhythmic pressure on his prostate, massaging persistently, *more, yes, there, more, more.* Evan kissed and nipped around the curve of Patrick's ass as his fingers worked his hole again and again with a steady pressure.

Without so much as a touch to his cock, Patrick's orgasm spread through his body, both languid and strong, as if it moved through his every inch, every cell, pulsing and easing and pulsing again and again, slow and steady and so fucking exquisite. With one final shudder, he fell to the bed, pulling Evan to him. He wanted to feel Evan all over him as he had felt him all *through* him.

"Fuck, Baby."

"Yeah." Evan smoothed his hair, his fingers tangling in the damp, unruly strands while Patrick fought to catch his breath. "You're incredible."

Patrick reached back again for a kiss, pressing his ass into Evan's hips and loving him there, soft and spent but still fitting just so. "You okay?"

"Yeah. Yeah, I'm sorry, I—"

"There's nothing to apologize for. You just sort of—I mean, I'm not complaining."

Evan wrapped his leg up and over Patrick, pulling him in closer. "I'm overwhelmed by you."

Patrick turned in Evan's arms, cupped his face in his hands and pressed a soft kiss to his lips, their legs tangling and pushing some unknown article of clothing onto the floor. "I don't understand how, but I'm glad."

"No one's ever—no one's ever loved me the way you do. You watch me. You *see* me."

"Then they've missed so much."

They rested there together, sharing soft kisses, slipping off to sleep for moments and startling awake only to sink under the covers and curl up closer together, flirting with starting another round but stopping to simply take each other in, to look and touch, closed off to all else.

Patrick closed his eyes as Evan's fingers combed through his hair. His touch was perfect on his scalp, a steady stroke to match his soft and comforting voice. "You said earlier that you got some clarity for yourself, too?"

Patrick's eyes fluttered open and he nodded, nestling into the crook of Evan's neck. He felt tucked away, warm. "I'm going to pocket it for now. This trip isn't about me."

"Okay." Evan tightened his arms around Patrick, soothing his back with his hand. "You'll share with me later, though?"

"Yes. Probably. I just—I need to process it a bit more." He unearthed himself from his temporary cocoon and kissed Evan's chin. "No worries, okay?"

Before Evan could answer, a phone vibrated somewhere on the floor. "Shit. Is that you?" he asked.

"No, that's you." Patrick snuggled in closer and grasped at Evan's hand to pin him down. "Don't answer it."

Evan didn't, nestling deeper into the mattress instead as Patrick began softly kissing his chest and running his fingers down the center of it. Evan flinched.

"Maybe we should wash up instead of tickling, huh?" Evan swatted at Patrick's traveling hand and laughed when he began a full assault: slow, unrelenting brushes along Evan's sides. "Patrick Sullivan, I take back everything I said."

"Oh, you do not." Evan's phone buzzed again and all motion stopped as they stared at the pile of fabric. "Go ahead. If they're calling twice."

"No." But after a few moments of silence, Evan swore and sat up. "I'm sorry." He bent over the bed to dig and Patrick smacked his bare ass. "Watch it... "

"I am."

"Unknown number. Fuck it." Evan tossed the phone aside and curled back around Patrick. "I need pizza."

"We're not going to find any worthwhile pizza here. Gonna have to wait until tomorrow—"

The hotel room phone rang and they froze in mid-breath. "Shit." Evan reached back to answer it and hit speaker before setting the receiver on the bedside table.

"Hello?"

"Hello, Mr. Stanford?"

"Yes, this is Evan."

"I'm sorry to bother you at your hotel. I was hoping I'd catch you before your flight back to New York."

"To whom am I speaking?"

"Oh, my apologies. I'm Jean McIntyre. Mildred Bishop's attorney."

VIII. Fromage

*A cheese board with selections of varying textures and
flavors accompanied by fruits, nuts and baguette.*

Evan walked into Johnny's and stopped cold, the door handle hitting him on the ass as the bell clanged behind him.

As he approached from the train station, he could have *sworn* he heard Elvis. But he'd also been up since six o'clock that morning, and just finished a particularly busy lunch rush and dinner prep, so his judgment might be in question.

Sure enough, Elvis was blasting through the diner, the waitresses bopping, patrons jiggling in their seats and of course, Patrick hip-checking Oscar and the dishwasher as they worked back in the kitchen.

The song ended, and Evan slipped into an empty booth while the restaurant settled back into its more typical routine. He dug into his satchel and pulled out two journals, startling when he heard a glass hit his table. He was greeted by Mimi's happy, sweaty smile as she slid into the booth across from him.

"Celebration or distraction?"

"Yes. Mr. Freeman dropped me a forty-dollar tip and two more burners went out on the six-eye."

"Ooh... "

"Yeah, it's been a day."

Evan took a healthy drink of water. He still felt sticky from the train. "So how much tip is necessary to get a private show around here?"

"From me? You can't afford it. From the boss? Seems to me you already know the answer to that one."

"Mmmm, that I do. Is he going to be able to get away?"

"Yeah, he's just giving Oscar some last-minute crap. You here for food or to steal him?"

"Both. Who made the chicken salad today?"

Mimi laughed. "Patrick did. I can't figure out what the fuck Oscar does to it, but people still buy it."

"Too much tarragon, not enough acid. Tastes like Twizzlers and mayo."

"It's not *that* bad."

Evan took a drink and raised his eyebrow over the rim of the glass and Mimi held up her hand in submission. "Okay, it's that bad. Challah, white, wheat or croissant?"

"Challah. Fruit too, if it's fresh?"

"You got it, Chef."

Evan cracked open the first journal he'd brought, a drugstore-bought blank book that probably hadn't been opened in fifteen years, if not longer. He smiled as he fanned through the filled pages, pausing to read the lists therein and blushing at the quality of some of the drawings that accompanied them. The book was full of his childhood doodles and dreams, and as he read they matured and changed along with his handwriting.

His food arrived by the time he got to his second journal, a binder filled with pages printed from a computer. The first page was in a pixelated Courier font. Subsequent pages progressed to higher-quality print-outs with swirly, overdone fonts finally to the last few pages that were more professional, complete with a makeshift logo and trademark.

He wiped a drop of mayonnaise from the corner of his mouth as Patrick slid into the bench across from him and squeezed his hand. "Sorry that took so long. Day from hell."

"Mimi said you lost two more burners?"

"Yeah. Fuckin' thing." Patrick shrugged and reached across the table for a kiss. "But, you know. When life hands you lemons... "

"You sing Elvis."

"I'm so glad you understand." Patrick's smile was as bright and contented as it would be had it been an ordinary day with happy patrons, good tips, a functioning kitchen and maybe even an offer to buy his cheesecakes wholesale.

"So, what are you going to do?"

"I'm going to go home with the hot guy at table eight, get naked and forget it all. That is, if he's interested... "

"Hmmm. He'll get back to you on that." Evan slid the half-eaten bowl of fruit across the table. "Get some vitamins. You've had a bad day."

Patrick sucked a piece of melon into his mouth and pointed to the journals. "Those from that box at Millie's?"

"Yeah." He cracked the first one open again and Patrick grinned at the childish attempt at a title page.

My Life List
by Evan Stanford
Second Grade, Mrs. Collier

"You did these for school?"

Evan shook his head, wondering at himself. "No. I started this with Mom as something to do in the summers. I think it was so ingrained in me to write that woman's name on every piece of paper pushed in front of me... " He paused, remembering Mrs. Collier's face. "I don't remember liking her too much. She never smiled."

"So these are like... bucket lists?"

"Yeah, Mom went to some conference and they were doing them. Maybe that's where the idea for the movie came from."

"So what does a second-grader put on his life list?"

"Well, that's what I'm finding interesting. I mean, it's fluid, obviously." He flipped the page to his first-ever life list. "I crossed out what I actually did—'Get a B or better for spelling before Christmas'—and scribbled out the stuff that I decided I wasn't going to do."

Patrick reached toward the book and pulled back. "Can—can I?"

"Yeah. It's just little boy wishes."

"Those are the best ones." Patrick swung the book around to read. "I wish I had something like this. It's a little like a diary."

"You never journaled, or... "

"Nah. My family wasn't much for dreaming. You just did what was expected."

"Hunh. I spent most of my childhood daydreaming." Evan got up and moved to Patrick's side of the booth. "I'm still trying to read some of the scribbled ones. I went to town with that damned marker."

See the Atlantic Ocean
Bake one batch of Christmas cookies by myself
Own a pug
Meet the Queen of England

They squinted and corrected, piecing the words together and back into boyhood dreams that didn't quite happen.

Pointing to the line about the pug, Patrick noted, "And you've done some of these anyway, even though they're scribbled out."

"Yeah, some things made a reappearance over the years. That's sort of what I'm looking for." Evan flipped through a few more pages. "After that first summer, I showed my list to Millie. It became our thing instead and she just kept the lists at her place. I'd make a new list and we'd go back and update the old ones."

"So why are some of the scribbled-out items circled?"

"Those are things she thought I should reconsider."

Evan stopped on his fifth grade list. It included the long-lost dream of finding Millie a boyfriend. "Needless to say, she was not interested in a boyfriend, because that one remained scribbled."

"So much for your matchmaking days."

"Mmm, I never was very good at it." He slowly skimmed through a few more pages and set that book aside, opening the notebook with printed-out pages.

Sip espresso at a café in Venice
Graduate with over a 4.3 GPA
Run for Student Council President
Conquer soufflé

"You went to Venice in high school?"

"No. Not until much later, but I remembered it and crossed it out."

He fanned through a few more pages and finally found what he was looking for. "Here it is." Evan pointed to the page. On a list made in his mid-twenties, in a bold typeface that had been scribbled out, circled, scribbled out again in another color and circled again with a very emphatic, "Evan Stanford, do not close this door," Patrick read:

Open my own restaurant—intimate, casual—my food.

"You closed the door anyway."

"I never had a door to open." Evan stared at the words peeking through the scribbles, remembering the day he'd first typed them. He was working at a trendy bar and grill in Greenwich. The executive chef was a horse's ass, the sous was incompetent and he was a simple line cook, most often filling the role of *garde manger,* responsible for the cold food service. He saw it as a steppingstone; it was nowhere near a goal he was shooting for.

He had graduated from CIA about a year earlier, and the lovely chef who had paid his way had since closed the doors of his restaurant, unable to keep up with the tanking economy and the demands of an ailing wife.

Evan was miserable. His creative juices had all but dried up; his love of being in a professional kitchen dangled by a very tenuous thread, and all he had left was his dream to simply do it himself.

So he and Millie plotted. And planned. And he hooked her up with email and a cheap phone so they could communicate with links and texts, ideas and proposals.

Evan: *How about a confit of chicken wings? Fried in duck fat? Still working on sauce ideas.*

Millie: *Skip the bar food BBQ—how about a fish sauce vinaigrette?*

Evan: *And mint.*

Millie: *Book my flight. I'm packing my bags.*

And then he got another job and his love for the work was back. But even still, there was always the burning, niggling feeling that there ought to be more, more, more, and his life lists proved it even when the goals were harder to define.

On the page made two years before his hire at Il Boschetto, he found this:

Advance to sous

Build your reputation—take risks—be sought after

Make them come to you.

Later, once sous was achieved:

Chef de Cuisine, dammit

And of course, the last item on that list:

James Beard?

After the question mark was Millie's distinct script. *Take that question mark off, mister.* Later, on his last visit with her, he responded by crossing it off his list and adding exclamation points instead.

He was sought after—check. He had a good reputation—check. He had his Beard Award—check. He was Executive Chef—check.

He'd made it.

The updating of the life lists stopped.

They hadn't stopped because he'd made it. But because he'd made it, his life changed exponentially. His routine of keeping up with Millie disappeared into a demanding schedule unlike any he'd ever known. His communications with her dwindled along with her health, and they only spoke on birthdays and Christmas, skirting anything important because her aging mind struggled to keep up. By then, he only wanted to hear her voice.

"Have you found yourself a man yet, Evy?"

"Millie, I was lucky to find my socks this morning."

"Now you're starting to sound like me."

Every dream Evan dared to dream before that final entry— before that last exclamation point had been added and the high-five had been shared—had been left to the pulp of the pages in front of him. Every dish he concocted with Millie, every testing of flavor they discussed, every creative notion Millie had nursed along was left behind to succumb to DiSante's demands for a static menu and the dust and occasional mildew of Millie's art room closet.

But Millie never forgot.

Evan retrieved an envelope from his satchel and pulled out the letter within, reading it for at least the tenth time since his visit to Millie's attorney's office.

For our restaurant. Your restaurant.

Never close the door to the house where you belong.

The trust was huge—more than he ever imagined Millie would have had. And while its beneficiary was decided in her later years, judging by the sheer enormity of it, it was obviously something she had set up when he was a child or even earlier. Ms. McIntyre told him there would be more, once Millie's estate was settled.

Evan rested in the crook of Patrick's arm and sighed, looking at the life list again.

Open my own restaurant—intimate, casual—my food.

Patrick rubbed his arm and let him rest there. These moments were quite frequent since their return from Quincy. "You know, I think Millie missed one thing, though."

"What's that?"

Patrick flipped back to a page from high school. Evan's makeshift logo decorated the almost professional-looking list. Patrick scanned the list and finally pointed to one particular scribbled-out item. "She should have circled this one."

"Arrive at school in a hot air balloon." Evan kicked Patrick under the table with his work clogs.

"Seriously—opening day? A big-assed rainbow balloon floating over the East River... "

"Figure out a way for Millie to arrive in it and I'll consider it."

▶•◀

"Did you get—"

"Pumpkin spice, of course." Patrick lifted his scone. "And a matching pumpkin scone, too."

Evan dropped his belongings and sank into the chair across from him. He picked up the spicy, hot latte and dared a sip as steam billowed around his face. "I don't care if it's only September, it's fall."

"Well, since we eat only the most seasonal of foods—"

"Every meal."

"Then, it is most definitely fall." Patrick broke off a piece of scone, popped it into his mouth and licked the glaze off of his fingers. "How'd the meeting with the financial advisor go?"

Evan pulled a tablet out of his satchel and booted it up. "Well, as suspected, she said I only have about half of what I need. And, for total comfort, I have about a third. I'm sure I could get a loan, but—outside of my condo, I've never really been in debt."

In his own private world of worry, focused on nothing else, Evan kept rambling. He pulled a folder of papers out of his satchel as he talked.

"I mean, this is exactly what I've been afraid of. Here's this pot—this huge pot of money to get started—and it's just enough to make the biggest mistake of my life. The risk is huge and I still don't feel like it's my money—" Evan stopped and looked at Patrick, probably for the first time since he walked into the coffee shop, and offered a weak smile. "It's simply not enough. Not now. I'll need an investor, or a partner, or—"

Patrick took a breath to speak, but Evan was back at it, fanning through the apps on his tablet with abandon.

"Ah, here it is. This is a breakdown of the expenses I'll need to plan for and a cushion to have at the ready, and all I can do is bring up lists in my head of people I've worked with. Previous owners. And then I get heartburn because I can't think of one of them that I'd want to work with in that capacity."

Still scanning through the spreadsheet, Evan took a sip of his latte.

"I'm just repeating myself; it's what I've been saying for weeks and I'm just—"

"For months, actually."

"For months. Yes." Evan sighed and continued prattling. "I'm afraid I'm going to have to just invest this for now and wait. It's not enough. It's not going to work." He flipped through his papers, looking for something specific, and gave up, his attention back on his tablet. "But I'm not getting any younger, and you know chefs have a very short life when it comes to full-time line work."

"Evan…"

"My knees already sound like they're going to explode out of my body every time I squat down to the lowboys, and you know my back is a fucking joke when it rains, and my right shoulder—"

He stopped when he felt Patrick's hand on his arm. There was a look he couldn't quite identify in his eyes, almost pleading, and it seemed to spread through every inch of his body. With a smile, Evan recognized it.

Don't look at the menu. Look at me.

And so he obeyed the now-wordless command. His life had already changed immeasurably since that moment, if not because of it. He stopped talking. He stopped calculating. He even turned off his tablet.

"Patrick?"

"Do you remember when we started seeing each other and Rosey told me your story? About how you saved him? And you said you were so happy you didn't have to save me from anything?"

"Vaguely…"

"And I said—"

Evan lit up with the memory. "You said I shouldn't be so sure about that. And I left it there because—because it didn't feel like the right time to pursue it."

"It wasn't. And I'm not sure it is now, but—"

"Patrick?"

Patrick fed Evan the final bite of scone they'd been picking at and smiled, running his finger down the line of Evan's jaw.

"I'm so very grateful for you. For the way you've been so open and vulnerable with me. I know—I'm guessing that's not easy for you."

"Not until you."

"I'm honored."

Evan let Patrick take his hands in his and trace the outline of his fingers and his knuckles, apparently still collecting his thoughts. It was about to drive Evan mad, but he trusted this man. He'd wait.

"When you're angry—that was the first time you let me in that way. When you're angry, you're crisp. Quick. Your words snap and your movements pop. Like this self-contained, crackling fire—alive."

"I'm not always self-contained. I've hurt you. I hurt—"

Patrick shook his head and rubbed Evan's hand. "And when you're sad, you pull in and shut down. It's almost like I can hear the soundtrack to you—you do have one, you know. It just falls in decibels, in pitch."

"Until you hold me—"

Patrick smiled and Evan's heart raced, waiting. Waiting for all Patrick had to say. "Then the music rises again, yes. And when you're afraid—that's when it all just falls apart in the most beautiful way. You bite and you snap. You close off to everything around you and I have to really make an effort to get your attention."

"Tunnel vision—I used to drive my mom crazy with it."

"You learned it from her."

Evan smiled, thinking about his mother and the moments when she became this whirlwind of words and gestures and emotions. His dad had simply to put a hand on her shoulder, grasp her face in his hands and firmly speak her name and she'd focus, take a breath and listen. He loved this about her, as exasperating as it occasionally was. "I did, didn't I?"

"And you make these grand gestures to try to erase your fear, and when those fall apart, you run and struggle and run and you hide sometimes, but inside you're always always always fighting it—"

"You know I've been afraid this whole time?"

"Not this whole time? But I think—I think you've been afraid since before I met you, yes."

Evan put his tablet away to gather this thoughts, more tangled than the numbers he'd been battling all day. "Patrick?"

"Yes?"

"I love you."

Patrick's smile spread across his face slowly, his eyes crinkling, his lips curling skyward. "I love you. So much."

"Are you ever afraid?"

"That's what I want to talk to you about." Patrick nodded at the door. "Let's walk and talk."

They cleaned up their trash and headed outside, beginning the walk back to Evan's home, hand in hand, silent until Patrick took a deep breath to begin. "My dad always taught me that when you have negative emotions, you should act the opposite until you feel the way you're acting."

"Sometimes that's what we have to do."

"Yeah, except this was always. Angry? Act at peace. Sad, put on a happy face. And afraid? Forget about it. Your fear is telling you that you shouldn't be doing it."

"That's kind of sa—" Evan stopped himself, realizing almost too late how rude it was. "Is this why I've never met your parents?"

"What?" Patrick tugged at Evan's hand to wait for the yellow light instead of making a run for it. "No. Not at all. My parents are... well, they're not much to speak of—" At Evan's judgmental look, he cut himself off and tried again. "Close your eyes."

"We're going to be crossing the street."

"We'll stay until I'm done. Close your damned eyes."

"Is this where you find me challenging or intoxicating?"

"A royal pain in my backside. Your eyes still aren't closed."

Evan closed his eyes.

"Picture this."

"I had to close my eyes for—"

Patrick's lips were on Evan's before he could finish his sarcastic comment. He brushed them over Evan's again as he spoke. "Keep them closed."

"Sorry."

"So, there she is. This stunning, *gorgeous* Brooklyn girl. Fancies an Irish Catholic schlub. Good guy. Sweet story. But now they're in their late sixties. Their favorite decade—the one in which they were born—is the 1950's. They still live there in their minds."

"Mmmm... I'm seeing a lot of rooster wallpaper."

Patrick laughed and tugged at Evan's hand to cross the street. "There was rooster wallpaper at one time, oh my God. So—"

Evan tripped over his feet and Patrick laughed again. "Open your eyes. You are impossible."

"I've been trying to tell you."

Evan kissed him quickly on the temple, just in case he really was being impossible, and sighed happily as soon as Patrick started up again. "Mom and Dad. Lovely people. Truly. Caring. Devoted. Frugal—to a fault. Hard-working. All the positive adjectives you can conjure up. They even did their best at being okay with a gay son."

"We're so lucky, you know."

"We are. So, I know this sounds awful. There's just—not much to meet? You will. Soon, if you want."

"I want."

"Okay. I'll have her make her famous turkey loaf." Patrick glanced up to Evan laughing softly as Evan grimaced. "Because watching you be gracious as you swallow that gelatinous crap will be worth everything."

"I'll only do it because I love you." They walked in silence for a bit, but Evan felt as if he'd lost the point somewhere along the way. "So, your parents... lead sort of a bland life? I mean, you met my folks. It's not Hollywood glamour out there."

"I'm afraid I'm becoming them. Not taking risks. Keeping my emotions so close to the collar that I just stand still. And I see you—" Patrick stopped walking and pointed in the general direction of his parents' home. "They have a good life, they do. A good enough one, you know? Nothing to be ashamed of. But... that's just it. It's good *enough*. And I need you to save me—from that."

"From good enough?"

"Don't get me wrong. Good enough has been good. It's been great, actually. And with you beside me it's—it's pretty fucking amazing, good enough. I get to make people happy every day. Every fucking day."

"Gentlemen—gorgeous day, innit?"

Hearing Roger's gravelly voice, Evan startled. He had been lost in their conversation and was unaware of where their walk had even taken them. He smiled and squeezed Patrick's hand, a silent message that he wasn't going to let this conversation drop. "Roger! We haven't seen you in a few weeks."

"Ehh, I've been sick, you know?" He sniffed for liquid effect and pointed to his window boxes. "The impatiens are getting a little spindly."

"Yeah, they do that." Evan walked over to them and brushed through some dead leaves to clean up the display. "You want me to get you some mums?"

"Naw, you don't have to. Not why I was telling you."

"I'll get you some mums. Next day off, okay?" He shared a glance with Patrick—Roger's color was a bit peaked. "You feeling better now?"

Roger pulled out a grayed handkerchief, blew his nose and shoved the wad into his back pocket. "Yeah, a little. Just a cold. I, uh." He looked back at his boxes. "My mother always used to have purple mums in the fall. Said she got tired of orange everywhere."

"Purple mums it is. You rest up now."

"Thank you, boys. Have a good evening."

They walked in silence, Patrick resting his head on Evan's shoulder as their hands slid together again. "Maybe I should stop complaining."

"I'm not hearing you complain, Patrick."

"I am lucky, you know? I could have been sitting at a desk at my dad's office pushing papers or, hell, like most of the guys from school, punching a clock at the navy yard or riding on the back of a garbage truck."

"But you didn't—you pushed beyond it."

"No, I got lucky. I fell into this like a klutz into a mud puddle. I mean, I have a great job with a great staff in a great community. I have a beautiful home and now—" He looked up at Evan and stopped walking. Then he stepped in front of Evan and cupped his face in his hands for a tender kiss. "Now I have this magnificent man who loves me."

"Very much."

"So, you know, *good enough* is damned fine. If nothing changes, if I died today, I'd die a very happy man."

"Maybe I'm being obtuse, but I'm not sure how I fit—"

"I've been watching you fighting with yourself all this time. Reaching and stretching and peeking over the top of what your life is—which is a damned good life, too."

"Maybe I should be satisfied."

"No! That's my point. You've been sticking with this job you've come to hate because you are afraid to move. It was the pinnacle. The final item on your life list. Closed the book and you were done."

Evan took a breath to correct him, but Patrick kept plowing forward. "And come to find out, even with that, it wasn't enough. *And* you knew that if you fought DiSante, you'd get canned and never reach it again. You'd end up—"

"I'd end up like Perci..."

"And now you've got this opportunity right in front of you, and you've been sitting on it and fretting over it for months, and now I hear you making excuses and maybe even giving up on it because it's fucking frightening. And you're scared of standing still, but moving forward is—"

"I'm not making excuses. I'm just trying to be reasonable."

Patrick pulled his hand away and dug into his back pocket. "I don't want to settle anymore. I've been acting like I'm satisfied to the point where I believed it, and the truth is, I'm not." He shoved a piece of paper into Evan's hand. "Oona hadn't bought a dress for herself since 1992."

"What?" Evan unfolded the paper and looked at it. And looked at Patrick and at the paper—a bank statement—again. "Patrick, this is more than Millie gave me. How the hell did she have this much money?"

"We think her father was rich, because as much as she stashed under her bed—and you don't want to know how much cash was there—there is no way she could have saved that much in her lifetime."

"Maybe she was a secret drug lord. Potato-based narcotics." Evan stared at the statement in shock. It wasn't so much that Patrick had been sitting on this huge nest egg, but that, if he understood properly, he was offering it. Offering himself. Offering everything.

Everything.

"And she gave it all to you?"

"Every penny. We talked, too. Like you and Millie. About a real Irish place. You know most of them in the city are—"

"Mostly bad. Yeah."

"And I could have used it for school, but that never felt right for me. Going back didn't, studying something else didn't."

"Why didn't you—Patrick?"

"I've been terrified, Evan. Terrified I'd become them by doing nothing and terrified of complete failure if I risked it all. So I followed Dad's advice and appreciated the life I have and didn't complain."

"And it's been good enough."

"Until you came and upended everything, yeah."

"Sorry?"

"No. Watching you, feeling you come alive when we went to Quincy—you've inspired me to stop settling. And this feels like—"

"You want to leave the diner?"

"I want to leave the diner."

Evan knew better than to pull out the "but you said..." comment. This had been a journey for both of them. You don't know all the answers while you're in the process, or even where you're going, but now Patrick was standing before him with the map. As if it were as simple as a diner menu.

"I love you."

"I—I love you, too." They arrived at Evan's building and Patrick pulled him to the wall, as he slid his hand up and down Evan's arm, an anchor between them. "I'm grateful for what Johnny did for me, but you're right. I don't owe him the rest of my life. I can be more than that place, partially because of him.

And I can help you be more than Il Boschetto. We can be more together."

Evan couldn't speak. He couldn't think. Only an hour before he was ready to hang this one up for a good long time, figuring he'd invest in a place, give it a name and a personality and hand it off to some young chef to either make it explode or run it into the ground, potential peril be damned.

"I know I'm not the quality of cook you're used to working with, but—"

"Shut *up*, I'd hire you in a minute and you know that."

"And I know you said that it was a benefit that I wasn't on staff with you—you had a safe place to talk—"

"This is different. This is—"

"I just want to see you do this. See us do this. I think we could be a good team." Patrick smiled, devilish and a little shy. "Although maybe we shouldn't put risotto on the menu."

Evan took Patrick's hand and pulled him inside, to the elevator and up to the twenty-ninth floor without a word or a kiss or a nod to all of the things running through his head. He swiped his key card and opened the door, kicking it closed as he pulled Patrick into his arms, taking him in a hungry kiss, his fingers sinking into Patrick's thick hair, pressing his body to him and longing for a way to say *I love you* as he'd never said it before.

When they broke free, foreheads pressed together to catch their breath, Patrick's eyes fluttering closed as Evan softly kissed his temples, Evan spoke the one remaining, resounding fear. "This could kill us."

"No." Evan started to argue and Patrick put a finger between them, taking a step back. "No. We're the priority. Never the business. If it goes down, we'll have each other."

"What if we go down?"

"That's not an option. If we do this, we have to agree that that will never be an option."

Evan stared at him, wanting more than anything to buy into it, but the risk—the financial gamble, the risk to their careers and, most importantly, to them—was almost unbearable to comprehend.

As if he could read Evan's mind, Patrick pressed on. "There's another thing with my family. They love. But"—Patrick took Evan's left hand and kissed his fingers, planting an extra, final kiss on his ring finger—"not like this. Not like us. It was convenient. They fell into it like a klutz into a mud puddle."

"You're a muddy crew."

"They fell into it and they just stayed. Because it was easier than dating and finding someone better. *Eh, he'll do*. Oona and Daideo, Ma and Dad. They had the forever part... "

"Just not the love."

"Right. It wasn't a conscious choice. And I'm standing here, with a fuck-ton of money in my back pocket... *choosing* you. And me."

"And a business."

"But mostly us. Because if this fails—if we're talking about making the biggest mistake of our lives and we have to settle back where we started, it's not going to be tolerable without you. Even *good enough* doesn't work without you."

"Patrick."

"I love you."

"You're crazy."

Patrick finally smiled, then, as if he'd won the jackpot and not just given it away. "They say most geniuses are."

▶•◀

Evan exited the Clark Street station with a smile. The boxed dinner in his hand was still warm, and the breeze was crisp and cool, the start to what he hoped would be a beautiful fall. Color tinged the edges of the leaves on the trees, and on the days or evenings he and Patrick could take a walk, they returned with noses nipped rosy with cold.

After a quick stop in a local pet shop for new socks for Dini, hearing Patrick's complaints about them already—*They have jack-o'-lanterns on them, Evan*—he made his way down the familiar road to see if Roger might be out.

And hungry.

And he was both.

"Ehh, you didn't bring me dinner again, did you?"

"I did. We had extra pulled pork tonight." The truth was, Evan had been making a concerted effort to get out of the kitchen at least three or four times a week, and based on what he'd learned about this particular dish, he changed his braising beer and tweaked the seasonings on the spiced apple sides. Now it was so popular, they were running out before the end of each night's service.

But, since he worked the lunch shift, he was able to plate up one good helping for Roger before dinner began.

Roger's eyes popped open wider when Evan lifted the lid to show him the goodies. "Ooh! Come look. I want you to see how your mums are doing."

As the weather cooled, Patrick and Evan worried that they'd see less and less of Roger. He seemed to remain perpetually one sneeze away from a sinus infection and one jacket shy of comfort. But he ate with gusto, always gracious, humble, kind.

"I ain't keepin' ya' from dinner with your sweetie or nothin', am I?"

"No, no. He's working late tonight." Evan picked through the mums, deadheading a few and making a mental note to bring a little more mulch to protect them from the cold. "How do you like the pork? I changed the recipe a bit last week and it seems to be taking off."

"It's delicious. I like the apples. Real fancy."

Evan rested back against the brick banister and looked around the neighborhood as Roger finished. It was quaint, quiet, somehow removed from the busyness of downtown Brooklyn, with beautifully painted row houses and brownstones tucked under overpasses and around paths to the Brooklyn Bridge. A business here and there, a rare restaurant, a small company's office all dotted the residential neighborhood. It felt like a hidden gem of old-school New York City living.

"So, I'm glad you stayed tonight, Chef. I, ehh... I want to show you something, if you have the time."

"I have the time." Evan took Roger's box and walked it to the trash can alongside the house. When he lifted the lid, a putrid, worse-than-rotting smell wafted up in his face. Evan choked, tossing the container in just in time to slam the lid closed. "Shit. Smells like something died in there."

"Yeah, yeah. I, ehh... you never know, you know?"

When Evan looked up, he found Roger digging deep into his baggy pants pocket for something. He heard coins, coins and more coins, and finally, with a yellow-toothed, snot-nosed grin, Roger pulled out a set of keys. "Now, your boy's a cook too, huh?"

"He is. At Johnny's down the way. He makes those cheesecakes we bring you."

"Yes, yes. I remember now. Well, I thought I overheard you two talking... "

Roger jiggled a key into the lock on the front door to the house where he always watered the flower boxes, whether the flowers were dead or alive. The house where the elusive "they" had convinced him to take care of the place while "they" were gone. "I think maybe they ain't coming back."

Evan could finally ask the question he and Patrick had always wanted to ask, but never believed they had a right to know, a right to intrude. "Do you live here, Roger?"

"Third floor walk-up. They let me stay rent-free, but... "After the first key didn't work, Roger cursed and tried the second one, giggling when it popped the door free. "I always go in back where the stairs are."

He stepped one foot inside and back out. "You, ehh... you have a handkerchief or something?"

"I do?"

"Might want to have it handy. It's... " He looked inside again and sighed, pulling his own grayed hankie of his pocket. "Have it handy."

Evan reached into his back pocket for his handkerchief and followed Roger inside the building.

And immediately slammed the cloth up to his face.

"Fuck! Roger! What the *hell*." Evan stood just inside the door while Roger opened blinds to let the remainder of the day's light into the room. As he did, Evan dared to lower his handkerchief and look around. "This was a restaurant?"

"Yeah, a café. I should have brought you in earlier in the day. They killed the power not long after everyone disappeared."

"Do you have power upstairs?"

"Sometimes. I still have water, though."

"*Roger...*" Evan took a few steps inside and glanced down at the dust-heavy glass case filled with candy bars and packages of gum, where the cash register sat. "How long has this been empty?"

"Coming up on a year now."

The front of the house was small. Evan did a quick count and estimated seating for about fifty. A crowded fifty—too crowded for a pleasurable dining experience. A bar of sorts stood in the back corner, but held no alcohol. There were plates and bowls set up at varying heights as though for a buffet.

"Sunday brunch?"

"Yeah, they never showed up to open. Ehh... knocked on my door in the middle of the night, told me to hold down the fort and I never saw 'em again." Evan walked further into the restaurant, covering his face with the handkerchief again as they got closer to the kitchen.

He turned to face the front of the room, and from this vantage point his breath caught.

The setting sun shone through the opened blinds and painted golden stripes across the tables and chairs, playing with flecks of dust dancing in its rays. He could easily imagine patrons talking quietly, sharing bites of each other's meals, laughing uproariously at their dining companions' ridiculous stories.

The room was light and airy, if not a little twee, but with just a few cosmetic changes, the removal of some tables, a more rustic theme, better art lining the walls—

"You want to see the kitchen? It's, ehh... small, but efficient. At least, that's what they always told me."

Evan turned to follow Roger and a flit of movement on the floor along the wall drew his attention away. He jumped and then laughed at himself; of course there would be rats. Among other things.

"Yeah, let's dive in."

It was clearly a "fuck it and leave" situation—the bank had obviously shown up right after close, leaving every end-of-day task stuck in a time-freeze, as if the owners didn't really believe someone would come and take their business, their livelihood, their dream.

But they did. And they did it swiftly.

Even as Evan clicked on his phone's flashlight and walked through, ducking cobwebs and eyeing the back door in case he needed a quick getaway to be ill from the stench, he could see it.

Through the all-encompassing, putrid odors from decaying meat and dairy in the shut-down refrigeration, through the stacks of grease-stuck pots and pans, food-encrusted knives and cutting boards, through the dry storage walk-in filled with fruit flies and various critters feeding on dried and rotted produce, through the shelves moving with scurrying cockroaches and floors sticky from rat excrement, Evan saw a well-equipped, amazingly functional kitchen.

It would fit two, maybe three cooks at a time, with no room or need for an expeditor—two to three worker bees making food dish by dish, order by order. After making a quick exit out back to catch some fresh air, Evan came back in and viewed the kitchen at a new angle.

"Did anyone consider knocking a hole there for a pass-through to the dining room? It'd really open things up in here."

"I—I don't know, Chef. I was just the night porter. When the bank came, it was my night off."

Evan nodded, lost in his thoughts and focused on not vomiting. He made it worse for himself every time he opened a lowboy only to find more rotted, dripping meats, or dared himself to poke at deflated produce stored in the reach-ins only to find a liquefied, bug-infested soup of rancidness.

"I think I've seen enough. I need fresh air."

"Sure, sure, Chef." Roger hurried over to the steel back door and opened it while Evan stumbled out of the fetid air of the kitchen, his gag reflex threatening to take over. "You okay?"

Evan bent over, choking and gasping, taking in as much air as he could, breathing deeply to regain some sense of equilibrium. "Yeah, yeah. That's just…" He clicked the flashlight off on his phone and grimaced at the low battery. "You live upstairs from that?"

"I—I do. It's not so bad if I keep blankets up against the door."

"Roger. You realize this is why you're sick all the time, right? All that rotting food—you're breathing that shit into your lungs."

"Do you like the space? I heard you and your boy talking about a smoked brisket poutine that made my mouth water, and someone needs to make this right."

"You're ignoring me."

"You're ignoring *me*." Roger blew his nose and pocketed his handkerchief. "Besides, I think I'm getting better."

"Who owns it now?"

"Citizens Bank sends a lot of mail."

Evan nodded, looked up at the street address and typed it into his phone. "I want to take you to my doctor."

"I'm fine, Chef."

Evan shoved his phone back into his pocket and buttoned his jacket, narrowing his gaze at Roger as if speaking to an insolent child. "You want to keep living like this? Want to go through another winter without heat?"

"No. No, Chef."

"I'll make an appointment for you this week. That's my first step in making this right, you understand?"

"Yes, Chef."

Evan reached his hand out for a shake, startling Roger into a nervous fit of giggles. "Thank you. I don't know what, yet, but something is going to change here, okay?"

"Okay. Thanks for dinner, Chef."

"Evan. For now, anyway, you can call me Evan." His words held a promise he didn't know he could keep, but the simple utterance of it made him want to make it so.

This place was perfect.

▶•◀

"Wait, wait, wait, wait. There is a *method* for this now." Patrick slathered thick butter on a slice of brown bread and handed it to Evan. With a pointed look, he lowered Evan's other hand—the one that was full of oyster. "This requires patience."

"There are oysters in front of me. Patience is an impossibility."

"Trust me." Patrick squeezed a bit of lemon juice onto Evan's oyster, gently shoving a nosey Dini out of the way. "Ready?"

"Patrick. I'm tipsy and I'm hungry and I still smell like decaying poultry."

"You smell like opportunity and promise. Now, throw back the oyster and then take a bite of the bread. You want them pretty simultaneously."

"Opportunity and—you are so full of shit." Evan looked at the oyster jiggling in its shell, and then the bread. "I'm impressed you can say *simultaneously* in light of how much you've had to drink already."

"I thought you were impatient." Patrick lifted Evan's oyster to his mouth. "Eat."

He sucked the oyster into his mouth, eyes closed as the salinity hit his palate. When he felt Patrick press the slice of bread to his lips, he giggled and opened his eyes to slowly chew, the flesh of the oyster resisting just a bit before his teeth sank into it and released the sweet body of flavor.

"Wash it down." Evan took the offered pint and drank, the heat of Patrick's gaze warming him as he swallowed.

"Oh. God." With another quick swallow, he smiled and lifted a shell for Patrick. "Eat. I feel like I'm tonight's show."

"You're gorgeous."

"You're intoxicated."

"You're still gorgeous." And with practiced ease, Patrick squeezed lemon onto the oyster Evan held for him, slurped it in, took a bite of their shared slice of bread and moaned when the combination of flavors and textures filled his mouth. He washed it all down with a slug of stout and smiled broadly, pressing in for a salty, buttery, bitter kiss.

And then he pulled back with a grimace.

"You still smell like decaying poultry."

"Thank you. You smell like bleach from trying to rescue the half-washed glassware." Evan took another oyster and prepared it for eating anyway. Stench or no, nothing was stopping him from this glorious food experience.

"Bleach beats decaying protein."

"Oysters and Guinness beat *everything*."

Evan had kept the news about the potential restaurant to himself for a few days, letting the emotions that had gripped him later that evening work their way through him: utter sadness at Roger's situation, heartbreak at the loss the previous owners had endured and paralyzing fear that, regardless of what he and Patrick decided to do about that specific property, the same thing could very well happen to them.

But the potential there, the promise that hid beneath the grime and the stench and the bugs and the rotten food, had kept him awake and distracted him so much so that, in the middle of an argument with Patrick over the benefits of Dansko brand chef's shoes versus Dickies brand, of all things, he'd blurted out that he'd found the place.

The place.

"Were you planning on filling me in or just hoping I'd show up on time to my first shift?"

"I'd still sort of appreciate it if you'd show up on time."

"So, the house you've been decorating for two seasons now…"

"Yeah. But—"

Instead of explaining the "but," Evan showed him. And after they said goodbye to Roger and reminded him of his doctor's appointment the next day, they headed back to Evan's, where a feast of oysters, brown bread and Guinness awaited them.

Except they started with the Guinness and still smelled like sewer rats. Even Dini couldn't stand it, having walked away in disgust and buried her face in her blankets.

"So, I've been thinking about what we'd call the place."

"We don't even have a place, Patrick."

"Regardless, we will." Patrick sucked the final oyster back after offering it to Evan, who only held his gut in reply. "And I know your affection for lists."

Evan rolled his eyes, more at himself than at Patrick's honesty. "I started lame—Evan's Eatery."

"Oooh, alliteration!" Patrick stole the piece of bread about to disappear into Evan's mouth and talked around it, sloppy, rude and adorable. "Patrick's Pastries."

"We're doing a bakery now?"

"I'm officially drunk. It's the best I can do."

Evan scooped his finger into the final shell and lapped up the last morsel of briny goodness. "We could go with a portmanteau—like… Stanivans."

Patrick curled his lip in distaste and then smiled that goofy smile that Evan knew to buckle up for, because whatever came next was going to be ridiculous. "The Running Duck."

"What?"

"You know, like how you said you felt at your first gig. So close to the water and yet not quite where you belonged." He shrugged, as if it were the simplest concept. "Like we've both been, our whole careers."

Evan lowered his glass after draining the last of his stout and looked at Patrick, his mouth slightly agape in surprise. "Patrick, that's genius!"

"People call me that a lot."

"What? A genius?"

"No. Patrick."

Evan stared at Patrick, sitting there with the most drunkenly absurd expression on his face. "Did you just... did you just quote Spongebob at me?"

"You helped."

"I'm going into business with a five-year-old."

"Hey now. You knew the reference. Don't act all high and mighty here."

"I think the proper word you've used for me before is *haughty*." Evan leaned over for a kiss. "It really is genius. How long have you been sitting on the name?"

"Since this morning. In the shower."

"You had your fingers up my ass this morning in the shower."

"No. I was alone—oh. Wait. *Yesterday* morning in the shower. I—yes. My mind was not—no. Yesterday."

Evan stuffed the last piece of bread in his mouth and picked up the tray to take it to the kitchen, shaking his head. "How soon they forget."

"Hey now. I'm drunk. Ish. And. And your ass rendered me... stupid."

"I don't think you needed my ass for that." Evan winked over his shoulder and did a quick step-ball-change to avoid falling over on his way to the kitchen. "I thought oysters sucked up the booze."

"I think our oyster-to-booze ratio might need some work." Patrick grabbed their glasses and scratched Dini's ears before following Evan into the kitchen. "So, The Running Duck. What about the food?"

"Ours. I want it to be ours. Yours. Mine. Millie's. Oona's. The community's."

"And you have a community all picked out, huh?" Patrick's smug smile told Evan he knew the answer to that question. He knew it as surely as he knew that Dickies brand shoes were good, but Dansko's were better, and as surely as he knew he was being obstinate just to have something to do on a Tuesday night.

"I've made a few calls. It's not officially on the market because of some weird paperwork log-jam, but knowing there's an interested buyer should push it through." Evan squirted dish detergent into the receptacle of the dishwasher door and sighed as he lifted it closed with his foot. "I don't think I'm ready to have this conversation when I'm drunk."

Patrick stepped into Evan's space, bracketing him against the counter with his arms and kissing him softly, his lips brushing over Evan's as he spoke. "You're not that drunk. You're scared. Still."

Evan kissed him back, looping his arms around Patrick's shoulders. He was an anchor. Solid, sure. Unwavering. "Aren't you?"

"Terrified. And interested. And we'd be the stupidest mother-fuckers in this city if we didn't look into it further."

"We're crazy. It's a pipe dream. I mean, we might have enough to buy the building and everything in it, but we have to keep it running."

Patrick stepped back with a laugh, taking a moment to start the dishwasher. "Do you know where the term *pipe dream* came from?"

Evan started to answer and stopped himself. "No, actually. I don't think I do."

"Plans made while smoking dope. Opium, to be specific."

"Seriously?"

"Are we smoking dope?"

"No, we are not. Our blood alcohol level is mildly questionable, but no. My days of smoking illegal substances ended about ten years ago."

"Pity. I'd love to see you stoned."

"We probably could have found a bowl and an old crusty dime bag at Millie's." Evan kissed the tip of Patrick's nose, pushed him back and pointed him to the couch, where they flopped gracelessly, hoping never to move again. Until morning. Or until their backs gave out and they had to take the party to the bed. "I'm still just afraid I'm reaching beyond—like I've lost my mind."

"What would Millie say?"

"Taste everything."

So Patrick tasted, starting with Evan's fingers and working his way to his wrists, kissing each browned patch of skin and reminding Evan of late night *sfogliatelle* and the first "I love you" bubbling out of him as if from a boiling cauldron. Evan giggled when Patrick nuzzled just over his armpit and into the heat of his neck, buzzing his lips on the salty skin there.

"You pass. Everything tastes delicious. What else would she say?"

"You're crazy."

"No, I'm trying to explain to you that I am indeed *not* crazy."

Evan sighed; he knew from the look on Patrick's face that he wasn't getting out of this. "Her favorite expression was, 'All of life's answers can be found in musicals.'"

Patrick sat back, cocky and annoying and sexy. Evan was fuzzy and horny and—

"Exactly. And what's the constant message in every single, solitary musical?"

When Patrick swung one leg over Evan's and settled himself perfectly on his lap, back straight with assurance and confidence, the answer right there between them, Evan had to concede. "To follow your dreams, no matter how far out of reach they seem at the time."

Patrick sat up even taller, his eyes locked on Evan's, waiting for him, waiting for his fear to give way to his dream.

"This is you pretending not to be scared again, isn't it?" Evan asked.

"Am I doing a good job?"

Evan looked into his deep brown eyes, alight with ideas and dreams and memories of where they'd come from all meshing together into this great story of where they could go. In the periphery he felt Millie and Oona, watching, waiting for him to catch up and let go and find his voice again. "The Running Duck..."

With one more kiss, Patrick's lips soft and warm and fitting perfectly against his, Evan sat back, and took in this beautiful, amazing man—this man who had reopened his world to help him see what he'd forgotten. To help him find his voice; remember his original vision. To remind him how to love freely, how to trust fully and how to be vulnerable and available for anything that might come his way. He would be a fool to consider anything but moving forward.

"This is going to take at least a year of our lives."

"Then I guess we'd better get started."

IX. Dessert

A closing course consisting of a sweet or fruit dish,
commonly light and small so guests do not feel too full.

"It is *not* puke green."

The property wasn't quite theirs yet, but Roger still had a key, so they were there, making some cosmetic decisions about the dining room. Evan was being difficult and Patrick was being entirely too cheerful.

"It's more of an apple... green."

"Patrick, this floor is puke green."

"Pistachio."

"Puke."

"Asparagus. And really, unless you've been barfing all day, who pukes green?"

"I have no—what goes on in that head of yours sometimes?" Evan sighed and smiled in spite of himself. "We're painting it or replacing it. I don't care what food color you try to name it."

And so it went. Evan's and Patrick's lives became a whirlwind of phone calls and decisions, too-frequent meetings with financial planners, attorneys and bureaucratic red-tape holders. Each time they swore they could say, "This is it. *Now* we can move forward," another piece of the puzzle would come skittering along, reminding them of another detail that needed attending to.

Eventually, the building was theirs, all three floors: Roger's apartment, the second floor for office space and storage and the lower level for the restaurant. And, while they began the seemingly insurmountable task of cleaning up the mess the previous owners had left, they maintained their jobs at their respective restaurants.

It was slow going.

The first two projects were to clean out the rotten food and to hire an exterminator to clean out the rotten everything else. That was, of course, after Patrick was completely convinced that they needed an exterminator.

"The varmints and bugs will just leave with the garbage. Wasted expense."

He was soon proven wrong.

On a particularly January-like day in January, Rosey, Angel and Roger joined Patrick and Evan at what would soon be The Running Duck to remove the very outdated and incredibly change-resistant pasted-on wallpaper. Unfortunately, Patrick was having trouble concentrating on the job at hand.

Evan was suited up in dark blue coveralls, a bandana covering his head, wearing work boots so heavy that every time he took more than two steps across the dining room floor, he sounded like Frankenstein's monster on the hunt for his maker.

To hear Patrick tell it, Evan was the most adorably fuckable thing he'd ever laid eyes on, what with the outfit—which seemed to fulfill some latent mechanic-fantasy of Patrick's—and the bandana and the sweat and the flexing muscles underneath it all, teasing at him. He took it upon himself to remind Evan of that fact approximately every thirteen minutes by traipsing across the room, planting a kiss somewhere on Evan's person and traipsing back, all while carrying a soapy sponge and dripping water and muck across the ugly "Paris Green" floor with each trip.

Evan was convinced Patrick had looked up that color on Wikipedia. *Paris Green. Honestly.*

It was on his fifth or sixth journey over for a kiss that it happened. Evan's job was to score the existing paper, and he had moved from the front corner of the room to the north wall, where he planned to put a bar. He was lost in his daydream of finding an antique unit, complete with stained glass corner pieces and simple but beautifully carved wood. *Cherry. No, mahogany. Maybe redwood.* And he was doing everything in his power to ignore Rosey, because if he sang the chorus to the already annoying "Staying Alive" playing from Angel's iPad as, "Ha, ah, ah, ah, steak and a knife, steak and a knife," one more time—

"Oh my fucking God, it's moving! It's moving!!"

Evan had known Rosey for twenty years, and only once before had he heard him *shriek*.

And when he had, it had to do with a bag of garbage and a dead rat moving about by the power of the ravenous maggots eating its innards.

So, to say he wanted to pretend that he didn't hear what he'd just heard would be an understatement.

Unfortunately for everyone working in the small, closed-in space, Rosey shrieked again.

Patrick jumped back, hands in the air, sponge dropping to the floor. "What the *hell*?"

Evan spun around to follow everyone's gaze. He sucked in a swallow of air and shivered. Not so shriek-worthy, but what he saw was pretty disgusting.

Roger and Angel came in, Angel's heels clacking loud enough to wake any napping toddler within a twelve-block radius. "What the hell is going on in here?"

Evan dropped his scoring tool and approached, squatting down at the corner with Patrick and Angel to get a closer look at where they were coming from.

Rosey shrieked again. "Don't touch 'em, oh my fucking God, what is *wrong* with you people?!"

And that was when Evan decided that, as annoying as Angel was, as loud and brash and stereotypically *Jersey* as she was, she would always and forever be worth his admiration.

With the speed of a trained sniper, she yanked off a heel and started hammering on the parade of cockroaches marching out of the wait station corner and into the dining room.

Unfortunately, most of them scattered, causing a ripple effect of jumping and hopping amongst everyone in the room. And another shriek from Rosey. The former high school wrestler. And thief. And set design painter.

Angel, however, just kept whacking away at the critters, chasing them as they fled, throwing Italian curses into the air with each swing of her arm.

Eventually, Evan had seen enough. "Angel. Hobble away from the cockroaches." He turned to Patrick with a glare. "And Patrick. We're hiring an exterminator, goddammit." He started muttering like his father. "Like I've wanted to all along. I don't care how much it costs."

And then his voice wound up right along with his frustration. "I won't eat for a week and Dini will sell off all of her slippers if that's what needs to happen. We're *hiring* an exterminator." Evan interrupted his lecture with a glance up at Rosey, who was scratching and pacing and muttering to himself like a meth addict looking for his next hit. "Rosey, go outside. Take a break."

"Someone better clean up the carnage before I come back in. I mean it."

"Get out. In fact"—Evan reached into his coveralls for his money clip and handed him two twenty-dollar bills—"grab your girl and Roger and make a sandwich and beer run. There's that little place up on Henry."

Rosey hustled a very confused Roger and a very wound-up Angel out of the building and they left with one more warning. "I mean it, Paddy! If I come back to a room full of—"

"We're on it. Go get food!"

Patrick side-eyed the corner one more time and looked back up at Evan, who was pinching the bridge of his nose and glancing at the mess himself, feeling more and more afraid that another parade might start at any moment.

"*Your girl?* I thought I knew everything about my girls' social lives."

"Surprise."

"I'm not sure whether to be disgusted or impressed. She's a tough one."

"I can't believe you didn't you see them making out by the reach-in earlier."

Just as they both looked at the corner, five more roaches skittered out and into the dining room, making them both jump back as if the floor were made of lava.

"Jesus fucking Christ." Patrick shivered. And looked at the corner. And looked at Evan, who was gulping down the experience as though it were bitter cough syrup. And back at the corner. "Let me call my dad to see about an exterminator who can come... now."

"Highly advisable."

►•◄

"Okay, so we're looking at a fall opening, right?" Evan closed his oven door with his foot as he rested the Dutch oven on the stove. He lifted the lid and smiled into it.

"Until something else goes wrong, that's the plan."

Evan's face fell. "What went wrong today? I'm having a good day."

"Nothing major. Roger thinks there might be a leak from his commode down the second floor office wall and into the kitchen. I took a look, but honestly, I think he just doesn't know how to aim."

"Wait, his errant pee is staining the office space *and* the kitchen?"

"No, his penchant for hyperbole is creating imaginary water stains in our office and the kitchen. I ain't seein' shit. This smells amazing." Patrick grabbed a couple of plates from Evan's cupboard and pouted when Evan shook his head.

"Tasting, love. We're working on our menu, not eating dinner."

"Okay, *you* might be working on the menu, but I'm fucking starving. What're we eating?"

"We're tasting cassoulet." Evan stirred his dish, lifting various meats from the bubbling cauldron of white beans.

Patrick peeked in. "Pork and beans."

"No. Ass. *Cassoulet.* These are cannelloni beans with duck leg, sausage, back bacon, aromatics... "

"*Protein* and beans, my apologies. No wonder you love that damned ice cream." Patrick jiggled his large plate in front of the pot again. "You're going to charge forty bucks a plate for this Cassie O'Lay, aren't you?"

"Cassie O—oh my God, what is *wrong* with you?" At Patrick's cheesy grin, he snatched the oversized plate from him and put it back into the cupboard. "Depending on the proteins, maybe thirty dollars?"

He moved into the incoming kiss on his cheek. "Does that meet your approval, or am I just going to have to take this entire pot to Roger, who—now that he can smell again—says my food is the best he's ever tasted?" He knocked the wooden spoon against the side of the pot and kissed Patrick's sassy smile. "Ever." And again. "In his fifty-five plus years." One more kiss. "Also, moisturize." He scratched at Patrick's scruffy chin. "You're 'poke-y'."

Patrick rubbed at his chin. "Roger's a very wise man." He offered up his empty hands and one more kiss. "But, you stole my plate."

"Because... " Evan reached up into another cupboard and pulled down a shallow, oval individual baking dish. "Let's do this the way I want to serve it."

Evan spooned a helping of beans into the dish, cut a good helping of duck meat from its bone and chunked a link of sausage, nestling it all into the beans. "I've got a quart container of bread crumbs in the pantry. Let's mix some with the leftover garlic and parsley."

Patrick mixed the ingredients and sprinkled it on the dish, moaning when Evan drizzled some of the duck fat over the top and popped it back into the oven. "Okay, ten more minutes."

"Ten more?" Patrick pouted.

"What?"

"Hungry."

"Child." He looped his arms around Patrick's shoulders anyway. "Ten minutes to kiss me."

"Oh. Yes. What was I thinking?"

And after kissing for a few minutes, Evan brushed his nose against Patrick's scruffy cheek. "You taste like work."

"I'm sorry."

"Don't be. Work is delicious." And after feeding Dini and making out for a few more minutes, it was finally time to taste.

Patrick looked at the steaming dish of food and poked at the bubbling edges with his fork. "Rustic. Hearty... "

"Right. So, like we've said, farm-to-table menu, changing daily based on the best our purveyors provide, right?"

"Yes." Patrick scooped up a forkful and ate. "Oh God."

Evan smiled and opened his mouth, pointing to it.

"What do you want?"

"Food."

Patrick fed him and forked up another mouthful for himself.

"Not bad—needs a little more cooking time, but here's what I'm thinking. The proteins in here change. Except I want you to make the sausage. All the different ones Oona taught you. And, hell. It's sausage. We can make whatever varieties we want. We can change the seasonings in the pot depending on the other proteins. Use a different wine, add tomatoes or not—" Evan opened his mouth again for another taste. "But the foundation stays the same, September through March."

"Did you mean for this to be an homage to your last meal?"

"No. Maybe? Not intentionally. God, that duck is amazing." Evan peeked into the pot, pulled more duck meat from a leg and dropped it into his mouth like a bird with a worm. "It'd be even better if we *confit* it, though." He took the fork from Patrick and scraped at the browned crumb topping around the edges of the pan, taking a bite and disappearing into a memory of running to Millie's one day after school, the fallen, drying leaves crunching and blowing under his feet as he went. He'd lost his sweater at school and was freezing by the time she opened the door for him. Inside was a bowl of Millie's Mess and an extra sweater he'd left there. "That's what we want to make though, isn't it? Our patrons' guilty pleasures. Or their last meals."

"Maybe even their best meal ever." Patrick pointed to another crusty bit and then to his mouth and smiled around the fork Evan offered him. "What's your best meal ever?"

"I haven't made it yet."

"That you've eaten."

"I haven't made it yet." Evan accepted yet another kiss. Now they tasted like the French countryside. "Maybe we need to make it together."

They cleaned the plate, sopping up juices with a chunk of leftover soda bread—now a staple in both their kitchens. Patrick leaned back against the counter while Evan tidied up. "Okay, so what other proteins could we use?"

"Just about anything. Pork belly, mutton, goose, pancetta. A good fatty beef shank would work. It's a great foundation and super flexible."

"I'm on board. That'll sell." Patrick pointed to the bags he'd brought in. "I got some pigs' feet. You up to learning about crubeens tonight?"

"Boiled and fried pork? Sweetheart, I'm ready for that every night."

"Too expensive for every night... and probably for the restaurant at all. I want to show you anyway. Oona's were the best." Patrick retrieved the bag and plopped it onto the counter.

"Could we swing them for special events? Or, too much at all?"

"I'm not sure—they're a pain in the ass, but so worth it." Not quite proving his point, he lifted up a trotter with a scowl. "Looks like these still have some bristles to scrape off."

"Some day we need to teach pigs how to shave their legs."

▶•◀

Roger was right.

Patrick was wrong.

There was a leak.

It involved all three floors of their business. The business they'd paid an outrageous amount of money for. The one that, after all of the cleaning and inspecting and exterminating and re-inspecting and re-exterminating, was finally shaping up into what would be a beautiful farm-to-table restaurant with a three-man kitchen, a twenty-five to thirty-seat dining area and the beginnings of a menu that would make world-famous chef, Daniel Boulud, proud—

"Honey, Daniel Boulud would never know we exist."

"He should. We're *that* amazing."

Perfect menu or not, beautifully appointed kitchen or not, exquisitely decorated or not, this new plumbing issue was going to cost a major fortune to fix.

"We didn't plan properly. I knew that damned accountant wasn't thinking long-term." Evan took the coffee Patrick served him, sipping without adding his traditional two creams and half teaspoon of sugar and even ignoring the offered kiss.

"Ev, he set aside backup capital."

Evan ran his left hand through his hair, his right hand busily scrolling and poking at his tablet as if the answers to the universe might be stored there. "We're going to have to cut costs from the top. Before long we're going to have salaries to pay—"

"I've been thinking about that, actually. A way to cut some costs," Patrick said.

"I don't think we're going to be able to follow through on only being open five or six days a week. At least not at first."

Patrick started to join him at the kitchen table, but stopped cold and turned on his heel to go to his refrigerator. "My timing might be off, but... "

"I mean, I know what we promised and I know it's important—*we're* important." Evan paused long enough to write a few numbers down and go back to his digital spreadsheet. "But we have to get this thing up and running and now we're going to be set back even further with time and—"

Evan finally stopped rambling long enough to look down at the slice of cheesecake that had magically appeared in his line of vision. "Patrick?"

Patrick simply smiled and handed over a fork. And then lifted a finger. "Wait. I forgot something." He scurried to the freezer and pulled out a container of what appeared to be homemade ice cream. He served a scoop of it on the side, stepped back and waited.

Evan looked down at the dessert and back at Patrick, sliding his tablet to the side. "Tell me about this. It looks… " He bent to inspect the cake more closely, finally dipping his finger into the jam-like topping slowly dripping down its sides. "Fig compote." He smiled back up at Patrick and took his hand as he joined him at the table. "Like Millie's jam."

"Yes. The cheesecake is just mascarpone."

"There is no *just*… " He forked a piece of the cake, inspecting it more closely. "What's the crust?"

"Almond shortbread."

"Dear God. And the ice cream?"

"Fennel. Would you hurry up and eat it? You're making me a wreck."

Evan smiled then, a genuine from-the-tips-of-his-toes smile. Once it warmed his face, he realized he hadn't smiled like that in weeks. He had been so overwhelmed with keeping his obligations at Il Boschetto, with the endless business of getting their new restaurant up and running, with trying to find time with Patrick, that he had lost track of what was important. Again. And now this plumbing problem loomed overhead—

"Evan. Stop thinking. Eat the fucking cheesecake."

"Oh! Yes. I—" Evan had the grace to look sheepish and finally took the bite that was on his fork. His eyes fluttered closed but he said nothing as he scraped from the mound of ice cream on the side of the plate, dipped it into the fig compote and gathered a little more cheesecake.

This time he moaned, ever so softly, wordless again. Then he speared another forkful, making sure to get more crust.

"This is perfect."

"Yeah?" Patrick finally took a bite. He opened his eyes after savoring it and immediately grabbed for more ice cream.

"Millie's in there and you're in there and that crust is absolutely—" Evan put his fork down and sighed happily. Possibly even peacefully, although he couldn't be sure. "We're adding this. Just a couple desserts a night, right?"

"Yes, but you think this is a keeper?"

Evan nodded and took one more bite and groaned around it. "It's a keep-uh."

"So, I had a thought about cutting costs?"

And with that, Evan grabbed his tablet and turned his focus inward, blindly nibbling at the cheesecake as he calculated.

"If—Evan?"

Evan didn't look up, just nodded and gave Patrick half of his attention, grumbling when the accounting application wouldn't fully load.

"If we only paid one rent between us—" Patrick said.

"Yeah, honey, I think if we close only one day per week. We can't—we simply can't take the revenue loss with two. Not at first."

"And I've been thinking it might be easier if I didn't have to fool with the train. I won't need to be that far downtown after I leave Johnny's."

Evan nodded again and flipped his notepad page over, starting a new list entitled, "Pros and Cons of a Full Bar."

"And you know how much I love Dini."

"You *tolerate* Dini. Do not make a mockery of her affection for you."

"Ah-ha! You *are* listening!" Patrick rolled his eyes and took the plate to the sink, stealing Evan's favorite bits of pressed crust and melted ice cream for himself on the way.

"Of course I'm listening. So, if we have the full bar, we get revenue from that, which is always good."

"Booze does bring in the money."

"But, if we just go with wine and beer, we don't have to pay a bartender, and we can probably get away with adding one, maybe two more tables."

"You really wanted a bar, though."

"And, with our small size, we need a quick turn. People will linger too long with a bar," Evan said.

"You practically painted a picture of it for me."

"Yes, but—"

Patrick kissed Evan's temple. "You're in a zone. I'm going to shower and maybe we could—"

"I can't stay tonight. I've got to figure this out and Dini hasn't been walked since dinner and—"

"Right. Okay." Patrick scowled and Evan went back to his calculations. "You figure it out."

Evan clicked off his tablet and began to gather his belongings. "Hey. Where's the plate? My crumbs... "

"Hunh. I dunno. Maybe you'll find it in your paperwork."

▶•◀

Two days later, Evan still couldn't get the taste of that cheesecake out of his mind. He also couldn't get the bitter sting of Patrick's last words to stop playing on repeat.

But after an appointment with a second plumber, their accountant and a much more experienced owner-chef, he had been able to calm down enough to at least sleep at night.

And think clearly.

He arrived at Johnny's during the lunch rush and waved off Angel's offer to clean a booth for him, settling down at the counter with a manila envelope secured under his arm.

Patrick could only wave from the kitchen. He was distracted, swamped by a cold, hungry crowd. This spring was taking its sweet time to arrive, just as it had last year when Evan had stopped in for his first meal.

To celebrate, he ordered a side of boxty with his tongue sandwich, which earned him a wink from the hot cook in back just as it had before.

He took his time eating, lingering over a slice of carrot cake— impeccably made, delicately decorated and perfectly spiced, nutted and fruited—everything he expected from Patrick's kitchen.

"You waiting on your boy?" Mimi wiped the counter around him and refilled his water.

"I am. Can he break free?"

"I shouldn't get him for you, ya' know? You're taking him away from us forever… "

"Well, you and… you have a new girl, don't you? You'll have to bring her over for a date now and then so you won't miss him so much."

"I dunno. He might turn all snooty and shit on us."

Evan swallowed the last of his water and looked at her, relieved to see a glint in her eye. "I don't think Patrick is wired for snooty."

"No, but I'm pretty wired for snotty. Have we figured out who to call and complain about this damned weather?" Patrick pointed to a patron waving her check in the air and grabbed a pot of coffee to refill Walter's cup before joining Evan. "You doing alright today, Walter?"

"Yeah, but your toast is dry. Are you getting stingy with the butter or something?"

Patrick turned and grabbed a few packaged pats of butter from a tub and a jelly caddy and put them in front of Walter. "Knock yourself out, buddy. No one should eat dry toast."

Just as he had that first night Evan came to Johnny's, Patrick took his breath away—all work-worn and sweaty with that damned red terrycloth headband pushing his hair into messy spikes. His five-o'clock shadow had made its typical early appearance, and his ease with people, his ready smile, his entire *person* made Evan fall for him all over again.

Don't look at the menu. Look at me.

When would he learn?

"Hi, Handsome."

Patrick reached across the counter and kissed Evan, smiling into it, out of it, pushing his headband up off his head. "Hi." He took Evan's empty dessert plate and dumped it into a bus bin. "Is the tongue good? Oscar is afraid he over-boiled it and I've been too swamped to taste."

"Taste *everything*, Patrick. And it was fine." Evan took a deep breath and slid the envelope across the counter.

"What's this?"

"I was listening. Dini and I had a talk and she said I was behaving rudely."

Patrick opened the envelope and looked inside. Then he looked back at Evan, curiosity etched into his brow.

"This is entirely her idea."

Reaching into the envelope, Patrick pulled out a plastic card with a photograph of Evan's condominium building on it.

"Evan?"

"I know you have the passcode, but the keycard gets you into the building after hours and the weight room, laundry facilities, storage. I mean, maybe we should talk about me coming down to your place instead because you've already given up so much for me, for our restaurant, and I'm willing to consider that, but my place is closer and I know you have more rustic furniture than mine but I'm sure we could make it work."

Evan took a breath. He felt himself babble and ramble, unspooling like a loose bobbin. And Patrick just stood there with a goofy grin on his face, waiting his turn to speak.

"I don't give a flying fuck about my furniture."

"Well, it's just furniture, but do you think you could live with—I mean will you be comfortable? At my place?" Evan sighed. It all weighed so much and he didn't want to say anything to make it all come tumbling down. "I want you to feel at home."

"Evan. My bare ass was skittering across your bathroom counter as you gave me a blow job this morning. I don't think I can be more at home than that."

Blushing and giggling, Evan grabbed Patrick's wrist and pulled him close, burying his face in his chest. "Patrick, people can *hear* you!"

Patrick chuckled low and deep, his baritone hitting Evan right in the gut. Just as it always did. He curled a finger under Evan's chin and lifted it to plant a soft kiss on his lips. "Then let's take this downstairs where we can talk more privately."

When they got to the bottom step of the musty basement, Evan took a deep breath in and rested against the concrete wall.

"This reminds me of the first restaurant I worked in. Old, dingy basement. Best, coldest walk-in freezer I've ever had."

"We've got the old and dingy, anyway. The walk-in's average." Patrick captured Evan in a searing kiss and broke it with a noisy smack. He looked up at Evan, a shy smile curled at his lips. "Remember the story of your neighbor's dog? And how, after chasing squirrels all evening, running home was the best part of his day?"

"Yes." Evan gently scratched at the side of Patrick's head, his fingers brushing at the short hair over and around his ears.

"And you said I was home for you and you worried that you weren't that for me—"

"And you foolishly said I already was."

"See, that wasn't foolish. It was true—even then." Patrick kissed him again, chastely this time, his eyes tracking Evan's face as if to memorize it. "It's just that I'm ready to come inside now, rather than staying chained to the porch."

Evan's eyes snapped out of their trance at Patrick's deep voice and sultry gaze. "Please tell me that by *chained* you mean the restraint of living in two separate places and not that I've kept you on some kind of—"

Before he could finish his rambling, panicking thought, Patrick's hands were on his jaw, whispering a definitive "*Shut up*" against his lips before pulling him in for another heated kiss.

Evan forgot where he was, the cold, dank air around him heating quickly with each kiss, with each press of Patrick's body against his. The contact rejuvenated his exhausted bones, his exhausted mind, relieving the undercurrent of fear that seemed to linger in every waking moment as they threw *everything* at this new business.

The noise from the restaurant overhead pulled them free from their embrace, both of them apologizing for getting so wound up in the first place. "I'm sorry I was so—self-absorbed the other day when you brought this up. I just feel like I'm constantly running."

"It's okay. You get insular and spinny when you're stressed."

Evan carded his fingers through Patrick's sweaty hair again. "I don't want to do this alone. I never mean to push you away."

"I know. We've both been alone long enough."

"You understand what we're committing to? Not just the business, but everything. *Everything.* Together."

Evan continued to stroke Patrick's hair and study his face, getting lost in the depths of his eyes as he stared back, unblinking, unflinching, assured and confident in the entirety of what he was asking of Evan. "I do."

Evan let those two words and all of their meaning hang between them—a pillow for their landing when the reality of all of this knocked them around. And it would. He knew it would. There was no way it couldn't. But the words were there, ready to cushion the realities that awaited them.

I do.

"Okay." It was but a whisper, but the message was loud. And clear. "Thank Dini for me?"

Evan smiled and breathed easily again. "Meet me at my—at *our* place at eleven tonight and you can thank her yourself."

"Maybe I'll come a little early so she and I can have some private bonding time. Or, you know, so I can start moving my cameras in."

"I, uh. I already cleared off some shelves in my office for you."

"You cleared off—" Patrick pressed in for another kiss, laughing softly and brushing his lips up Evan's jaw. "Fuck Dini." He tugged at Evan's earlobe with his teeth. "You're getting all my gratitude tonight."

▶•◀

The reality of restaurant ownership did knock them around.

The plumbing problem in Roger's apartment was less costly and time-consuming than Evan had feared—his fears were admittedly pretty extreme—but the repairs still put a hitch in their timing. Balancing their other restaurants while trying to get The Running Duck in place was hard enough, but they had found a rhythm and this put them on the fun house walk again as they tried to find solid ground.

Evan got snappy. Patrick avoided the snappy by taking extra shifts at the diner until the plumbing was fixed.

"I can deal with your spinny, but you're a fucking tornado right now."

Then there was the incident with the convection oven that they'd won at auction—top-of-the-line model, only three years old. They paid a third of a wholesaler's going cost. When it was delivered, it wouldn't fit in the door, and since the delivery company only *delivered*, they left it on the front walkway for Evan and Patrick to deal with—provided they could stop arguing long enough to come up with a solution.

Passersby watched as they measured and yelled, made phone calls and yelled, paced the street and yelled and finally called the seller and begged him to take it back.

Which he wouldn't do.

Evan finally swallowed his pride and called Theo, who showed up with a toolbox and a level head. With some creative door removal—from both the restaurant and the oven—they were able to get the piece in, and somehow Evan and Patrick were able to fall into the same bed that night and neither planned to kill the other in his sleep.

While challenges seemed to arise at every turn, the energy of the impending opening day also buoyed them as they created dishes and greeted neighbors who peeked in as they worked. They asked what kind of place would be opening, when they'd be opening; they joyfully accepted samples of trial dishes with requests for preparation instructions. Which of course they never received.

"Come visit us in the fall and it will make a menu appearance!"

Evan figured that if he kept saying "in the fall," it would remain true. Some days that was harder to believe than others.

But at the end of each day, with Patrick fully moved into Evan's apartment, they met in bed, in the kitchen, in arms of comfort and rest when their weary muscles and aching feet felt as if they were about to crumble.

It was on a rare morning together in the summer—a calculated scheduling feat combining contracted work on The Duck's not-avocado-green floors and days off at their respective restaurants—that they were able to reconnect. No financial considerations in the way. No contractors.

"No Roger."

"God love him." Patrick lifted his T-shirt over his head and wondered why he'd bothered to put it on at all after their shower. There was one goal for the day, and it did not involve clothing. He crawled onto the bed, mimicking Roger's deep, gravelly voice. "Well, the guys who owned this before... "

"Didn't know how to pay their bills, so shut up, Roger." Evan simply stood at the side of the bed, lounge pants slung low on his waist, their tie already undone because again—why bother? "Oh, and no Rosey."

"Heh. You said 'hard'—you guys gonna go fuck now?" Patrick knelt in front of Evan, his eyes dark, his fingers running up and down Evan's muscled arms, sliding between them to reach into Evan's pants where he was rock hard and thick beneath the fabric, and took him in his hand.

Evan hissed and struggled to continue mocking their caring but annoying helpers. "Yes, Rosey. Wanna watch?"

"I bet he would—he and Angel." Patrick paused to smack his gums, echoing Angel's incessant gum chewing. "They could learn a thing or two from us." Patrick started right in on Evan's neck, smiling as his lips landed on the stretched skin there.

"Although I might miss Mimi calling Rosey *pendejo* for a day. That's sort of a highlight."

"Stop talking."

Evan took a step back, smiling at the small pout it earned him. With a glint of want and need in his eyes, he pushed Patrick back onto the bed, trapping him between his arms, between his legs.

And then it was just as it should be—just Patrick, hard-muscled and smooth-skinned, his coarse chest hair brushing Evan's cheek as he mapped Patrick's abdomen with his mouth, memorizing each valley because he didn't know when they'd have time like this again.

There were giggles and cursing as they awkwardly shed the rest of their clothing, and then Patrick's arms were firm and warm around Evan's back, gently guiding him down to settle between his legs, his breath hitching and ass lifting off the bed when Evan's tongue traced the line from his inner thigh up to his hip.

"Missed this. Miss you."

Evan gently bit at the flesh of Patrick's hip, humming happily as Patrick sucked in air and bucked up again, his hands reaching for Evan's hair. "See? We *need* to close two days a week," Patrick hissed, as Evan's hot breath and lips brushed against the underside of his cock. "God, your mouth..."

Evan lifted up and looked down at Patrick, smiling at the man beneath him. His hair already looked as if he'd been well-fucked; his was face flushed, his lips swollen, eyes blown as if the anticipation alone was all he needed. "You just want two days off for sex."

"You caught me." Patrick reached up and pulled Evan down for a kiss, running his hand down his back, kneading the flesh of his ass as he deftly flipped them both over.

And then it was hot need firing between them, Evan's body stretching and pulling as Patrick kissed and nipped at his jaw and settled into the curve of his neck, their cocks lining up as he pressed him into the mattress, their bodies melting into it, into each other, sweat from the heat of the summer sun streaming through the window slicking their skin as they slid together, smooth and needy.

Evan reached between them and grasped the throbbing heat of Patrick's cock, gripping them together as they moved awkwardly and so, so desperately. They had all day. He wanted all day. He wanted all of him now. "Patrick... "

Now Patrick lifted up and looked down at Evan, his smile bright and comfortable even as Evan stroked his fingers over the head of Patrick's cock, catching the moisture there. Looking into the eyes of this beautiful man, Evan's mind fired with memories of kisses under the slide and neck-nuzzling in their new kitchen, of breakfasts in Patrick's home kitchen and cheesecake at the diner, and of course, the moments like these, when he was aware of how the palpitations of new love and connection had been replaced with familiarity and comfort and love.

So much love.

And when Patrick straddled him and hovered his ass over Evan's cock, which jutted impatiently from his body—having put on a show of absolute masculine sensuality as he prepped himself—and then sank down onto Evan slowly, steadily, his head tossed back in pleasure, the brush of the hairs on his thighs catching on Evan's as he lifted and sank, Evan was reduced to a gasping, clawing mess, desperately caught between wanting to thrust up into Patrick, fast and hard, and wanting to lie back and watch Patrick pleasure himself on his body all day long.

For now, he watched, and admired the muscles of Patrick's thighs flexing and tightening as he lifted himself, the tight heat of his ass surrounding Evan's cock. Pleasure rippled through his gut, circling his chest when Patrick's eyes, so warm and full of promise, met his.

I'm yours. You're mine. I want for nothing more.

He had a man, a life, all wrapped up together in this business that was zapping their energy and firing their imaginations with possibility, and at the end of the day, of every day, he had this love—all-encompassing, beautiful, strong, loyal—that never wavered. Never hesitated. Never questioned.

Evan lost himself to it, to the beautiful man above him, to their intertwined fingers. Patrick lowered himself for a kiss, for a rest as their sweat-slick motions slowed. And then the fire flashed in Patrick's eyes when he sat up again, and slid back to prop himself on Evan's thighs, his cock bobbing between them as Patrick used him, riding him hard and fast. With the soft call of his name, Patrick came back to him and their bodies pressed together, Evan rolling them over, their giggles mingled with grunts as they rearranged, moans and curses filling the room when Evan sank in *right there, right there*, perfect and hard and *now, yes now*, thrusts and strokes until they were both drained, spent and sweaty and curled together in a heap while Dini's indelicate snores pierced their sighs and shuffles to prop the pillow and kick off that last corner of bed sheet.

"We are so fucking good at that." Patrick kissed Evan's head, hitting somewhere between his forehead, an eyebrow and a stray tuft of hair.

"So good we put the dog to sleep."

"*Lulled* her to sleep. Because we're good."

"Okay, yes. Lulled." Evan snuggled into the crook of Patrick's arm and sighed as Patrick smoothed his hair with his fingers. "You're going to lull me to sleep if you keep that up."

"Breakfast?"

"Soon. I've forgotten what stillness feels like."

So they rested in stillness, tangling legs and soft kisses punctuated by the snorting inhalations of Dini, dreaming, and after one stomach growl too many, Patrick slid from Evan's arms to make breakfast.

"Want my help?"

"No. You be still." He hiked up a pair of lounge pants, shaking his ass when Evan pouted at his disappearing nakedness. "C'mon, girl." He clicked his tongue for the dog and waited for her to grumble herself out of her blanket pile. "Just want a parfait?"

"Yeah. Use up those raspberries, huh?"

Evan sat up and sighed peacefully as Patrick led Dini out of the room, closing the door behind him. He looked around his bedroom—now theirs—and thought about how so much of Patrick was woven into his life now: his vintage cameras warmed the cool contemporary décor of the office and living room, his clothes were neatly tucked into drawers and hung on his third of the closet—a third for Evan, a third for Patrick, a third for the T-shirts and sweats they shared—and their toiletries mingled on the sink and in the linen closet.

Because film needs to be refrigerated and the door is the best place, the butter in his refrigerator had a new home, and it was now of the Irish variety, richer and—Evan couldn't deny it—much more delicious. Coarse-ground whole wheat had a permanent home in his pantry and the stack of tubs of dried fruits and nuts would make Millie blush in its excess.

But his favorite additions to his home—besides the man himself—were the photographs on his walls. Patrick's work decorated every room, the abstract work and the realism, black and white and color blending into the life Evan had already built for himself, the previously unknown missing pieces making it feel complete.

His eyes landed on one particular photograph and he shuffled out of bed to pull it from the wall. Patrick had taken it the day of their picnic, over a year before. Evan had been unaware of the shot until he'd seen it developed and framed. It had hung prominently in Patrick's bedroom until now.

At a glance, it was simply the Manhattan skyline, the Brooklyn Bridge framing the right edge of the image. But in the bottom left forefront of the shot stood Evan, his hair blowing in the early spring breeze. His body was turned toward the East River and into the city but his gaze was tossed back in Patrick's direction with a slight smile, as if to say, "Put the camera down and join me." Evan had no memory of the moment, but Patrick did and he wanted that picture in *their* bedroom the night he moved in.

"My heart felt so good that day. I knew we'd be together."

"Oh you did, did you?"

"I did. It's like the promise of everything is right in that picture."

And if Evan was honest with himself, he knew it that day too. They had covered their feelings with the sentiments of friendship and camaraderie, taken a cute phone picture that still alerted Evan of Patrick's calls and texts, and discussed their mutual desire to admire children from afar and never to have any of their own—all platonically, of course.

But there was a comfort with Patrick—and a burning desire—the combination of which he'd never experienced before.

He knew.

So when Patrick told him what that picture meant to him, Evan moved an old painting of Millie's that had followed him from his bedroom in Quincy to every New York apartment he'd lived in so it would have a special place.

And now, as he hung the picture back on its hook, he also knew what would make the restaurant come to life with the love that they shared—beyond the food.

They had two months before the scheduled opening. So much to do. So many details to finalize. And hearing Patrick singing a made-up song to Dini and her ridiculous socks—"Your feet are dressed in purple; your face I want to slurple"—he decided that the details would wait one day.

Today was just for them.

▶•◀

Patrick tucked the money bag under his arm and dug into his pocket for his keys. "I don't understand why you always feel the need to go through the front door—especially tonight. I'm not even sure I have that key here—"

The loop of keys dropped to the ground and Evan stooped to get them, his bashful smile a vain attempt at softening the irritated glare on Patrick's face. "Trust me?" He flipped the keys in his hands to find the brass-colored one, bright and barely used. "I just want—"

With practiced ease, Evan located the key and shoved it into its slot, taking a deep breath as the tumblers moved under his turning hand. "It's opening night. I just want to... *open*, you know?"

He pressed a soft kiss on Patrick's cheek. "We're both nervous. Let's not bicker."

Patrick sighed and rested his head on Evan's shoulder, slipping his hand into Evan's pocket to twine their fingers together. "You're right. I'm nervous. And getting cold."

He reached for the door handle and Evan lovingly swatted his hand away. "Wait, wait, wait. God, you were like this at Christmas last year, too. So impatient." Evan slipped the money bag from under Patrick's arm and opened the door, putting up a hand before Patrick could walk inside.

"What? You want to carry me over the threshold?" Patrick

wrapped his arm around Evan's back and made to jump into his arms, laughing before he could get the lift to do so successfully.

"Just—hang on. Let me get the lights. Make sure it's—"

"You know why I'm like a kid at Christmas? You're that annoying dad who has to set out the eggnog and turn on the tree before the kids come and destroy it all anyway."

"There will be no destruction, mister. Our whole life is behind this door."

"And we're back to nervous." Patrick flapped his hand in dismissal. "Go. Do your—thing. Dad."

"Kiss me one more time."

Patrick cupped Evan's face in his hands, his eyes speaking comfort and assurance, even though Evan knew the nerves were right under the surface. "I love you." His lips were warm in spite of the cold autumn air, a salve on the pressing anxiety of the evening.

"I love you." Evan kissed the tip of Patrick's nose and stepped inside, hitting the lights to illuminate the front half of the dining room.

It was just as he had imagined a year before. Seating for twenty-five, thirty if absolutely necessary—casual, comfortable, inviting. The colors were warm, the décor simple and meaningful to them, with pieces from Millie's home and memorabilia from Oona's kitchen—Oona's teapot shelved next to a hand-thrown pottery vase of Millie's. They were bound together even though they'd never met.

He took a deep breath and stepped in farther, tossing the money bag onto a table before opening the blinds to let in the early afternoon sun.

"We finally did it, Millie." He spun around to take it in one more time before finally letting Patrick in. "Welcome to The Running Duck. I hear the cook is super hot."

Patrick closed the door behind him and kissed Evan's cheek. "Yeah, but you should see the chef. Nice ass."

Evan stepped back to let Patrick look around, guiding his eye with his own gaze, quietly coaxing him to take in all the final details, details they'd left for Rosey and Angel, Mimi and Roger, their partners in overtime, over-grime, tasting and testing and cheerleading when the task of just getting to opening night without committing a murder seemed impossible.

"Oh! Evan. This is—I love it." Patrick reached up to a grouping of pictures near the door, touching the frame of a photograph of Oona. Evan had asked for one months ago and Patrick had provided a favorite that he'd taken shortly before her death. Next to it was a photo of Millie, beaming brightly, her yellow-white hair straw-dry and wild around her face. Nearby were the required inspectors' certificates, a ridiculous photo of Dini in duck socks and an empty frame. "Evan?"

"For our first dollar." He knew it was corny and ridiculous and probably passé, but he didn't care. They'd worked hard to get here and that first dollar was going to be worth millions in sentimental payback.

Patrick looked around the rest of the dining room, taking in little wispy breaths each time his eyes landed on another of his photographs. Evan had also asked him to contribute these, but, being overwhelmed with final details—creating potential menus and booking inspections and meetings for marketing and promotions and preview nights and, and *and...* he'd simply forgotten and let Evan take the front-of-house as his project.

"These look amazing. They fit right in."

"They do. Better than I'd imagined. Rosey recommended the framing store and they were so helpful—"

Patrick took two steps in one and almost threw himself at Evan, arms wrapping around him as if he were afraid Evan might float away and leave him to fend for himself. "Thank you. This is all so—it's perfect. You're perfect." He kissed Evan fiercely and pulled back to look at him as if seeing him for the first time. He shook his head, kissed him one more time and stepped back to take it all in again. "I mean, look at this." He walked to a string of pictures along the north wall—where the bar might go one day. "This was the day Roger almost hung himself trying to take that godawful chandelier down, wasn't it?"

"I think so, yes." Evan looked more closely at the image and smiled. "Yes. You can see the wires behind him—he said he didn't sleep at all that night. Kept having dreams he was being strangled."

Patrick took in another picture and then another, both abstract and simple snapshots of their renovation of the building, of Patrick's life in New York, of their life together. The slide in the park, with a lovely curly-headed girl posing on the ladder; the batch of *sfogliatelle* and the excess powdered sugar decorating Evan's apron. A soup pot from Johnny's that had been used for generations, Oscar's calloused hand gripping a spoon above it to stir something delicious. Evan in his coveralls, his cheek paint-smudged with a lip print smack dab in the middle of it *and* a blush visible even in the black and white image.

It was their story, as told by Patrick, done only to capture the memories as they came.

As Patrick perused the photos, Evan slipped away to the darkened wait station and grabbed a long black bag. He walked up behind Patrick and dangled it in front of him, "A great cook needs his own knives—and I only work with great cooks."

"What?" Patrick took the bag and spun around, his eyes bright and shocked—truly a child at Christmas. "Evan—we have knives here." He opened the roll anyway, almost giggling with excitement. "These are exquisite"

"And they will remained sharpened at all times."

"Yes, Chef. Absolutely." He pulled each knife out and ran his finger along the blade, weighing each one in his hand just as he'd hold it and putting it back, doing the same with the next, motioning with the tourne as if turning a potato, on and on with each blade, thanking Evan over and over again.

"And I have one more surprise." Evan pulled the last knife out of Patrick's hand and put it away, kissing his pouting lips.

"Ev, you didn't—this restaurant is our gift."

"Just one more thing, and I hope—I hope this is right." He motioned for Patrick to stay put as he walked to the back wall.

"If not, we can—" Evan swiped a sweaty hand on his pants and reached for another light switch, biting his bottom lip.

When he flipped the switch, the newly built pass and kitchen lit up and a ceiling spotlight beamed down onto the wall to illuminate his final gift.

Patrick followed Evan's gaze to the wall and gasped, his hand to his mouth, tears instantly filling his eyes.

"Evan!" He mouthed the Irish words painted above the pass-through, then again, whispering them and closing his eyes in disbelief. "*Grá anois agus go deo*."

"Is it ok—"

"Love, now and forever. Evan. It's—you're—how did you—oh my God, I love you so much." He didn't throw himself at Evan this time, but walked deliberately to him, his eyes ablaze with a love Evan had never seen before, freezing him in his spot and bringing prickling tears to his eyes. "It's perfect. It's—"

"You said your family had the forever... "

"But not the love, so much."

Evan nodded and tucked his fingers into Patrick's hands cupping his cheeks. "But we do. And I want everyone to know what built this place." Patrick's lips were on his, soft and sweet, mumbling utterances of love and Oona and pride and everything, everything, *this is everything*.

They looked around some more, coming together in the middle of the room to kiss again, breaking to look at photographs or tchotchkes and finally the painting above the pass again.

"I mean, even separate from the meaning—it's just beautiful. Who did the lettering?"

"Rosey."

"He did not."

"He did. That's one reason I had to come in here first. I wanted to make sure he didn't paint "Buttfuckers Forever" or something."

"Oh my God." Patrick walked to the front door and looked back; it would be the first thing people saw when they entered the restaurant. *Love, now and forever.*

Some would ask who it was for, what it was about, and they'd tell their waitstaff to answer honestly. To tell their story.

Evan finally made his way into the kitchen and stopped in his tracks. "Patrick? Did you have your own surprise up your sleeve?"

"No? Why? Did he graffiti our ovens?"

Evan laughed and popped open the chilling champagne just as Patrick pushed through the door. "Seems the painting isn't all they left. The note says to check the reach-in."

"They?"

"It's Roger's chicken scratch. Mimi, Angel, Robin, Theo, Oscar—everyone signed. Even Johnny and DiSante."

Patrick opened the reach-in. "Evan. Look at this." He pulled out a tray of long-stemmed, chocolate-dipped strawberries, rose petals decorating the plate and fluttering into the lower shelves of the refrigerator.

Evan poured two flutes of champagne and took a strawberry from the tray, weighing the options of eating it, feeding it to Patrick or drinking. Patrick pressed a strawberry to his lips to decide for him and he moaned and opened his mouth, biting into the sweet, succulent fruit. "How did they find fresh strawberries in October?"

"Who cares? Shut up and make a toast." Evan fed Patrick a strawberry, chasing the taste from his lips with a soft brush of his tongue, their lips smacking loudly in the quiet room.

"Okay." He lifted his flute, heart pounding at the potential of the night before them, the enormity of the risk they were taking, the joyride they knew they were poised for. "To Millie. To Oona. To Us."

"*Sláinte.*"

"*Cin cin.*"

They sipped the champagne, eyes locked on each other, sharing another strawberry before taking one more drink.

"They'd be so proud of us, Evan."

"They would. This is what they loved us for."

"*Grá anois agus go deo.*"

"Now and forever."

X. Digestif

A spirit consumed after the meal to aid in digestion.

"So, I finally give Robin the answer of her dreams and tell her I'll do prep a few hours every night. You know, 'cause I'm a generous bastard."

It was supposed to be a toast. It started out as a toast.

But in pure Rosey form, it was quickly unraveling into one of his stories.

"You just wanted the pay raise so we could move into that place on East Thirteenth." Angel tugged on the hem of his borrowed jacket to shut him up. Even though they had been together more than a year now, Evan still laughed at how naïve she was when it came to shutting down Rosey's stories. By the time he'd uttered the word "so," it was a done deal—the story was happening.

"And that. So she gives me some knife lessons. Makin' sure I don't cut off a limb… "

"Or your neighbor's."

"Oh, shut it—" Rosey looked toward the voice and stopped himself. It was Theo, the new sous chef to Robin's executive chef at Il Boschetto. "B—boss." Rosey offered a nervous smile and continued. "Or my neighbor's. Right."

"Exceptin' Rosey here ain't a great study, even for the fact that he thinks he knows everything." Angel grabbed at Rosey's left wrist and held his hand up, showing off the large, bulging bandage on it. "Dumb-ass almost screwed it up so I couldn't put a ring on it."

The group sitting around the table laughed, everyone used to Rosey's hubris, everyone loving him for it.

In the kitchen, Evan and Patrick worked, quietly whispering words of direction to each other while their attention stayed in the front of the house and they were as present with their guests as they could be.

It was a special day for the staffs of Johnny's, Il Boschetto and The Running Duck. A blending of families. A wedding. The ceremony was a simple one in the upstairs banquet room of Il Boschetto and the meal afterward, upon Evan's insistence, was at The Duck.

He knew a gathering such as this worked well here, because only months before, he and Patrick had hosted another one just like it; they'd had a quick civil service in Central Park and—again at Evan's insistence—a gathering of loved ones at The Duck, served by the grooms themselves. Because it's what they did. It's what they loved. It's how they thanked. And they had so much to thank these people for.

So, since it was Rosey and Angel's day, Rosey had the floor. And from all appearances, he wasn't giving it up any time soon.

"So, I hear the gasp before I see anything. Before I feel anything."

"Yes, because I always gasp at a paper cut." Robin rubbed her very pregnant belly and propped her feet up just as Theo slid a chair over for her. "But please. Do continue."

"I would if you all would quit interrupting me."

"Oh for Gawd's sake, Rosey. Just cut to the chase." Angel tugged on Rosey's jacket again and stood, wobbling on her five-inch stilettos and smacking her gum. "He sliced the tip of his finger clean off. Hanging there by a thread and dontcha know, Miss Chef over there just tells him to wrap it and keep working. Finished his whole shift bleeding like some sorta stuck pig."

She sat down with a plop and downed the rest of the wine in her glass, lifting it to no one in particular for a refill.

"I—" Rosey looked at his bride and at the unimpressed crowd, finally tossing a glare at the kitchen because the snigger had started there. "You all think this is funny! I coulda died that night! You should have seen the amount of blood!"

"Wait, wait, wait. Angel, you didn't *finish* the story." Theo got up, retrieved the wine bottle from the wait station and filled glasses as he talked, topping off Evan's and Patrick's through the pass and whispering to them before he continued with the crowd. "You need an extra hand back there, Chef?"

"Why, can't stand to be out of the kitchen, can you?"

"No."

"Tell the rest of the story, because I know with that cast of a bandage, it's got to be good." Evan tested the doneness of the pork medallions in his pan and nodded to Patrick. "We're good. Let's start plating."

"Mash smear, put 'em around the outside and—"

"Yes, sauce it and brussels will go in the curve."

Patrick kissed Evan's cheek and grabbed for the root vegetable mash. "Yes, Chef."

"So, what Rosey's leaving out of the story is that the asshole passes out at the sight of blood." Theo set the wine bottle in the center of the table and rejoined his wife with a kiss on her swollen belly.

"I do not—"

"Okay, since Rosey's such a stickler for accuracy, allow me to rephrase. He passes out at the sight of *his own* blood."

"Ehh, I can verify that. Slammed his knee into the corner of the reach-in while we were cleaning this place and cried like a baby for an hour." Roger ducked and giggled when Rosey made to toss a roll at his head.

"All right, what the fuck, man? It's my wedding day. Can't I at least have a story to myself?"

"No!" For a crowd that excelled at carrying on more conversations at one time than there ever were people in them, that answer, that word, was in complete unison.

And so was the laughter. And so were the oohs and aahs when dinner was served. And so was the resulting silence as everyone dipped into their meals, a murmur beginning between Mimi and Natasha and spreading to Ross and Oscar, different schools of training and venues of service merging in this one place to celebrate the union of two hilariously odd people.

Evan and Patrick stayed in back, eating from the same plate, content, happy and at ease, observers and participants all at once.

"So, Rosey? What's with the hole in your hair at the back of your head? Knife slip?" Evan laughed in spite of Rosey's glare. "You know, I should be offended. You always refused to work the line for me."

"The hole's on account of he passed out." Angel pointed to Theo, confirming his story. "Cracked his cement head on the cold station on the way down."

"Thank you. *Wife.*" Rosey offered her a pained smile and unwrapped his bandaged hand, the charade over. His pleas for sympathy were lost on this crowd, these veterans of burns, cuts, stabs and slices, all for the love of their jobs. The love of the craft. The love of toughing it out to have a great story to tell at weddings. "And Chef, you'd already done enough for me. I—I couldn't be indebted to you further."

They shared a look, the noise of the crowd disappearing in the moment. Evan felt Patrick's warm touch on his back. "Evan, Rosey. It's been a year. You can call me Evan now."

"No. You'll always be Chef to me." Rosey lifted his final forkful of food as if in salute.

"Okay, is this going to dissolve into some kind of warped gay alliance love-fest? Because I've been missing Patrick's desserts. Where's the wedding cake?" Mimi tried to stand mid-tirade, weaved into Roger's space—almost onto his lap—and sat back down clumsily. "And I need a refill."

As everyone finished their meals, Patrick put the final touches on the cake, a fall-inspired caramelized apple and spice number complete with marzipan garnishes in the shapes of fall produce, leaves and acorns—"Just a few, not too much, I promise." It was simple and lovely. Perfect for the occasion.

Evan watched Patrick delicately place the marzipan, such a dainty touch for such masculine arms and hands, his wedding ring hitting the light in the room like a lighthouse guiding Evan's heart right where it needed to be.

He wiped his station clean and glanced out at his friends—a ragtag group if he'd ever seen one—as they chatted and sipped their wine.

Natasha conspired with Ross and Oscar over the dinner preparations. "I think it was just a *confit* of garlic in between the tenderloins. Divine."

"Cone-what?"

"*Confit*. You just wrap unpeeled cloves of garlic in—" Ross tried to explain, but as soon as he saw the blank stare on Oscar's face, he gave up.

Roger, their ever-faithful night porter, cheap maintenance man and third floor tenant, sat quietly, keeping a fatherly eye on Mimi. She continued to drink and bemoan the sappiness of the day, her heart having recently been broken. Again.

Robin and Theo curled into each other, as if remembering their own wedding day. They were now anticipating the arrival of their third child and enjoying a night off their feet as the guests in another's kitchen.

Angel and Rosey, of course, wandered between being so involved with each other that they forgot they were in a group setting and being so blitzed on wedding jitters and too much wine that they just didn't seem to care.

Evan looked out beyond his guests and deeper into the dining room, at the framed write-ups from Zagat's and Michelin—they had been awarded the Bib Gourmand, for the best restaurants with meals under forty dollars a plate—and at the spread from the *New York Times* Dining & Wine section. He looked at their first dollar, paid to them by his parents, who had surprised him on opening night; at photographs Patrick had taken during their first year in business and photographs of their wedding, some of which had replaced photographs from their opening, some of which had just blended in.

A journey in black and white.

And just when he thought he might pop from emotion, from satisfaction—and, if he cocked just so on his left hip, from exhaustion—Patrick appeared in his line of vision with a forkful of cake and a smile—the smile that had offered Evan more than a simple potato pancake so many months before.

"Hey. You zoned out for the cutting of the cake."

Evan ate, eyes closed as he tasted the sweet spice cake, wondering if he'd ever stop being surprised at the magic in Patrick's expertise.

With one more glance out at his friends, he smiled and took the fork from Patrick's hands to lick up the remaining icing.

Patrick took Evan's hand through the pass and lifted it, wordlessly inviting him to come around and join them all up front. When they met in the wait station, Evan folded himself into Patrick's awaiting arms, welcoming the breath of laughter against his neck.

They pulled back from one another, Patrick's eyes shining bright and full with the promise of everything before them and the security of how far they'd come.

"You good?"

Evan ran a finger under Patrick's apron strap and tugged him in for a kiss, a seal to his answer.

"I've never been better."

THE END

Acknowledgments

For those who believe writing is a solitary activity, I'm here to tell you differently. It takes an army of people, all of whom deserve my utmost gratitude.

First, I'd like to thank the amazing team at Interlude Press for taking a chance on all of us. More specifically, for believing in this story that, when you first saw it, was in mid-chaos. Annie, I have learned so much from you, not only about piecing a story together, but also about my characters—ones whom I thought I was already pretty intimate with. It has been a great pleasure getting to know you as a professional and as a friend. C.L., your marketing and promo expertise pushed me into my biggest *dis*-comfort zone and I am eternally grateful. It was the most joyful anxiety I've ever experienced. And Lex, you are a true gem. Your constant availability and readiness not only to help, but also to play when you sense my stress, never ceases to amaze me. We must meet up at a Jeni's storefront one day. And finally, thanks to RJ and Abby for a cover beyond my imagination. Thank you for understanding the importance of detail and whimsy and making my boys come alive. I adore you both.

I can't forget my family, who has taken the biggest hit from my scattered time and attention. Alex, you have been my greatest cheerleader for three decades. I could not imagine a better partner, friend, traveling companion and first set of eyes. I love you. My amazing kids, I tell this to others but now it's time you hear it: If I had to have two adult kids living in my house, I'd still pick you. You are stellar human beings. I love you, too. Son, laundry? Today would be good. And Mom and Dad, your support has meant the world, even when you're not sure what it is I'm doing, exactly. It's okay. Oftentimes I don't know what the hell I'm doing either.

I almost forgot dear Cartman. The male model to the loveliest girl in the book. You will always have the most smooch-able chin on the planet. We all miss it.

Where would we be without friends? I need to thank you, Becky, for coming to me two years ago and offering first your talent, and then your friendship. This ride wouldn't have been tolerable without you. You listen, you laugh, you encourage, you kick my ass. Cindi, your courage and strength center me every day. I'm so grateful for your support and unwavering belief in me, even though up until now you've never read a word I've written outside of text messages (although, let's be honest, I'm damned hilarious via text.) To all my other lovely friends who ask how things are going and tell me I can do it when I look discouraged, thank you.

And Lisa. You were the first person to tell me that I expressed myself beautifully through the written word. While I'm sorry you left us before you saw this all happen, I know you've been with me all along—even if I can feel you side-eyeing me a little. It's okay. The slice of white chocolate raspberry cheesecake is for you. I won't even ask for a bite.

I must thank the food professionals that helped embellish this book with detail and accuracy, anecdotes and good food. A huge thanks to Hannah, a lovely senior line cook from New York who offered to consult with me. Your help was immeasurable. And thanks to Richie, my Brooklyn inspiration. By simply being yourself, you brought color and personality, character and vibrancy to this book—and to my life. With the offering of a single pastry I'd never heard of, you earned a permanent spot in the telling of this tale. You've been a gracious consultant, a wonderful host and an absolute joy. And if you need a ghostwriter for that "Dumb Sh*t People Say at Richie's" book, I'm your girl.

And finally thanks to you, the reader. If you've read me before, your words of encouragement and praise rang through my ears as I worked. And if this is your first time reading my words, I hope you enjoyed my little world. I enjoyed creating it for you.

interlude 🧩 press

A Reader's Guide
to
Chef's Table

Questions for Discussion

1. Contrast and compare the influences of Oona and Aunt Millie and how they shaped Patrick's and Evan's approaches to food.

2. Why didn't Patrick finish culinary school after Johnny, his boss, got back on his feet? Do you think this was in his best interest, or should he have stayed with it?

3. The inner workings of a professional restaurant kitchen seem rough and unforgiving in *Chef's Table*. Why do you think this is? Is it the same for the diner? How is the work atmosphere different between the two, and why?

4. Patrick is comfortable settling for "good enough." Evan is not. How does this cause conflict in their relationship and ultimately help both of them grow?

5. Patrick is quick to correct Evan when he describes Patrick as a "chef." Instead, Patrick considers himself a "cook." Do these defined roles they play in the food industry affect their relationship? How do you think this would play out in the long run?

6. What does Evan see in Perci that troubles him? Is it just her poor performance in the kitchen?

7. On one of Evan's early visits to the diner, Patrick says "Don't look at the menu. Look at me." How does Patrick help Evan focus on what's important?

8. How do Evan and Patrick communicate with food?

9. In Aunt Millie's house, Evan finds an old bucket list that he abandoned after winning his James Beard award. How do you think he would update the list? If you could compare your goals of ten years ago to your goals of today, how would they differ?

Also from interlude  press ™

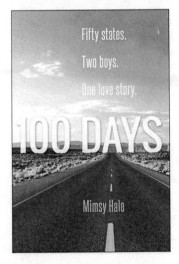

Now available from

interlude 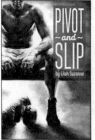press™

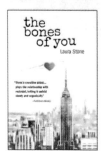
One **story** can change **everything**.

www.interlude**press**.com

interlude press

One Story Can Change Everything.

interludepress.com

Twitter: @interludepress *** Facebook: Interlude Press
Google+: +interludepress *** Pinterest: interludepress
Instagram: InterludePress